D1784249

INSIDER OUT

'Christopher Hudson writes with sophisticated
flair ... A convincing narrative aided by an
authentic suspenseful showdown'
Publishing News

'Christopher Hudson's writing has what it takes
to make a good thriller: pace, tension, timing.
Highly intelligent, the very best of good reads'
Financial Times

'A tough, realistic espionage story, with a plot
that grips to the end'
Mail On Sunday

'An exciting and terrifying glimpse into the
ruthless world of top level espionage'
Daily Express

INSIDER OUT

ABOUT THE AUTHOR

Christopher Hudson was born in 1946, and educated at the King's School, Canterbury, and at Jesus College, Cambridge, where he edited *Granta*. In 1971 he was appointed Literary Editor of the *Spectator*, for which he also reviewed films. He left to work with Stuart Cooper on the screenplay of *Overlord*, which won the Silver Bear at the 1975 Berlin Film Festival and the *Evening News* Special Award in 1976. Since 1977 Christopher Hudson has been a regular contributor of editorials and reviews to the London *Standard*, of which he is now Literary Editor.

**Also by the same author,
and available in Coronet Books:**

The Final Act

Insider Out

Christopher Hudson

CORONET BOOKS
Hodder and Stoughton

For My Parents

Copyright © 1982 by Christopher Hudson

First published in Great Britain 1982
by Michael Joseph Ltd

Coronet edition 1984

British Library C.I.P.

Hudson, Christopher
  Insider out.
  I. Title
  823'.914[F]   PR6058.U313

ISBN 0-340-33995-0

Printed and bound in Great Britain for
Hodder and Stoughton Paperbacks, a
division of Hodder and Stoughton Ltd.,
Mill Road, Dunton Green, Sevenoaks,
Kent (Editorial Office: 47 Bedford
Square, London, WC1 3DP) by
Cox & Wyman Ltd., Reading

The First Week

MONDAY

It was dark in the woods. In the green uniform of a Park Warden the man was camouflaged against the trees. He took off his peaked cap and wiped the sweat from his forehead. Then he raised the heavy binoculars once more and focused them on the Castle gatehouse, which cast afternoon shadows across the wide green of the inner bailey. The lake was still; the green was empty. There was no sound to be heard, except for the honking of geese flying overhead.

The man lowered his chin and spoke softly. The sound went through the tiny microphone round his neck and down the plastic-coated wire to the aluminium transmitter the size of a box of kitchen matches in his pocket. Immediately a voice crackled through the small white bead in his left ear. He muttered again, angrily, and looked at his watch. The shadows on the Castle green were lengthening. The man he was waiting for was due to walk across the bailey, go through the old gatehouse and take the road to the car park. He was already nearly twenty minutes late.

With his binoculars the man in the uniform swept the empty stretch of road through the golf course to where it disappeared in the trees. Four minutes had passed since he had spoken down the microphone. The main Castle door swung open. Three men came out and stood in the doorway.

'Chocolate Whizz, please.'

Leaning out of his serving hatch, Arthur Norman took the two 10p coins and put a chocolate confection in the grubby upstretched hand. Nothing like a Bank Holiday for pulling in the custom. Past four o'clock and still the kids and grownups were trudging up to his Mr Softee icecream van in the picnic area. He'd completely sold out of Orange Meteors. Another hour like this and he'd be down to his last dozen icecream cornets.

As he sat down for a moment to take the weight off his feet, there was a loud chatter of static from a nearby radio. It was the young couple who had been sitting out of sight round the back of the van for the past hour or so. Irritated, Arthur Norman switched on the Mr Softee loudspeaker jingle to drown them out. A familiar strident nursery tune carried out over the families from Maidstone stretched out on the warm grass with the remains of their holiday picnics, half-eaten ham sandwiches, plastic plates, empty soft-drink cans and apple cores, over the soccer players, frisbee-throwers and sun-worshippers, all the way down to the stream in the woods.

'Next please', shouted Arthur Norman.

He was closer now. Through the binoculars he could be seen distinctly as he stood talking to the other two at the end of the Castle bridge. In his neat blue polyester suit and brown leather shoes with a carefully folded handkerchief in his breast pocket, he could easily have been one of the conference delegates — an anonymous salesman of bulletproofed limousines or of electronic jamming devices. But the man in the Warden's uniform had seen the photographs. The narrow shoulders, the light brown hair balding at the crown . . .

It was Martin Commoner all right.

The man waited until Commoner made his farewells and started down the barbican alone. (The policemen paid him little attention, he noticed, except to give him a quick salute.) Putting away the binoculars, the man wiped the sweat out of his eyes and spoke into the transceiver round his neck. Then he stood up and hurried away.

Arthur Norman leaned over and held out the cornet with its smudge of vanilla icecream. Before the small Indian boy could grab it, the candy-striped van suddenly jerked forward. Arthur Norman slipped; the cornet flew out of his hand. He grabbed vainly for the hatch, fell back and hit his head against the side of the electric generator.

Dazed, he scrambled to his feet and lunged towards the

8

driver's cab. It might have been his head spinning, but the van seemed to be turning in the road as if to make up towards the Castle. There was a girl at the wheel, a girl in a long skirt, he'd seen her somewhere before.

He shouted, 'What the bloody hell . . .'

Too late he saw out of the corner of his eye the broad-shouldered figure in the passenger seat, its arm already raised. The blow hit him above the left ear with a force that cracked his skull. His knees gave way. Heavily he sat down, in a scattering of cardboard boxes. He opened his mouth but a sudden blare of music from the van loudspeaker drowned whatever he was trying to say before the blackness came.

The man in the Warden's uniform came full tilt through the bracken, the transceiver thudding against his heart. As he ran over a small wooden bridge and came out into the open, he staggered, his cap fell off. Not daring to look over his shoulder he plunged on, wheezing and panting, running as if every battlement of the Castle behind him was manned by archers loosing arrows at his back.

In the shelter of the woods, he slowed to catch his breath. Almost at once he heard the blare of the icecream jingle. He shook his head in disbelief and stumbled on through the trees.

Below him, the bank sloped down to the Castle drive. The icecream van stood opposite a beech tree growing out of the bank, parked so that it half-blocked the narrow road. Its serving hatch was lowered. A girl in a blue summer skirt leaned against it, holding a raspberry icecream cornet.

The man caught his breath and bellowed. She looked up, frightened. He came slithering down the bank, his face puce, his dark hair sticking up in clumps. The girl stood staring at him.

'Turn it off. You want the whole fucking place hears?'

A deep slow voice came from inside the van. 'But I thought you said . . .'

'Forget what I said. Just turn it off. Okay?'

The music was switched off. In the sudden silence, a clipped voice spoke behind them. 'In a spot of bother, are you?'

The man in the uniform wheeled round. The car was right there, a brown Rover, arrived from nowhere. Beside the open door stood a man in a grey lounge suit, wearing a chauffeur's cap. He advanced, scowling. 'What's this van doing here anyway?' he demanded angrily.

The girl dropped her icecream. It made a raspberry splash on the tarmac.

At the same instant, the man in the Warden's uniform snatched out his gun, and smashed the butt down hard on the chauffeur's skull. The chauffeur gave a loud cry. He clawed at his jacket. Again the gun came down. The chauffeur fell to his knees, clutching at his head. His cap came away in his fingers. Grasping it, he sprawled face down at the side of the road.

Holding the gun out stiffly in front of him, the man moved towards the Rover. There was a shape in it, the figure of a tall, fair man in a blue suit. He was clambering out of the back into the driver's seat, reaching for the ignition. As the gun levelled at him through the window, Martin Commoner shoved the car door violently, catching the Warden in the midriff and sending the gun spinning out of his hand.

The icecream van had started moving. It was reversing towards him. Commoner revved the engine and jerked at the unfamiliar gears. Somewhere, a girl was screaming. He couldn't find the goddamn reverse. The van was on top of him. He turned to leap sideways. As he did so, the crash threw him against the door.

He was unconscious before he hit the road.

Its loudspeaker silent now, the Mr Softee van trundled out of the Castle grounds, through the picnic area towards the London road. The picnickers lay dozing in the sun.

There were two ways Mrs Lomax in the outer office could attract the General's attention. She could flash one of the lights on his mahogany desk console, or she could set off the high-pitched bleep on his intercom and risk a gruff rebuke if the message turned out to be anything less than high priority. For the call that came through at midday Washington time, she bleeped and went on bleeping until the Director of Central Intelligence flicked the intercom switch.

It was James Parrish, head of the London station of the CIA. 'We've got a spot of trouble here, Director.' There was a pitch of

10

distress in his voice which the understatement failed to disguise. 'It's Martin Commoner. He's disappeared.'

'What's that supposed to mean?'

Parrish gave him the news which had come through to him a few minutes earlier from the Home Office. The General interrupted him.

'Let me get this straight. You're saying Martin's been *kidnapped*? In an *icecream van*?'

Parrish cleared his throat nervously. 'The police are down there now.'

'When did this . . . goddamn!'. The General closed his eyes tightly and opened them again, bringing himself under control. '. . . when did this happen?'

'We think about thirty minutes ago. About 16.30 Greenwich time. The police are putting out an alert.' Parrish hesitated. 'About Commoner, sir. Is there anything I need to know?'

'No. You know the drill. Right now I want this handled like he was any other senior Government official.'

'Yes, sir.'

'And James? Keep in touch. I want to know what's happening, and I want an update every hour until further notice.'

The General put the 'phone down and contemplated the gallows and noose he'd doodled on the paper in front of him. There were contingency plans for this. Codes could be changed. Agents could be shifted. Operations could be cancelled or frozen or put on the back burner. Vince Addams, head of the Middle East division, would have to be consulted on BeeSting. Thoughts flickered through his mind without cohering. He could hardly fathom what he had just heard. It would take a little time before the significance of it began to sink through.

From what Parrish had told him, Martin could have been kidnapped with a plastic gun and a wad of chloroform. The President would be asking to know why he wasn't better protected. What could he say? No top official of the Central Intelligence Agency had ever been kidnapped before. It was the kind of thing that happened in the other branches: to an ambassador in Paris, to a consul in Honduras, to a Nato military attaché in Italy. Not to the CIA. There was a gentleman's agreement against poaching the senior intelligence operatives of the other side. If it were to be broken, every one of your own top men would be fair game. The General had been in

11

intelligence work of one kind or another for forty years. His nickname had stuck since his days in the OSS. He found it hard to believe that the KGB — many of whose senior operatives were as familiar to him from their names and photographs on his files downstairs as his own neighbours at home — would suddenly, inexplicably break the rules. Their own men in Washington were too vulnerable for that.

He came to a decision and pressed his intercom. 'Get me Vince Addams,' he said. 'And call Max Hemming in.'

After the General had told him what had happened, Addams was silent for a moment. The DCI could hear the small sucking noises he made when he was uncertain, drawing his lower lip under his front teeth. 'What's your reading of it?' he asked eventually.

'I don't know yet. We can't afford to sit on our asses until a ransom note arrives. I think we should move to reassure the Israelis. They're going to be mad as hell. BeeSting was a risk to start with. It could go badly wrong if Commoner's taken out. It was his baby.'

'I know.'

'Unless we defuse it now.' Addams meditated. 'If we can get the President's agreement to pull Fisher out of Jerusalem —'

'Too dangerous.' The General knew the rivalry between the two men. He suspected it would cause Addams no great pain to see BeeSting aborted. 'If you agree,' he went on, 'I'm going to suggest to the President that we put BeeSting in deep freeze for a day or two. We keep Fisher sitting in the Embassy, and tell him not to put his face out the window until he gets the word. If we have to pull him out fast and destroy the ground-plans, the Israelis won't forgive us in a hurry. But at least we won't be caught with our pants down. What do you say?'

Addams grunted. 'Remember, we fixed the President a sure-fire escape route. The whole idea of the mission, if it became public, was simple surveillance.'

'It won't wash and you know it. It's not just the President I'm thinking about. It's Senator Traill and the Intelligence oversight committees. Jim Traill's looking for a stick to beat us with. If BeeSting gets blown, he'll have both Congressional Committees up in arms demanding prior notice of all our covert operations again. I don't know about you, Vince, but I'm too old to be tied to anybody's apron-strings.'

There was silence on the line. The DCI smiled grimly. If anything was calculated to patch up Agency rivalries, it was the threat of outside interference.

Sure enough, Addams adopted a more conciliatory tone. 'I guess that's right, Jack. If you don't get a lead on Commoner —'

'I can't hang around. The President should be in the air by now, on the way back from Florida. I'll get out to Andrews Air Force Base and nail this down as soon as he climbs off the plane.'

The General put the 'phone down with a sigh and spoke to his secretary again. Then he got up, leaning his hand on the desk as he felt the sharp familiar pain in his back which came whenever he was tensing under pressure. Hands in his pockets, he went across the room to the wide seventh-story corner windows overlooking the woods and the Potomac river. He wanted to think about Martin his colleague, drugged maybe, bound and blindfolded, his life in danger . . .

But there was no time for that. He had to think coldly about the options open to him. He'd been DCI long enough to know how Presidents and their political sidekicks operated: if you can't deliver the intelligence, you'd better deliver the action.

He'd send someone to London straight away to push the search along and keep control of the information output. Parrish was no use. Parrish was not ruthless enough for what . . . for what might be needed; besides which he was too cosy with British intelligence. Who were the good anti-terrorist men? Allen Vanderbyle? He was as tough as a Texas cowpuncher; he even looked the part. Senior enough to take over the London end without Parrish pulling rank on him and behaving like an old woman. He'd send Vanderbyle over on the afternoon Concorde flight . . .

'Director?'

The DCI started. Max Hemming had come in noiselessly and was approaching with short quick steps across the green carpet. Even at close quarters he was unobtrusive. His staff made a joke of it, calling Hemming 'the man in the empty suit'. A slight figure with blond crewcut hair and an eggshell-smooth face, even with pouches under his eyes he looked younger than his forty years — too young, certainly, to be heading one of the most efficient departments in the Agency. Brought in off the Middle East desk to work on Soviet infiltration, Hemming had been made directly responsible to the DCI's office. Since then, four senior CIA men had been quietly retired or shunted to other jobs, and at least one had been left where he was to feed false information to the Reds. As a result, Counter-Intelligence was getting back some of its old reputation.

'Max, thanks. Sit down. We've an emergency.'

Hemming gazed at the General while he was talking, with an intensity which disconcerted the older man. When he'd finished, Hemming simply nodded.

'What do you want me to do?'

'You know Martin well. You used to work for him. That's why I've sent for you. I want a complete report on him. All the personality data: who he sleeps with, who his friends are, how many Scotches he drinks before dinner — you know the kind of thing.'

'Understood.'

'That's the 48-hour assignment. What you can get me straight away are the facts and figures on file here — his background, career in the Agency, operations up to now — I'll need that before I see the President. I'll give you written clearance to take out Martin's polygraph file as well. I want your own assessment of it on my desk by eighteen-hundred-hours today, and a psychiatric assessment to follow.'

'You think he could have gone over?'

'I don't think anything.'

Max Hemming took off his steel-rimmed spectacles and tapped them into his breast pocket. 'I think we should bring, er, Miss Koscinski back here on the first accessible flight,' he said, with an appearance of embarrassment.

'Miss who?'

Hemming was sitting on the edge of the one hard-backed chair in the room. He kept his eyes fixed on his shiny leather shoes on the carpet, but the DCI didn't miss his smile.

'Her name is Nancy Koscinski, Director. Miss Koscinski is a lawyer here in Washington on Senator Traill's staff and she's Martin's, uh, paramour. She's been staying at the Capital Hotel in London for the last week.'

'Is she a security risk?'

'Probably not.' Hemming looked discomfited at the General's pointed question. 'We've been keeping an eye on her.'

'I was just wondering,' said the DCI, with an upward

14

inflection of his bushy eyebrows, 'how the Agency ever survived in the late '70s without a CI division to look after its morals.'

He held out the clearance for Martin's flutter file. Max Hemming bounced off the chair and stepped across the room to take it. There was a frown on his face. As he reached the door, he hesitated and turned back. 'The work Martin's beeen doing,' he said, 'doesn't he have something going on right now?'

The General had begun to fill his pipe. He went on pressing down the dark tobacco. Hemming stood intently by the door.

'You're still our permanent representative on the National Security Council's Staff?' asked the DCI.

'Yes. But, if you remember, Martin attended one Council session which was exceptional. It was closed to all but the Special Co-Ordinating Committee. No minutes were taken. No staff members were present.'

'How much do you need to know?'

'Anything that will help an assessment of Martin Commoner's state of mind.'

The General had finished filling his pipe. Putting up both hands to light it, he felt again a sudden twinge from the old wartime injury. Looking straight at Max Hemming, he asked 'Do you know who I mean by Peter Fisher?'

'By sight. Head of the Israeli desk. Used to be Martin's assistant.'

'He's in Israel right now. Martin sent him over two days ago with some photos.' He paused. 'Do you know anything about BeeSting?'

Hemming shook his head.

'I'll tell you what you need to know. The AWACS high-altitude pictures that Fisher's envoyed over show details of a military site in Asia. We couldn't wire them, they might have been intercepted. If anybody finds out they've been passed on to Israel, it would give the Reds the biggest propaganda victory they've had in years.'

'This mission — was it Martin's idea?'

The General nodded. 'You see what I mean,' he said.

Hemming left the room as quietly as he had come in. The DCI wondered briefly if he should have given him the full story. But until they knew who had taken Commoner, it was best to keep even Counter-Intelligence as ignorant as possible of what the real sting in BeeSting might be.

The military site shown in close-up detail on Fisher's ground-plans was a uranium fuel-fabrication plant in Pakistan, not many miles from Islamabad. What the Israelis were proposing to take out, with the guidance of the CIA's satellite photographs and drawings, was nothing other than the Moslem bomb.

And they had a week — maybe two weeks — to do it in, before the plant went on stream.

The General drew on his pipe until he could feel the acrid smoke on his tongue. Then he called up Vanderbyle.

The unmarked police car, a dark blue Rover 2600, picked up speed in the fast lane of the A20 dual carriageway and silently flashed its headlamps to get right of way. A light drizzle was falling, as it had most days this autumn in the late afternoon.

Sitting beside the driver was a plump youngish man, prematurely balding, with a round shiny pink face and baby-blue eyes, fixed now in an abstracted gaze. Detective Chief Inspector William Pomfret was looking at the falling rain. He imagined it tapping on the window of some room in which Martin Commoner lay blindfolded, perhaps the only sound that was keeping him in contact with the outside world.

William was on his way to Maidstone, where the kidnap Operations Centre had been set up. Maidstone police had found the kidnap van (it had been decided to treat it as a kidnap from the start) abandoned under a railway bridge just over a mile from the Castle, and by now should have dusted it over for dabs. Arthur Norman, the icecream seller, was in Maidstone General Hospital with a skull fracture — still too badly concussed for William to see him.

He glanced down at the black-and-white photograph he'd been given of the CIA man. There was something typically American about the face — unlined, boyish, conventionally handsome, with a firm mouth and a direct gaze — the kind of face illustrators used to draw on Wing Commanders in *Boys' Own Paper* stories about the Battle of Britain, distinguished and anonymous at the same time, a good face, he thought, for the CIA.

What he knew about Commoner was hardly any more than that; no more than what Parrish had told them an hour earlier

16

in the Cabinet Briefing Room. His job at Langley was DDO or Deputy Director of Operations, which meant in effect that he ran all the CIA's foreign missions under its Director, the DCI. He was in his mid-forties, married with one teenage son, and lived in Georgetown, Washington DC. He had come over on a private visit to give the keynote speech at a business convention in Leeds Castle, organised by a friend from college days. Parrish had shrugged, then, as if to say — what more can I tell you? — and that was that. He'd been lucky to even get the photograph.

It wasn't the sort of case William was used to. The Commander, at the meeting, had introduced him as one of his 'experts' on the American scene. That was a laugh. His expertise was mainly with the hammer and sickle mob. Most of what he knew about the States had come out of back numbers of the National Geographic. It was simply that he happened to get along with Johnny Wax, one of the FBI people who doubled as legal attachés at the US Embassy in Grosvenor Square.

But the CIA in Britain tended to keep a low profile, even to the Yard. Parrish he'd never even met, before the meeting in the Cabinet room. A small nervous man in a check jacket which was too loud for him, he'd given them the minimum of information and then clammed up. He'd had to have his arm twisted by the Minister ('conditions of censorship' . . . 'unacceptable public concern') before agreeing to let an alert go out. And then he'd revealed that, as they sat there, his men were busy hustling Commoner's girlfriend, Nancy Koscinski, out of the way on to a Pan Am flight to Washington.

Martin Commoner. Just another intelligence expert maybe (he wouldn't give a brass farthing for the lot of them). Why couldn't they look after their own? Christopher Knight from M15 had sat in on the meeting, and taken notes. But he hadn't once opened his mouth. It was all distinctly curious. There was something else going on, something in the background, he could smell it. Just before he set off this afternoon, Parrish had come back to them to say he'd had a priority message from Washington, ordering him to keep the whole thing under wraps. But by that time the news of a missing US 'diplomat' had already gone out to the Press Association. There was no way the news people would hold the story back now.

It meant that he wouldn't get home for hours — and Bank

Holiday Monday, too. Jenny — Christ, he'd forgotten — Jenny was having some people from the council round to supper! Or was it tomorrow night? Either way, she wouldn't thank him.

He sighed, and gazed out at the suburban houses in their obedient rows. His gut feeling was that the lads who kidnapped Commoner had scarpered before the cordons went up. They could be anywhere by now.

Judy Gelb, in pink trousers, was sitting fanning herself with a cardboard folder when Barbara came out with the tray, walking across the raked gravel on to the round of green grass in the middle of the garden.

'My dear, I think you've done wonders with this backyard,' she said, as Barbara put down the two tall drinks. 'It's so difficult in gardens this size to get any impression of *space*. You ought to ask the Committee to put it on the Georgetown Garden Tour next spring, as the perfect miniature garden.'

Barbara smiled. She had known Judy Gelb too long to get riled by her compliments. 'It's no smaller than most other Georgetown gardens in this area,' she said. 'Martin likes a lot of gravel, he says it's easier to hear an intruder coming through the back.'

'Don't you miss Spring Valley?'

'Oh, sure. It was smart. But, you know, John grew up, and you get tired of rattling around in a big house, just the two of you. You both must have found the same in Chevy Chase.'

Judy flushed with annoyance. Their old Chevy Chase house, as Barbara knew, had been cramped and dingy. Barbara went on swiftly. 'How is your better half? We never see him these days.'

'I know the feeling.' Judy Gelb gave a mirthless laugh. 'He staggers out at dawn to the Office of Measurement and Control or whatever it's called now, and gets back at nine looking like Banquo's ghost. I give him food and shelter and bank the paychecks.'

Barbara laughed aloud. This was why she tolerated Judy, for the flashes of self-deprecating humour which leavened the usual litany of petty slights and jealousies. 'I feel the same way about

18

Martin sometimes,' she confessed. 'Now. Can I get you anything else before we start work?'

Judy sipped her drink and made a face. 'Is this stuff neat?' she asked. She opened the folder on her lap, which was the same shade of pink as her trousers, and brought out several sheets of paper embossed, *The Washington Center for Autistic Children.* Putting on her spectacles, which hung on a silver chain around her throat, she began ticking off the notes she had made. Barbara yawned. The sun and the whisky were making her sleepy. For a moment, she imagined she was back in Spring Valley, in the tall garden, listening to Martin and John pitching a baseball on the lawn under the trees.

In those days she still thought of herself as a New York girl washed up in a Southern backwater, a sleepy humid company town in which everything moved at the speed of a Southern drawl (except in the heavy luxuriant dozy heat of summer when nothing moved at all). Her monthly columns on Washington life for *Harper's Bazaar*, which now struck her as febrile and skittish when she re-read them, were laced with ironies about the snobberies of Washington's upper crust and the provincial dullness of its sober-suited bureaucrats and politicians. She had invented a fictional character, Walter Righteous, a congressman from Nebraska. He squired her on the social round of soirées, concerts and gallery openings, and could always be relied upon to exclaim, 'Gee, wasn't that something!', in wide-eyed admiration at the end of every hick party, much to the amusement of her New York readers.

She had travelled out with Martin and the child for two rather boring years in Buenos Aires — and already, by the time she returned, Washington was no longer merely an administration sitting on a swamp; as a capital city it had a long way to catch up on London or Paris, but it was a whole lot better than Bonn. The cave-dwellers remained, the old élite of the city, whose unblinking crustacean vigil over Washington society never shifted or broke. But the atmosphere had changed. Washington had a cultural confidence it had lacked in the past; and there was the money to back it up, more money than ever before. Walter Righteous had given his dowdy suit to charity and taken the sheepish smile off his face. Now he was to be seen in a natty lightweight two-piece, his working wife dressed in something fashionably European from a smart M Street boutique, the two of them off to listen to the Chicago Symphony Orchestra at the Kennedy Center or take in the latest theatrical import from London's West End.

As Washington had begun to move faster, so Barbara had slowed down. She did not take up jounalism again: there seemed nothing worth being scathing about in the world she had once observed with such easy disdain. John was in high school. Martin was spending long hours at Langley and wasn't disposed to talk about his work. Her parents had died, and left her independently wealthy — wealthy enough that she could no longer work at a job without being gossiped of by her friends as being ambitious, a *canard* which she had no intention of provoking. There were other ways she could expend her energies — in good works, for example, helping the poor and the underprivileged, of whom, she now discovered, there were a good many in Washington . . .

Judy's voice broke in on her thoughts. 'Barbara? I've broken the figures down. We've banked 13,000 dollars in donations, as at September 20. The Junior League's committed another 11,000 dollars to the Program. That means that with three more barbecues, including yours, with 40 dollars a plate going to the project, we'll have met our Christmas target of 28,000 dollars. That's enough to pay the salary of a Director of the Evening Program at the Center, plus costs of initiating one season's recreational activities for the children, plus the two hours a week services of either the music teacher or the art teacher — which do you think?'

'Did you see what the very wonderful Mrs Julie Comstock said in the *Washingtonian* about people like us?' asked Barbara. 'She said that voluntarism was a one-way ticket to self-pity. She said she preferred to do something that contributed to her husband's career. Can you believe some of these women?'

'You can believe it of the Comstocks.' The heat was sticky. Judy Gelb shifted in her chair and plucked at her trousers. 'She married Comstock because she thought he was going places, and he's still legal assistant or something at Interior. If Julie doesn't start contributing hand over fist to his career, she's not going to be very wonderful much longer. There's no money in a divorce there. Listen, I must go see the steering group about all this. What do you say, music or painting?'

The front door bell chimed. Barbara put her drink on the

tray, spilling some of it. 'Music,' she said. 'I mean, autistic kids can listen to music, can't they? I mean you have to be deaf not to enjoy music, don't you?'

She crunched over the gravel and went into the cool of the living room, shaded by the raffia blinds she'd pulled down at lunchtime. In the distance she heard Judy Gelb calling out towards the house: 'Don't worry, I can let myself out.' There, she thought, is the perfect Voluntary Coordinator, for whom charity work was husband, household and child all rolled into one. If Judy hadn't been left so much money, she might have had quite a successful career.

On the step was a chubby young man she didn't recognise, with the neat brown suit, dull eyes and bright smile of a door-to-door salesman.

'I'm afraid there's nothing I want right now,' Barbara said at once, slightly slurring the words.

'Mrs Martin Commoner?'

'Barbara Commoner, yes.'

'Pardon me. I'm Paul Shusterman, from your husband's office. May I have a few words with you inside?'

Barbara swallowed. She led Shusterman into the living room and pulled up one of the blinds. Judy, she was glad to see, had let herself out the side entrance.

'Can I get you a drink?'

'No, thank you.' The young man's expression had changed in an instant from cheerful to mournful, like a ham actor's. He sat down on the other end of the camelback sofa from her and crossed his legs.

'Mrs Commoner, I'm Max Hemming's assistant, I think you know who I mean.'

She nodded. Hemming? Martin never told her anything.

'Uh,' he stumbled for the phrase. 'I'm sorry to say we have a problem with your husband.'

'A problem?' She was beginning to get impatient.

'Yes.' He was twisting the large gold signet ring on his finger. 'He's disappeared in England. We think he has been kidnapped.'

Barbara looked at him blankly. The words made no sense to her. Kidnapping was something she had schooled herself to think about years ago in Buenos Aires. Since their return to Washington, the possibility had not crossed her mind.

21

'Martin? Kidnapped? Don't be absurd. Who would want to do that?' she heard herself say.

'We don't know.'

It was a moment before the full horror of it was borne in on her. Confused, she could think of nothing except that she would have to cancel the barbeque.

'But you were smiling,' she said at last. 'And now you tell me . . .'

Shusterman lowered his eyes. 'One of our rules,' he said. 'It's never advisable to look like you're the bearer of bad news. The neighbours get interested.'

It was the familiar banality of this remark that restored her to her senses. Martin had been kidnapped. The salesman wasn't pulling her leg. She sat bolt upright.

'When did it happen?' she asked.

'About two hours ago. About 11.30am our time.'

'Two hours! You've known about it for *hours*?'

Her drink was outside; she held on to her anger instead.

'Why? Why wasn't I the first to be told? I'm his wife, aren't I? He's not married to you people.'

The chubby young man looked comically dismayed. He scratched one of his sideburns. 'I'm sorry, Mrs Commoner. I guess it was procedural. I mean,' he corrected himself, 'we needed to be sure, we didn't want to give you a false alarm. If there's anything we can do —'

'Sure. I understand.' Barbara reached for a cigarette, but her fingers trembled. Procedural. One of the rules. She understood. These were the kind of people Martin worked with. She had known them all her married life. Max Hemming, she suspected now, worked in Counter-Intelligence — which meant that this gofer confronting her, with his bland, earnest face, did the same. Martin had told her about people like this. They bugged the headboard in people's bedrooms and then drove round the block all night monitoring the conversations and recording them on tape.

The CIA man was on his feet. In a panic she said, 'What am I supposed to do?'

'Nothing. You're okay, Mrs Commoner. We've got someone watching the house from now on. We'll let you know just as soon as we hear from your husband. Or whoever is holding him.' He extracted what looked like a visiting card from a thin leather wallet and wrote a number on it in pencil. 'This is a number where you can reach Max Hemming or myself during office hours. Mr Hemming will be round to see you soon, but if there's anything you want to tell us meanwhile, that's the number to call. Uh, one other thing.' The dull eyes regarded her dispassionately, like a sea-creature. 'If you plan to leave Washington at all, please will you give us a call on that number anyway?'

He seemed anxious to go. Barbara nodded dumbly. Shusterman muttered another awkward apology, handed her the card and went out without turning back — maybe so as not to let her see him fixing the smile on his face for the benefit of the neighbours.

Standing where he had left her, the cigarette between her fingers, she heard the front door close quietly behind him. Curious, she turned his card over. It was blank on the other side.

Martin Commoner's file lay beside him on the back seat of the limousine, as crisp and shiny as an unused envelope. Sighing, the Director of Central Intelligence picked it up again and took out the terse typewritten documents.

They told him that Martin Commoner had been born in Hagerstown, Maryland, in 1936, the younger son of a moderately successful corporate lawyer. Both parents had been dead some years. Apart from an annual exchange of Christmas greetings he had no close contact with his one sibling, Richard, an Army officer who had graduated from West Point and been decorated in Vietnam. Martin himself had gone from high school in Hagerstown to Princeton where he had got into the Colonial Club, majored in political science at the Woodrow Wilson school, and graduated *cum laude* in 1956.

Thereafter, the DCI noted with a nod of approval, Martin had not gone straight into the Agency, downy-cheeked out of college like most of them nowadays, but had made his own way in the world for six years, first as a law student, in deference to his father's wishes, and after that, rejecting lucrative offers from a couple of distinguished Maryland law firms, as an editorial writer on *The New Leader*, the New York-based political journal. It was in this period that Commoner met and married Barbara Cobb. Their first son, Edward, had died of leukaemia. Their second and surviving son, John, was born eighteen years ago.

Their photographs were attached. The General glanced with a new interest at the woman his Deputy was allegedly unfaithful to. Barbara's was a strong-boned face, handsome rather than pretty, framed in thick corn-blonde hair which fell straight to her shoulders like that of a woman half her age. What saved it from heaviness (Cobb — Irish? German?) was an intelligence around the china-blue eyes, and the remains of laughter lines around a mouth which had set in disapproval for the CIA photographer. The same life and intelligence showed in the son John, a lanky, gawky youth with unruly carrot-coloured hair spilling over his long quizzical face.

His own son had looked that way once. Not any longer.

The limousine turned off the highway and drew up at the main gate into Andrews Air Force Base. There were extra security guards on duty, a precaution always taken when the President's jet was due to land. As his limousine was waved through and went on down towards the Base Operations Building with the runways to its right, the General turned back to the file.

He skimmed through the next couple of pages of testimony about the radicals and left-wingers Martin had consorted with as a journalist (there would have been more ground for suspicion if he hadn't made any radical contacts in that job) and went on to his first direct connection with the CIA, after the Cuban missile crisis, when he had been the first reporter to point out that the CIA director John McCone had got it right about the missile sites all along. It couldn't have done him much harm, the General reflected, when he applied to join the Agency in December 1963, a month after Kennedy's assassination.

It had been in Vietnam that Martin had first begun to make himself indispensable. He had been rewarded for his long stint in Saigon by being made the youngest station chief in any major capital. Back in Washington, Martin had risen steadily in the Agency hierarchy. By mid 1973, he was in the right position to become chief of the covert action staff in the Deputy Director of Operations' Middle East division and then head of the Western

Hemisphere division, from which he had been promoted to run the Directorate of Operations last year.

That was it. The information in Martin's file was painstaking, detailed and almost certainly accurate, and it told the DCI precisely nothing he didn't know already. Up until this moment, Martin had always been the right man in the right place at the right time — a patrician, a WASP, well educated, but also the kind of savvy, hard-nosed guy you could rely on not to louse things up. The DCI had never stopped to ask himself how Martin voted, how many bourbons he drank before dinner or how he conducted his private life. You didn't ask Martin that sort of question. He was the sort who cut his own grass and shovelled his own snow: always in his office by 8.30, always leaving at 6.30 with a clean desk . . . and this was the man who a few hours ago and three thousand miles away had been violently torn from his well-ordered existence, kidnapped and maybe taken hostage. At this moment he could be steeling himself to face torture or the bullet in the back.

The limousine stopped again, outside the squat, unglamorous terminal to which the American government welcomed visiting heads of state. The General got out, and was greeted by an Air Force colonel who took him up to the control tower where two traffic controllers, wearing headphones, were watching the President's airplane on a radar scanner.

There was no time to waste. Shaking his head to the colonel's offer of iced coffee, the DCI settled himself in a chair and took out of Martin's file the hasty notes he had scribbled on a pad before leaving. Under *Motivations* he had pencilled three headings: the first, *Money (Blackmail)*; the second, *International Terrorism*; and the third, *Islam/KGB*. The first possibility he had dismissed in a few sentences. It was highly unlikely that some criminal gang in Britain would have kidnapped Martin in order to ransom him to the US government. There was a similar problem with the terrorist theory. There was no Pakistani terrorist organisation known to him. The only known terrorists who could have a strong enough motive were Palestinian and Arab groups. And that brought the Director on to his longest note, under *Islam/KGB*.

This, he knew, was what had got Vince Addams chewing his lip. If the Reds had somehow got wind of the current mission (the word BeeSting did not appear in his pencilled notes), there

25

could be one hell of a price to pay. If they had even an inkling of it, kidnapping Martin would be an ingenious way of discrediting the entire thing. And the worst of it was, Parrish had let the London police put out an alert. The 'phones hadn't stopped ringing in the CIA press office since. Martin Commoner was now big news.

On his pad, the General wrote down the word *Consequences*. Then he crossed it out again. It was stretching hypothesis too far to imagine what might happen if Fisher's satellite photographs fell into the wrong hands. The United States had joined in the expression of outrage after the Israelis had neutralised Iraq's Osirak reactor. If they were found out to be actively conniving in a similar act of war against Pakistan, another non-aligned country, it would destroy America's credibility with Islam for a generation. That was why the meeting of the National Security Council which had deliberated the idea had been pared down to its five principals plus Martin, and closed even to the Council's permanent staff. As happened very rarely, the Undersecretary of State had withdrawn from detailed discussion of BeeSting rather than commit State to supporting it.

Airport One was taxing slowly towards them. After much thought, the DCI added one last addition to his notes: *KGB*, he wrote — *Commoner setting up his own kidnap in order to defect?*

Before he could formulate an answer to this, the elevator doors opened and the Air Force colonel stepped out. 'Sir, the President is coming across here now,' he said. 'He asks that you should meet him in the helicopter right away.'

The General's heart sank. It meant briefing the President eyeball to eyeball on his way back to the White House. It was a free ride he could have done without.

The journey south through the Bank Holiday traffic was painfully slow. The roadblocks which had been set up after the kidnap had only been lifted half an hour before. It was past seven by the time William Pomfret arrived at Maidstone Central Police Station where the Operations Centre had been set up.

He was too late to talk to the Chief Superintendent in charge of the local investigation, who had exchanged his uniform for a black tie and left a few minutes ago to attend a civic dinner. Instead he was shown round by a young CID Inspector, an arrogant, good-looking six-footer to whom William took a dislike on all three counts.

In the flat tones of a professional lecturer, the Inspector explained the police photographs pinned on the board. 'The tyre marks on the grass verge are those of the van used in the kidnap. Bloodstains on the road — here — match the driver's blood group —'

'Any others?'

'None. But a fair old number of dabs, which we're checking now. Plus other traces, hairs, the usual fluff, which Forensic is analysing. We're still checking isolated buildings in the area —'

'Chance'll be a fine thing.'

'And there have been reports of possible getaway cars, including a Morris Marina parked under the railway bridge. Now on this map over here —'

'Talking of getaways,' said William, looking at his watch, 'I've got to make a 'phone call, in private, if you don't mind.'

To his relief, he was left to himself in the Superintendent's empty office. Next to the 'phone on the desk was a television. He switched it on. A coloured map of the Middle East came up on the screen, with an inset picture of the President of Pakistan. It changed, and an Israeli general in army fatigues was banging his fist and shouting down a microphone.

William picked up the phone, and put it down again. On the screen was a blurred newspaper photograph of Martin Commoner. He turned up the volume.

' . . . police say that Mr Commoner, a senior US diplomat who was on a private visit to this country, may have been kidnapped by an armed gang. A van apparently used in the getaway was found a few hours ago abandoned near the kidnap scene. The driver who was attacked and injured is in hospital and said to be resting comfortably. Maidstone police are anxious to interview anybody who may have seen the van or have any information. There was an exciting finish to the Chelsea-Everton match at Stamford Bridge tonight when Chelsea goalkeeper —'

'Bugger that,' said William aloud, switching off the set. Chelsea were a lot of nancy-boys anyway. He was a Fulham Rugby League supporter himself.

He rubbed his eyes, feeling suddenly tired. But he was damned if he was going to get elbowed out on this case — even if it did mean staying up all night here at the Operations Centre and dosing himself with strong tea, while rookie detectives moved coloured pins around on a wall-map and tried to impress him with tall stories.

He picked up the phone again and dialled his deputy at the Yard.

'John Little speaking.'

'John, do me a favour. Give Jenny a call at home, will you? Tell her not to expect me back tonight.'

'Yes, sir.'

'Oh, and John?'

'Yes?'

'Break it to her gently, all right?'

'Red socks?' queried the General incredulously. '*Bright* red socks?'

'With respect, sir,' said the man standing in front of the Director's desk. 'You asked me for the whole picture. An individual can reveal his true predilections in any variety of unconscious ways. It doesn't mean that Martin is a Soviet agent. The fact that, while always conservatively dressed in dark suits, he has been known on occasion to wear red socks, is merely the kind of thing my people are trained to observe.'

'Max, I'm more interested in his vulnerability to blackmail,' said the Director of Central Intelligence shortly. He had had a demanding day: it was not over yet; and he was in no mood to appreciate the subtler *arcana* of Counter-Intelligence. 'This stuff about Martin having once served on the Agency's Fine Arts Commission — are you really suggesting to me that Martin is secretly homosexual?'

'I'm not guesstimating beyond a factual observation. Make of it what you will.'

'Zero, a round zero, is what I make of it. Why, Martin has a wife, a son, he even has a mistress so you tell me.'

'In CI's experience over the years, a man's having a mistress is no gauge of his sexual orientation.'

Seeing the DCI's expression, he went straight on. 'Okay, in

general Martin's polygraph answers over the years indicate a fairly high percentile of physical courage, although that wouldn't aid him for long in a modern interrogation situation. His imaginative faculty seems to be about average. Conversely, he has a high sensitivity response on what we loosely call the conscience questions.'

'Conscience questions?'

'Yes. When he was fluttered in 1975, and again in 1980, Martin had stress readings on questions relating to his participation in the Phoenix counter-terror programme in Vietnam and on the treatment of Montanero terrorists in Argentina. Since he was completely in the background, in Saigon and in Buenos Aires, we have to assume there's a moral issue here, Director.'

There was silence in the room. To the General, everything about the man standing in front of him radiated conviction, from the way he stood with his shoulders back and his arms by his sides to the calm pale eyes behind the steel-rimmed spectacles. He liked a man who knew his own mind, he told himself, but there was an implacability about Max Hemming that disconcerted him. He was not the kind of man you talked baseball scores with.

What Max was suggesting, he knew, was that Martin had a dangerous weakness. Trained interrogators were like death-watch beetles: they would search the fabric patiently for a single point of rottenness or insecurity, burrow in, and bring the whole edifice down. If Martin was vulnerable on moral guilt it would not take his interrogators long to find out, just as Max had done.

He stood up. 'Let me think about all this,' he said, waving his pipe to show that the discussion was over. As Hemming turned away he added, as an afterthought, 'Max, you worked for Martin. What's your impression of him?'

Max Hemming halted, blinking rapidly. Then he gave a sudden barking cough of amusement. 'I was working with Martin when he had to fire a man on the Middle East desk for getting too friendly with the Russians,' he said. 'I told Martin I'd always had the impression he was one of our most reliable people. Martin said, "That's the time to start worrying. Impressions are only useful for telling you what people want you to think."'

29

'So?'

'My impression of Martin Commoner is that he's the most efficient and trustworthy operative you've got.'

It was 19.15 by the General's watch. In London, past midnight; in Jerusalem, the small hours of Tuesday morning. The sun was touching the oak woods that surround the great glass and concrete palace of the CIA. The shadow thrown by the tall red-and-white-checked water tower in the middle of the compound had almost reached the chain-link fence. The General had 'phoned his wife to cancel their tennis doubles, and had sent down to the cafeteria for a club sandwich. There had been no word from Fisher.

He got up restlessly and roamed the antiseptic corridors. Staffers carrying memoranda shot him startled glances and hurried on their way. Like any other limb of the bureaucracy, the Government's chief intelligence-gathering service went on auxiliary motor after six pm. Circuits in its giant brain went to sleep; its neural responses became more selective. Information from human and electronic spies all over the globe continued to pour in, second by second throughout the night, but unless it was given priority marking it reposed until the following morning in cables, taped messages and telex print-outs on a thousand unoccupied desks. Since, as the General was well aware, only a fraction of one per cent of it was of the slightest value, it made little difference.

It was this fraction of a percentage point that the vast bulk of the CIA with its 26,000 operatives had been built up to detect, analyse and pass on in simple form to its impatient masters in the White House. Fisher was part of it; and yet there was still no word from Jerusalem. The General stopped at an open door at the end of a corridor, crossed a large square room with maps hanging above grey filing cabinets, and went into a cool partitioned office on the other side. Vince Addams were waiting for him.

It was way past the time Addams was usually free to tip back his first scotch of the evening, and his heavy face under the grey hair slicked down over his forehead had a sallow, puffy look. The General suspected that he drank secretly in the office, but a security guard given a pass-key to his private safe had found no evidence of liquor. Like many brilliant Arabists, Addams was

30

something of a loner; a morose, suspicious man, three years into his second marriage with a beautiful Druze girl whom he treated brutally (so Agency rumour had it) when the drink got on top of him. But his ability as an intelligence analyst was almost intuitive: he alone had appreciated the full significance of the Ayatollah's broadcasts from exile, and in the departmental shake-out which followed the Shah's downfall he had risen quickly to the top. He sat now, hunched over his untidy desk, a small cigar protruding from his clasped hands, making no move when the DCI came into his office except to gesture him to an armchair.

'What news of Martin?' he asked.

The General who expected greater deference from his junior officers, remained standing and shook his head. 'What is Jerusalem saying?'

'Golding on the Israeli desk has been pulsing our people there. Fisher paid a courtesy call early this evening on the Prime Minister to lay the groundwork. After that he was being entertained to dinner at Air Force Headquarters. He was due back at the Embassy ten minutes ago. I'm expecting a message any moment to say he's arrived.'

'Once he gets there I want him to stay there. I don't want him out of that building without my direct permission.'

'You really think there's a connection?'

'Do you, Vince?'

Addams hesitated. He leaned forward and squashed out his cigar in the small okapi-foot ashtray given to him, so he claimed, by one of the Saudi princes. Gruffly he said, 'Martin knows Fisher better than I do. He hired him to run the Israeli desk and he wanted him for this mission of yours. Don't ask me where his loyalties lie.'

The General turned away to hide the twitch of amusement on his face, and peered at a framed photograph on the wall of Addams with the late Shah of Iran — taken not in Teheran, he noticed, but in St Moritz. There was no love lost between Addams and Commoner. Addams regarded Martin as an upper-cruster — the kind of Eastern establishment figure who gets promoted above his mid-Western colleagues because he's regarded by the old hands as *one of us*. It was nonsense, of course, but it was the kind of discrimination Addams liked to keep alive. Martin, after all, had gone to Princeton, as had

31

many of the old-timers like the General himself — the 'wine and cheese brigade' as Addams liked to call them, though not to the DCI's face.

'I don't ski,' said Addams' voice behind him. 'I hate the goddamn snow. It was the only place the Shah would consent to talk to a spook like me.'

'Fisher can be trusted.' The DCI turned round. 'Counter-Intelligence has gone through Fisher's background since his first year at Yale. He's as clean as a bayonet. You know MOSSAD trusts him. That's why Martin sent him out with the pictures.'

'His first street job for us was in Beirut.'

'So?'

'I'm speculating. The Arabs could have had him wrapped up all this time. What then? Suppose copies of those photographs suddenly turned up in Islamabad with our fingerprints all over them? The flareback could destroy this whole Department.'

Before the General could answer, the electrically-operated door swung open. A young man with a pink face and a weak chin came into the room. 'Your message from Jerusalem, sir,' he said, glancing at the Director and half-consciously straightening his string tie.

Addams snatched at the paper. He waited until the gofer was out of the room. Then he stood up and handed the message to the General, his face animated for the first time.

'Fisher hasn't returned to the Embassy,' he said. 'The contact number he left was a restaurant which closed an hour ago. The Air Force people say they know nothing. Fisher's simply disappeared. The same way as Commoner.'

The General read the message silently, standing straight as a ramrod to ease the stabbing in his back. It said nothing about the AWACS photographs. No reason why it should. But he knew damn well what had happened. The Israelis were holding on to Fisher as a guarantee. They wouldn't let him go until the nuclear pictures were in their hands.

The whole thing had become a time bomb. It could go off in their faces tomorrow or it could go off a year from now, whether they got Commoner back or not. As the President had said, they were walking barefoot through a snake farm and if they didn't keep moving they were going to get bit.

'I want copies of all further communications with Jerusalem

sent up to my office without delay,' he told Addams, who was lighting a fresh cigar.

Feeling suddenly very tired, he crumpled the cable in his fist. The White House would have to be told. It occurred to him that if Martin Commoner got out of this alive, he was going to have a lot to answer for.

TUESDAY

Waves of nausea brought Martin to the surface, choking. His eyes were sticky; he blinked them open into a blank greenish whiteness and felt a stab of panic: they had left him here to die. His limbs were paralysed. The screens were up around his hospital bed. He couldn't move or shout out that he was still alive.

He closed his eyes as a blinding pain shot through his head. When he opened them again he saw there were no screens. He was lying inside a tent, an ordinary campers' tent with a pole in the middle. His wrists and ankles were tied with cord, which was why he could not move them. He was stripped to his shorts and lying on a blue corrugated plastic air-bed. Painfully turning his head, he saw with no more than mild surprise that what he had taken at first to be grass underneath was green carpet: it explained the relentless cold light penetrating the tent walls and disorientating him.

He had been kidnapped. He was in a room, probably somewhere in the south of England. Holding on to those two facts brought him out of the nightmare of semi-consciousness and strangely comforted him. He had been hit over the head — when was that? The last thing he could remember was leaving the Castle and getting into a car. He must do better than that. It was a Monday. He had left early to go and see Nancy in . . . some town nearby. The driver — his face — no, he could remember only a peaked cap and a grey coat. They had gone back past the Castle on the right, past the lake and the golf course . . .

He turned his eyes away from the whiteness and rested them on the green carpet. Faintly in the clangour of his headache a nursery jingle played. His hand was raised, shading his eyes from the sun. Beside the van his driver was pitching on his face. A girl in a blue-patterned dress was standing over him. A man in a green uniform was running towards him holding a gun.

He groaned involuntarily and stared at the carpet two inches from his nose. Out of the corner of his eye he saw the tent-flap open. A girl came in. He saw only her blue trousers and tennis shoes. He opened his mouth to speak to her, but could not. In a deft movement she lifted his head and took away a white towel. He had not known it was there. He saw that it was caked with dried blood, blackish-brown in colour. It meant he must have been lying there for at least twelve hours. Probably longer.

This time a sound escaped his lips, although his wooden tongue could not make it sound like 'water'. The girl let his head fall back and took the towel away. A moment later she came back with another rolled towel and, thank God, a cup of water. Holding his head, she put the water to his lips. He drank greedily, the growth of beard on his chin rasping against the cup. As he did so, a man came into the tent, silently and so quickly that he had time only to see a dark beard and the thin wiry arm which gripped his arm and plunged into it a hypodermic needle.

He jerked convulsively. The girl was leaning on his bare chest and holding his head. Her long black hair was in his open mouth. He looked up in outrage at an oval face, beautifully shaped with high cheekbones but sallow and spotty, out of which a pair of hazel-brown eyes gazed down at him fearfully.

'Why you . . .' he began. She shook her head and put her finger to her lips.

He struggled to speak again, but the drug was taking effect. His sphincter loosened and he passed a trickle of urine into his shorts, like a baby. He turned his head away from the girl, closing his eyes in disgust. Darkness flooded over him; he slumped unconscious.

Martin's mouth was furry and tasted of vomit when he awoke, many hours later. But his head was clearer. The blinding flashes had gone. There was now only a dull constant throbbing, overlayed by a sound like musical strumming on a guitar. The light inside the tent was unchanged. He had no way of knowing how

35

much time had passed. The heavy rancid smell of urine in the air — that was different. Mortified, he realised that his captors intended to let him lie and rot in his own excretions.

He was still pathetically weak. It was the classic treatment of course. He'd seen it done in Vietnam to Viet Cong. Strip him of everything: his sense of time, his sense of being somewhere, his dignity. Especially his dignity. After a long period of isolation he began to talk. That was the way it had gone with Pham Trang after they'd caught him in Bien Hoa and brought him down to Saigon. Nothing specific at first. Just a few mono-syllabic responses to his interrogator, less to communicate than to prove to himself he was human and not an animal shunned by men. But once that silence was broken, the psychological relief was too great to stop there. It was like taking an arrow out of a deep wound and letting the flow of blood wash the pain away at the cost of life itself. Out of the exchange of words with his interrogator grew a relationship; and out of the relationship, dependency. Scattered remarks built day by day into conversations. The dreadful fear grew of losing this one link with humanity and being thrown back into an isolation more hope-less than before. As the interrogator showed signs of boredom, Trang started throwing in personal details, names, dates, any-thing to keep his interest, even to the extent of inventing fictional stories to whet his appetite. But by this time the blood had run out; Trang was a husk, his usefulness at an end. The operation that followed, against a VC network in Bien Hoa, was one of the few clear-cut successes Phoenix could lay claim to.

But that was Saigon in wartime. This was England. Martin was not an agent or a spy, he was a bureaucrat: nobody could mistake him for anything else. Why kidnap a bureaucrat? What information did he have that would not already have been rendered useless by the Agency by the time it was forced out of him? Only BeeSting. It had to be BeeSting. But who? The Russians? Surely the KGB would not need to resort to these crude, amateurish tactics. The Pakistanis? Hardly. One of the Palestinian groups perhaps? The girl looked as if she might have Arab blood in her. But how? It was absurd. He was distraught. He couldn't think straight. He jerked his legs and his bound arms in a spasm of rage.

The tent flap was pulled back. The girl came in. Martin stared

36

at her. She was wearing a quilted cotton jacket stitched with an oriental design in black and red, and blue velvet pantaloons. She had pulled back her long hair and tied it with an elastic band. She wrinkled her nose.

'God, what a smell,' she said.

They were the first words Martin had heard. It was an English voice. Painfully, he eased himself into a sitting position against the back of the tent.

'What time is it?' he asked hoarsely.

The girl ignored him. She called back over her shoulder: 'Luke? Get me the bucket, there's a love.' Turning back to Martin she smiled at him. There was none of the malice and fanatical bitterness he had been expecting. In her eyes he saw only a wide childish sympathy.

'We love you,' she said.

'Who are you?'

'We are the Family.'

'You won't get away with it. You'll be caught. Do you know who I am?'

'Yes.'

'Then you know you don't stand a chance in hell,' he said between his teeth.

The girl shrugged and smiled at him again.

A shadow fell against the tent wall.

'Esther,' a man's voice called.

Esther ducked out of the tent. She returned a moment later with a plastic bucket in one hand and a mug of coffee in the other.

'Drink this,' she said, cupping his tied hands around the mug. 'You look like you need it.'

The coffee tasted acid: ten-to-one it had been drugged. But he didn't care. It must be the first real nourishment he had had in days. The girl was still gazing at him. He said gently, 'Esther, is it? Please tell me, Esther. How long have I been here?'

She shook her head, not taking her inquisitive brown eyes off his face. 'I'm going now,' she announced, in the same matter-of-fact voice. 'I'll be outside, if you want to use the bucket.'

She retreated, a yard at most outside the tent, and sat cross-legged on the carpet, watching him. Behind her, through the open flap, he could see a wall of the room he was in, papered with a green trellis pattern. Standing against the wall was a mahogany dresser with a silver-framed mirror and an empty blue glass vase on it.

The girl was staring at him and mouthing something. He could not hear what it was. The drug was beginning to dull his senses. The girl was rocking slightly, backwards and forwards, her head swelling and receding. It was her face he was looking at — her *face*, not a mask. She had never been masked in front of him, nor had the man who injected him earlier. It was a known fact (in his giddiness it seemed to him an axiom beyond dispute) that all kidnappers masked their faces except those, like the Sicilian bandits, who intended to kill their captives anyway. This thought, as he stared into the face of his murderer-to-be, paralysed him with an abject fear, the more gripping because of its suddenness. He felt sick and breathless. His hands shook uncontrollably. Nausea rose through him. He retched violently, heaving and spewing.

'God, help!' he gasped, and blacked out, as the girl got off the floor and moved towards him.

The Travellers' Club in Pall Mall had a mothy, slightly sweetish odour about it, as though generations of Empire-builders had not only expired in it but been buried just underneath its frayed carpets. The porter made William Pomfret feel that he should have been wearing a hat and carrying a cane. Since he had neither, he handed over his rolled gaberdine raincoat awkwardly, like something wrapped in newspaper, and proceeded up the stairs.

It was typical of Christopher Knight's sense of humour to have chosen a place like this as neutral ground for their first strategy conference. William was in no mood for humour. After a fruitless night in Maidstone, he'd catnapped for an hour in the car taking him back to London, and his brain was still signalling him back to sleep. Unshaven and bleary-eyed, he was going to cut a poor figure beside the M15 man with his dry-cleaned suit and his trim moustache. He was being cast in the role of the humble police officer, waiting to be told what he ought to be investigating.

What the hell, it was all mystique with the Security Service anyway. Mystique and bloody privilege. The Intelligence Corps badge in World War II, a small flower against a background of foliage, had been known to its critics as 'a pansy resting on its laurels'. As a description of Knight and his team of wet-behind-the-ears public school types, it was still the best he knew.

Arriving in the dining-room, William traced the sweetish smell to kippers, and his spirits rose. Knight, for the sake of appearances, was sitting at a corner table with his back to the wall. His pale heavy face was pinker than usual. He looked ill-at-ease, fiddling with one of his cufflinks inlaid with a gold K on a black background. The man sitting beside him was tanned and rangy-looking, with bleached hair, a thin mouth and a long nose which had been broken at least once and mended badly, giving his face a beaked, disapproving expression. This must be Vanderbyle. He was wearing a pale blue suit and a bright pink shirt on which a club tie had been awkwardly planted.

Christopher Knight's manner seemed to William strangely deferential, almost obsequious. 'You know why Vanderbyle is here,' he said to William after the introductions had been made. 'I want you to give him all the help and assistance he requests. I need hardly emphasise to you, Pomfret, the enormous importance his government and ours attach to clearing this case up as expeditiously as possible.'

'I'll have two kippers, toast and a pot tea,' said William to the waiter who had materialised at his elbow.

'We are particularly anxious — correct me if I'm wrong, Vanderbyle — that the investigation should be carried forward as confidentially as possible, with the minimum of information being made public. I have conveyed this point to your Commander.'

'That's right.' Vanderbyle leaned across the breakfast table, so close that William could smell the mint on his breath. 'I don't want any asshole journalists screwing this up. Whoever lifted Commoner, I want them hunted down while they're still on the move. No newsmen. No television cameras. Just in and out.' He looked at Knight. 'Isn't that right, Chris?'

'Yes. Yes indeed.'

The kippers arrived, and William ate in silence for a while. He thought of pointing out that while the investigation was head-quartered in Maidstone only the Chief Constable of Kent had the power to authorise a security blanket — but if he started explaining that, he'd lose what little bargaining power he had. He was buggered if he was going to be used as a front-runner by

Knight and Vanderbyle while they sucked him dry of information and gave back none in return.

Eventually he said, 'Don't worry. I'll keep the wraps on. But I'm going to need one or two things from you gentlemen.'

'What do you mean?' asked Knight.

'Communications, for starters. I don't want to get my wires crossed. For instance, is M16 in on this?'

Christopher Knight glanced at Vanderbyle, and with a fussy gesture brushed invisible crumbs off the sleeve of this dark grey suit. William suddenly began to understand the earlier deference towards the man from Texas. There was a power struggle going on here.

He pricked up his ears. 'Better kept in the family,' Knight was saying. 'I've been explaining to Vanderbyle that from the British point of view this is strictly an internal security matter which need not affect the other Department.'

'But what about your six dozen permanent agents over here?' William asked Vanderbyle. 'They've been reporting to Parrish, who passes on the titbits to M16 in Century House, isn't that right?'

'They stay out of this,' said Vanderbyle succinctly. With a toothpick he was extracting bits of the Club breakfast from his teeth. 'I've got my own team over with me, and I'm calling the shots. We've had our fill of double-agents in the CIA: Kampiles, Bisley, Barnett, Clarke. The kind of people who kidnapped Commoner play hardball. I've worked against the big boys in this game, I know how they operate. As soon as you penetrate their back-up apparatus they cut out and move on. You gotta travel light and travel fast. Or else you get off the mat.'

It sounded impressive. Knight was nodding, like a city slicker listening to a cowboy.

'What kind of people are we looking for? In your view?' asked William.

Vanderbyle took the toothpick out of his mouth. 'I'll tell you what I think. My hunch is that we're up against international terrorists, probably hired by a foreign intelligence service. I am not in a position to amplify that at this moment in time.'

'You see, Pomfret?' said Christopher Knight unnecessarily. His face was wearing an important smile.

'I see,' said William. He did indeed. Knight was lining up with

Vanderbyle. It was the kind of procedural game civil servants loved to play: manoeuvre the board so that every piece of information passes across your desk first, and then take the credit. Well, Knight was welcome to play it against M16. But he sure as hell wasn't going to play it against William Pomfret.

As he was thinking how to get around the Maidstone problem, the waiter appeared at his elbow again, carrying a salver. William dug into his pockets for a tip.

'I think you have a message,' said Knight, allowing an edge of condescension into his voice.

When he came back from the telephone, the other two were waiting to listen to him. He stirred his coffee and drank it before speaking.

'My assistant at the Yard,' he said casually. 'It looks like we've found the getaway car. In Lewisham, a dark-blue Morris Marina. It was hired yesterday from Hertz Rent-a-Car at 200 Buckingham Palace Road, on a stolen driving licence. The Hertz assistants are off duty. We've got detectives travelling to their homes now. It's an early break, earlier than they can have been expecting —'

'Unless it was a plant,' said Knight.

William chose to ignore this. 'It gives us the initiative,' he went on, looking at Vanderbyle. 'The Commander has told Maidstone that we're handling everything now from the London end. What I must have from you now is the full picture on Martin Commoner. Photographs, habits, mannerisms: anything that will help particularise him in people's minds. Plus all the background that could be relevant. I've got to follow this up right away.'

All his tiredness gone, William studied the American, wondering if he'd judged him right. Obviously Vanderbyle didn't care for Parrish; it shouldn't matter to Vanderbyle if he put the CIA chief-of-station's nose out of joint. And William had the executive powers of the police behind him. These two needed his cooperation right down the line.

Vanderbyle picked up the end of his tie and studied it. Knight flushed. Didn't they cultivate poker faces up in Curzon Street? 'Surely Parrish told you yesterday all you need to know,' said Knight.

'He told me who Commoner was and where he came from.

41

He didn't give me any clue as to why a gang should want to kidnap him on a private visit to England.'

'Because he doesn't know. Any more than we do.'

Vanderbyle was playing with the butter knife. William tried again. 'I've got five hundred undercover men and women out there, in squatters' houses, radical groups, fringe politics, IRA, Arabs, you name it. If I can point any one of those in the right direction, we'll get some action, I promise you. I need something to work on.'

'Let's take a walk.' It was Vanderbyle who spoke. He stood up, rattling the teacups, and strode out of the dining-room. The two Englishmen followed in his wake.

Outside the Travellers' Club, they turned left and left again, towards St James's Park. It was still early for the tourists. A gardener was weeding the green verges. An old woman was feeding bread to the ducks and pelicans. As Vanderbyle talked, in a generalised way, about Commoner and the Middle East, William glanced at Christopher Knight out of the corner of his eye. Knight might be unhappy about it, but Vanderbyle was treating him on a par with the M15 man. Jostling for advantage in the information game, William was in pole position. He wasn't intending to relinquish it.

Nancy Koscinski had tidied round the apartment, made the bed, washed up her solitary dinner from the night before and stacked all her work papers into a neater-than-usual confusion on her desk. Now all she had to do was wait. And try to relax. She put Vivaldi's *Seasons* on the Music-center and took down off the shelf a favourite book of Japanese woodcuts. Before she could stop them, the row of books slumped sideways along the pine shelf, knocking the photograph of Martin on to the carpet.

With a cry she knelt down to pick it up. But the glass was unbroken. Martin looked up at her with the expression she had seen a hundred times across the dinner table — thoughtful, intelligent, the self-mocking grin (she had teased him about spooks hating to have their picture taken) not hiding the wary seriousness around the eyes. With her fingernail she traced the lines around his mouth. They went upwards. Which was a good sign.

Remembering who was coming she did not replace the photograph but put it away in a desk drawer. Tears came unexpectedly to her eyes and she blinked them away. Dumb to think of it as an omen. But it had been one of those days when nothing had gone right. Her Havasupai weaving had fallen off the wall mysteriously during the night. There were no cabs and she'd had to wait ten minutes in the rain for a bus down Connecticut Avenue. One of Senator Traill's committee meetings on the Hill had had to be chaired at short notice and without a full brief. Then to top it all, when she'd wanted a quiet lunch to prepare herself for this afternoon's interview, Laura Cohen had come and sat beside her and talked on and on about Martin, until she'd burst into tears over her caesar salad and had had to leave.

It frightened her, this crying. She had not cried at all when Parrish had told her what had happened and put her on the plane, tidying her away to Washington like she'd just tidied Martin's photograph into the desk drawer. Dry-eyed, she'd been driven home from the airport by one of Martin's colleagues and told to keep her mouth shut and behave normally, which was exactly what she had done. Until the night before last, alone in bed, when she'd smoked eight cigarettes in a row and had to 'phone up her mother in Brooklyn in the middle of the night, which was something she hadn't done since she was, well, a teenager.

The record had got round to 'Winter'. It was coldly soothing this music, the plucked strings like the slow dripping of icicles from the eaves. She hoped she wouldn't start crying when the CIA spook arrived. So embarrassing suddenly to burst into tears and snivel into a handkerchief. It had been difficult enough choosing the right clothes to wear. She wouldn't feel on top of things if she looked sluttish; but anything too smart might suggest that she thought there were more important things than Martin. She'd decided on a Calvin Klein sweater and a very ordinary pair of slacks. That should make her unclassifiable.

She got up to tuck a handkerchief in her sleeve. The door-bell rang. She checked her appearance in the hall mirror, running her hand through the thick black hair which framed her pixie face with its wide mouth and brown serious eyes. Her face was pale and her eyes were red-rimmed, but it was too late to do anything about that. After a last hurried look around, she opened the door.

The pale blondish man standing in the corridor was not much taller than her own five foot four. But he stood so stiffly with his arms at his sides, and looked at her so intently through his steel-rimmed spectacles, that she took an involuntary step backwards.

'Yes?'

'Miss Nancy Koscinski?'

'Yes.'

He put out his hand, lifting his arm from the elbow. The smile on his face reminded her of the icicles she'd just been listening to.

'Hi, I'm Max Hemming. I expect Martin has talked to you about me.'

He was carrying a briefcase, she saw now for the first time. She cleared her throat nervously.

'Mr Commoner has never discussed Agency people with me.'

'May I come in? Thank you.'

He followed her into the living-room and stood motionless just inside the door. She wondered if he was the shy type, a bachelor perhaps; then she noticed his eyes darting round the room, registering the two Japanese paintings and the woodcut on the wall, the little Bonsai tree and the fan box on the low glass-topped coffee table, the long-leaved Kentia palm in the corner, the big white paper lampshade hanging low over the cushions on the floor. She felt invaded. In a moment, the darting eyes would come round and rest upon her.

'Go ahead. Anywhere,' she said, indicating places to sit down. 'Can I get you a drink? A Scotch?'

'Do you have a cup of coffee?'

'Sure. Come through.'

She led the way into the kitchen. Hemming sat down promptly on a hard chair and opened his briefcase on the kitchen table. Resting her hands against the stove to steady herself, Nancy asked, 'Is there any word yet? About Martin?'

'About Mr Commoner?'

'Okay. You caught me off guard out there.'

'We have received no communication from the kidnappers. Always presuming he was kidnapped.'

'What do you mean?'

'We have not yet established what happened.'

He had not looked at her yet. He'd taken a pad out of the briefcase and was writing something on it in a small bunched script. There was no sound in the kitchen except the rasp of his white shirt cuff across the paper.

'Was he . . .' Her voice was trembling. She had cigarettes in her purse. She fumbled for them and lit one from the grill. She started again. 'Was Martin hurt?'

'That's interesting you should ask that. There was no evidence of any struggle taking place.'

'What's so damn interesting?' He was like a mortician sitting there. 'Of course I'm interested. Martin was . . .'

'Yes?'

'Well, I love him.'

Hemming looked straight at her for the first time, and smiled. It was a disarming, rather boyish smile. 'Good. That means you'll help us, does it?'

'Of course. Anything at all.' Her throat was fluttering again. Hearing the kettle boil, she turned and poured out the coffee, glad to have her back to him.

When she turned back there was a microphone facing her on the table, its lead snaking back into the opened briefcase.

'Let's begin with last Monday,' Hemming said. 'I need to know your movements in detail.'

'Okay. Milk?'

'Black. No sugar.'

She brought the two coffees over and sat down at the table opposite him.

'I'd flown over the day before. I stayed the night in the Capital Hotel in Chelsea —'

'Any particular reason?'

'Nope. I stayed there once before. The name seemed kind of apt, coming from Washington. So. After breakfast at the hotel I went shopping in Harrods. And gave up when I found a dollar wasn't even enough to buy a box of pins.'

'Did you have any sensation at any time you were being followed? Or watched?'

'No.'

'Then what?'

'I decided to have an early lunch, a ham salad I think, at a snackerie on the other side of the street.'

Hemming stared at her. 'Are you telling me you passed the whole morning in this store, Harrods?'

'What? Oh. Well, I mean yes. Sure. You know, I got up late. Anyway, it's a big store.'

'You were alone all this time?'

'Yes. After lunch I took a subway to Victoria Station, and caught a train to Maidstone in Kent. I arrived there about 3.00 pm and took a cab straight to the Kings Arms Hotel.'

'Why there?'

'This was . . .' She hestitated. 'I thought you knew. This was by prior arrangement with Martin. He made the booking before he left Washington.'

'Did you inform anyone you were going to be there?'

'Did I? No. But I'm sure Martin would have told you people. I mean, the Agency.'

'What was the hotel like? Describe it to me.'

'Oh . . .' Nancy smiled wanly. 'You know. One of those dinky English inns you read about. Where the floors slope away from you, and you can't get out of the sack in the morning without banging your head on a Tudor joist. We were planning . . .' She trailed off. Her throat was tightening again.

'You were planning?'

'We'd planned just to use it as a base, and to spend the weekend, you know, seeing the countryside. I went up to the room. It was number 36. I freshened up. Martin was supposed to be arriving about 4.30 —'

'He said that in Washington?'

'It's what we arranged. And I waited. And at 5.00 he hadn't arrived. I started thinking maybe something urgent had come up. Or Barbara had flown over — you know, his wife. But I kind of knew he'd have 'phoned me. And I thought maybe I should go look in the bar, although Martin hates bars as a general rule, he's not the socialising kind. So I went downstairs. And that's when the phone call came through.'

'From Parrish in London?'

'Whoever. He didn't tell me about Martin. He said, go back upstairs and wait. But I knew . . . I knew.'

There was a long pause. She said dully, 'What do you need to write for, with the tape machine going?' Hemming didn't answer.

'Is Martin a friend of yours?'

The cuff stopped rasping across the paper; the hand was still. 'Martin is a colleague,' said the even voice. 'What happens to him matters to all of us. Now can I ask the questions?'

'Oh. Sure.'

'Your maiden name is Nancy Braun?'

'Yes.'

'Age 33. Born in Brooklyn, father a jeweller. Studied law at Columbia. Married Stefan Koscinski, a professor of jurisprudence —'

'Sure, okay, okay. You've got the right file card.'

'If you don't mind me asking, why did you disassociate from him?'

'Oh, Jesus!' She sighed. 'Are you married? Sorry, I asked a question. How many reasons do you want? I married too young; it was a teacher-pupil relationship; Stefan left his clothes all over the floor; he wanted me to have babies, I wanted a career — a hundred and one reasons why it wouldn't work. The marvel is it lasted five years. I think he told good Polish jokes, that was it.' Seeing no reaction from Hemming, she added, 'New Yorkers appreciate humour, you know. Even more when they go to Washington.'

'Did you disassociate from him because of Martin?'

'Did I? No. No, I didn't. Listen, I've told you why —'

'You met Martin in New York?'

'Yes, but —'

'You started seeing him again as soon as you got here?'

Nancy moistened her lips with the coffee. It had gone cold. 'So what?' she asked. 'There's no law against it. I'm sure I was checked out at Langley just as soon as Martin was seen talking to me in an intimate voice. Do you want more coffee?'

'No. When did you become Martin's mistress?'

'I don't know what you mean. That's not a word I use.'

Hemming blinked at her. 'Pardon me. When did you start sleeping together?'

'Are you trying to make me feel dirty, or what? Martin and I have been close friends for eighteen months, maybe more. What we do in bed is none of your business.'

'Did Martin talk to you about his wife Barbara much?'

'No.'

'Did he ever say he'd mentioned to Barbara about your relationship?'

47

Nancy stood up abruptly, stubbing out her cigarette in the saucer. 'Is it okay if we go next door? I'm tired of this room.'

'I'd just like to finish my questions if you don't mind.'

'To hell with your questions!' She was trembling, close to tears. 'It's Martin's life at stake, Mr Hemming. I'm not here to answer prying questions about my sex relations with him. What do you take me for? I'm not guilty of anything.'

Max Hemming surprised her with another sudden smile. His voice was conciliatory. 'I'm not accusing you of malfeasance, Miss Koscinski. Please sit down.'

She sat, knocking her coffee cup. He leaned across the table, close enough for her to see with a shock that his eyes were not at all amused; they were angry and hard.

'Let me get this straight with you,' he said softly. 'Martin Commoner has an extremely high security clearance. He has ... disappeared. On the way to see you. That makes you very important to us, Miss Koscinski. It makes you very important to the whole United States Government. If it hadn't been for you, maybe Martin would be safe —'

'You can't say that!'

'I am saying it. He could have been blackmailed. You tell me nobody else knew you were meeting him in Maidstone. Well maybe his wife knew, maybe she was jealous —'

'That's absurd!'

'And what about the Senator you work for? Traill? What did you tell him?'

'I told him I was taking a long weekend off. That's all.'

'Off to England for the weekend?'

'No!'

'Your mother? Girlfriends? Colleagues? It's something to boast about, isn't it? Off to Europe for a dirty weekend?'

'Fuck you!'

'Who did you tell, Miss Koscinski?'

Hemming pushed the microphone a few inches closer to her. She stared at it, like a rabbit at a cobra, and shook her head speechlessly. The kitchen light burned down on them. 'You have no right ...' she said, choking.

'No right? To put you through this? Do you know what Martin could be going through now, because of you? Shall I tell you what they do to turn people like Martin round? It's an art in itself, making people —'

48

'Shut up!' Nancy stood up blindly and turned from him, but the tears came anyway. Gripping the sink, she sobbed aloud. She was so defenceless, that's what she couldn't bear. She had no idea she was so vulnerable to something like this . . . this calculated cruelty. How dare he —

A hand rested lightly on her back. A handkerchief was offered. She took it and dabbed her cheeks; it smelt of cough pastilles. 'Please accept my apologies,' said Hemming's voice in her ear.

'Get out of here, you bastard!'

'I understand how you feel. It's how we're all feeling right now. I'm just as tough on myself as I am on you. We should have taken better care of him.'

Nancy turned on him, angrily. Hemming took off his spectacles and tapped them into his breast pocket. He gave her a small apologetic smile. 'You're right, let's go next door,' he murmured. 'I hate these strong lights.'

She went through in front of him and sank on to a cushion, still holding the handkerchief to her face. 'Can I get you a drink?' Hemming asked.

'A Scotch. In that cupboard. Glasses above.'

He poured her out a stiff whisky, holding up the glass like a waiter and measuring out the dosage. Ignoring the cushions, he brought out of the kitchen a hard-backed chair which he placed squarely in front of her and straddled.

'Here's to Martin's homecoming,' he said.

'What are you drinking?'

'Perrier water.'

They drank to Martin, and she stared at his shiny brown shoes. She felt drained of emotion. 'What more can I do?' she asked.

'You want Martin back alive, don't you?'

She nodded.

'Then please help us. I want your full co-operation. Will you give me your full co-operation?'

'Yes.'

'Then here's what you do. Think of anything Martin said that might have been nagging him. Problems at work. Problems at home. Any anxiety or insecurity. Any smallest thing that might be picked out in deep interrogation and used against him.'

'Really?'

'A good interrogator can start with a pin that he can't feel pricking, and build it up into a knife that twists in his gut. We need those pins, Nancy. We need your help.'

Nancy nodded, serious now. Sipping the neat whisky, she was beginning to revive. It was for Martin's sake; she could see that clearly.

She reached for another cigarette. 'Give me some time,' she said.

He came awake very suddenly in darkness, his senses at fever pitch. The blackness was absolute. There must be boards on the windows, or heavy black-out curtains. His kidnappers had not moved him: he could feel the invisibly stifling presence of the tent walls. If he put out his hand . . . but his hands were tightly bound still, and his legs.

There was no sound. Maybe they had left him here. Maybe they had had to make a run for it. More likely they were testing his sanity. Or else they had left him here to die.

His situation was not hopeless. He could inch his way out of the tent. If the glass vase was still on the dresser he could somehow reach it and smash it, and use the glass to cut away whatever it was they had put over the windows. But he was very weak. If he could first loosen his bonds, that would help conserve his strength. He raised his hands to his mouth and ran his tongue over the cords, trying to identify the knot in the darkness. With his teeth, he began tugging.

After he had worried at the cords like a dog for a long time, he felt them begin to loosen. His mouth was full of blood from his gums abrading; he spat it out and continued until he thought his front teeth would fall out. At least they had taken his watch: he didn't have to bite on metal. Flexing his wrists, he felt the cords begin to slip and slide. Panting, he clenched and pumped his fists. He could move his hands apart now. It would not take long to have them freed altogether.

At that moment he heard footsteps on the stairs, and felt a split-second of regret at being rescued before he could make his own escape.

'In here!' he yelled. 'Martin Commoner! Help me!'

A door opened; the light went on, dazzling him. The man

sitting watching him through the open tent flap must have been there silent and motionless for hours, sitting where Esther had been, keeping guard. He smiled now, and rose to his feet, a great bear of a man built like a quarterback with long blond curls falling around his wide moon face and through one ear a small silver earring looking absurdly delicate on that huge head.

'Hiya, Mr Commoner,' he said, in a slow Californian drawl. 'I'm Luke. It's a pleasure meeting you.'

'I was asleep,' Martin muttered, half to himself. Indeed, in his confusion he did not know if he had been dreaming his attempted escape. The sharp pain as Luke tightened the cord around his hands brought him back to his senses. The large figure bending over him was hardly more than a boy, he realised, hardly into his early twenties at most.

'What do you want with me?' he demanded weakly.

'We're going to educate you. Save your soul.'

'Don't give me that crap,' Martin's wrists were throbbing. 'You've got me here. What do you want?'

He was shivering. Luke smelled of machine oil. He was wearing blue overalls with a yellow *Jesus Loves You* badge pinned to them. It made no sense at all.

'Hey, are you cold?' Luke shouldered his heavy body out of the tent. A minute later, he was back with a woollen blanket which he draped laboriously over Martin's legs and chest. 'I'll get your breakfast,' he said, and disappeared again.

Martin was grateful as much for the relief from indignity as for the warmth the blanket gave him. It was the first real mark of humanity his captors had shown. When Luke came back and sat him gently upright against the back of the tent, he gave him a grateful look, opening his mouth like a baby when Luke lifted the bowl of Weetabix with milk and sugar to spoon-feed him.

As he was fed, Luke recited in a sing-song voice: ' "There is nothing from without a man that, entering into him, can defile him: but the things that come out of him, those are they that defile the man." *Mark* 7,15.'

The tea that followed was hot and strong, made in a pot, English-fashion. After the pain of the first mouthful, Martin let it trickle carefully down his tongue, keeping it away from his sore and bleeding gums.

'Are you expecting to keep me here?' he said.

51

'Sure.'

'Until when?'

'When your heart is full of repentance.'

They were playing a game with him he didn't understand. But at least this one was talking. The manuals and the public safety programmes he had read years ago in Buenos Aires, when kidnapping was a real and constant threat, were coming back to him. He knew what the statistics were on hostages. If they managed to survive the first three days, 90 per cent of them lived to go free. Even from the Red Brigades in Italy. However long he'd been in captivity already, he must act as if this was the first day. He must talk to his kidnappers and go on talking, try to involve himself in their lives and relationships . . .

Luke was leaving the tent. Martin said hurriedly, 'Will you teach me what I must do?'

The big youth shook his head. 'God teaches. You must listen.' There was a Bible on the carpet beside him. He sat cross-legged, like Esther, and began reading from the Sermon on the Mount, in the same sing-song voice: '"Blessed are they which do hunger and thirst after righteousness: for they shall be filled. Blessed are the merciful: for they shall obtain mercy. Blessed are the pure in heart: for they shall see God. Blessed are the peacemakers: for they shall be called the children of God."'

He stopped reading at this point, and looked up. Martin stared at him. 'Who sent you? Where are you from?' he demanded.

Luke shook his head again and smiled good-naturedly. 'That doesn't signify,' he said. 'It's where we're at now that signifies.' He scratched his blond curls.

'Are your parents alive?'

'Parents? We don't have parents any more. Like, we're all children of God. Peace-makers.'

'Is this how you keep the peace? By kidnapping people and drugging them?'

Luke's large placid features clouded for a moment. He seemed to be searching for something in his mind. 'I *John*, 2, 18,' he pronounced slowly: "Even now there are many antichrists."'

A chill struck through Martin's heart. He was talking to a lunatic, to someone high on drugs, certifiably insane. How did you relate to a madman? He decided to humour him.

'I am a Christian too,' he said slowly. 'I believe in God. Do you know Washington DC? There is an old Episcopalian church in Georgetown, St John the Baptist. My wife and I go to church there every Sunday —'

A door opened somewhere on Luke's left.

'Okay, Luke,' said a flat voice.

'Okay, Zed.'

Obediently Luke scrambled to his feet. Without another glance at the tent, he went out of Martin's line of vision. Into the frame of the triangular tent-opening which was Martin's only contact with the outside world stepped a man he hadn't seen before: tall, with a dark headband to keep the long black hair off his narrow forehead, and calf-length boots with a flower pattern picked out in leather. He was carrying a cushion under one arm and a guitar. The guitar explained the sounds Martin had heard after he came out of his last drugged sleep.

'Are you Zed?' he asked.

'Yup.' The man arranged himself on the cushion and rested the guitar across his knee. He fiddled with his hair and took out of it an object which Martin recognised as a guitar plectrum.

'Have you known Luke long?'

Zed regarded him balefully. 'What kind of question is that, man?'

It was another American voice. Another of his own countrymen. It baffled him. 'Who's paying you to keep me here?' he asked.

Zed, tuning his guitar, ignored the question. In a burst of rage, Martin threatened him. 'You know they'll kill you. If the police find you here, they'll shoot first and ask questions later!' he shouted hoarsely. 'If you want something from me, ask me —'

Zed interrupted, reciting in that same flat voice, '"All that will live godly in Christ Jesus shall suffer persecution. But evil men and seducers shall wax worse and worse, deceiving and being deceived."'

Martin leaned back against the tent wall and closed his eyes in weariness. 'I am not an evil man,' he said.

He received no answer. Into his burning mind the notes of 'Amazing Grace', picked out on Zed's guitar, fell comfortingly, like rain. Could these people really be religious wierdos as they appeared? It would explain why they couldn't engage with his arguments. It was like being on drugs, this fanaticism, like being constantly high on God. He'd seen people who'd suddenly converted to religion — to Catholicism, for instance — go quiet and

53

intense when they entered the faith, as though they were switching off a part of their minds which was no longer needed.

Zed had moved out of 'Amazing Grace' into a dreamy rendition of the hymn, 'Morning Has Broken'. Martin leaned forward to attract his attention. He said 'You really get off on music, don't you?'

'Aural hashish, man.'

'I have a son, about Luke's age, who listens to rock music.'

'Oh yeah?'

'Do you play rock music?'

'I make music to praise the Lord.'

'What about *Jesus Christ Superstar*?'

Zed hesitated. Then he began to strum a medley of tunes, expertly played, from the rock opera. After a while he began to hum, and to twitch his feet and his head in time to the music. Behind him, the door opened. Martin could not see who was standing there. All at once, as Zed began to play the familiar, simple melody of Mary Magdalen's song to the sleeping Jesus, Esther's high clear voice joined in, singing the words. Zed smiled and carried on. Martin listened to the child-like recital in amazement and fear. Such conviction. He had a sudden vision of Abraham binding his son Isaac to the rock and raising the knife, at the instruction of an unseen God. He shivered, and shivered again as the cold sweat trickled down his bare flanks.

Zed put down his guitar. Martin said hoarsely, 'You know, Jesus teaches that God is love.'

Zed fixed his dark stony eyes on him, and said nothing.

'It is not Christian, what you are doing. To kidnap me and treat me this way is not an act of love. God will punish you for it.'

Zed sprang to his feet, knocking the guitar which gave out a hollow sound. His pitted face dark with blood, he leant back against the dresser, grasping the blue vase as if he wanted to hurl it at Martin and smash his face in. 'That's a lie, man!' he cried. 'You're the sinner. You're the one who needs saving. We're gonna make an example of you, oh yes, sir, we're gonna make you an example for all your kind.'

It was preposterous. 'How? By this silly kidnap game?'

'It's not kidnapping! It's an outreach. Love is not enough. Evil has to be driven out before the sinner will repent. Ishmael will

54

tell you. If this work is not of God, it will come to nothing. If it is of God, nothing will stop it!'

'Which one is Ishmael?'

Zed fell silent, as if he had said too much already. He stepped forward and knelt to pick up the guitar. Peering at Martin through the tent flap he said craftily, 'Jesus said: "When sheep walk into the den of the wolves, they should be as harmless as doves and as cunning as snakes."'

The electric light was hurtful. Martin closed his eyes again, shutting out the unreality of it all. They were obviously under the control of this Ishmael, whoever he might be. He must have convinced these dumb bastards that kidnapping a senior CIA officer was a short cut to heaven. Unless it was all some mad hysterical joke, it wasn't spiritual guidance they'd brought him here for. He was being primed for something, half-starved, filled with drugs and left to stew in this tent until he was ready to give them whatever it was they were after. But what was that?

He may have slept then. In any case, when he felt his bare foot being tugged and opened his eyes, Zed had gone and Esther was crouching in the tent flap.

'I was pulling your leg,' she said, trilling a laugh. 'Get it? Pulling your leg. Say, here's your tea.'

'Please. Get me some food. I need to eat something.'

She shook her head, eyes sparkling. 'It'll do you good. Soften you up. You're looking kind of peaky.'

'Soften me up for what?'

'What? For the question game of course.'

'What question game?'

'Ishmael's going to interrogate you.'

With a stab of panic Martin asked again, 'Who's Ishmael?'

'Ishmael. He's one of us.'

'So who are you?'

The girl shook her head sadly, still smiling. 'Don't you know that yet? We're here to save you. To teach you God's love.'

'Okay, okay,' Martin was choking with exasperation, 'but who the hell *are* you?'

Esther's smile vanished and was replaced by a sulky frown. 'It's when you stop asking questions like that that you'll know who we are,' she declared.

Martin groaned. He raised the mug to his lips and drank, cautiously, tasting for narcotics.

'Are you married?' Esther asked suddenly.

'Yes. I have a wife. And a son aged eighteen.'

'What's your wife's name?'

'Barbara.'

'Barbara.' She savoured the name for a moment. 'I guess that's okay,' she said nodding. 'I used to know a girl called Barbara.'

'Where?'

'In my old life. In Carmel.'

'But you're English. What were you doing in California?'

Esther tossed her hair and looked up at him, her head turned slightly aside and her lips parted. 'How do you know I'm English?'

Martin realised with astonishment that she was flirting with him. 'Because of your voice,' he replied.

'Do you like my voice?'

'It's a very sweet voice. What were you doing in Carmel?'

Esther studied her fingernails, and licked one of them which was bitten down to the quick. She had small hands with slender fingers. If she took more care of herself she would be very attractive.

'Well?' he asked.

'Not the yucky tourist town. Behind it. Do you know Carmel Valley?'

'Yes.'

'I was at a Jesus festival. That's where we met, Zed and me. I was a dancer. I danced for Jesus. You know Salome?' She pronounced it Saloam. 'I did Salome dancing before Herod, with the veils. I was erotic.'

'Zed —'

'Sure, he was reely turned on. He said I was the sexiest chick since Mary Magdalen.' She giggled, revealing a row of sharp little teeth, then put her fingers over her mouth in mock contrition.

'Was Zed at school in Carmel? Was that how you meet him?'

'Zed? Nah, Zed dropped out of college. He was doing gigs along the West Coast. We hitched up to do a song-and-dance routine. Did you hear me just now?'

'Singing? Yes. You were great. Terrific.'

Esther flushed with pleasure. She shifted herself on the cushion closer to the tent; he could smell the cheap scent she was wearing. Her quilted jacket had fallen open so that he

56

could see that she was wearing nothing under her thin green rayon shirt.

'Zed thinks my voice is reely sexy. He said so. It was Zed who turned me on to Jesus. I used to get my head off on grass and acid, you know? And then Zed showed me this article in the *San Francisco Chronicle* which made out there was a link between drug-taking and damage to unborn babies in the womb. Heavy stuff.' She nodded. 'Getting high on Jesus is less of a health hazard, see what I mean?'

'Is that when you met Ishmael?'

'Nah. It's when Luke joined us. How do you rate Luke? Don't you think he's nice?'

'Is he the one who zapped me on the head?'

Esther laughed, deftly by-passing the question. 'Some way to make friends, isn't it?' she said. 'No, Luke's a real incredible guy. He's very loving, you know? He loves everything, even car engines. He's got *Jesus Loves You* decals on his toolbox.'

The blanket had slipped down Martin's chest. He plucked at it with his tied hands.

'Esther, have you ever loved anyone? Apart from Jesus?' he asked her gently.

The girl looked at him askance. 'Why?'

'I just want to know.'

'That's dumb. Of course I've loved persons.'

'Then you can imagine . . .' he paused and phrased the words carefully, '. . . can you imagine what it is like to have someone you love taken away from you, and not know whether they are alive or dead?'

'You mean Barbara?'

'Barbara and my son.'

She considered the question, winding strands of hair around her finger. When she looked up, her eyes were wide. 'I don't think you reely love her,' she said. 'I mean, apart from fucking. I mean, Ishmael told us about you. You're an evil man. You killed people.'

'*What?*'

She was looking at him with glittering eyes. Her voice had taken on a purring, husky note. 'You're like Herod. You've activated hundreds of people to die. Maybe thousands, I dunno. Real true love can't live with evil. It can't just live with it. So you can't love Barbara, until you repent. Except sexily.'

Martin's mouth was dry. He licked his lips. 'I need to go to the john,' he said hoarsely.

Esther got up. She crawled into the tent on her hands and knees, and squatted beside him. 'Shall I pull your pants down for you?'

'*I will not use that bucket*,' he spat.

She recoiled at his anger. 'Shit in your pants, I don't care.'

Tears of rage and self-pity stung Martin's eyes. He lunged at Esther, knocking the bucket out of her hands. Before he could shout out more than a handful of obscenities, the girl had rammed the bucket down over his head and run out.

Two men entered the tent. He heard the heavy tread of Luke, and a lighter cat-like tread he didn't recognise. While Luke held him in a bear-like hug, the other man plunged the hypodermic needle into his arm. The bucket was taken off him and a heavy hand clamped across his mouth. He was lifted up, his shorts were pulled down, he was sat upon the bucket like a rag doll in a nursery.

Through his giddiness and humiliation he heard the girl say something to Ishmael. So they were all looking at him. Helpless in Luke's arms, he drew back his lips in a snarl. 'Now you can all lick my ass,' he heard himself cry.

He was out before he heard any answers.

John Little was waiting for William when he got back to his partitioned-off cubicle in the anonymous-looking building on Victoria Street. He was in no better shape than the Chief Inspector, unkempt and red-eyed, his pasty complexion paler than ever. 'We've turned up sod-all on the getaway vehicle,' he said without preamble. 'No question that it's the right one.'

'The licence?'

'Stolen from a woman who lives off the Brompton Road. A wee actress. Doesn't know when; she didn't even know it was missing.'

'A description of the girl?'

'Useless. All the two Hertz people remember is a typical Sloane Ranger type — medium height, dark hair, dark glasses in round plastic frames and a white belted mac, the kind you pick up anywhere from Harrods to Peter Jones. CID are still down there with Hertz. They've dressed a woman in the same clothes —'

'They'll get bugger all from that. People are so blind you can walk a man with a shotgun under their noses and they'll think they saw it on TV the night before.' William took the cup of tea his secretary brought in and swilled it moodily around its plastic lip. 'Any rings? A necklace? A scarf?'

'They don't know.'

'Wonderful. Okay John. So what else is new?'

'We've got the appeal ready to all landladies who've had suspicious-looking Arab lodgers in the last two months. It's going out on the World at One and on all three TV channels tonight. Also, Mr Knight's been on the 'phone.' Inspector Little's narrow Scots face twitched into the beginnings of a smile.

'Has he indeed?'

'He wanted to know if we'd started turning over some of the squats. I said it would have to wait for you, sir.'

William flushed. What did bloody M15 think it was up to? Briskly he said, 'Let's you and I follow the normal procedures. I've got you use of a video terminal next door. It's linked to the Immigration Control computer recording all arrivals in Britain and their conditions of stay. I want you to start checking through the last four weeks before the kidnap for arrivals belonging to any extremist political organisations — you know the coding.'

Little grimaced. 'Do you have any notions on what I should be looking for?'

'Yes, John. You're looking for a KGB terrorist who has a grudge against the CIA, likes icecream and has Islamic sympathies.'

'Thanks a lot.' Little hung back in the doorway. 'Like M, is he?'

'What?'

'This man Commoner. Like M in James Bond, is he?' John Little smirked to show he didn't take this spy stuff seriously.

'Nothing so cute. He's more like me and you. A bureaucrat who pisses and gets pissed on, that's all.'

After Little had sloped off, William went back to his desk. Grudgingly, he started on the thick folder of undercover agents' reports that had been mounting on his desk since the special alert had gone out that morning. As he had feared, there were few leads and none of them very promising. Christopher Knight had bent his ear about the Socialist Workers' Party, but that was typical M15 paranoia. This wasn't an SWP type of operation. In a way it was disheartening how few of the young radicals were going on about the CIA any longer; it was all nuclear energy and arms control. Even the kids nowadays had stopped believing that wars were started by secret agents delivering guns in a newspaper. It made him feel old.

International terrorists, Vanderbyle had said. Easier said than acted upon. He could type a query about suspected IRA activists in Britain on the computer terminal and it would come back immediately with a long list of names and addresses, along with distinguishing marks, hobbies and the pubs they frequented. Type in a foreign terrorist organisation like the Red Army Fraction or Black September and what he'd get on the screen would be references to foreign computer data and a whole lot of dead history.

He sighed and ran his head through his receding hair. He'd been getting stale recently, and he knew it. He'd spent too much time on routine paperwork, and the dreary round of co-ordinating reports from his men in the field about how many Communist lecturers were teaching at the North London College for Further Education, how the Trots were planning to take over local government in Hackney and which new London property the National Front was trying to set up its headquarters in.

In the old days, it had been different. Okay, that was ten or fifteen years ago when he'd been in his mid-twenties. But it was true that before they took away responsibility for the ports and airports, and set up special squads to deal with IRA terrorism, protection of diplomats and public order, there had been a real feeling of the Branch being in the front line. The Angry Brigade, Stoke Newington, the anarchists ... he'd even had one spell himself, when his waistline was trimmer and his fair hair still successfully covered his scalp, of being infiltrated as a sleeper into an anarchist group.

Stuffing his hands in his pockets, William went to the window and stared gloomily through the shatter-proof glass at the Board of Trade. In those days he could pass the buck. Now he had no excuses, no let-outs. The Commander had shovelled this one into his lap and it lay there, stinking at him. He needed a break, and he needed it quickly.

Martin was roused from unconsciousness by a hand shaking his shoulder and a cupful of water thrown in his face. The electric light burned down through the tent on his reddened eyes. It seemed to him he had been asleep only for seconds — a few minutes at most.

'What time is it?' he asked in confusion.

'Time for you and me to have a talk, old buddy.'

It was a new voice. An educated Boston voice. Martin raised his head. The man sitting on a chair in the tent entrance he had seen before. He had seen him dressed in a dark green uniform, pointing a gun at him through a car window. He had seen him out of the corner of his eye, sticking a needle into his arm while Esther held his head. Now he was sitting in full view of him, a man in his late twenties in frayed blue jeans and grubby white T-shirt, his beady eyes observing him critically through wire-rimmed spectacles. It was a narrow censorious face, which suddenly widened at the top into a bulbous cranium on which fuzzy black hair sprang out in clumps around a bald white crown. He seemed to recognise it from a long way back.

'You are Ishmael,' Martin said.

Ishmael bent down and pressed a button on a small black machine between his feet. A tape recorder. This was to be his interrogation. Martin felt less apprehension than relief that there was at last to be some purpose in this crazy charade. He pushed back against the tent wall until he was sitting upright and able to look at his interrogator in the face.

'You mean to kill me, ' he said.

'Why?'

'You're not wearing masks.'

'We've nothing to hide,' said Ishmael with a touch of scorn. 'You keep the secrets, Commoner. Not us.'

'If you think I've got secrets to give you, forget it. I'm a bureaucrat. Not a secret agent. That's why you got me so easily. I'm of no value to anyone.'

'You're of value to us,' said Ishmael, staring at him. 'That's why we brought you here. You are the top spy-runner for the

61

American Central Intelligence Agency. You have directed or been involved in world-wide operations which have caused the suffering, oppression and death of thousands of innocent people, mostly in the Third World. You are here to answer for your crimes before a people's court.'

'You're full of garbage. And I don't recognise the legitimacy of your people's court.' Martin recalled the CIA version of the wartime code of conduct: in hostile situations provide the enemy only with name, grade and Langley parking-space number. But this was no more a war situation than Gulliver bound with threads in the land of Lilliput. It was a joke, sitcom stuff. The only mystery was why the police and his own people hadn't yet put an end to it.

Ishmael had taken a notebook out of his pocket. He made notes in pencil was he spoke. 'Commoner, you first came to light as a journalist and CIA contact in New York —'

'Wrong.'

'— in 1963. After Kennedy's assassination you joined the CIA full time —'

'That had nothing to do with it.'

'— and after eighteen months training in propaganda, terrorism and related intelligence activities in Washington, you went out to Vietnam to help organise the Phoenix so-called counter-terror programme against Vietnamese peasants in the demilitarised zone . . .'

Martin remained silent. Ishmael leaned forward on his chair, as if to get within spitting distance of his victim.

'What was the word you used back in 'Nam? Pacification. That was it, pacification. Like you pacify a baby by holding it, except your men held people down under water until the bubbles stopped, and you held them over fires until their flesh roasted, just so you could wring a confession that the poor bastards gave food to a VC, yes sir, because he was holding a gun to their head. You pacified them all right — by exterminating them, like you exterminated the Meos in Laos, and the Montagnards. And if by some mistake you brought them back alive, you stuffed them into tiger cages on Con Son island, where if they didn't die of dehydration their legs rotted away because the cages were too small to stand up or move about in. Some *pacification* that was,' he spat the word out. 'You were the original Man from UNCLE who stands up at a Hearts and

Minds conference and says, "To save their souls we must first destroy their bodies." Well now it's your turn, old buddy, to see what it feels like.'

'You're talking nonsense.' Martin kept his voice deliberately calm and reasonable. 'I had nothing to do with the Montagnards, or with the Meos. I never saw a tiger cage, and I never put anyone into a tiger cage. Whatever you might think about pacification, the fact is we were fighting a war, a people's war. And we were a goddamn sight more kid-gloved about taking the war to the people than the North Vietnamese were, believe you me.'

'Kid-gloved. Yeah. I suppose you call kid-gloved killing 40,000 people on the Phoenix programme alone.'

'That's a myth, like the others you've picked up. The South Vietnamese doubled their head-counts because they thought that's what we wanted to hear. Most of the Vietcong infrastructure was terminated by the police and military, and the number of deaths was 20,000 maximum.'

'I guess you're proud of that, aren't you Commoner?'

'I'm proud that we did what we set out to do. We won the war in the countryside.'

Ishmael scribbled in his notebook, his pencil pushing down hard on the paper. 'The prisoner pleads not guilty,' he muttered to himself.

'What's that?'

'You had your blooding in 'Nam, didn't you old buddy? You came back ready for anything. So they send you out as a hatchet man to Argentina, to help prop up the fascist regime of Peron. You were in your element there, weren't you old buddy? The masses were beginning to rise up and throw off their chains after years of exploitation and brutality. The Junta were getting scared. They imported Mr Phoenix Commoner to set up a whole new apparatus of repression to keep the masses to heel —'

'Who feeds you this junk?'

'You must have learned enough in Saigon to be pretty useful to those guys. How to interrogate people so it didn't leave any marks on their skin. How to use *agents provocateurs*. How to wire up all that police computer hardware they got at a discount from IT & T.'

'You've been seeing too many movies, Mr Ishmael. I was in Buenos Aires as Chief of Station, and that's the same as being

Chief of Station anywhere else in the world. You keep your eyes and ears open. You co-ordinate intelligence reports and send them back to Washington. The garbage you're talking is a lot of Commie propaganda.'

Ishmael let his jaw drop open. He took off his glasses and stared at Martin through pale protuberant eyes.

'Man, you're off the wall. You know that? I mean, where do they programme you turkeys? You knew what was going down in Argentina. And in Chile. And in El Salvador and Guatemala. You would have had Allende shot if Nixon had told you.'

'That's a hypothetical question.'

'Answer me, Commoner.'

'I would obey my President, whatever.'

'Yeah, that's what I mean. You're a contract killer, Commoner. No principles. Only duties. Fuck who you kill for, it's not important. You killed in Saigon, and you've killed since. You're a murderer, old buddy. A government murderer.'

Martin watched as Ishmael put his glasses back on with trembling fingers, took out his notebook and began to scribble. 'The prisoner pleads not guilty,' he heard him say again under his breath. He forced himself to remain calm. He had seen this technique used before, of course. It was one agents were trained to recognise: the sudden violent outburst, which either put the fear of God into the subject or misled him into thinking the interrogator had lost control of himself. He knew better. It was a way of softening him up before the serious questioning began.

Ishmael had gone off on another tack. 'Let's go back four-five years to when you came home from Buenos Aires. You remember the Hudson Plan?'

Martin allowed himself a smile. 'If you've brought me here for a lecture on domestic politics in the Nixon years, go right ahead,' he said. 'If you're talking about me, my only contribution in the area was to help prepare a report entitled "Foreign Communist Support to Revolutionary Protest Movements in the United States". We found there wasn't any.'

'This is no joke, old buddy. You better believe me, you won't be so smart in a day or two. I'm talking about you. You're as guilty as hell. Personally. Morally. You take full responsibility.'

'And God has set you up in judgement over me. Is that it? I suppose God also told you to beat my driver to death, and whoever else it took to get me here.'

'They're not dead. They're okay. And don't you talk to me about murder. *You* murdered often enough.'

Martin sighed, and closed his eyes to rest them. In the background he heard the girl call out Ishmael's name. Without pausing, Ishmael switched from one vocabulary into another. 'We shall cast out Satan and drive him down into the pit,' he intoned. 'You will be reborn in Jesus, to bless and praise his name.' In a low voice he added, 'Stay where you are, old buddy. I'll be back.'

While Ishmael was away, Martin thought rapidly. His interrogator was not a Jesus freak like the others — that much was obvious. That he seemed to find it necessary to act like one when the others were around was something to pick away at. The problem was to know who he was dealing with. Ishmael had done some homework. But his questioning was amateur. Even as softening-up, it was amateur. It was more of a debate than an interrogation. The mock trial he was undergoing was a hoax. Their minds were already made up about him.

This conclusion plunged him into melancholy. He did not look up when Ishmael padded back to his seat, but slumped back against the tent wall, sweating in the warm, fetid atmosphere of the tent.

Ishmael changed the tape on the machine between his feet and droned on, reciting a catalogue of grievances against the CIA as if he had read them in a book and committed them to memory. He talked about secret armies, about undercover medical experiments, about bribes to Third World politicians, about extensive laboratory research on new poisons, student drug programmes, wire-tapping and black-bag jobs. He talked about the CIA as a multinational whose product was repression — a product exported to an archipelago of client regimes in South-east Asia, Latin America and the Near East.

He talked about 'the infra-structure of imperialism' and 'ideological complicity'. He arraigned Martin as the chief advocate of America's repressive foreign policies. He accused him of abuse of power and cynical disregard for human rights, charging him with hypocrisy, deceit, callousness and homicidal aggression such as all the Nazi defendants at Nuremburg had not been able to muster between them. Every now and then the notebook would come out and another indictment would be pencilled in.

At last, when Ishmael's voice had grown hoarse, and his thin body drooped with the exhaustion of his fury, he brought his grand proceedings abruptly to an end. Leaning forward and peering through his spectacles like a Boston brahmin, he addressed Martin.

'Prisoner, do you have anything to say?'

'Yes. Bug off. Go play in the traffic.'

Ishmael grinned, without humour. 'That was just part one,' he said. 'You ain't seen nothin' yet.'

He slid off the chair and stood up, outside the tent. Martin opened his eyes. He said in a firm voice, 'If I am your prisoner, I demand the basic prerogative of any prisoner, guaranteed under international law. And that is water, and solid food, and sanitation.'

There was a pause. Then Ishmael's footsteps went away, treading lightly over the green carpet.

Martin again closed his eyes. He was surprised by a sudden weakness in his limbs. What if his body gave way and his mind began failing? Would he end up confessing a multitude of imagined sins, like the victims of the show trials in the 1930s? Would they have him on the altar, praying for salvation, before the knife came down? A succession of shudders ran through his body; he fought to suppress them as the footsteps returned.

A heavy weight on his chest. A hand over his mouth. Ishmael's voice: 'It's a prisoner's prerogative to be fed.' He felt the needle plunged into his arm, and tasted the bitterness in his mouth. As his consciousness receded, he noticed in detachment that his body was putting up less of a struggle against the drug than it had before.

The brochure he'd been handed as he stepped on to the foot-bridge described Theodore Roosevelt Island as 'a wild vignette'. As far as the General was concerned, it wasn't wild enough for the man he was going to meet that afternoon. He would happily have thrown him to the wolves.

Senator Traill, the ranking Democrat on the Senate Intelligence Oversight Committee, had rung him early, as soon as the morning papers had come out with their headlines and photographs of Martin Commoner. The DCI had refused to meet him immediately, claiming it was a matter of top-level national security. Then Traill had mentioned the word BeeSting . . .

The General was not prepared to go up the Mall, nor Traill to come down to Langley, so they had agreed to meet halfway. Theodore Roosevelt Island, so late in the afternoon, was almost deserted. The General found Traill at the great concrete memorial set down among the yellowing bushes. A tall, broad-shouldered, red-faced man with a prominent fleshy nose, he was gazing up at the rooks relieving themselves over one of America's better-loved presidents.

'What do you know about BeeSting?' asked the DCI after the two men had exchanged frosty greetings.

'Enough to be confident of the accuracy of my sources. I want to know why the Congressional committees have been kept in the dark.'

As the General explained what was at stake, it became increasingly plain that Traill after all knew almost nothing about BeeSting — possibly no more than its name. That was a relief; it meant there had not been a serious leak. But the Senator's disingenuousness infuriated him nevertheless. Traill was well aware that covert activities involving the security of Israel always aroused dangerous passions on the Hill. It would have been suicidal to have given the committees advance warning.

Either side of the Roosevelt statue were wide cobbled stairways with granite balustrades, leading grandiosely up to nothing and down the other side. Surveying the view from the top of one, the General said quietly, 'I need your word, Senator, that none of this goes further. I can't stress too highly the crucial importance of this mission, to Israel and to us. If Pakistan activates a nuclear weapon in the next few days, it would neutralise the Israeli response. Islam could move in for the kill.'

Traill stubbed out his cigarette and flicked it into a marble urn. 'Why don't you just hand over the ground-plans?' he growled.

'Too risky. If BeeSting's gotten out and Israeli planes are shot down over Islamabad, the Russians get their biggest intelligence coup in history.'

'That's Jerusalem's problem. Not ours.'

The General looked at his watch. It was 17.45; the gate would soon be closing. 'Senator, I appreciate you have a substantial Jewish vote in Rhode Island. But you don't know a damn lot about covert operations. You saw the papers this morning. Rumours are already getting round that Commoner is in Tripoli or Beirut. Now I happen to think he's still in Britain. But it doesn't alter the fact that he planned BeeSting, or that the man held by the Israelis, Fisher, is his close associate. In the CIA, coincidences teach us to tread on the brakes.'

A couple of German tourists were strolling back past the presidential statue. Traill turned his back on them, cupping his hands round a fresh cigarette.

'If you ask my opinion, it stinks,' he said. 'State obviously think so; they're steering a wide berth. And what stinks more than anything is that you should take a gamble of this magnitude without consulting anyone on the Hill. You must see that this whole thing could have been set up to put Israel in a bad light and give her enemies the excuse they've been waiting for.'

'You're forgetting one thing. Jerusalem has got Fisher under wraps. If BeeSting gets blown wide open, it's the United States Government that gets framed by Israel. Make no mistakes: I know how they operate.'

Traill gazed at him, more in sorrow than in anger. 'You've got to trust your allies occasionally,' he remarked, and set off down the steps.

'Do I have your word?' the General called after him.

Traill paused. 'I'm your ally,' he said. 'Try trusting me.'

WEDNESDAY

A photograph of Martin Commoner was propped up against the marmalade pot on the pine kitchen table. William Pomfret swallowed a mouthful of scrambled egg and went on staring at it. If he closed his eyes he could picture Commoner's face in the smallest detail, down to the small mole on his left cheek. It was a method he'd used before (he'd got it from a clairvoyant) to establish the physical presence of the person he was looking for. It meant he could dismiss nine out of ten alleged sightings and not waste time and manpower chasing them up. Sometimes it worked; sometimes not. This looked like it was going to be one that didn't.

'Urgh, it must be disgusting.'

'What?'

His wife, Jenny, made a face at him across the breakfast table. 'The scrambled eggs. You've let it go cold.'

'Damn. I'm sorry, love.' William pushed the plate aside and poured more tea. Jenny had put the paper down and was considering him; her small round face under the purposeful fringe was set in an expression of determination. She had put on a jersey and trousers today, which meant she was in a no-nonsense mood. He wondered if her colleagues in the local council planning department had come to recognise the signals as well.

'Willy, you'll have to try and get more sleep.'

'Mmm?'

'You were up half the night. And when you did come to bed you tossed around like an old beach-ball.'

'I did not.'

'Yes you did, darling.' She got up and began making toast for the children's breakfast. 'Seriously, I don't see why you should do the Americans' dirty work for them anyway,' she went on with warmth. 'I mean, they've got FBI people over here. Johnny Wax. Why don't they put the FBI on to it?'

'There are only two of them.'

'By the way, Willy, I've got the boiler man coming today to check the boiler. He said he'd be here before 9.45 so I can get down to the Town Hall.'

'Yes.' Jenny was right. It was time he had a word with Johnny Wax. The chief FBI legat always had his ear to the ground. And there would be no love lost between him and Vanderbyle, more than likely.

'One thing I'd love you to do for me is check the radiators. We haven't had them on since March, so they might need bleeding.'

'Bleeding?' He started.

'The radiators.'

'I'll check them tonight.' Hospitals — of course. If Commoner's head wound was bad ... it shouldn't have taken him this long to think about it, especially when he was just off to see the van driver, Arthur Norman. He'd put a call out to check every hospital dispensary in the London area for people asking for bandages, liniment, blood-clotting agents ... and they'd have to call on all the chemists as well, that would keep them busy for a while. He groaned.

'Willy?'

'I'm off.' He stood up. Commoner stared at him from the marmalade pot. There was something appealing about that face, the lines of humour around the eyes and mouth. A man he could get on with. If he ever found him.

Jenny, holding a toast-rack, kissed him on the lips. 'Shout up to Eddie and Cathy on the way out, will you? Tell them they'll be late for school.'

'That won't get them down. I'll tell them breakfast's being cleared away.' He smiled at her expression. 'Don't worry. I'll try and get an early night.'

When William arrived, Arthur Norman was out of bed. He was sitting at a table at the far end of the ward, playing checkers with a very old man in baggy blue pyjamas. As William came up to them the old man raised bushy white eyebrows and stared at the newcomer. Then silently he swept the pieces off the board, got up and hobbled away.

'It's his age,' said the icecream salesman. 'He can't stand to finish anything.' He smiled at William apologetically. His heavy turban of bandages was spotless, but his left eye was bloodshot and his hands were trembling.

'How are your eyes?' asked William.

'Okay. They're focusing again. I got a skull fracture, you know,' he said with pride.

'How long are they keeping you here?'

'Not as long as they think. The doctors want to keep me in bed. I told 'em, I said I don't sell icecreams on the National Health. I got a franchise: every hot day I'm in here I lose bread.' Mournfully he squinted up at the morning sun streaming in through the high slatted windows. 'Plus, it's right in the middle of the season.'

'Is it a good money, lad?'

'I don't know what you coppers think is good money. It's good enough for me. You see, I knew the Castle pitch was up for grabs. That's how you do it. Get the right pitch.'

'It wasn't the right pitch for you last Monday, was it lad?'

Arthur Norman grinned painfully. 'I've been thinking about that.'

'Yes?'

'It's no good. I just know I saw the girl before. I just know.'

'Nurse!'

The nurse William had beckoned finished tidying the next bed and came over to them. She was medium height, rather sallow, with long dark hair.

'Nurse, would you do me a favour, love?'

William fished in his pocket and produced a pair of dark glasses with round plastic tortoiseshell frames. 'Just put these on for a second and look at my friend Mr Norman. That's right.'

Arthur Norman stared at the nurse for a moment with a puzzled look in his eyes. Then he said slowly, 'The couple on the grass. How did you know?'

'What couple on the grass?'

'That's right.' The icecream man flushed as the memory came back to him. 'I'm bloody daft, that's what I am. They were sitting on the grass round the back of the van. I saw them when I went off for a pee — excuse my language, nurse!'

71

William pocketed the glasses, not taking his eyes off Norman. 'Yes?'

'The girl. And a man with her, quite a big fellow. He was playing a guitar, I think. Yes.'

'What was he playing? What tune?'

'Tune? I dunno. Anyhow, he'd stopped when I came back. He was fiddling with a radio. Getting a lot of static.'

'Are you sure it was a radio? How big was it?'

'Didn't see. I just supposed it was a radio.'

'You're doing fine. Just keep thinking. What were they wearing?'

Arthur Norman screwed up his eyes. 'Cor, you're making my bonce hurt,' he said with a weak grin. 'Let me see. The girl was in a long skirt. Can't remember the colour. Wearing a straw hat an' all, very la-di-dah. The man was, you know, shirt and trousers. Nothing special. He had boots on. Why do I remember that?'

'Did they look foreign, the boots?'

'No . . .' The icecream man scowled in thought, tapping a draught on the table. 'I can't think,' he said finally.

William cocked his head. 'Did you know you were playing a tune then?'

'What?'

'Tapping on the table. "John Brown's Body."'

William tapped it out with his knuckles, humming the tune self-consciously; he couldn't remember the words.

Arthur Norman listened. Then he burst out singing in a powerful voice — '*Glory, glory, hallelujah! And his soul goes marching on!*'

The ward went quiet. William glanced round. The nurse was staring at them. An old man propped against the pillows raised a withered hand and crossed himself.

'That's it!' Arthur Norman exclaimed triumphantly. 'Marching. That's why I said his boots. He was doing that hymn on his guitar.'

William had followed up Jennifer's suggestion and arranged a pub lunch in Victoria with Johnny Wax. The big FBI legat with his cabbage ears and red good-humoured face was an old friend. After William had joshed him, once, about Hoover's G-men wearing spats, he'd bought a pair of white socks and showed

72

them off to William under his conservative grey suit. But this afternoon he seemed uncharacteristically morose.

'We're redundant, William,' he said. 'Who needs detectives when a silicon chip can tell you a person's life history from a single credit card? You're young, you'll adapt, you can take the corners. I'm the one who's gonna be phased out.' He frowned and changed the subject before William could interrupt. 'I'm not so past it I don't know who I have to thank for this lunch. Our friend from Leeds Castle, am I right?'

'As always.'

'This is CIA territory. You know that?'

'Yes. They've sent over this man Vanderbyle —'

'I've heard.'

'And I get the feeling, you know — just an impression — that he's been sent over as much to restrict the information output about Commoner as to help the investigation. Sort of in a *dis*information capacity. Of course I might be absolutely wrong . . .' He paused.

'I doubt it.'

'But if I find Commoner, any help I get will be credited in the right quarter.'

Johnny Wax swept up the empty beer glasses and marched up to the bar. When he returned to their settles in the corner he was grinning.

'William, you got to understand my position,' he said with mock humility, placing fresh drinks on the table. 'Like every servant of the Federal Bureau of Investigation, past and present, I have total unstinting respect for the CIA. Anything I can do to help them along I will, including kicking the sons-of-bitches up the goddamned ass. What can I tell you?'

William leaned forward. 'Who might have wanted Commoner this badly?'

'I don't know.' Wax stared into his drink. 'If the Agency is giving you the runaround, it means they're scared about a current operation. All I can tell you is they think there's another war coming up in the Gulf. And our friend used to head up their Middle East desk.'

'Palestinians?'

'I would guess not. They go for political solutions. Not kidnapping backroom boys. If you want my guess, they're scared because they think Commoner's gone over to the other side.'

'*Defected?*' This was something that hadn't crossed his mind.

'Don't you bright boys read the papers? The Russkies have started putting up dirty stories about us. One: that the US has secret underground arms depots in Oman. That was in *Tass* this morning, apparently. And *Pravda*'s just printed a nasty little rumour that our flights over Cambodia in 1970 were not with B52 bombs but Agent Orange defoliant, wiping out hundreds of square miles. They even give the dates: March 26 to the beginning of April.'

'Sounds pretty stale to me.'

'Not Oman, if it's true. Nor the other one, which is that the CIA is trying to destabilise the left-wing government in Greece by funding the opposition. Plus you've got to remember, Commoner was in Vietnam in 1970.'

The FBI man let the implication hang in the air. William shook his head and took a long drink, putting down the glass Wax had brought him with a sour expression. Americans never knew the difference between real ale and the ordinary poison. He said, 'It's no concern of mine, what his politics are. My job is to find out where he is.'

'You asked me. I'm telling you.'

'Okay. I appreciate it. Johnny, can I ask a big favour of you?'

'Uh-huh?'

'Your list of Americans over here. I'd like to have a shufti at it.'

'List? The list of American nationals in Britain is kept by the Embassy, you know that. You've got an automatic access to it through D section of the Special Crime Branch, haven't you?'

'You know what I'm talking about. The special Bureau list. The ones you think could be trouble.'

Johnny Wax finished his beer and put the glass down with a bang. 'You want me to get fired,' he said, shaking his head. 'There's no list I can show you. But there's one thing I will do. I'll check out all the names I've got for connections with what we've been talking about. Fanatics, Moslems, Christians, KGB — anything that comes up I'll get across to you under plain cover. Hell, we're going to make Vanderbyle look like a beginner.'

William raised his glass to him, smiling. 'Make it as soon as you can, Johnny. I'm running hard and getting nowhere.'

The FBI man belched loudly. 'Aren't we all,' he said.

The Battle Hymn of the Republic. William hummed it all the way back to the office. What had Johnny Wax said? *Fanatics* . . . *Christians* . . . It was a connection. He was superstitious about connections. As soon as he reached his office he summoned Little in.

'John. There's something might be worth following up.' William briefed him quickly on Arthur Norman.

Little looked puzzled. 'Religious groups?'

'It's a possible. Jesus freaks can be violent. Look at the guy who shot John Lennon. I want the names and descriptions of all the religious cults in Britain, Christian ones heading up the list. Plus the addresses of all their branches in the London area.'

'Then what?'

'I'm going to raise your consciousness, John. We're going to get search warrants and pay them a visit.'

'Christ.'

'That's right. You can forget about the Moonies and the Scientologists. If we're dealing with religious nutters here, it won't be the sort who prey on the insecurity of rich people. Kidnapping is guaranteed to scare off the bank-rollers. We'll go for the smaller groups. The ones with nothing to lose.'

'Why?'

'Why what?'

'Why should religious types want to kidnap a CIA chief?'

William looked at Little through half-closed eyes. 'You're a Rangers man aren't you, John?'

'Aye, I'm a Presbyterian.'

'Well, lad. For you this is going to be a walk on the wild side. I covered one of these outfits years ago when they were just getting popular. They operate identical to the militant lefties. They push leaflets in your hand. If you respond, you get invited to one of the houses they've conned off a rich admirer, for a discussion on the secret of happiness. You get a glass of watered wine and a piece of home-made cake and it's all very friendly and family-like. And when you're ripe and ready, you're invited to an internal meeting and sworn to secrecy. After that, you're hooked.'

Little looked disbelieving. 'Sounds like a cross between *Jaws* and *The Exorcist*.'

'That's about right. I made my excuses and left at the fruit-cake stage. But I stayed long enough to find out one thing — the British aren't the only suckers in the world.'

'Eh?'

'It's mostly young Americans in Europe who go crazy over fringe religions. Like with Jim Jones. Away from their homes and families they take up just about any souped-up garbage that's going the rounds. You know, burning the joss-sticks, chanting the Koran, following ley-lines to Glastonbury, that sort of caper . . .'

William stopped as he saw the scepticism on the canny Scots face in front of him. 'Of course it's a hunch,' he admitted. 'It's all we've got to go on. Bob has got fifty people down at Maidstone interviewing everybody in sight of Leeds Castle on Saturday. I've got another forty here going over every man, woman and child seen near the Lewisham supermarket. I'm taking twenty off, as from now, to help us case the religious communes. Okay?'

He glanced up to find the Inspector looking at him curiously. 'It's a gamble, John, I know that. If it fails, we try something else. Let's hope it doesn't.'

THURSDAY

A hand shook him until he moved and opened his mouth. He felt the mug clink against his teeth, and the hot tea swill in his mouth until he could get his throat to swallow. He kept his eyes tightly shut. Then he lay back in a half-doze, twitching as the dreams came.

In a moment, it seemed, he was awake and listening. His head was aching badly. There was the sound of hymn-singing, coming from the next room. He thought of Sundays in Hagerstown: the cold wind blowing across the cemetery and the parking lot, the distant prayers for the soldiers who had gone across the sea to fight in France, his mother in a small round hat with a long jewelled hatpin, his father in the suit he wore to hearings. Sunday, it meant he had been here eight days already, but that couldn't be. He heard Esther's voice clear above the others: 'Morning has broken, Like the first morning. Blackbird has spoken, As on the first day . . .' To the pure all things are pure, he thought grimly. Including sacrifice.

For once there was no-one on guard outside. Morning prayer-meeting must be compulsory. Listening to the music, the filth of his surroundings suddenly became more than he could bear. Writhing feebly, rocking his body from side to side, he inched towards the tent flap. His swinging arms knocked the plastic bucket, but he managed to grab it with his fingers before it fell and spilled its foul-smelling contents. Feet-first, punching his limbs like something breaking out of its caul, he wriggled into the middle of the room and lay stranded on the carpet, catching his breath.

From the occasional outside sounds he'd heard, he knew he was in an upstairs room. Now he saw it was a bedroom, perhaps a spare bedroom, quite large, and genteelly furnished with a white-painted wooded bed pushed into one corner, a white-painted closet, the dresser with its blue glass vase, the chair Ishmael had used, and two watercolours of the Pass of Glencoe on the walls.

His tent was pitched against the outside wall, between two large squares of black paper taped over the window recesses. At either end of the opposite wall were two doors. The hymn singing was coming from behind the left-hand door. As he listened, gathering his strength, the singing stopped and what sounded like a muttered Bible reading began. If he was going to make a move, he had to make it now.

Twisting his head and shoulders, he gauged his distance to the other door. It was maybe a yard closer than the nearest window, but for all he knew it might lead into a broom closet. If he could get to the black-out paper and punch it through, there was at least a chance he could break open a window and attract the attention of neighbours or people passing in the street below.

Rolling himself underneath the window, he eased round until the base of his spine was flat against the wall. Then he dug his heels into the carpet and began inching himself painfully upright. He now had his back to the black-out paper, which crackled loudly under his weight. Shuffling his feet, he turned to face it. His legs were trembling, and a pulse beating in his head drowned out the muttered prayers. With a huge effort he lifted his bound fists, tore the paper wide and swept open the heavy curtain on the other side. Through the window he looked out on emptiness. There were no houses, no street-lamps. And it was the dead of night.

For a second, he hesitated, his bound wrists raised like a supplicant. Then he lunged forward. As he did so, he felt himself being picked up from behind like a baby. Carried back, away from the window, he heard Luke's voice in his ear, soothing, unflustered.

'Mr Commoner, you could hurt yourself.'

The next thing he knew, he was back in the tent. Esther was sitting in her familiar position outside on the carpet. She had brought with her a newspaper and Ishmael's cassette recorder. She gave him a kittenish smile.

'You're a lucky guy, you know that?'

'What?'

'Ishmael wanted to punish you. He said we should put sticky tape over your eyes and cottonwool in your ears.'

Martin said nothing.

'But Luke said it was our fault for not guarding you properly. And Zed and I agreed. So how about that?'

Martin remained silent.

'Anyhow,' Esther persisted, 'I wanted you to hear something.' She picked up the newspaper and opened it — a *Daily Telegraph*, he couldn't make out the date. 'It says here, they're all after you. But they aren't getting nowhere.' She read slowly: ' "Scotland Yard has set up a special Operations Centre to coordinate the investigations. D11, the branch of the Metropolitan Police trained in weaponry and assault tactics, has been placed on full alert. Security checks are being run at all Britain's ports, air-ports and private airfields." How about that? But they haven't got any leads, Mr C. That's what it says. Not one single lead to the kidnappers. So you see,' she put down the paper, with the same skittish smile on her face, 'you're safe with us.'

Martin remained expressionless. Inwardly, he felt the fear in his belly rise towards his throat. How long had he been a prisoner here? Four days? Five? An amateur operation would have been blown wide open by now. The British police had a good record when it came to tracking terrorist gangs. Were they negotiating? No chance. Don't believe them if they tell you so. He'd seen the TV pictures of the SAS going into the Iranian Embassy. Britain and Israel were the two countries in the world that never made concessions to kidnappers. They sure weren't going to make an exception for him.

He was racked by a fit of coughing. The police had to be close. These wierdo kids must have left prints all over the icecream van. Trouble was with the computer. He'd warned the General often enough about relying on all that goddam high technology. Look at the Weisbaden computer in West Germany. The most advanced goddamned police computer in the world. But it hadn't been able to find Schleyer in time. Or Aldo Moro. Was that how he was going to end up, pumped full of bullets in the trunk of a stolen car?

He thought he heard a police siren. Thinking about the police . . . he must have imagined it. But no, it was getting louder.

And Esther had heard it too. She was half-rising, looking over her shoulder, wondering whether to call the others. What would they do — shoot him? Try to escape? And if the police broke in . . . He moistened his lips.

The siren faded away in the distance. The police car must have been at least a block from them. He breathed more freely and looked across at the girl, who was squatting again, calmly picking her feet. In any case, better the British police should get to him before his own people did. He knew what it was to be 'denied to the enemy'. Something very simple, that they were all trained to do. If there was any risk of losing him to the other side, the clear instruction was to shoot him first, think about his kidnappers afterwards.

With the back of his hand he scratched the days-old stubble on his chin and gazed out at the girl, who had begun to comb out her long black hair. His face was itching. So were the backs of his legs and hips. If they kept him on this filthy bed much longer, he'd get bed-sores. He lifted his arms to get Esther's attention, then dropped them. If she wouldn't let him piss in private, there was no way he was going to get a shave. Maybe he should start another conversation. But he hadn't the energy. He was too tired to talk.

His beard, it wasn't growing at normal speed. That must be the drugs. It was a two-day-old beard, he reckoned, but he must have been lying here at least three days, including the time they kept him doped insensible. His life in Washington was a world apart. It was a fantasy. Bringing it into his mind was like looking down the wrong end of a telescope.

The General — what would he be doing? Those fifty feet of windows looking over the Potomac . . . whenever he visualised the DCI, it was to see him in his office standing against the light, a bluff, stocky figure, his feet planted squarely on the carpet, pressing down his pipe tobacco with a blunt thumb while he searched for an apt military metaphor to express what was in his mind. Martin's kidnap was the kind of raid behind the lines that would have moved him to a blind fury.

It was the principle of the thing, as much as the neutralising of his Director of Operations. The General was a man to whom principles mattered. But when the chips were down, how much did any single operative count for? None of them was indispensable. For the sake of his own prestige, he would not allow

Martin too much credit when he reported to the President. If his body was found in a ditch in a day or two, the DCI would have to call up his career file before making the memorial speech. Just to be on the safe side, memory being what it is in an ageing man.

Come to that, what did he matter to any of them? Take Addams, for instance, envious son of a bitch. Vain, too, with expensive tastes. It showed in his appearance, the care he took with his suits and his fingernails, the Porsche in the carport, the way he brushed his hair in silver wings over his ears. There was a picture in his office of him skiing with the Shah. It was vanity which made Addams resent Martin's command of Middle Eastern affairs, vanity and hurt pride that Martin as DDO could go over his head to the Director. He would weep a few crocodile tears for him, before taking out his handkerchief and dabbing his cheeks to make sure the wetness wouldn't leave wrinkles in his Bahamas tan. He could see them now at his funeral — Addams, Max Hemming and the General, bowed in thoughtful silence before the nailed-down coffin, calculating the damage.

Max. Surely Max would feel for him? He'd given Max all the breaks he'd ever had in his life. Pulled him into the Agency from a dead-end lawyer's job in San José, after the Californian office recommended him. Got him a plum counter-intelligence job straightening out the Middle East division, when it turned out that MOSSAD was getting to see every piece of paper that passed over the desk, down to cable schedules. Finally, after Max had done a great job of closing Middle East down like a clam, he'd set him up in Counter-Intelligence with a direct line to the DCI. Since then, they'd worked hand in glove on several operations — except for the occasional project like BeeSting which was too sensitive to be filtered to Counter-Intelligence.

Max would be loyal — he had a great capacity for loyalty. He'd already be weevilling in the Langley fabric looking for conspirators, burrowing for clues. The last time he'd lunched Max on Capitol Hill (how long ago? . . . he couldn't recall . . . he'd lost track of the days) Max had boasted to him that he'd got the whole outfit sewn up so tight, a marble could drop to the floor and he'd know which direction it was rolling in. But that was the other side to him —

'You wanna pee?'

'No.'

Martin shifted his eyes off the girl and struggled to concentrate. His train of thought, he must keep with it. Concentrate. Max Hemming. That was the other side of him, a coldness, a ruthlessness. Goddamn, it wasn't loyalty he needed now, it was friends, and that wasn't Max's strong point, friendship.

He was a cold bastard, from his crewcut hair to his shiny shoes. At Berkeley in the mid-sixties, so Martin had been told, Max had paid his way through college by informing on student radicals. That was how the Californian office had got to know of him. Sometimes as they worked in partnership, agreed with each other, compared notes, Martin had felt those rapidly-blinking eyes behind the steel spectacles alight on him with detachment and sum him up as a dilettante. He'd said to Max over lunch at the Cosmos Club — what was it? — 'Macnamara climbed over the fence to get in here once.' Ironic, that was all, and Max had given him one of those glances, cold, almost scornful, which had stopped him dead for a moment and made him reach for his wine-glass.

What if he did enjoy a social life? He had nothing to defend or apologise for. Max would register his death with a moment's silence, a flicker of genuine emotion, and then busy himself with the mechanics of finding his killers, his loyalty already transferred to what Martin stood for rather than Martin himself.

To hell with him. To hell with all of them. He knew where to find his friends. And his pleasures. Nancy would be grieving for him. She would have left Maidstone that same evening and gone back to London, and be waiting for him, thinking about him. Maybe she'd have checked out of the Capital, which was expensive, and gone to some little hotel that James Parrish had found for her while the police asked their questions. She would be sitting up in bed, with half-smoked cigarettes filling the ashtray and newspapers scattered on the comforter and on the floor. She'd be hoping for the bedside phone to ring, and dreading what it might tell her. She'd light another cigarette, noticing that she hadn't put any nail polish on her nails in days and what the hell, and she'd pick up a magazine or one of the Congressional transcripts she was checking for Traill. Then she'd think of him, sending out messages of love to her perhaps for the last time, and she'd throw the magazine down and rub

82

her fist in her eye in the little child-like way she had when she was solemnly thinking . . .

Of course she would be wearing the black nightdress he'd given her, to set off her pale skin and her dark hair with the lights in it that glimmered when he stroked it. She would be remembering the gift and the giver, running her fingers down the black silk strap which rose over her firm little breast, and letting her fingers go on further. But it was no good thinking about it. She would reach out, instead, for the pink comb on the bedside table, and start running it through her hair, pulling it until it hurt and the pain brought her back to the present —

He looked up. Esther was combing her hair, the same withdrawn expression on her face.

'Nancy,' he murmured.

'What?'

'A woman I know. You look alike.'

'Is she pretty?'

'Yes. Very.'

'Do you fuck her?'

She came close up to the tent. He could see her small breasts clearly outlined under the thin shirt. She had on the long blue dress she was wearing at the Castle. There was a rust-coloured stain on it in a crescent shape around her groin — that must be where she'd taken his bleeding head on her lap in the getaway. That scent again, there was something of cinnamon in it, it remained him of the whores in Saigon.

Her eyes inquisitive and bright, Esther asked again, 'Do you fuck her?'

'That's none of your business.'

'Aw, shit, come on Mr C. What's wrong with fucking? You think it's a sin or summink? There's nothing in the Bible against it. In the Bible it's called knowledge, like in the Tree of Knowledge. So when Jesus says he knew Mary and Martha it means he knew them sexily. He fucked them.'

'You think so.'

'Yeah. I mean, God invented sex, didn't he? So if Jesus had said that sex was a sin, he would have been blaspheming against his father. Get it?'

'I hear what you're saying.'

'So then. Sex is no sin, even for old people like you. Sex is

83

knowledge and knowledge is power. Sex is the way to loving God.'

Martin stared at her, fascinated. Esther was squatting at the tent entrance, hands clasped between her legs, swaying slightly from side to side like a snake-charmer tempting out a snake. Where her skirt was drawn down tightly between her thighs, he could see that she wasn't wearing panties either. Only the skirt and the T-shirt, and on her feet tennis shoes and socks rolled down to her ankles like a schoolgirl.

He tugged the blanket over his legs. He said, 'I've got my own ideas.'

'Oh reely? What are your ideas, old man? What do you think of when you're fucking a woman? Do you think that she's in your power? That she's helpless? That you can do anything you want with her?'

The girl put out her hand and touched his bare foot. He felt a shock go through him and jerked his legs away violently, forgetting that they were bound and nearly falling on his side. Esther giggled. She opened her lips and ran the tip of her pink tongue along her teeth, tilting her chin to let him see her effort of seduction.

Roughly he said, 'Who do you think you are? Marlene Dietrich?'

'Marleen who?'

'Forget it.'

The girl leaned forward, so that her breasts slid against her shirt. This time Martin made no attempt to get away from her hand stroking the hairs on his legs. He had control over himself. He watched her stonily.

'This woman who's like me. What's her name?'

'Nancy.'

'Is she good? Is she sexy? Does she do what you want? Does she take all her clothes off, very slowly, while you watch, and then kneel in front of you and take you in her mouth?'

'Get away from me.'

'And you grab her by the hair and pull her head back. Slap her around a bit, give her a few bruises. Gettin' a bit excited for an old man, aren't we? Throw her down on the bed then, do you? Over the table, on the floor, it doesn't matter by then, you're ready for anything, ready to go, aren't you Mr C?'

Her fingernails pressed deep into his flesh, enough to have

drawn blood if she hadn't bitten them. Panting slightly, not taking her eyes off Martin, she reached behind her for the tape cassette on the carpet and pressed the *Play* button. The sudden clamour of George Harrison chanting 'My Sweet Lord' filled the room, ringing in his head like a pagan hosanna.

'I'm gonna show you something,' said Esther.

As Martin watched, she took off her tennis shoes and peeled off her socks. She had long delicate feet — like Nancy's, he thought, unable to take his eyes off her. Backing away from him, she stood up in the tent entrance, brushing her hair from her oval face. Her eyes glittered. He thought she was going to call him a murderer again.

'I'm gonna do my dance for you,' she announced. 'This is Salome dancing before Herod.'

His throat tightened. Deliberately in time to the music, Esther put her hands on her hips and began to rotate her stomach like a belly-dancer. To the wailing incantations of *Hare Krishna!* she raised her arms up above her head and wriggled her slim body sinuously, from her neck and shoulders down to her hips. With her heels she stamped on the carpet, the hem of her blue dress flowing around her bare ankles.

Bringing one arm down, she fumbled with the buttons on her shirt. Her cheeks were flushed and a mask of absorption had come down over her face, though she never took her eyes off Martin in the tent. He wanted to shout at her to stop it; he wanted to tell her roughly that he had seen better strip artistes in a Buenos Aires back-street; but speech deserted him. Not losing the beat of the music, the girl slipped off her shirt. She had thin shoulders and pale, rather pointed breasts, and a pink birth-mark in the shape of a scarab on her rounded belly. Suggestively, as she danced, she ran her hands over her breasts and played with her nipples as she had played with her fingers across Martin's legs.

The birthmark. That was one for the police if she ever got away. But the thought slipped from him. The rhythmic chanting of the song went on and on; it pounded in his head. Esther, still moving her body as if in a trance, dropped her hands to her skirt and caressed herself around the crescent stain of blood on her groin. To his horror and confusion, Martin felt a stirring between his legs. He lay transfixed as the girl let her skirt fall and danced before him entirely naked, still caressing

85

herself, her eyes closed now and her lips parted, her head thrown back in ecstasy. Her long-legged body, waif-like with swelling belly and narrow hips, affected him powerfully: she was appealing and sexy in her very defencelessness. Shimmering, bare, she came closer still, falling on her knees in the stink of the tent and reaching out to give his swollen member ease.

'Oh God,' he groaned, screwing up his eyes so she would not see the tears, 'Oh God!'

'My sweet lord,' she said.

As he raised his bound arms in an arc — to embrace her or to send her away he did not know — the tape ran out, the music stopped. In the sudden hush he heard voices murmuring encouragement. He opened his eyes in disbelief. Ranged round the tent-flap were the grinning faces of Luke, Zed and Ishmael.

In his shock and fury he felt himself go limp. Tears of rage and humiliation coursed down his cheeks; he screamed curses at them until he choked on his sobbing breaths.

Esther looked at him impassively. Her eyes were blank and unfocused, as if she had danced herself into a state of catalepsy. Trance-like, she turned from him and held out her arms: Zed reached into the tent and drew her to him.

'Come to me, baby,' he said in a soft voice. 'Let's show him how the Family love one another.'

He laid Esther gently on the carpet. Sitting beside her, he began yanking off his flowered boots. Then he stood up, grinning at Martin, and lowered his trousers.

Martin turned his head away and closed his eyes. He heard a click, and then his own voice, hollow and quavering.

'What time is it?'

'Time we had a talk, old buddy.'

Ishmael had switched on the interrogation tape. Martin struggled to listen to it, to assess his replies; but shame engulfed him and ruined his concentration. Over the two voices, Ishmael's sneering, his own quiet, sometimes almost inaudible, he heard the sounds of love-making a few feet away. Esther was moaning softly. Zed was grunting and muttering under his breath.

He opened his eyes and dully watched them, beyond arousal or humiliation, or even anger now, as he might glance at the copulation of stick-insects. In his weakness he found himself grieving that people could behave in this way — not peasants or

86

savages but his own countrymen. To beat and torture him for information — that he could understand. What he had been subjected to in the last few days was not in any of the manuals.

'*We did what we set out to do. We won the war in the countryside.*'

'*The prisoner pleads not guilty.*'

Esther's moans reached a climax. She cried out, 'Oh! Oh! Oh! Oh!'

'Praise the Lord!' shouted Zed, humping over her. 'Praise be to Jesus!'

They fell apart, and lay side by side on the carpet. Ishmael appeared in the tent doorway, carrying the syringe. 'Part One is over, old buddy,' he grinned. 'We've got some more questions for when you wake up.'

'Not without food. For God's sake!'

'Take it easy. It's a weaker shot.'

Martin could make no effort to resist. He did not feel the needle go in. His thoughts were racing ahead, out of control; he felt like a husk blown after them. They were children. He must understand that. Innocents picking the wings off a moth. They were not responsible. The girl was not responsible for her behaviour: she was a child, a primitive, coping with her fears and insecurity by asserting herself in sexual play. Zed was the same. And Luke. Frightened, simple-minded children looking for father-figures to protect them. A leader to lead them back to the womb. *Unless you become like a small child, you shall not enter the kingdom of heaven . . .*

Discipline. Think about affirmative things. Ma had always told him that as a baby. Give yourself strength, she chided him; don't let it come from others. Old friends. Geoff MacLaren, his squash partner. There was someone to rely on. Always good for a bit of bar gossip. Who was out, who was in. Cock-and-bull stories. Plans for retirement.

The Toy Factory, Geoff called it. Langley. He could remember it perfectly. You came down in the elevator to the ground floor and walked into the main hall. Marble walls. One wall made of glass and looking out to the inner courtyard with its landscaped garden. When the magnolia trees were in bloom, you knew you could take your jacket off as soon as you stepped outside. Maybe the guard at the desk was checking briefcases and you had time to look around a little. On the opposite wall was a row of paintings borrowed by the CIA Fine Arts

Commission. Usually abstracts nowadays. Hideous uncontrolled daubs of orange and yellow. When he'd been on the Commission, he'd got pictures where you could understand what the man was saying. That Andrew Wyeth he'd negotiated so long to borrow — that was his greatest coup. There was a painter. A small boy in short trousers at sea in a yellow cornfield. Corn rolling. New England sky stretching away in all directions. Freedom.

Inscribed in the marble wall above the entrance desk, as proudly as the words in the Lincoln Memorial — 'And Ye Shall Know The Truth And The Truth Shall Make You Free.'

Right outside by the Agency parking-lots, the bronze statue of Nathan Hale, American patriot awaiting execution, his hands tied behind him with cord. The truth did not make you free. It bound you in oaths of secrecy. It got you taken prisoner —

He began to sweat heavily again, and tremble all over. The sky. Wyeth's sky, the New England sky — what colour was it? He could not picture it. Was it blue? Was it white? The last time he looked up at the sky in Washington ... he could not remember, so long ago. He tried to put himself in the place of the boy in the cornfield. What was he looking at?

He was looking up into a tent of white. And falling.

The Operations Room at Victoria House was a hubbub of voices, clacking typewriters and ringing telephones. On an investigation this big there was normally too much information; it was all they could do to winnow out the useful leads. But all William Pomfret could hear, as he walked through to his office, was a deafening silence. Silence from the kidnappers who had made no contact, not even telephoned a message to the national papers. Silence from his grasses — in fact from the entire villains' grapevine. Silence above all from the Americans on the subject he needed to explore more urgently than any other at this point — what the motive could have been for kidnapping Martin Commoner.

So far, he could have been kidnapped out of thin air. All the hundreds of man-hours that had gone into the case since his own interrogation of Arthur Norman had produced no facts of any real significance. William himself, turning a blind eye to peremptory telephone messages from Christopher Knight, had spent the last twenty-four hours discovering that there were more cult movements in the forty square miles of metropolitan London than he had dreamed possible.

He had familiarised himself with the soul-travellers of the Satsang Society in Campden Hill Road, the Hare Krishnas in Oxford Street, the Aetherius Society in the Fulham Road who believed that Jesus was a Cosmic Master, the disciples of Bhagwan Shree Rajneesh who wore a picture of the Bhagwan on sandalwood beads round their necks and practised rebirthing at their meditation centre in Belmont Street, and other centres of curious and esoteric faiths based in houses across London from Tennyson Road to Rutland Gate.

In person he had visited some of the harsher, rawer cults that might attract the kind of people he had built up a picture of in his mind — angry, frustrated, bewildered and fanatical. The more extreme the demands made on the celebrants — to give up all their material possessions, to cleanse their minds of everything except the Way and the Truth — the more the hostility and violence of suppressed fanaticism hung in the air, disturbing and faintly menacing, like the presence of silent strangers . . .

Back in the Operations Room a telephone buzzing on the desk beside him made him think of Vanderbyle. Every moment he paused, the Terrorist Theory gained ground on him. He left the Operations Room and walked along the corridor and down the stairs to the Special Branch Registry, to see how the manual card-search was progressing.

'What's the score?' he asked the young Inspector who was coordinating it.

The Inspector shook his head.

'Any Americans?'

'One Californian in one of the address-books. Nelson Winthrop. I'm running it through now.'

'Let me know right away on that.'

As he strode impatiently back to his office another message was pushed into his hand. Filed information on a newspaper cutting dated a year ago. A man called George Archer, 42, had been found and put on probation for two years for ripping off a religious sect call the Jesus Children (who the hell were they?), by selling them a London house he didn't own.

'Where does this come from?'

'The National Police Computer, sir.'

'Then it's probably out of date. Check it against the Thames Valley computer. Wait. On second thoughts, I'll do it myself.'

William went into his office, where a computer terminal sat bright and new on top of a metal trolley. He tapped in George Archer's name and age, and the few other details the card provided. After a moment, via the eight yellow-topped computers in a small carpeted annex beside the Operations Room, the man's name came up in flashing green capitals on William's video screen, followed by the words INFORMATION NOW. In lines of neat green typing came George Archer's address, the description and numberplate of his car, and various other facts including the maiden name of his wife and details of all his previous convictions. William noted down that the fraud offence against the Jesus Children involved dollar payments. He also noted that George Archer was currently inside, serving a two-year sentence at Durham Prison.

He swore softly, and looked up to see John Little standing in the doorway, carrying a folder stuffed with lists and pamphlets.

'John, have you heard of people called the Jesus Children?'

The Inspector shuffled through his lists.

'Jesus Children — yes, I think they must have folded. They don't answer enquiries to their postal address. No mail gets delivered.'

'They were going about a year ago. Check it out again. What about the others?'

The Inspector laid the folder on William's desk. 'It's all in there, sir. Cuttings on fringe religious groups in the national and local UK press, dating back nine months. Newspaper photos, where taken — they're a pretty sad-looking bunch of screwballs, most of them. Magazines and leaflets. And here,' he took three cassette tapes out of his pockets, 'supplementary interviews with journalists, a couple of local vicars, an employer and a social security official.'

'Any leads?'

'I don't know what you'll make of it, sir. One of the vicars is quite interesting. We're a long mile from the Red Army Fraction, that's for sure.'

'When I want your sarcasm, Scotty, I'll ask for it.' William was flicking through the opened folder. It was all the same kind of stuff. Youngsters arrested on an obstruction charge for handing out literature in the streets. Crudely roneo'd warnings that the end of the world was at hand and the time to repent was now. Photographs of plain women in shapeless dresses holding up babies to the camera; occasionally a man, sometimes the bearded guru himself, glowering at the unwelcome publicity.

'It takes all sorts,' said Little.

'That's right. Get this lot off to Registry and see if it tallies with any of the names they're working on.'

His green telephone was ringing. Little picked it up, and passed it over to William, raising his eyes heavenwards to where the Commander had his office on the floor above.

'William?'

It wasn't the Commander. It was Johnny Wax. 'If it's any interest, my friend, I hear the Agency is wetting its nappies over Commoner.'

'What?'

'That's what I'm getting from Washington. They're running around like blue-assed flies at Langley. There's something big going on. If Vanderbyle breaks his silence to you, I'd like to know what he says. Be seeing you.'

'Yes.' William slammed the phone down. No wonder Vanderbyle was so much in evidence. Knight obviously had an idea what was going on. There was collusion between the two governments at some level. So why the hell weren't they giving the Detective Chief Inspector in charge of the case a proper briefing?

There was snow on his boots. It was bitterly cold, so cold that he couldn't feel the rifle in his gloved hand. The young roebuck he had shot hung across his shoulders like a heavy overcoat. The blood still dripped out of his soft mouth.

He plodded on steadily through the plantation of spruces. The sun sinking behind him threw his shadow hugely over the snow. He could hear nothing over the crunching of the boots on the ground and his heavy breathing. John was with him somewhere. Without stopping and looking round he called out over his shoulder and trudged on.

The load across his shoulders was growing heavier. John must be with him — where was he? He began to walk faster, calling out, 'John! John!' Ahead was a large clearing. He broke into a stumbling run, shouting for his son: not daring to look round, not even out of the corner of his eye, for fear of what he was carrying on his back.

He was not in the forest any more. He was in CIA headquarters, running along a corridor towards his office. It was midnight and people were staring at him. Embarrassed, he slowed to a walk. There was blood all over his coat, John's blood. How had it got there? Around him the security guards were scurrying like ants. All the colour-coded office doors were open and he could see the guards busily writing out demerits for overflowing trash baskets and unlocked safes.

He arrived at his office. The door had been taken off its hinges. Inside a phalanx of security guards awaited him. His safe was wide open. Classified documents were strewn around the floor. The chief guard came forward. It was a face he recognised — an oval face with hazel-coloured eyes, framed in long dark hair. Without taking her eyes off him she pointed to the two signs on his wall. *Knowledge Is Freedom*, said one. The other, *Vigilance Is Strength*. Obediently he took off his clothes and stood on the desk, waiting for orders. Faintly at first, then closer and closer, he heard the sound of a creature howling in pain.

'Hey! Hey!'

A hand was shaking his shoulder. Half in the nightmare still he muttered, 'Get me out of here.' He heard Ishmael's precise New England voice answer him:

'A man who gets on with dictators can get on with us for a few days.'

Martin opened his eyes. Ishmael put a mug of hot tea to his lips. When he had finished drinking he asked hoarsely, 'How are the negotiations going?'

'With God? The others are praying for you every day.'

'I mean for my release. Ransom.'

Ishmael took off his rimless glasses and rubbed his eyes. 'That depends on how you answer my questions,' he said.

With an enormous effort of will, Martin brought to mind what he had planned to say. He hadn't heard of BeeSting. BeeSting did not exist. He would be prepared to admit to his interrogator everything he would be able to discover for himself from unclassified material at the Library of Congress: the existence of a Pakistani nuclear programme which might or might not have a military application; and the existence of US surveillance satellites and AWACS capable of sending back series of detailed aerial photographs. What he would *not* admit was that any such photographs had been taken over Pakistan; or that any such photographs might be used to help Israel against the threat of an Islamic nuclear strike.

Ishmael switched on the cassette recorder. 'Your people have given up on you, old buddy,' he said. 'According to the papers, they think you're dead.'

'Is that so.'

'How do you think we'd have got you here if it wasn't for them?'

'Who?'

'You know who I'm talking about. People who want you out of the way, Commoner. You know how easy it is for the CIA to get rid of people when they try.'

'You don't impress me.' Martin paused, waiting for Ishmael to go on. Then he said, 'Prove it.'

'Okay. Let me give you some names. Fidel Castro. Eight separate attempts chronicled by the Church Committee, including a poisoned wet suit and an exploding cigar.'

Martin gave a weak chuckle. 'Castro's still alive. That speaks for itself.'

'Okay. The President of Vietnam, Ngo Dinh Diem.'

'Not the CIA. Try the State Department.'

'Patrice Lumumba. The CIA man drove around with his fucking body in the trunk of his car.'

'Lumumba was killed by the Congolese. There was no evidence of any Agency involvement. I've read Stockwell too: it doesn't prove a damn thing.'

'Proof? You want proof?' Ishmael shouted at him. 'I'll give you proof. President Trujillo of the Dominican Republic. Ambushed and killed with a .38-calibre pistol and .30-calibre carbines handed to the killers by the CIA.'

'I don't know anything about that. It's before my time.'

'Okay. Let's bring it nearer home, old buddy.' Ishmael leaned forward, his voice lower, more intent. 'Ever heard of Rene Schneider?'

'Yes.'

'You bet you have. Chilean general. Friend of Allende. Murdered by soldiers with CIA connivance in October 1970, six hours after CIA weapons had been given to them. The weapons then handed back and deep-sixed by the CIA —'

'I was Chief of Station in Buenos Aires, not Santiago. I heard nothing about the plan to kidnap Schneider until afterwards. The plan was bungled. It wasn't the Agency's idea in the first place. It was a cock-up. That's all there is to say.'

'I haven't finished yet, Commoner. I've just established that the CIA knows how to get rid of people. I've got one more name for you.'

Ishmael stopped abruptly and stared at the carpet, plucking fretfully at the straggly growth on his chin. He seemed agitated, as if mastering some strong emotion. 'I've got one more name for you,' he repeated, looking straight at Martin now. 'David Bisley.'

'Who?'

'He's dead, Commoner. You can talk about dead agents, they're out of reach. He was one of the best you had, wasn't he? You said so yourself.'

'Bisley?' Martin was confused. What did Bisley have to do with it? The drugs had weakened his grasp on coherent thought. Of course he remembered Bisley, one of the most successful street men behind the Iron Curtain the Agency had ever employed. A short, pale man with unruly black hair and a sharp nose. He went. A lousy business. But what was that to do with —

'You knew David Bisley. He worked for you.'

'Sure he did. So what?'

'So what?' A red flush spread across Ishmael's sunken cheeks. 'You're a heartless sonofabitch aren't you, Commoner,' he snarled. 'A real Nazi. I should have expected that. You killed him, Commoner, that's so what. You had him executed.'

'Executed?'

'Oh I'm sorry, you don't understand these simple words. Termination with extreme prejudice, that's what you call it in the CIA.'

'You're crazy. Bisley committed suicide. He shot himself on a hunting trip. His son was with him. He found him with the rifle in his hand.'

'Fuck that. You killed him Commoner. As surely as if you put the bullet through his head. But you were a clever bastard, weren't you. First you disgraced him, to give him a motive for suicide. Two months later he was a dead man.'

'We dismissed Bisley for security reasons. What happened after that was a tragedy, I accept that. But it wasn't our business to hold his hand.'

A door opened and shut. Ishmael lowered his voice and spat his words out. 'David Bisley was a hero. Any other service would have decorated him. But you, Commoner. You called him a traitor. You drag his name through the mud, destroy everything he built his life on. All because of allegations that weren't even proved against him.'

Martin struggled to alert himself. Something was going on here. Ishmael wasn't reciting the old stories any longer. He had suddenly zeroed in on something specific, something that wasn't common knowledge.

He said casually. 'What allegations?'

'You know damn well what I'm talking about. The Soviet double agent who pissed off to Moscow. George Mitchum, from State. You got a report that . . . that David Bisley was a friend of Mitchum. That he tipped him off to flee the country.'

'Bisley was a friend of Mitchum's. He admitted it to me himself.'

'Yeah. He also swore to you he never tipped Mitchum off. He couldn't have. He didn't know Mitchum was working for the Russians. Or that you were after him.'

'My information was different. Bisley knew more than he let on. Mitchum left him an air ticket to Beirut.'

'He pleaded with you.' Ishmael was almost whispering. 'Why is it always the victims who have to prove their innocence? He put his whole career on the line.'

'There was too much at stake.'

'So you terminated him.'

'Dismissed him, yes.'

'But then you thought he knew too much. He might follow Mitchum to Moscow. So you had him killed —'

'Not true.'

'You had him shot.'

Ishmael was trembling all over. He unbuttoned his denim jacket and drew something out of it. A kitchen knife. It had a black handle and a blade about six inches long tapering to a sharp point. He balanced it in the palm of his hand, watching the blade shiver.

Ishmael said softly, 'David Bisley trusted you. He was really

95

loyal to you, Commoner. He said you were his buddy. He said you were one of the only good guys at the top. Then you disgraced him. Then you killed him. And now you're lying to *me*.'

Martin struggled to hold Ishmael's eyes. They were deep-set, staring. He said, steadily, 'Every word I've told you is the truth.'

'His death? You said his son was right there with him. That's a lie, old buddy.'

Ishmael was staring down at his hand. It had stopped trembling. The blade was still.

'I was quarter of a mile away,' he said in a muffled voice. 'I heard a shot. I found him dead and carried him back to the cabin. I don't think he killed himself. I think you murdered him.'

It was suddenly very quiet in the tent. Martin said nothing. In the stillness he could hear his heart pounding, slowly, like the heavy tread of a man being led to the gallows. He drew up his knees. He saw, in slow motion, Ishmael's hand tighten around the knife. He heard him say, *I was gonna be next in line. Now it's you instead.*

Holding the knife blade downwards, Ishmael sprang. In the same instant Martin, his shoulders on the ground against the tent wall, kicked out high and hard with his legs. The kick caught Ishmael in the groin and knocked his legs from under him. He fell heavily across Martin's body, plunging the blade into the airbed beside his left shoulder. Too weak to dislodge him, Martin beat on his assassin's head with his bound fists, cawing. Ishmael's face was inches from his own. He could see a kind of triumph in it, a terrible satisfaction. The son killing the father: it was the wrong way round. It was crazy. He couldn't die this way. Found in his underwear. Murdered by a bunch of kids in a suburban bedroom.

'You're crazy!' he cawed, 'you're crazy!', as Ishmael pulled up the knife —

And then the face was gone, with a look of surprise, lifted up and away from him. Luke was stooping in the tent entrance, hugging Ishmael like a baby. His moon face was screwed up in embarrassment.

'Hey, c'mon man,' he kept saying. 'C'mon brother.'

Bisley's son struggled to free his pinioned arms, his thin legs kicking out in tantrum.

'Kill the bastard now!' he shouted.

Luke set Ishmael on his feet outside the tent. 'It's in God's hands, not ours,' he muttered. Shyly, he took the kitchen knife from him. After a moment, as Ishmael gazed at the man he wanted to kill, Luke added, 'It's time you checked the other house, do you think?'

Ishmael turned, without another word, and walked out of the room. Luke stooped into the tent, and lifted Martin back on to the airbed, which had shrivelled like a wrinkled bladder.

'Are you okay?' he enquired.

'He was going to kill me.'

Luke looked doubtful. 'God has a terrible swift sword to smite his enemies,' he declared with a frown, as if uncertain it was the text to fit. He backed out of the tent and sat down on the carpet, at an angle to the tent so that he could see the door out of the corner of his eye.

Martin stared at him. He could see the doubts in Luke's face as clearly as clouds moving slowly across a wide landscape. How much had he heard? How much did he know about Bisley? There was an opening here: something to exploit. If he was given time. The delayed shock caught up with him and he began to shiver uncontrollably.

He blurted out, 'C-can I have another blanket?'

Luke rolled forward on his haunches and got to his feet. 'Hold on there,' he said, and went out, grinning as if he had made a joke.

Martin looked up at the tent roof and struggled to concentrate. If Ishmael was Bisley's son, his name would have come up on the CIA computer by now and been forwarded to England along with others. It meant that finding him could only be a matter of hours away. But what evidence was there that Ishmael was telling the truth?

The details were filtering back. It was a year ago, almost to the day. David Bisley had taken his son on a hunting expedition in the Alleghenies. He'd left his son (what was Ishmael's real name? he couldn't remember), he'd left him behind in the cabin and walked a long way into the hills before blowing his brains out. But the son had learned from the father how to stalk. He'd stalked him, so he said, until he lost him. Then he heard the gunshot, and found his father, dying, with the rifle beside him.

It tallied. And Ishmael had Bisley's features, that was what had seemed so familiar — the black clumps of hair, the strangely narrow face broadening suddenly at the forehead. He remembered the last interview well, with the vividness almost of hallucination. David Bisley was in a pale grey suit, both hands in front of him resting palm-downwards on the long walnut table. He was blinking, and his hair was sticking out more untidily than usual, as though he'd been dragged out of a hole in the earth into the unaccustomed sunlight.

He had denied everything, in a firm voice. The polygraph had been inconclusive, as it often was with agents accustomed to living a life of subterfuge, and Bisley must have expected that his unblemished record would see him through. But the evidence all pointed in his direction. Mitchum had been tipped off by somebody. He had fled within forty-eight hours of the final decision to bring him in. He was seen with Bisley only a few hours before he walked through the gates of the Soviet Embassy in Washington. As a friend, Bisley was one of the few people who could have known or suspected what was going to happen. And then the air ticket, and a note, had been found among Mitchum's things.

Bisley had taken the verdict without a flicker of emotion, although he must have known immediately what it meant; dismissal with a negative reference, the word going out that he was not to be trusted, his career in ruins. He had stuffed his hands in his pockets, nodded jerkily and walked out of the room, and that was the last Martin had seen of him. In retrospect it might have been wiser to have kept tabs on him. Dismissed agents needed careful handling. But Bisley was not the snivelling kind. He could be trusted to take the rap and not complain. Even in his death he had behaved in the proper manner by not leaving room for suspicion that it wasn't suicide. His wife had moved to the West Coast and remarried . . . a businessman who had a franchise for selling salted popcorn, so she had told Martin when the unofficial compensation had been settled. The son just disappeared; no-one suspected the long fuse that had been lit within him.

He was still shaking all over, unable to keep his limbs still. Luke came back with a red woollen blanket which smelt of mothballs. He lifted Martin up like a bird and wrapped the blanket round his body. Martin felt tears start up in his eyes. He wanted to lay his head against Luke's broad chest and weep, like a baby nestling against his mother for comfort. Turning his face away, he said hoarsely, 'Tell me what I have to do.'

'In the Bible it says all they that love Him shall have eternal life.'

'I'm talking about life here and now.'

Luke stuck out his lower lip and shook his head, with an air of sagacity. 'All our lives are in God's hands.'

'Yes, but mine —'

'All of us. That's what Ishmael's been telling you, right? God is taking charge of His world again. All the signs of the Apocalypse have been fulfilled. Volcanoes erupting. Comets in the night sky. Nuclear leaks. God is preparing us for punishment. The work of the Family is to announce the coming of the reborn Jesus to smite the heathen.'

Martin stared dully at his captor. 'Okay, so why aren't you out on the streets of London announcing it?'

Luke screwed up his face unhappily. 'All prophets are persecuted,' he explained. 'John the Baptist was persecuted. It's a sign that we're speaking the truth.'

'Is this what Ishmael says?'

'He says there is no turning back. He says we must root out Satan and prepare the way of the Lord. He says you're an agent of Satan. If we can succeed to save you, we can succeed with all the agents of Satan.'

'Luke, you're wrong about Ishmael. He's making fools of you. It's not what he says to me. He thinks I killed his father — me! That I killed his father! That's why he's tried to kill me ... Luke!'

Luke was backing out of the tent. His face had closed into the sullen expression of a child refusing to accept what it cannot understand.

'Luke, listen,' Martin shouted after him in desperation. 'Goddammit, he's a killer! He's going to kill me, don't you see?'

'The prophet Amos says — "Woe to them that are at ease in Zion."'

'Murder ... he's going to murder me —'

'"If you confess with your mouth the Lord Jesus, and believe in your heart that God raised him from the dead, you shall be saved." *Romans* 10, verse 9.'

Martin made another attempt and another to break through. But Luke droned on, mouthing the catch-phrases printed on

99

the hoardings outside churches and in the literature handed out by Christian cultists on the streets, invoking them like a cowl of spiritual protection against the ideas Martin was throwing up against his mind. '"He that does not believe is condemned already,"' Luke recited, fixing his eyes on the far wall. '"And whosoever was not found written in the book of life was cast into the lake of fire, and shall be tormented day and night for ever and ever." *Revelations, 20*.'

They were trying to make him like one of them: no past, no future, a reborn Christian; just time to be baptised before the knife went in. Light-headed with fear and exhaustion, Martin could keep watch for Ishmael no longer, and closed his eyes.

Among the smart little Volkswagen Rabbits and Honda Accords in M Street, Max Hemming's dark blue Ford Mercury nosed like a whale shark among porpoises. It accelerated hard away from the lights at Wisconsin and cut in front of a yellow Fiat Panda, the colour of its elegant driver's hair. Hemming lived less than two miles east on Capitol Hill, but Georgetown to him was a world away. He made no secret of his dislike of Georgetown. It was superficial and expensive; a dinky-toy ghetto which put up price barriers and class barriers against the sprawling city beyond its well-defined borders. Its shops were full of French crockery. Its movie theatre showed trendy European sex films with sub-titles. Homosexuals he saw everywhere.

He turned up 33rd Street, away from the shopping traffic, and bounced along the cobbles, parking a few yards up from the intersection with P Street. Twisting his rear-view mirror, he located the Peugeot and the red-haired Agency man sitting at the wheel. A black kid of about twelve, in sneakers, came flopping down the brick sidewalk with a *Washington Star* which he thrust in through the Peugeot window. Money changed hands. The boy put his finger to his baseball cap and shouted 'Yassuh!' before running off grinning. On Hemming's side of the road came a very thin black man in shades, with red bangles on his wrist, strolling a rich woman's borzoi on a gold-link chain.

Getting out of the car, Hemming identified himself with a sign to the CIA operative, and walked back the short distance to Commoner's home. It was a box-shaped pink brick house with dark green shutters. Above the front door jutted out a dark green balcony with sparse green fingers of ivy trailing around it. It was the kind of Georgetown house the realtors rhapsodised about — well-established, comfortable, discreetly wealthy — in an area where even the babysitters had unlisted numbers. It made sense that Commoner should have developed misgivings about the Vietnam war. That polygraph test Hemming had told the DCI about dated from the time the children of Georgetown folk started getting draft notices. The shocking idea that people in homes like these might have their sons coming home in coffins had brought the war to an end faster than all the student demonstrations could have hoped to do.

A silver grey Honda Civic was parked outside the door — Barbara's runabout, they had a description of it out to police in case she left town in a hurry. Hemming went up the three brick steps and tapped politely with the heavy brass knocker. The door was opened by a woman he didn't recognise, a middle-aged blonde with her spectacles on a silver chain under her lifted chin. She smiled at him short-sightedly. 'You must be dear Mr Hemming from the CIA.'

'That's correct.'

She held out a hand, heavy with rings. 'I'm July Gelb. Barbara's expecting you. Come along in.'

She led him through a narrow hall which smelled of furniture polish. An old turn-and-spindle desk, with a silver tray on it for visiting cards, stood against one wall under an eighteenth-century English engraving of a hunting scene.

'She can't go out, you see,' the Gelb woman was explaining over her shoulder. 'What if the 'phone rang, and it was Martin's kidnappers, and she was out buying the broccoli?'

'Are you living here?'

'No. I just come round to hold her hand and do the groceries.' She ushered Hemming into the drawing-room. 'I'll just go fetch her. She's in the kitchen. Make yourself comfortable; I'm sure you'd like a good look round.'

With this parting shot, Judy Gelb bustled out. Hemming could hear her calling out to Barbara in the bright voice of professional sympathy. He scanned the room. He had not yet been invited here socially, but it was plain to see that Barbara had kept the same pleasant and expensive Early American style as in their old house in Spring Valley — pearl-grey walls, dark red

101

rugs on the wooden floor, a wooden-framed early American naive painting of a boy and a dog over the mantelpiece, a built-in bookcase with a broken pediment molding, and raffia baskets of plants and flowers on a nineteenth-century wooden blanket chest. The books were mostly hardback American history and current affairs, plus novels by the expected people: Updike, Pynchon, Bellow, Styron . . .

'Do you approve, Mr Hemming?'

He spun round. A tall, striking woman with an expensive complexion and thick blonde hair swept back from her forehead like a young girl, was standing in the doorway. 'Approve of what?' he stuttered.

'The novels of mine. My husband doesn't read novels. He says he gets enough plots in his working hours.' Barbara smiled faintly and gestured Hemming to a leather wing chair before seating herself on the camelback sofa. She was wearing a well-cut woollen dress which went with the decor. Her lipstick looked fresh: she could have put it on a moment ago.

'I hope you don't mind me asking for this private meeting, Mrs Commoner,' he said glancing at the open door.

'Don't worry, Judy's gone for the groceries. I had to promise her that I wasn't frightened of the big bad wolf.' She smiled again, but he was close enough now to see the tension in her face. 'I haven't rung the number I was given —' she began.

'That's quite all right, Mrs Commoner —'

'There was nothing to tell you. The news, I think, is going to come from your side.'

'I don't know. We've heard nothing. We're assisting the police in England. We're doing everything we can, I want you to believe that.'

'Oh, I do.'

Again the fleeting smile, perhaps ironic. He went on hurriedly. 'Mrs Commoner —'

'Call me Barbara. We've met socially.'

'Uh . . . has *anything* out of the ordinary happened? Any 'phone calls, for instance, when the 'phone has been put down the other end?'

She shook her head. 'Not even a heavy breather.'

'When you go out — have you ever thought you were being followed? Say, at the supermarket?'

'Supermarket? I don't shop at the supermarket.'

She stared at him, suddenly biting her lip, and stood up, reaching for a cigarette out of the box on the mantelpiece. 'I'm sorry,' she said. 'I'm sorry.'

'Mrs Commoner —'

'How could I have been followed? You know I don't go outside. You've got a spook out there in a car who tracks my every movement — ask him. *They* might call. Martin might call. How the hell do I know what's going on? I'm just cooped up in here, getting fat. I can't even go to my exercise class. Jesus. I need a drink.'

Barbara went to the sideboard and poured herself a stiff whisky. Hemming watched her and asked, 'What about John? Doesn't your son come round?'

'Do you want a drink?'

'Just a Perrier, please.'

'I'm out of Perrier, Mr Hemming. I finished the Perrier in the whisky last night. You'll have to make do with a fucking mineral water.' She brought it across to him, as he sat perched in the wing chair. With the drink in her hand her eyes were already brighter.

'To answer your question. John comes round every lunchtime. We go through the papers together. He says all his friends in college think that Martin must have defected. Nice friends they must be.'

'Why do they think that?'

'You ask me that? How should I know? Ask them.' She paused in her restless travel around the drawing-room and looked at him uncertainly. 'Is it true? About these underground military depots in Oman? And destabilising the Socialists in Greece?'

She was accelerating. Hemming smiled and spoke slowly, in a calm voice. 'Martin must have told you, the Soviets will say anything to make an effect. The Kremlin will lie just for the sake of it. I know enough about that. Just recently they spent hundreds of millions of dollars producing the most detailed large-scale maps of the Soviet Union ever published. We checked them against our satellite photographs and found they'd located all the major targets and big towns ten miles off from where they really are.'

'What was the point of that?'

'So our missiles would come down ten miles off target.'

'You're kidding.'

'That's the kind of people we're dealing with. You must have met one or two Russians, Mrs Commoner. Diplomats.'

Barbara looked puzzled. 'Maybe. I could have done. At an Embassy party.'

'Martin knew several of the Russians in Washington. *Met socially* to use your term. Did he never bring them back here? Introduce you to them?'

Barbara went to the sideboard and poured another measure of Scotch. She began: 'What you're asking me —'

Hemming cut in swiftly. 'Of course we've no evidence the KGB is involved in this yet. I'm looking for people who might have tipped off his kidnappers.'

'Is that what you meant?' She did not look at him or come back to the sofa. Sipping the whisky she moved restlessly around the room, touching a picture straight on the wall, patting a chair cushion, putting down her cigarette and picking it up again. She came to a stop in front of a silver-framed photograph of a baby boy, perhaps two years old, sitting on a stoop and turning his face up towards the light. She put out her hand and traced around the photograph with her finger.

'Feinstein says to be calm and rational,' she said in a low voice. 'She says that hope is the most affirmative emotion we possess.'

'Feinstein?'

'My psychiatrist. One smart lady. We talk on the 'phone every day at quarter of ten.'

'Is that your son John?'

She gave a start. 'This? No, this is Edward. Our first son. He died a couple of months after this picture was taken. Of leukaemia.'

Hemming bounced out of his chair. Taking the chance to establish contact, he placed the flat of his hand lightly on her upper arm.

'I'm sorry,' he said to her, his voice gentle. 'You've lost a child. I promise you won't lose a husband too.'

'You sound like Feinstein,' she said.

'Come back and sit down. That's better. Let me get you another whisky. Here's something you might know. Is there any history of amnesia, or psychosis, in Martin's family?'

She flinched. 'Nothing he's ever told me.'

104

'Tell me about John. How is he taking all this?'

'John? I rather expected him to think it was a gas. The headlines, the publicity. Instead I think he finds it . . .' she searched for the word, 'An *embarrassment*.'

'Kind of a hostile reaction, in fact.'

'No it's not.' She looked at him sharply. 'Were you ever eighteen, Mr Hemming? You're majoring in political philosophy at Georgetown University. You're very serious about it. It suddenly becomes common knowledge that your father's in the dirty-tricks business. How would you react?'

Hemming gave one of his disarming smiles. 'I guess I hadn't thought of it that way. Do you talk to him much about his work, when he gets home at night?'

'Is that a serious question?' Barbara gave a short laugh. 'If John comes back here to sleep, it's usually the middle of the night. The nearest I get to a motherly conversation with John is yelling at him to turn the light off after he's fixed himself dinner at one in the morning.'

'What does Martin say about that?'

'What should he say? He's just as bad.'

'He really gets home late?'

'You people should know. You're the ones my husband married.'

Hemming ignored this. 'I can't say I work that late.'

Barbara swilled the whisky round in the glass and took a long sip. Her mouth was slackening. 'Then you're a good little boy, Mr Hemming. Either that or you don't have anything to prove to yourself. Most men in government stay at work long after normal hours, otherwise it might imperil their sense of importance. Self-importance is a very precious thing, Mr Hemming. Secretaries are much better at looking after it than wives.'

'I'm sure you would do wonders for any man's self-importance, Mrs Commoner.'

'You're too kind. Help yourself to another mineral water.'

'Does it ever occur to you that Martin may have . . . other interests . . . which keep him away from home?'

'Such as?'

'I don't know, I'm asking you.'

'Oh c'mon, Max. It is Max, isn't it? You're a full-grown intelligence agent, you know the ropes. You don't have to be coy with me. If you mean, does Martin go screwing other women, then say so, and don't be po-faced about it. Of course he does. Most men do. You've all got your brainless little bunny stashed away somewhere for when you want a bit of uncomplicated adoration. If telling you that is going to bring Martin back to me, I freely admit it.'

Hemming leaned right forward, until his knee was almost touching her grey woollen dress. His voice was intimate.

'Barbara, don't think I'm prying. Your husband means a lot to me. I've got a personal stake in getting him out as well as the security angle, believe me. Now we've established that Martin has a private part of his life which he doesn't share with you. Haven't we?'

She nodded.

'And that he doesn't talk to you about his work, or bring it home with him?'

She nodded again, as if drowsy from the alcohol.

'Okay. Try to think back over the last few months. Let me ask you again. Did Martin ever bring back home people you never got to see? People who maybe telephoned and asked for Martin and didn't leave a name?'

There was silence. He waited anxiously. Barbara drew herself upright on the sofa. Her eyes focused on Hemming and held his gaze.

'I don't understand what you're saying,' she pronounced slowly. 'My husband is an honourable man. He has his faults, plenty, but dishonourableness is not one of them.'

'I'm not saying —'

'Everyone gets freaky 'phone calls. But you can count me out, understand? I've nothing to do with the Agency. I do recreational and charity work. My line is checking the flower arrangements to see they match the tablecloths. What Martin does is his own business. So what if he's got a floozy on Connecticut Avenue? It doesn't mean,' she said with dignity, 'he keeps from me the things that really matter.'

Hemming stood up abruptly. A small frown wrinkled his baby-smooth forehead.

'I'm sorry you've been getting undesirable 'phone calls,' he said. 'We should of course have routed all your incoming calls through our operator. I'll see that's done right away.'

'Is that all?' Barbara rose graciously to her feet, at the last

106

moment putting out a hand to the back of the sofa to support herself. 'I'm sorry you've come all this way for nothing. You probably think I'm as boring about keeping secrets as Martin is.'

'I don't think you have any secrets to keep from me, Mrs Commoner. I'll let you know as soon as we have any news.'

'Mr Hemming? Max?'

He turned at the door. Barbara was standing in the middle of her drawing-room, surrounded by her flower displays and old wooden furniture. Her mouth was working, and there were tears in her eyes. 'I want to know what you think. Do you think Martin's still alive?'

'Probably,' said Max Hemming. 'Don't worry. I'll find my own way out.'

When Martin woke again, after vivid broken dreams, Luke was gone and Zed was sitting in his place. The thought of his sexual humiliation came back to him and he bit his lip. But there was no malice in Zed's expresssion. He was sitting with the guitar in his lap, dreamily gazing at the carpet and letting the guitar plectrum wander over the strings.

'Zed?'

'Oh. Hi, man.'

'You remember telling me what Ishmael said?'

'What?'

'He said: if this work is not of God, it will come to nothing.'

'Oh. Yeah.'

'Well you'd better listen to me. He's taking you for a ride. He's making you keep me here so he can kill me.'

Zed did not look up. His long black hair was curtaining his eyes, hiding his expression. At length he admitted, 'He got angry with himself. He said he wasn't getting through to you, you were too evil to be brought to Jesus. We told him . . .' he hesitated.

'You told him?'

'About Saint Paul. The most evil persecutor the Christians ever had. But when God took a hand, on the road to Damascus, he was converted, see? Just like that.' He snapped his fingers. 'So he's gonna try again.'

'To kill me. He's going to kill me.' Martin pleaded: 'He doesn't talk about God. Why don't you listen to him? He talks about his father. He thinks I killed his father.'

Zed strummed some more. Still sitting, he eased himself furtively across the carpet. In the tent, Martin leaned forward. His heart beat faster. He waited.

'Mr Commoner, I want to ask you a question.'

'Yes?'

'Esther and me. You see, we've done a lot of sets together. And we sound real good on tapes. I mean, professsional, you know?' He inched closer and lowered his voice. 'Who do you know in the recording scene, man?'

'Recording scene?'

'A guy in your position must know some top record producers, right? And like, we need finance, man. We need *contacts*.'

Martin felt the hysteria rising from his belly. He tried to stop himself. It was a chance he could use. But he was too weak. The laughter rose like a fountain; it came spewing out of his mouth. He lay back against the tent wall and laughed and laughed until the tears ran down his sunken cheeks, and the laugh pitched over the top into a heaving breathless moaning cry. Zed had gone. His chance was gone. They were all lunatics, every one. They would laugh him to death. He would die howling with the crazy goddamn humour of it. Too much, as John would say. Too much.

He let his head fall back. The tent above him was floating. Maybe it was something they had injected in his veins. It was a conspiracy. It had KGB backing, for sure. They were driving him mad, so he'd never know what he told them and whether it mattered. The recording scene. Recording . . .

His head was throbbing. He lapsed again into a feverish doze.

FRIDAY

William got into the office early and sat for a long while with a sheet of paper in front of him, writing down names and crossing them out. Then he rang Johnny Wax at the Embassy.

'Johnny?'

'How's it shaking down, young fella? I hear you've got religion.'

'You could say. Johnny, I need some information. Double agents in the CIA —'

'Easy. I've got a whole long list of devil-worshippers in the Vatican too.'

'I'm not kidding. Vanderbyle tells me in recent years four CIA men have been denounced as traitors — Kampiles, Barnett, Bisley and Clarke. Would they or their families have any reason to get back at Commoner?'

'Ask Vanderbyle.'

'Vanderbyle stonewalls me. It's like I told you, I've had no clearance for security information from the CIA. They think everyone who isn't in Intelligence is in the pay of the Russians. If you ask me, it's the other way round.'

Johnny Wax chuckled. 'Hang around,' he said. 'Let me go to the cupboard where I keep the skeletons.'

William waited. When the FBI man came back, his voice was crisper.

'Only Bisley and Clarke were in Commoner's time as Deputy Director,' he said. 'And here's a nugget for you. Bisley had a son, Jonathan, who could be in England. Age about 26 now. He's got no record, so he's not on the list I gave you. But we kept an eye on him in the States, with that kind of pedigree, and the last report I've got on him is he told someone he was coming across to join the family.'

'To join his family in England?'

'I guess England, I'll check. But he could be halfway round the globe by now. His Pa left him money.'

'What about Clarke?'

'Clarke. Let's have a look. Two daughters. Lucy, 20. She's married to a floor manager in Bonwit Teller's in Washington. The other, Amy, is 14 and at school in Maryland. Neither of them sound like pistol-packers.'

'Thanks, Johnny. That's a help. Be seeing you.'

He looked up to see the Commander standing by the video terminal. A solid muscular man with a bulbous nose and thinning hair, he tapped with blunt fingers on William's desk.

'I've had a communication from the Home Office,' he said gruffly. 'To be exact, an official bloody instruction. They want you to drop your line of enquiry.'

William stared at him. 'What do you mean?'

'On the fringe religions. The Cabinet Office committee met again this morning. Nothing I can do about it. They want us to dovetail with M15's line of enquiry. That means putting all available men on to left-wing groups.'

'Christ Almighty!'

'Sorry, William. You've not had any breakthroughs with the cults.'

'We're not halfway through.' William scowled at him. 'It's the Americans, isn't it? We're letting Vanderbyle behave like bloody Eisenhower.'

The Commander shrugged and was silent. A good policeman. A loyal civil servant.

'I'm beginning to think,' said William bitterly, 'that we aren't intended to find Commoner alive.'

Somewhere they were playing *Jesus Christ Superstar*. Esther was speaking.

'You feel you want to stop the record and take Jesus off the Cross. Then everything would come out all right.'

Esther had been here. That was right. Telling him some story about the Family, how the leader of the colony made her feel guilty if she didn't get rid of all her leaflets on the street —

'He wanted to fuck me.'

'Uh-huh.'

'But I didn't see why I should believe someone who wasn't very nice to me.' She was pouting. 'That's when Ishmael came. But I was gonna split anyway. I want my baby delivered in a proper hospital, not a grotty house in Camberwell, you know?'

A baby she'd said. Unless he'd dreamed that too.

Zed was there at times, and Luke. They brought him liquids to drink. They tucked the red blanket round him when he kicked it off in a frenzy. Where were the police? Where were his own people? They had Ishmael's facts on file. He must have been brought up in London while David Bisley was stationed over here after the War. They couldn't miss him.

They could. He knew the figures. Computers screwed up. They hadn't got to Schleyer. They hadn't got to Moro. Dear God, he was dying in their very arms, if they would just look down and see!

Hymns. A prayer meeting. Were they praying for the strength to kill him? All he wanted was to be left alone. More hymns: Zed's baritone, Esther's soprano —

> *He's got the whole world — in his hands*
> *He's got the whole world — in his hands*
> *He's got the whole world — in his hands*
> *He's got the whole world — in his hands*

'Just leave me alone,' he cried. They smiled and gave him something to drink. 'One more day,' said Ishmael.

He felt the needle searching for a vein in his upper arm.

The office was in shadow, except for a small triangle of sunlight on the regulation green carpet. William stood in the centre of the triangle and gazed out of the window in the direction of the Thames. He could not see the river. In fact he did not have a clear view whichever way he looked. On the left, he was blocked by the blank anonymous concrete of the Department of Trade. More government buildings rose in front of him, and on the right, where the light was coming from, were the tall terracotta towers of Westminster Cathedral. Hemmed in by

Church and State, he thought resentfully. Blocked. Obstructed. Made a fool of.

It was six o'clock and the sun was still warm, he could feel it on his face. He ought to be in the country, starting a long weekend with Jenny and the kids, cherishing the last of the summer before it slipped away. Instead he was incarcerated here, bound hand and foot by the politicians. It was small comfort that Maidstone had got no further with the investigation than he had. Switching the enquiry to political extremists was turning up all the old faces, as he had known it would. Commoner was as far out of the range of most of these half-baked pamphleteers as a man from Mars.

He looked at his watch. Little should be back by now. On cue, the familiar freckled face looked round the door. 'Nothing on that Turkish bleeder you asked about,' it said.

'A bloody waste of time.'

'He left ten days ago, I checked with Immigration. His girl friend just had a postcard telling her not to follow him. It was genuine enough: she was bawling her eyes out.'

William stuffed his hands into his pockets and moved away from the window. The towers of Westminster Cathedral disappeared from view. He said tiredly, 'Did you ever find out about the Jesus Children?'

'Who? Oh yes, the Jesus freaks. They changed their name, that's why they slipped through the net. They call themselves the Family now. There's a group of them in Stockwell Park.'

William took his hands out of his pockets. 'Did you say the Family?'

'Yes. The other check I ran was on Nelson Winthrop, the Californian connection.' Little took a notebook out of his pocket and read from it: 'Jamaican-born. Studied social science at UCLA. Now a trainee probation officer in Hounslow. Clean as a whistle.'

William hardly heard him. Rummaging through the files on his desk, he had brought out a single sheet of paper. It was headed FBI — CONFIDENTIAL, and contained six neatly typewritten lines. Staring at it, he became aware that Little was still talking. 'Wait a moment,' he said.

He picked up the green telephone on his desk and dialled on a direct line. Johnny Wax answered.

'According to the note you sent me on Jonathan Bisley,' said

112

William, 'he doesn't have any close relations apart from his mother in California. His father's dead. There are no brothers or sisters.'

'Okay. So what?'

'Can you check on that report exactly? Did he say he was coming across to join *his* family? Or *the* family?'

'Hold on. I've got the card right here.'

William waited.

'William? It says *the* family. That mean anything to you?'

'Could do. Thanks, Johnny.'

He breathed out, and put the receiver down gently as if he was afraid of breaking the spell. He had a feeling — he'd described it to Jennifer once as something all hunting animals must know — not of a scent exactly, but of a quickening in the atmosphere, a change in the wind that might bring the scent with it, clear and strong and to be followed.

If he'd had a hunting horn he would have raised it to his lips. Instead he handed the FBI note to John Little with a casual air. 'Have one of the artists do an Identikit of that description,' he said. 'We're going to take a trip to Stockwell Park.'

The police car switched off its siren after they'd crossed the Clapham Road. William knew Stockwell Park from the days when he'd covered political meetings. Sandwiched between three trunk roads, it was a strange, shabby, dignified little backwater, brooded over by a high-rise council estate which crowded 4000 people into its tarmac surrounds. Next door, along Stockwell Park Road, a row of incongruously large and splendid early Georgian houses surveyed through burglar-proofed windows what had once been parkland and was now a small square of dirty green on the end of a children's playground.

Alongside it ran Lorn Road, a street of high, grimy Victorian houses as desolate as the address they answered to. Developers had forgotten this street; either that, or the council had bought up property in it and run out of money. Half the houses were boarded up. Undergrowth from untended front gardens spilled out through cracks in the fencing and took root in the pavement. Avoiding a broken milk bottle, the police car pulled in halfway down the road, outside a detached house in better condition than most.

'This is the one,' said Little, scrambling out. William followed him down a loose brick path to the front door, stepping over the rusty skeleton of a toy pram. The front curtains were drawn; the building looked deserted. Little knocked loudly and waited. When there was no answer, he tried to look through the letterbox. It had been fastened down.

'I've got the warrant,' said William. He turned the door-knob and pressed his shoulder to the peeling paintwork. To his surprise, the door broke open easily: it had been tied shut with a piece of string.

The hallway was completely bare. Through the open doorway to the sitting-room they could see that was empty too. Somewhere in the back, a telephone was ringing. William hesitated for a moment, sniffing the fresh air. The walls were clean; so was the linoleum on the floor. Someone was using the house and cleaning it. Or else it had only just been vacated.

Cautiously they proceeded through empty rooms to the telephone, which they found on the floor in the kitchen. It stopped ringing as Little bent to pick it up.

William beckoned him. 'Look at this.'

He was gazing out of the window. In the middle of the garden stood a large white caravan with blue curtains and a gold cross spray-painted on the side. Smoke was coming out of the chimney and drifting across to them, with the sound of voices. In front of the caravan a blonde girl, heavily pregnant, in a blue-and-white check pinafore dress, sat playing on the grass with two naked toddlers. A neatly-bearded young man in jeans and a T-shirt reclined against the sloping trailer arm, his eyes shut, soaking up the last of the September sunlight.

The sight of two middle-aged policemen in raincoats and heavy black shoes plodding across the grass did not appear to disturb the blonde girl's serenity. She smiled up at them, shading her eyes.

'Are you the Family?' asked William curtly.

'We're all the family.'

'I'm looking for Jonathan Bisley.' William showed her the Identikit drawing of a man with bushy black curls and wire-rimmed spectacles. 'Do you know who I mean?'

The girl, still smiling, shook her head. She pulled one of the infants away from William's shoe-laces. 'He's at the age when he loves playing with people's feet,' she explained. 'Don't you, my

114

little one?' Looking up again at their set expressions she said, 'Matthew might know. Matthew!'

The youth on the trailer arm got up and came over to them, scowling. He gazed with slitted eyes at the picture and shook his head.

William asked politely, 'What's your name, son?'

'Matthew.'

'Matthew who?'

'Just Matthew.'

'You'll have to do better than that, son. Is this where you live?'

'Yes.'

'Let's go in, shall we?'

Sullenly, Matthew led the way. Bisley was not in the caravan. Everything else was: pots, pans, dirty plates in the sink, clothes on the floor, a cupboard stacked high with pamphlets, a thin red-haired girl suckling a very young baby, and, facing them, a bulky man with a bushy black beard, dressed in a T-shirt and underpants, who was ironing his trousers on a wooden table. The cluttered space smelled of cabbages and milk; Little kept the door open.

'Who are you?' asked the bearded man. His voice was soft, and sounded American.

William produced his warrant card. 'Police officers. We're looking for Jonathan Bisley.'

The man glanced at the Identikit picture and went back to his ironing. 'I don't know him, man.'

He had flashed a glance at William before dropping his eyes. The Chief Superintendent bent down and removed the plug of the iron from the wall. 'What's your name?'

The man put the iron down, but did not let go of it. 'I am called John.'

'You belong to the Family?'

'Yes. The Family of Peace.'

'Well then, John.' William was carefully examining the pamphlets. 'I am a man of peace as well. I want you to think very hard about Jonathan Bisley. It means a lot to me. Look at the picture. Take your time.'

'I told you, man. I've never seen him.'

Little happened to knock some of the dirty plates on the floor. They smashed in pieces. The baby started crying.

'You're American, aren't you, John?' William asked.

'Yes.'

'Do you want to stay in Britain?'

The man knitted his eyebrows in anger. Without replying, he began putting on his trousers.

'Answer me,' snapped William.

'Sure I do, man. What are you going to do to stop me? I've got the papers.'

'I can do plenty.' Checking to see that Little was back in the doorway, William moved across to the stove, opened it and began feeding religious pamphlets on to the coals. 'I can charge you for letting out black smoke in a smokeless zone. See? I can charge you for placing a dangerous obstruction on your front path. I can have you up on criminal charges —' the man's hand, which had tightened on the iron, relaxed, '— for threatening to assault a police officer.' For the first time he looked directly at the black-bearded man, his face darker than its usual pinkness. 'Listen, my friend,' he said roughly. 'I can cut your balls off and send you home in a packing-case if I have to. Now this is serious. Either you tell me about Bisley, or it's a deportation order. You choose.'

The man stared at him. The red-haired girl came up to him and buried her face in his shoulder. He put his arm round her. William held his breath. He couldn't carry the hunch much further.

'They left,' said the man.

'Who left?'

'Him. Ishmael. I don't know about Bisley. He came to us as Ishmael. He took the other three with him.'

'What other three?'

'Esther. And Luke. And Zed. They left a month ago.'

'Why?'

Another voice. 'They were heretics, that's why.'

William turned his head. It was the blonde girl who had spoken. She pushed past Little into the caravan and went to John, protectively. 'Ishmael is cast out from among us,' she told William solemnly. 'He refused to accept the Master's teachings. The Family won't have him back.'

'Where did he go?'

The girl shrugged. She said without looking up, 'Esther said they were going to a pad in Forest Hill. I dunno. She said it was all fixed up.'

'Anything else?'

'She said they had a mission. I dunno. Is there a mission in Forest Hill?'

He heard the sound of cars going past in the open air. Once he thought he heard the shouts of children on their way to school. He knew where they were going: down the long Hagerstown hill, slippery after rain, with the young cherry trees set neatly in the grey pavement and Mrs Elliott's spaniel peeing through the protective netting; down to the main road, where the noise started, with the Esso station on the corner and then the nickel-and-dime store (no candy in the window, by arrangement with the school), and the realtor, and the undertaker where he'd hung around the back with friends a few times to see the coffins come in.

Voices again.

The commandment. It says. Thou shalt not kill.

A hush. Ishmael's voice.

The Bible also says: the wages of sin is death. I vote he dies.

They were children. Mindless kids. *Forgive them, Lord for they know not what they do.* But John. John was a good kid. He had a sense of duty. He would take care of Barbara if anything happened to him.

She had brought him up well, Barbara. Thinking about her, painfully, reluctantly, he groaned with remorse. There were things he wanted to say . . . He hadn't given her an easy life. He should have made allowances. He should have loved her more. If he got out of here alive he'd make it up to her. He'd take her on a vacation to the Virgin Islands.

I don't think you reely love her.

He looked up, startled. Esther's eyes, wide, innocently cruel —

But that was days ago. He was seeing things that weren't there.

'He goes tonight then.'

'Who takes him?'

'We all take him. I'll tape his face over.'

'No need for that.'

117

Luke was squatting in front of him. A Bible was open in his lap. He began reading aloud, following each line with his forefinger and raising his voice above the muttering behind the door: '"For whosoever will save his life shall lose it; but whosoever shall lose his life for my sake and the gospel's, the same shall save it. For what shall it profit a man, if he shall gain the whole world, and lose his own soul?"'

'*They start in six hours. He's done for, then.*'

'*He can take his chances on that.*'

SATURDAY

It was shortly after 1 am when his official car delivered the Chief Inspector back to his home in Shepherd's Bush. William slammed the front gate; he very nearly slammed the front door too, remembering the children asleep upstairs just in time to bruise his fingers stopping it. He had picked up the scent. Coming away from Stockwell Park he had felt himself to be almost within sight of his quarry. But still it eluded him.

In Forest Hill and its environs every potential squat, every hotel and almshouse, every religious or charitable building in which Jonathan Bisley could have taken refuge, had been searched from top to bottom. Thousands of copies of his description and picture were now circulating around London and the South-East, along with descriptions and sketches of his three companions. Armed with these, hundreds of police officers had been making house-to-house enquiries throughout the area, breaking off at 10.30 pm and due to start again in about six hours time. All three TV channels had put up Bisley's picture. His description had gone out on the air.

And not a dicky-bird had tweeted.

He sat in the kitchen now, eating the soup which Jennifer had left on the stove in a saucepan for him to heat up. Thoughtfully, she had left Commoner's photograph propped up on the table between the salt and pepper. A full week since he'd disappeared. He snatched it up and threw it out of sight on the sideboard.

Could the Jesus freaks in the caravan have led them astray? It wasn't likely. John Little had gone over their story again when he'd stayed behind to collect descriptions of Esther, Luke and Zed (bloody silly name). Perhaps Bisley had rented or borrowed a place to stay: but unless he'd dumped Commoner already by now, surely somebody must have been alerted to arrivals and departures. England was a country of neighbours. That was the great hidden asset to people in his business: the legions of old grannies, invalids by the windows, sharp-eyed housewives and nosey little kids, who knew almost by instinct the moment something out of the ordinary happened in their street.

But none of them had come forward. Not this time.

William sucked up the last of his soup. Perhaps England was going the way of America: people in their little boxes seeing a homicidal assault in the street below and no more thinking of calling the police than they would after seeing it on television. The thought depressed him further. He would not be able to sleep in this frame of mind. After a moment he got up from his chair and went into the sitting-room. He selected a recording of Rachmaninov's *Second Piano Concerto*, put it on the record player and plugged his headphones into the amplifier. Then, picking up his white plastic conductor's baton, he went and sat in his favourite wooden ladder-backed chair, midway between the two speakers, and began waving the baton in time to the music.

At first, the wand made little feeble drooping motions in the air. Gradually it gained confidence, slashing in longer sweeps about the room. By the Allegro Scherzando, the chair was shaking in sympathy; the wand rose and fell with imperious assurance. Order restored in the universe, William went to bed.

Jenny was not asleep. Sitting up against the pillow in her red cotton dressing-gown she was reading a novel by Margaret Drabble. He watched her, sucking in her cheeks, nodding and occasionally frowning, as if she was taking issue with a particularly well-written report from the Hammersmith Parks and Recreation Department.

'You shouldn't have waited up for me,' said William.

'Did you finish the casserole?'

'Casserole? I didn't see any casserole. I had the chicken soup.'

'That wasn't soup. That was chicken stock.' She sighed and put down the novel. 'Poor Willy. You must have had a lousy day.'

Unlacing his shoes, unhitching his braces, William told his wife the kind of day he'd had. 'Just as I get the Commander on

120

my side,' he finished, 'he gets a call from the bloody Home Office to say that the MP for Vauxhall has put down a question in the Commons tomorrow about us victimising community squats. It makes me puke. If someone kidnapped the MP for Vauxhall you can be bloody sure they'd be on us to ram the Special Patrol Group up the backsides of every community squat in London.'

Jenny was silent. After a moment, taking off her reading glasses, she asked, 'Did you say you'd been checking the empty houses?'

William got into bed and gave her a peck on the cheek. Then he turned off the light above the bed, already half-asleep before his head hit the pillow.

'I told you,' he muttered. 'We've checked out every empty house in Forest Hill.'

'What about the ones being pulled down?'

William's eyes opened.

'I don't know about Forest Hill,' Jennifer continued. 'I know in Hammersmith demolition jobs go on a separate list. As far as the Council planning division is concerned they become non-properties, like non-persons. Just for the few days when they're boarded up and've had the floors taken out, before they're smashed to rubble.'

William switched the light on. He looked at her. 'Contractors always check before they move in,' he said hoarsely.

'They're supposed to, darling.' She looked at him in alarm. 'Where are you going, Willy?'

William was pulling his trousers on. Once he was respectable enough to speak with authority, he dialled the Operations Room.

'Inspector Little. Yes, John, are you still there? Send a car round for me, and get the Lewisham Chief Planning Officer alerted. I'm going to open up the Town Hall.'

Little sounded dog-tired. 'Sir, do you know what time it is?'

William looked at his watch. It was 2.15 in the morning. 'I'm sorry, John,' he said hoarsely. 'This one can't wait.'

'SHUT UP!'

Martin's shout, tearing out of his lungs, silenced all of them.

121

Exhausted, he lay back and fixed his blurry eyes on Luke. 'Leave me alone,' he said hoarsely. 'Let me die in peace.'

But they would not. They gave him a bowl of tomato soup. They came and stood outside the tent, like carrion crows, unwinking.

Ishmael seemed to smile. 'We're taking you out of here,' he said.

'Where to?'

'It won't make any difference to you.'

'I . . .', he struggled to speak, 'I have a request.'

'What is it?'

'Pen and paper. To write a letter to my wife.'

Ishmael began to demur, but Zed cut in. 'No sweat, man. You give us the letter, we'll deliver it.'

They were all solicitude. Esther brought a note-pad and a biro. Luke untied the cords around his hands and chafed his wrists: but still his fingers could not hold the pen. He gave the writing things to Esther and sent the others away.

'Address it to Mrs Barbara Commoner,' he said. 'Care of Mr James Parrish, United States Embassy, London.'

'Hold on.'

He waited patiently. Then he began dictating in a slow voice. '*Barbara, my darling: This may be the last you hear from me. I have been held prisoner all this time. I don't know where. Now they are taking me away. In case I don't come back, I want this letter to carry all my love to you. And to John.*'

He paused. He thought tenderly of his wife, but when he put out his arms to her it was . . . Nancy, this was no time to think of Nancy.

He went on slowly. '*Remember for me all the good times we had together. The day 'Harpers' took your first article and we borrowed Bob's boat and went sailing in Long Island Sound. Remember that? And the weekend we went to that ranch upcountry in Argentina and gave John his first ride on horseback. He fell off, but he didn't holler. We have shared so many memories together, don't let them fade.*'

Esther was sniffing. It was a good letter. He'd show them how to die. He went on, his voice growing stronger. '*I want you to know that I have no regrets. I have done what I thought best. I have given my life to serving my country in the fight for freedom, and, in the end, freedom will prevail, however many times its agents are betrayed. God Bless you. God Bless America.*'

There was a long silence. 'Is that all?' asked Esther.

'Yes.'

'Do you want to sign it?'

'If I can.'

She passed the letter across to him. She had written it in block capitals, in a naive attempt to disguise her hand. The circulation was returning to his numbed fingers, and he managed to correct some of Esther's spelling mistakes and to make a fair attempt at his signature. The nearness of death had sharpened his mental faculties. Watching Esther lick the envelope with her small pink tongue, an important thought occurred to him. He plucked at her.

'The letter. Will you put a stamp on it?'

'Sure.' She smiled. 'Just leave it to me.'

Luke and Ishmael came into view carrying a length of carpet. They unrolled it in front of the tent. So this was to be his winding-sheet. He called out, almost cheerfully, 'I'll be lighter to carry than I was before.'

Luke answered him politely, 'You're no trouble, Mr Commoner.'

An ambulance siren sounded in the distance. The reality of what was happening to him struck him like a knife in the bowels. His smile twisted on his face but he kept it there. Control. He would not let them see his fear. As Zed approached with the syringe, he addressed him. 'Is this it? If so, I want to be told.'

Zed avoided the question, 'We're moving you to a new address. It's your bag after that, man.'

He withdrew the needle. Martin beckoned him closer. 'Before I see you again,' he whispered, 'take some singing lessons.'

'Funny joke, man.'

Savagely, Zed bound his hands again. The drug worked fast this time. Martin felt himself being lifted and carried out of the tent. A hand came down and taped his mouth. He breathed deeply. The stink had gone. There was something sweet in his nostrils. With a shock he realised that they had taken the blinds off the windows and opened them; it was fresh air he was smelling. Before he could take another breath of air, he felt himself being rolled over inside the carpet, wrapped in the suffocating darkness.

He was not dead yet. He could still feel his limbs and the

pounding of his heart. He wanted to pray to God — not their God. What then? A vision came into his head. Suddenly calm, he was in their bed at home, gazing up at the nineteenth-century child's sampler on the wall, its words picked out in blue wool on the faded cloth:

Be with me Lord this night I pray
And hold me safe till light of day . . .

He repeated it to himself. As he was starting it a second time — 'Be with the Lord' — the darkness rushed him like a murderer.

The Lewisham Chief Planning Officer, blinking and yawning in a blue dressing-gown, referred William and his deputy to the Borough Architect. The Borough Architect lived in Norwood, right the other side of the district. By the time the police car had ferried them to Lewisham Town Hall, and the nightwatchman was awakened from his deep slumber, the sky was already beginning to lighten over Catford Road.

William, standing in the lobby, greeted the Borough Architect with the warmest smile he could muster. 'Mr Hoover? Please accept my apologies for getting you out of bed.'

'I didn't have time to put my watch on,' said Hoover fretfully. He was a tall, stooping man with a fringe of grey locks around his bald pate. 'I can't imagine I can be of any use to anybody at this hour on a Saturday.'

William explained what they were looking for, and showed him the sketch of Bisley. Hoover studied it with a critical eye. Eventually he said, 'I recognise the accent.'

'What?'

'An American, you said. Well a young American man did come and see me about a fortnight ago. But he didn't have a beard. Dark curls, yes. Glasses, yes, but wire-rimmed, not these black-framed ones.'

'What did he want?'

'He wanted to see some Housing Area Information Proposals. He was interested in the "A" list.'

'What's that?'

'It's our priority list. Houses about to be demolished. He

124

wanted to know if any of them were actually in process of being pulled down.'

'Did you *give* him this information?'

Hoover looked mildly offended. 'Of course. It was his right, under Section 16 of the Land Charges Act of 1925.'

William looked at John Little. He knew that his Chief Inspector was thinking the same thing he was. He said heavily, 'Perhaps, Mr Hoover, we could just go up to your office now and have a squint at this list of yours.'

The lifts were not working ('public spending cuts', suggested Hoover). They accompanied him up four flights of stairs and down empty darkened corridors to the Borough Architect's office.

Hoover pulled up a blind and brought out of an unlocked drawer a thick loose-leaf binder with street maps and typewritten planning proposals neatly arranged by date. Rubbing the sleep out of his eyes, he began to explain the planning schedule on demolitions. William cut him short.

'What houses did you show Bisley?'

'Bisley? Oh yes, the American. The "A" list would have been the same. I told him we've only got three active demolition jobs on hand; he sounded disappointed. This one in Peckham, near the junction of Asylum Road and Meeting House Lane. It's unsafe, should have been pulled down long ago. This two-up two-down in Brighton Grove beside New Cross station, it's having to go to make room for an extension of railway sidings. The third one is in Honor Oak — One Tree Close, on the edge of One Tree Hill, but that won't interest you.'

'Why?' asked William.

'It's a shell. The other two have been boarded up, pipes out, floorboards out, stairs destroyed, the usual kind of thing to discourage squatters. But you could still get someone inside, using a jemmy. This one's just a cellar full of rubble with four walls and roof timbers waiting to come down on top of it.'

Hoover looked at his watch. 'It should be gone by now. It's a small contractor and he likes to start at first light.' He paused. 'Now look, I need some coffee. Can I —'

William had thanked him and was halfway down the corridor before Hoover could get out the rest of his sentence. 'John, you take Peckham and New Cross,' he ordered. 'Ring for assistance. I'm going to Honor Oak.'

A pale orange sun had risen above the housetops by the time he got away. There wasn't much on the roads yet, except for buses carrying cleaning ladies to work in the City and vans packed with vegetables from the market at Nine Elms. But a heavy lorry had entangled itself in roadworks in the Stanstead Road and William, cursing his luck, had to go the long way round Blythe Hill Fields along Brightling Road and Stillness Road to One Tree Close. He couldn't find the house at all at first, until his driver saw a heavy lorry with a load of rubble backing out of a narrow driveway almost hidden by bushes.

For a moment, William had a disturbing vision of Commoner's body lying under the rubble, torn and battered out of recognition by huge chunks of masonry bulldozed on top of him. It was absurd, of course. Contractors didn't risk that kind of lawsuit. They made a thorough search before starting in with the ball and chain. All the same, he couldn't get the thought out of his mind. He remembered the woman's corpse they had found tipped out with building rubble on the Isle of Grain. Eventually they had identified her, by a filling in her teeth.

Rounding the corner, he saw to his relief that some of the walls at least were still standing. It looked like the remains of a big Victorian private house, perhaps once the vicarage of the church nearby. Its old yellow-brown bricks were in good condition and the contractors, wanting to keep them clean and usable, had spent valuable minutes fixing a wire rope with a noose to pull them down outwards on to the grass.

As soon as the workmen saw the police car, there was a scurry of activity to get the rope off. It was technically against the law, William knew — the shock waves of a wall falling in great slabs could fracture underground pipes — but he was not in a mood to argue. If they had smashed inwards with an iron ball swung from a crane, there would have been no chance of getting anybody out from under there alive.

He got out and hurried to the site. The doors and windows were still tinned up with corrugated iron, although they had nothing to protect except a dusty yellow graveyard of rubble, planks, broken glass and plastic sheeting. In the early morning sun a punk message — *God Rules OK?* — sprayed in crimson on the corrugated iron, gleamed with phosphorescent brightness.

The foreman came up to him, as he gazed through a hole in the brickwork at the silent desolation within. 'There's no pipes under One Tree Hill,' he said, a trifle surlily.

William flipped open his warrant card. 'Your name, please.'

'Edward Higgs. What's this in aid of?'

'Mr Higgs, have you checked every inch of this basement?'

The man stared at him. 'What? There's nobbut rocks down there.'

'Have you checked that?'

The foreman summoned over a gawky youngster in giant boots. 'Bill? You had a look to see there was no itinerants in here?'

The boy nodded. 'Yeah. Yesterday evenin'.'

'Okay, Bill. You go off now.' Higgs turned back to the Chief Inspector. 'We check at every stage,' he said in a pained voice. 'When we sheet it up. When we strip the fittings off, and before we take the floors and joists out. If a rat moved down there we'd cop an eyeful.'

William nodded. It had been a long shot. Maybe John Little was striking lucky. Or Bisley had gone to Wandsworth or Southwark for his demolition site. Or his instinct had deserted him, and he wasn't even warm.

'Can we start balling it in then?' asked Higgs. 'We've got another job at midday.'

Willian nodded again. 'It looks like a bomb-site,' he said, half to himself, remembering how, coming back as a kid after the Blitz, they had been still digging the bodies out. He walked round the side of the house, followed by the unwilling Higgs. A windowless bay looked out over the thick undergrowth which ran wild up the side of One Tree Hill. A small gap had been knocked through the brick in the middle of the bay, and the grass had been trampled down around it. 'Is this your way down?' he asked.

'Yes.'

'Been down this morning, have you?'

Higgs shook his head. 'Haven't needed to.'

William dropped to his knees in the gap. He felt along the jagged edge of the brick floor. On his fingers he brought up minute silver shavings, which glistened in the light.

'Use an aluminium ladder, do you?' he asked, glancing up at the foreman.

Higgs watched him, frowning. 'We allus use wooden ladders,' he said. 'Much more reliable.'

William stood up and dusted his hands. 'Do me a favour, Mr Higgs, and bring one round. I'm going to take a look.'

The foreman scowled. He complained. He warned what might happen to the Chief Inspector if the planks and rubble gave way and pinned him down. He abjured all responsibility for the Chief Inspector's life and limb. But the ladder was brought. William descended.

Watched by the assembled demolition workers, he picked his way carefully along a plank balanced on heavy chunks of concrete. Bits of rusted iron, twisted out of recognisable shape, lay in his path. He detoured around them, bending low in case his foot slipped. An old rotting door lay propped on its side against the basement wall. Beyond it, a square of green plastic sheeting lay like a tent across two timber joints that had been thrown from the roof. William went over to it and tore the sheeting away.

Underneath there was more rubble.

He turned away, coughing with the dust in his throat. His driver had not come over. That meant that Little had not had any luck. On the horizon above One Tree Hill he could see the vapour trail of an aircraft silently vanishing into cloud. There was not a sound to be heard, except for his coughing and the faint hum of cars passing on the road below. Standing there he felt a strange disturbance, as if ghosts were walking the vanished house, looking for the rooms they remembered. Nobody could be alive under this rubble he told himself.

He heard a faint sound behind him and turned. Nothing had moved, unless it was the shadow, on the yellow bricks, of the demolition crane overhead. He waited. It came again, a scratching sound. The old wooden door settled at a shallower angle against the wall. He ran to it stumbling over the bricks, careless of the danger. He pulled it away from the wall. An old roll of brown felt lay underneath. It was tied with string. Cutting the knots with a penknife, he unwrapped it —

A middle-aged man, half-naked, his wrists and ankles bound with cords, stared up at him blindly. His eyes were sunken; his face was chalk white and covered with stubble, but William knew it like his own, from the photograph on the kitchen table.

He yelled to the men watching, and then bent over the motionless form.

'Can you hear me, sir?' he asked.

For a moment he feared he had come too late. Then the eyes blinked, and the dusty lips opened.

'Get me the hell out of here,' said Martin Commoner.

The Second Week

SUNDAY

'I don't know what you're all making so much fuss about.'

Martin realised at once that it sounded like the kind of weakly irritable remark invalids make, and he glanced up with a half-smile at the impassive face bending over him.

Unwrapping the blood-pressure tourniquet from his arm, the doctor said, 'You can't be too careful at 30,000 feet.'

He was a CIA doctor. That figured. For the last twenty-four hours the Agency had not let Martin Commoner out of its sight. He'd barely had the chance to razor the growth of beard on his chin. After a lengthy check-up in hospital, and questioning by the British police, he had been driven under guard to the US Embassy where he'd stayed overnight, sleeping fitfully. This morning, he'd given the same brief statement to Vanderbyle that he'd made to the English detective who'd found him, William Pomfret. The rest could wait till Washington.

He looked out of the airplane window. Below he could see the broad sweep of the Delaware River, glinting in the late afternoon sun. Crossing the Delaware. In less than an hour he'd have his feet on American soil. The thought uplifted him, and dispelled the deep tiredness in his limbs and brain. He had won through. He was coming home.

'Unbutton your shirt, please.'

Baring his chest, he thought of his long nakedness. Ishmael and the others had tried their hardest to humiliate him. They had forced him to perform his bodily functions in public, and to do . . . other things. But it hadn't scarred him for life. If anything he felt stronger for the experience. They would be caught soon and jailed, that was inevitable. A term in the penitentiary would teach them what it was like to be on the receiving end.

The cold imprint of the stethoscope made him catch his breath. Obediently he breathed in and out, grateful for the curtain that was shielding his forward compartment from the other passengers on the commercial flight. In a moment the doctor would shine a pencil-light into his eyes to look at his pupils. In a moment of irrational panic he had refused to let them do this in hospital; he was suddenly back in the tent with the light shining in. But he was rational now. Calm. Much stronger. Quite trim round the tummy, too, after that starvation diet. Nancy would approve. Barbara, even, might notice.

Holding his eyelids open, the doctor beamed the pencil-light at him. His breath smelled of peppermint. Grasping the arm-rests, Martin asked him, 'What drug were they pushing into me?'

'We won't know until the tests are completed. From your description, I would guess they used a barbiturate, probably amylobarbitone.'

'What will that do to me?'

'Amylobarbitone in small quantities has no lasting after-effects on someone with a normal medical history. A couple of cc's injected intravenously knocks you out. You feel pretty high for a short time after you come round.'

'That's right.'

'I'm going to give you some capsules to take, Mr Commoner. But the primary requirement will be to have a complete rest.'

Martin laughed, light-headedly. 'I wish I could,' he said. 'By the time I get back, my desk will be piled this high with things that don't wait on vacations. I'll probably have to hire a second assistant to get through the paperwork.'

The CIA doctor made some non-committal reply. Martin scowled at him. Who did these goddam doctors think they were anyway? Anybody would think it was a candy store he was running, instead of a vitally important department of Government. It must be the fear of malpractice suits that made them behave like cosseting nannies.

Straightening his tie, he looked out of the window again and his ill-humour fell away. The Boeing in its descent towards

134

Dulles was flying low over the Potomac. In the pinkish-orange light of the setting sun, the confident lines of Pierre L'Enfant's master-plan were clearer than he had ever seen them. Jefferson and Lincoln, the White House and the Capitol. President Lincoln at the head of the cross, Congressmen at the feet — a feudal relationship which had not survived Watergate. A dip of the wing framed in his window the Iwo Jima statue beside Arlington National Cemetery, a monument to the most famous staged photograph in history.

So much marble. So much grandeur. It had seemed presumptuous in the nineteenth century. The speaker of the House had groused about a Greek temple set down in a swamp to be admired by bullfrogs. But the centre had held. Washington had outlasted all its critics. With the power had come the glory: it deserved its acropolis.

The doctor leaned across and tapped him on the knee. The seat-belt light had come on. Strapping himself in, Martin thought of Ishmael binding him with cord. He was the dangerous one. Probably insane. Counter-Intelligence should have kept an eye on him. People should not be left to brood on grievances. David Bisley too, he must have brooded, long and bitterly. He must have broken the rule of silence and talked to his son about it — about how George Mitchum was a friend of his, and how, if loyalty to your friends and colleagues meant nothing, what was there to live for?

Martin checked himself sharply. The real issue was not loyalty, it was treason. Mitchum was a traitor. He had walked into the Soviet Embassy with valuable State Department material on restarting the SALT talks. Bisley must have understood that the circumstantial evidence was enough to implicate him. It made no difference that he was one of the best, or that Martin Commoner, DDCI, knew him and trusted him. In the Agency you played by the rules, or you got off the field.

An air hostess bent over him on the way to her seat. 'Are you okay, sir? You look kinda pale.'

'I'm fine thanks.'

'You're welcome.'

Her skirt brushed his arm as she moved on, leaving a flowery scent behind her. He forgot about Bisley. The next woman he would have speak to him would be his wife. Thirty hours ago he thought he'd never see her again.

The Boeing taxied to a point some distance from the terminal, where a black limousine with smoked windows was waiting on the warm tarmac. Shaking off the doctor's hand, Martin went down a set of airplane steps from the forward hatch, while the other passengers, waiting for their access coach, peered at him through the portholes.

Out of the limousine stepped a dark-suited figure with a pink shiny face, bushy grey eyebrows and receding silver hair. Martin smiled broadly. The General was not a man to make empty gestures. For him to have come out to Dulles was an exceptional mark of friendship and respect. They clasped hands, silently.

'You sure have lost weight,' said the DCI. 'What did they feed you on — borsch and vodka?'

Martin laughed aloud. 'Hell, no. English tea and barbiturates.'

The General followed him into the back seat of the limousine and closed the driver's partition. 'Barbara's at the arrival building,' he said as they started away from the plane. 'We did it this way to avoid the newsmen and photographers. We've been under siege from the press since the rescue story broke yesterday. I've roughed out a couple of sentences for you. Are you up to reading this out, while they take their pictures?'

Martin glanced at the piece of paper. 'I'm up to anything. I feel 100 per cent.'

The General gazed at him. There was a speculative look in his eyes.

'Don't let them take you off guard,' he said. 'Let me handle the questions. If anyone asks about the President, say he's invited you to meet him at the White House, Tuesday.'

'*Has* he?'

The DCI's face broke into a grin. 'You're lucky it wasn't ticker-tape down Broadway. Just wait till you see what's ahead of you. You're a hero, Martin. The angle is, you've given the CIA a human face. You've whipped the Reds. We'll have to get you kidnapped more often.'

The car stopped outside a baggage-loading bay. Four airport policemen accompanied Martin and the DCI down carpeted back corridors towards the VIP lounge. Over the whirr of the air-conditioning Martin could hear what sounded like a group of girl choristers at the baggage check-out. Back from abroad, they had broken into a shrill rendition of 'The Star-Spangled Banner'. He grinned. God bless America.

Up some steps, through a couple of doors, and Barbara was waiting for him, in a shroud of cigarette smoke. She looked tired and strained. As the DCI went on tactfully ahead, she burst into tears and flung her arms round him. He clutched her round the waist, like a dancing-partner.

'To put you through all this ... I'm sorry,' he said, awkwardly.

'You're safe. And well. That's all I care about.'

'And John?'

'He's fine. Life goes on,' she said, smiling at him, wiping her cheeks with the back of her hand. 'We're both going to need a shakedown period.'

'The General says I'm a hero.'

'You don't look like one.' She dusted his jacket in the affectionate way she once had had with him. 'Who lent you these rags?'

'Someone at the Embassy.' Looking over her shoulder, he saw the General studying his watch. 'Come on,' he said. 'Let's get this over with.'

The airport conference room, as plain and impersonal as one of the transit lobbies, was packed with journalists. When Martin walked in, holding Barbara by the hand, the flashbulbs crackled round the room like ball lightning. The TV networks had taken the best vantage points, leaving many of the newspapermen to stand on chairs to get a better view. There was a scattering of applause, which stopped when the DCI stepped up to the rostrum to speak.

'My deputy, Martin Commoner, has been through a very grave ordeal,' Martin heard him say. 'He will make a short statement, but you will appreciate that he is in no condition to answer any questions at this moment in time.'

Martin came to the rostrum. The stuffy atmosphere and the bright lights reflecting off the white walls made his head spin. For a second he imagined he was back in the tent, stammering out his defence against the hanging judges ranged before him. He studied the paper that the General had thrust at him in the car.

'I am sure you will all understand that as of now I can make no substantive comment on the events of the last few days,' he

137

read out. 'Except to confirm that I was kidnapped by certain persons, and interrogated,' he paused, '...*questioned* over a period of time. I have nothing but praise for the way in which the British police conducted their investigation, which resulted in my release. I am in good health, and looking forward to returning to my desk in Langley in ... in due course. Which is to say,' he amended, pocketing the Director's notes, 'tomorrow morning. Thank you for your attention.'

The babble of questions rose at him. He grasped Barbara's hand and registered a smile on his face.

'Was it the KGB?'

'Did they give you a truth drug?'

'Why did they pick on you?'

'Did you tell the Russians about our military depots?'

'... Agent Orange?'

'... seeing the President?'

The General was at his elbow. 'The President will be meeting with Martin personally on Tuesday, to get a first-hand account. Now I'm sorry, gentlemen —'

'Mrs Commoner?' A cheerful voice from the back. 'Will you take Martin off sailing again, like he wrote in his letter?'

Martin's hand tightened on Barbara's. His smile faded. What bastard had had the goddamn nerve —

The General pressed his arm. They were out of the conference room, protected from the photographs by a ring of airport police. 'Let's go. I've got a car for you. Barbara, honey, look after him. We need him back.'

MONDAY

When Martin woke up, he had the strange sensation of being at home. It was morning, and the sun was shining through the loose-weave curtains on to the striped blue-and-white wallpaper. Then he realised it was no dream; there was the old pine closet, the Ben Shahn painting on the wall, and Barbara's unmade bed beside his, with the framed wedding photograph of them kissing in the rain on the table in between. In a daze he stumbled to the window and peered through the curtains. Reporters and TV cameramen were patrolling on the other side of the street.

So it was all true. It had really happened.

He glanced at the time, and hurriedly washed and dressed. When he came down, Barbara was in the kitchen preparing a breakfast tray.

'I should have been at Langley an hour ago,' he said by way of greeting, giving her a quick embrace.

She stared at him. 'Darling, you're kidding. You've just been dug out of a hole in the ground.'

'That doesn't make me an invalid.' He made a face. 'But that coffee smells terrific, all the same.'

'Must you really go in to Langley today? John was coming round for lunch.'

She poured out the coffee and brought it to him at the table, her flat slippers slapping on the quarry-tiled floor.

'I've got a lot of catching up to do. I'll see him tonight.'

Barbara laughed and lit a cigarette.

'What's funny?' he demanded.

'You are, darling. I was just thinking what Feinstein said on the 'phone the other day. Her usual mysterious self. She said —

Don't expect your husband to be the same man he was before. I thought she was talking baloney, but then that wonderful romantic letter arrived yesterday from the Agency. I really got a fright. But you're just the same, darling, you haven't changed at all.'

'Did you give that letter to the papers?'

'God, no! I haven't even seen the original yet, just a copy sent round by special messenger from Langley. I took it upstairs, and cried all morning.'

He looked up at her as if about to say something, and then glanced away. 'They had no right to release it,' he said.

'I can understand why.' Barbara poured herself out some coffee, slopping some of it into the saucer. 'I understand a lot more now about how your fellows operate. It's smart publicity for them, isn't it? It makes you out to be the great American patriot. It gets people on their side.'

He frowned. But she was probably right. The hot coffee was relaxing him; he was starting to think straight. He reached for an English muffin on the tray and bit into it greedily. 'So tell me, Babs. What's been happening around here?'

'Oh. The usual kind of week for when your husband's been kidnapped. A couple of hundred 'phone calls, interviews —'

'Weren't your calls routed through Langley?'

'Against my will.' She looked indignant. 'There could have been a ransom message. How was I to know the Agency would pass it on?'

He nodded, amused. His wife had never conquered her liberal suspicions of the CIA.

'Two of your colleagues came round. Max Hemming, and before that a strange lumpish youth called Shusterman.'

'Did they bother you?'

'No.'

She shook her head and stood clasping her coffee cup. He knew that frown. He said gently, 'So what is it then?'

'It's nothing. It's just the — it's the *prying* that bugs me. That security type who stands at the bottom of the steps, and the other one who sits in his car all day, watching the windows. The questions . . . Hemming asking questions about you —'

'It's his job,' Martin said, more sharply than he meant to.

'Oh I know it is. And the business about incoming calls being monitored: the feeling that you can't say anything without some anonymous spook taking notes in the background. Judy gets tongue-tied just 'phoning about the groceries.'

'It was for your protection, Babs.'

She looked at him through half-closed eyes, tilting her head and blowing out cigarette smoke. She had a striking face still, even if it was getting a little loose under the chin. And she hadn't put on that affection at the airport. Maybe something like this would bring them close again.

'Martin?'

'Yes?'

'Don't you think it's time you told me what happened?'

'Of course I'll tell you, Babs.' He rose, pushing his coffee cup away. 'Let me get it straight with the General first.'

'You mean, so I get the authorised version?'

He grinned at her. 'Would you be a honey and tip off our watchdogs? I'm going to drive myself in today.'

Without waiting for an answer he left her sitting at the table and went out to pick up his coat. On his way to the garage he paused and took a look at himself in the hallway mirror. It would do no good to arrive at Langley looking like a busted flush. His face was very pale, with dark rings under the eyes. His cheekbones were more pronounced than usual, or maybe his cheeks had sunken — but it was recognisably him all right. He wasn't likely to get stopped and held at the front gate, a stranger masquerading as the Deputy Director of Central Intelligence.

It was a beautiful morning. In England it was already autumn, but here it was the best part of the summertime, when the muggy heat had lifted and the first cool breezes had begun. Martin was grateful for the breeze. His bodyguard, whom he could see tailing him out of the rear-view mirror, had insisted on giving him a heavy bullet-proof waistcoat to wear under his jacket.

Waiting at the M Street lights he saw a blackboard inside a shop-window announcing New Arrivals From Europe — copperware and porcelain soufflé bowls from France, and tasting spoons. It had been there the last time he'd passed this way; so had the poster next to it, advertising a Leonard Bernstein concert at the Kennedy Center. He realised with a slight shock that nothing had changed. The time he'd lived through slowly and agonisingly in London had barely happened here at all.

It made no difference. The sun was shining on the blue Potomac as he crossed Key Bridge. Traffic was light. Turning down Memorial Parkway he switched on the car radio. A girl with a banshee voice was singing, 'In my rhinestone-studded boots I guess I was a sight to see.' He imagined her in tasselled cowboy boots and a short skirt, big-breasted like Dolly Parton and hummed along with the refrain.

Before Langley, Martin turned up Spout Run and stopped at a gas station. First things first. Walking to the telephone booth at the side of the forecourt, he dialled Nancy's number at the Devonshire. After three burrs it clicked on to her Answerphone.

He was disappointed. He had wanted to share with her the triumph of his freedom. 'Nancy, I'm supposed to be alive,' he said to the machine. 'But you and I know I won't come alive until I see you. Let's have lunch. Tomorrow. I'll book a table at the Angler's Inn.'

Out of the corner of his eye, he could see his bodyguard, waiting patiently. He signed off, and got back in the car, saluting the forecourt attendant as he went by.

At the main gate into the CIA, he stopped at the sign which said 'US Government Property' and showed his red-tabbed identification badge to one of the General Service Administration guards. The man checked it against the list he carried, and peered through the window of the Volvo. 'This badge has been withdrawn,' he said.

'What?'

'Sir, I can't let you through with this.'

Behind him, the bodyguard got out of his car and hurried across the grass. After a brief conversation with the blue-uniformed guard, the gates were opened. The bodyguard came over.

'They weren't expecting you,' was all he said.

Martin accelerated away from him up the long tree-lined drive. As a security measure it had been the right thing to do. But his clearances should have been re-validated the moment the news of his release came through. His secretary should have seen to that as a matter of course: he would have a word with her. Slowing to a more sedate pace, he drove round to the front of the enormous plate-glass building and parked in his designated place in the tree-lined square, opposite the silver beehive dome of the auditorium where he had once attended a church service after the botched attempt to rescue the American hostages in Iran.

He got out of his car and stood for a moment leaning against it. He thought he saw the General gazing down at him out of one of the recessed windows on the seventh floor. But it was too far away to tell; it might have been a trick of the light.

His guards would have telephoned ahead, so they would be expecting him. So long as they hadn't assembled the Agency band in full regalia to serenade him indoors with 'America the Beautiful', he would be all right. Max would probably be down there in the reception committee, along with any of the division heads who'd come in. Walking past the statue of Nathan Hale, with his tied stone hands, he wondered momentarily what kind of questions Max had been asking Barbara.

To his surprise there was no reception committee awaiting him in the main lobby, formal or otherwise. The only person who stepped forward to greet him was the doctor who had examined him on the plane. 'Welcome back, Mr Commoner,' he said gravely. 'Would you mind coming with me? It won't take long.'

'What's wrong? Am I contagious?'

'You weren't expected here today. I was coming up to visit you in Georgetown. You've saved me a journey.'

In the Agency clinic Martin had his third medical in thirty hours. Armed with three sets of different vitamins he went on up to the seventh floor, suddenly grateful that there weren't many people around to give him curious stares and embarrassed greetings. The General was in his office, talking on the telephone. When Martin came in, he cut the conversation short abruptly and came round the desk with his arms wide.

'You were just about the last person I was expecting to see today,' he said with a grin.

'I've come in to get away from the crowds.'

The DCI grasped his arm solicitously and led him over to the couch, like a blind man who'd lost his white stick. 'First out, I want you to know it's really good to have you back with us. It was one hell of a thing to go through, but it was pretty bad for us too.'

'I appreciate that.'

'We pulled out all the stops. But I don't mind telling you,

there was one moment when I called the padre up here and we got down on our knees and prayed.'

Martin shifted uncomfortably. From his kidnappers he'd had all the prayer he could stomach. Before he could think up a gracious reply, the General carried on smoothly, 'We're instituting a news blackout for the next few days. I've had your cover story from Vanderbyle, and I know there's a great deal more you'll want to tell me. Would you object if I brought Max Hemming in on this?'

'How much does he know?'

'About BeeSting? Not much. I gave Senator Traill the full story because he'd heard something already. That's all.' With his back turned while he worked the intercom, the Director asked casually, 'What's the latest you have on BeeSting?'

'Zero. I haven't had a chance to talk to Peter Fisher yet.'

'Nor have we.' Tersely, the General brought him up to date with the situation in Jerusalem. 'I got a cable from MOSSAD last night. It's what I was afraid of. Those assholes think someone's double-crossing them. All they're interested in is the ground-plans to the nuclear reactor and the yellowcake. If we keep the plans back, lock 'em in the Embassy or whatever, they could use Fisher to tell the world we've been taking holiday snaps of the Moslem bomb. So it's deadlock. Until they get irrefutable evidence you're cleared — that's their phrase, not mine — they've got Fisher in safekeeping, as they call it. Allowing us no contact with him.'

Martin stared at the DCI. He could not keep the incredulity out of his voice.

'You mean, the Israelis are holding him hostage? To blackmail us?'

'Wouldn't you have done the same?'

'No. Jesus, no.' Martin felt his face flushing with anger. 'I've known their military top brass for ten years. I've been out shooting in the desert with their Defence Minister. I took the Iraqi plan out to Jerusalem and went over it with him, point by point. He trusts me —'

'That's right.' The General pointed the stem of his pipe at him. 'That's right, they trusted you. That was the whole reason BeeSting went ahead, because of mutual trust. Then you get kidnapped —'

'By a bunch of crazy Jesus freaks, barely out of school!'

144

'That's what we've got to convince them of.'

'May I join you?' Max Hemming had appeared in the doorway, silently as usual. Grinning his boyish grin, he came forward, clicked his heels in mock-salute, and shook Martin's hand. 'Welcome to the returning hero,' he said.

'I'm not so sure any longer,' replied Martin with a smile, studying him. Max looked paler than usual; his hand was sweaty. The kidnap had probably put him under a lot of pressure. It was the biggest challenge he'd had to face.

'You had the Operations Center here looking like the *Washington Post* newsroom on the day Nixon resigned,' said Hemming. The grin was fading, but a little anxious wrinkle of it remained in the corner of his mouth.

'I'm sorry I gave you the runaround.'

The General and Hemming both started to speak at once. Hemming finished.

'It's our fault. We should have taken better care of you.'

Martin stood up and looked at them both. He felt a little dizzy. It must be the rarefied air up here in the DCI's office: he had never heard so much bull-shitting politeness in all his life. 'As I see it, BeeSting's success depends on getting my story over to the Israelis in short order,' he said. 'Let me give you the whole thing now, as I remember it. Max, why don't you take some notes. Then we can work out a statement for Jerusalem, and produce David Bisley's son, when he's caught, as proof, living or dead. What do you say?'

The General and Hemming exchanged glances. 'Let's do it,' said Hemming. 'But not with notes. Notes can be misinterpreted.' He took out of his pocket a tape recorder, the size of a pocket calculator, and placed it on the DCI's desk.

Martin drew up a chair, and talked across the desk to his two colleagues, starting with his afternoon at Leeds Castle. As he talked, a curious numbness came over him. He felt the tent around him; he saw the faces of Esther and Luke, Zed and Ishmael as they argued with him and cajoled him; but they were insubstantial, like actors on a stage after the curtain has come down. Sitting in this seventh-floor office, at the nub of the most powerful intelligence service in the world, his time in captivity already seemed as remote and dreamlike as Washington had done when he lay drugged and pinioned on a floor in South London. He had to touch the rough scar on his head to remind

145

himself that it had really happened. The best way to put it out of his mind as rapidly as possible was to tell the whole story, leaving out only the confusing irrelevancies like Esther's seduction attempt. Max and the General could make of it what they chose.

When he finished, there was a long silence from the other side of the desk. Hemming got up and walked over to the window.

'They gave you a hard time,' said the DCI eventually.

'Professionals would have given me a worse one.'

'They were professional enough when they lifted you.'

Martin shrugged. 'It was in a couple of local papers I was going to be at Leeds Castle. All they had to do was to find out when.'

The Director frowned. 'You make it sound too easy. Max, what do you think?'

Hemming turned away from the window. With the light behind him, Martin couldn't see his expression. 'I don't understand why they let you go,' he said. 'If they had the balls to capture you, they surely had the balls to kill you if they wanted to.'

'I've given you my analysis. They were kids. They were frightened. They weren't getting anywhere. Murder is against their religion, that's why they pulled Ishmael off me.'

'Yes.'

Martin realised Max had left the tape recorder running. That didn't matter. He had nothing to hide. He had acquitted himself very well. He looked at the DCI and raised his eyebrows. 'Do you think that gives our Israeli friends what they're after?'

Hemming interrupted. 'You must have considered this. Is it your belief that anybody here at Langley could have been involved?'

Martin shook his head. 'You're the counter-intelligence expert. You had my schedule. I should be asking you that question.'

'I'm thinking of, uh, a political connection. Someone in Washington who wants to give the CIA a bad name.'

'By kidnapping me? I don't see it. Like I said, I told Ishmael nothing that isn't already on public record.'

The DCI raised his hand. 'Gentlemen. I think that's enough for now. Martin, you look exhausted. While you're taking your vacation, Max and I will collate this stuff and get a summary off to Jerusalem.'

146

'Vacation?' Martin frowned. 'I don't need a vacation.'

'Your doctor would dispute that. He says you need to rest, to recover from trauma. Just three days, Martin. I'm sending you and Barbara up to one of our safe houses in the Catoctins. Potter's Key, I guess you know it. By the time you're back here on Thursday, we should have sorted out the Israelis.'

The General rose, as if the meeting was over. Martin got up, feeling the same disorientation he'd had before.

'I can't go there,' he said. 'I'm seeing the President tomorrow.'

The DCI cleared his throat. 'I was going to tell you. I got a call from the White House this morning. The President's schedule has had to be rearranged to fit in with a visit by Queen Juliana of the Netherlands, or something of the sort. We figure you'll get a presentation medal instead.'

Martin grinned. The cunning old bastard. Perhaps that accounted for the shifty look in his eye when he was talking about vacations. 'I can live with the disappointment,' he said. 'Now it's a matter of getting home before Barbara goes out to buy herself a whole new outfit.' And of postponing his lunch with Nancy, he might have added, but did not.

'Good. I'll have a car sent round to the house at 1400 hours to take you to the Observatory pad.' The Director smiled cheerfully and slapped his Deputy on the back. 'Have some dinner with me here, Thursday night. Take care now. And good fishing.'

As Martin went out, he saw Hemming pocket the tape recorder. Max couldn't be faulted for secrecy, that was for sure. It was a reassuring thought. If it got spread around that the Deputy Director had spent the last few days sitting in his own shit surrounded by a gang of loony bible-punchers, it would not enhance his reputation.

Smiling at the thought, he walked down to the door of his own office. It was locked. Betty, his secretary, was not in her room. There was a cover over her typewriter. Puzzled, he returned to the General's outer office. Mrs Lomax was working at her IBM console.

'Do you know where Betty is?' he demanded.

Mrs Lomax looked surprised. 'The Director gave her leave of absence. She'll be at home, I guess.'

'Okay. But I haven't got my clearances. I need my security clearances restored.'

The look of surprise did not leave Mrs Lomax's face. 'That's automatic, Mr Commoner. They'll be waiting for you just as soon as you get back from Potter's Key.'

Superior bitch. He smiled at her politely. 'Then perhaps, Mrs Lomax, you would be kind enough to give me a duplicate key to my office? I need it to open the door with.'

There was a second's hesitation, a momentary glance towards the inner office where the General and Hemming were still talking. Then Mrs Lomax lifted her spectacles over her forehead, rummaged in a drawer and handed over the key.

'May I have it back when you're through?' she asked.

Martin winked at her, and went out without answering. Going back to his office, he went in and sat at his desk. At once the vague uneasiness he had experienced all morning fell away. He had slotted himself back into place. The layers that had been stripped from him in the tent could begin to renew themselves. The telephones on his desk, the maps and photographs on the wall, the filing cabinets, the safe, the books on the shelf, the television in the corner, everything he needed to re-establish his communications with the real world . . . only the unnatural silence reminded him that he was still officially a non-person. That, and having no clearances. Which meant that he couldn't yet check out Bisley's file and see what he could learn about the man who'd reached back from the grave with a six-inch kitchen knife.

His internal telephone rang. It was Addams, weekending on the Middle East desk, gruffly welcoming him back and angling for details. Several more calls followed, after he'd notified the switchboard that he was in his office. Reaching out his hand for his appointments diary, he found it was not in its usual place. He discovered it eventually in a desk drawer. It puzzled him; he made a habit of always putting things back where they belonged. On impulse, he went over to his safe, where the BeeSting material was secured, and rolled the dead-bolt combination lock.

The safe refused to open. The lock had been changed.

He returned and sat at his desk for several minutes. It was the logical thing to do, he told himself. Security demanded it. As soon as he disappeared, everybody in the Agency automatically came under suspicion. His sudden return had caught them off guard; well, that was understandable too. The game would be to see how thorough they'd been. Carefully now, chuckling to himself, he scrutinised the working surfaces in the room, pulled books out of the shelves and checked the papers in his drawers. There was no doubt about it. Everything had been minutely inspected. His photographs had been taken out of their frames and replaced. Even his crimson chair covers were brand new — not just cleaned, as he'd thought. It occurred to him that his external 'phone hadn't rung once since he'd been there. He picked it up. The line was dead.

To hell with it. The General was right — he needed a vacation.

William Pomfret had shunned press publicity all his working life. Now that he couldn't avoid it, he was actually finding it rather enjoyable. On Saturday afternoon, the Assistant Commissioner had called William into his office on the other side of Victoria Street and warmly congratulated him, in front of the Commander. He had then suggested that a press conference — in which William could reveal, in the most general way, the collective effort that went into an investigation of this kind — would be useful publicity for the Metropolitan Police.

'Focusing on the detective work put in by the CID,' added the Commander.

'In particular, the Special Branch,' said William. Seeing the look of disapproval on the Assistant Commissioner's face he added swiftly, 'Not for its own sake, of course, sir, but to underline the efficiency of police intelligence in reaching those parts which other intelligence services cannot reach.'

In the general merriment which followed, the Assistant Commissioner seemed to forget whatever restrictions he had been about to impose, and William was able to take the personal credit which, he admitted to himself, he thoroughly deserved.

Yesterday, at approximately the time Martin Commoner was landing in Washington, the *News of the World* had carried a quarter-page photograph on its front page showing William at the demolition site, with a caption underneath reading, '*Detective Chief Inspector William Pomfret of the Special Branch points to the spot where he found Commoner alive*'.

Today, to the chagrin of John Little and the combined investigative teams in the Operations Rooms in London and

Maidstone, further photographs of William had appeared in the tabloid press, along with graphic stories of his single-handed, eleventh-hour, edge-of-the-abyss rescue of the American spy-runner. *Newsweek* was preparing a short, flattering piece about William as the typical selfless unassuming British copper. A British news magazine had interviewed him for a longer article, which was to be accompanied by a photograph of William at home in Shepherd's Bush with Jenny and the children around the fire. (Jenny herself had been interviewed by a reporter from the *Guardian*, which printed more interesting things than she'd remembered saying, about the adjustments that had to be made in a marriage like hers when a blue-collar husband developed into one of the professional classes.)

The only thing that nagged William in all this, as the Assistant Commissioner reminded him when he put an end to it, was that his triumph was only a partial one. The kidnappers were still at large.

Apart from confirming Jonathan Bisley's rôle, Commoner had been a disappointing witness. William had put in a strong plea to hold him for further questioning, but he'd been over-ruled by the Home Office, probably bowing to pressure from the US Government. The descriptions he'd given had been sent out immediately to all ports and airports. Nothing had come back: which meant either that the kidnappers were still somewhere in Britain, as John Little thought, or, more likely, that they had got abroad before the alarm was raised. They had left nothing behind. They had fallen through the social net. Even the local social workers, perhaps recognising a higher calling, steered clear of religious groups. They had made themselves as nearly anonymous as it was possible for foreigners in Britain to be.

William had instituted a watch on the other main colonies of the Family, in Liverpool, Glasgow and Dublin. He had sent the descriptions Commoner had provided to the police computer centres in London and Wiesbaden, West Germany — but no cross-references had come back. Driving home to Shepherds Bush for the magazine photograph, he was wondering how much Martin Commoner had left out of the testimony he'd given.

It was then that the first breakthrough came.

It arrived in a routine message on his car radio. A young police constable doing house-to-house enquiries in Brixton had turned up an unoccupied house in Brailsford Road, backing on to Brockwell Park. A woman answering to Esther's description had been using it. Two men had been seen with her on various occasions: they fitted Commoner's descriptions of his kidnappers.

By the time William reached Brailsford Road, John Little was waiting for him. The young constable filled in the details. The house belonged to a Mrs Gwynneth Jones, a woman in her late sixties. Three weeks ago, she had lent it to her grand-daughter Margaret to house-sit, while she went into hospital for an operation on her arthritic hip.

After several skeleton keys had failed, two policemen jemmied open the front door. William went inside, carefully wiping his boots on the doormat.

At first he thought it was just another false alarm. It was an old person's house all right, spotlessly maintained, with an unvisited air. In the hall corridor, an Edwardian stained-glass hanging lamp cast rainbow colours on a highly-polished umbrella stand containing a collection of walking-sticks. An open door into the drawing-room gave a view of overstuffed velveteen armchairs with embroidered antimacassars, looming around a tiny two-bar electric heater in the hearth.

But there was something out of place. He didn't know what it was at first. Then he realised it was the smell. There was an acid scent in the air, not civet exactly, more like urine. He sniffed it like a dog, and went up the stairs, following his nose.

This was where the girl and her friends had lived. There was a ring of dirt around the bath: Mrs Jones would never have stood for that. In the first bedroom he came to, there were all the signs of a hurried departure: a roughly-made bed, the curtains only half drawn back, a couple of cigarette papers on the carpet.

'Up here!' he shouted out to Little, leaning over the banister.

There was another bedroom, which also bore all the signs of recent use, and then a flight of stairs to the attic rooms. The sewer smell grew stronger. At the top, it hit him like a blow in the face.

The attic room was dark. He pressed the light switch and was dazzled by a 150-watt naked bulb hanging on a long flex four feet off the floor. It was a bedroom, he saw, when his eyes had got accustomed to the glare. In the corner was a white wooden

151

bed, with a cupboard beside it. On his right was a chest of drawers, and another door on the other side. The two windows, which would look out over Brockwell Park, had heavy curtains pulled across them. On the green carpet, half-covering a broad dark stain of urine, torn squares of blackout paper lay. Nearby was an old cough-pastille tin with ash and cigarette ends in it.

A floorboard creaked behind him. It was John Little. He had his handkerchief over his nose. 'We've found the tent,' said his deputy in a muffled voice. 'It was in the cellar.'

William nodded. 'This is it all right. Poor bastard.'

'Unless they faked it, to fool us.'

William stared at him. John was beginning to sound like Vanderbyle, obsessed with plots and conspiracies, cut-outs and letter-drops. He must have taken up reading spy stories, instead of his usual *Sporting Life*. He said curtly, 'Let's get forensic in. I want the lot. Semen. Blood. Nail-clippings. Hair on the pillows. Sweat marks on the bedding. I want them identified right down to their favourite breakfast cereal.'

'Should we put out a public alert on Margaret Jones?'

'You do it, John. And round up a few more neighbours. I'm going to have a word with her grandma.'

It happened just before the afternoon recess. Another five minutes and she'd have been able to escape to the women's room and not make an exhibition of herself. But it came on too suddenly. One moment, Nancy was sitting with the other legislative aides, behind Senator Traill in the small committee room on the third floor of the Capitol, making notes on the Senate hearing for the bill authorising appropriations for US Intelligence. The next, for no good reason, she had keeled over and was lying on the carpet, staring up at the Government service chandelier hanging from the ceiling, while people bent over her in inquisitive sympathy.

It was Jack Traill himself who had insisted on accompanying her home. He had steered her out of the Capitol and hailed a cab (it was too ridiculous, really, she could just as well have gotten a bus), and was now sitting beside her in the back seat, staring out of the window at the trail of joggers in running shorts and trainers pounding along beside the tourist stalls which lined Union Square.

'Still feeling lousy?' he asked her.

'No. Much better. Thank you.'

Traill stubbed out the Marlborough he was smoking, and tapped another from the packet straight away. 'You'll give me a bad name, Nancy. Word will get around I work my staffers harder than I work myself.'

'There's not much chance of that,' she answered, smiling. And indeed there wasn't. Jack Traill's nervous energy was a legend even in the Senate, which had more than its share of driving, ambitious workaholics. His whole life was politics. He worked the corridors. He did deals in saloon bars, lobbies, dining-rooms and back parlours. He lived on black coffee. To drum up support for a piece of legislation he would stay up all night by his bedside phone, if need be, arguing and cajoling until he got his man.

It was not a healthy life. To her mind it was positively a dangerous one. Jack Traill was a big man with a prominent, fleshy nose and a high complexion. With his sleeked-down grey hair turning to white over his ears, he looked older than his forty-six years. That was one of the penalties for pushing his brand of politics. Being a Liberal Democrat in a Senate full of right-wingers was bad for the blood-pressure from the word go.

She was about to say, *You're the one who should be taking it easy,* when the cabbie braked suddenly and burped his horn at two black girls in tight green pants sashaying across an intersection. Oblivious to the exchange of insults which followed, Traill turned to her and said seriously, 'What's your judgement of how the hearing is progressing?'

'Today?' She collected her thoughts. 'I think you're going to have trouble with Eisner.'

'Hah! Maybe. I don't think so. Eisner's a bubblehead. He figures that if he does enough grandstanding on behalf of the CIA, Galucci will reward him with a committee chairmanship. But Eisner's out on a limb, and Galucci knows it. He doesn't dispense favours to people who can't bring home the bacon.'

She nodded. 'You're pretty darn sure it's going your way.'

'Sure I'm sure. The days when we shelled out millions without knowing what we were getting for our greenbacks are over.

Surveillance satellites, you know what you're getting. You can see 'em, run 'em around the sky. That's Galucci's attitude. He doesn't give a damn about the CIA. He wants all the money to go on hardware.'

'I thought you didn't want to see the NSA getting a bigger slice of the budget?'

Traill grinned and punched his cigarette in her general direction. 'I don't. But here's something Galucci doesn't know. I've got Kent on my side. He's a real hardhat. But even he's appreciative that if we build up the NSA it's at the expense of the Pentagon. I'm telling you, we'll end up putting a freeze on the CIA's budget and then come round and do the same to the NSA. Divide and rule, Nancy.'

He lay back on the seat rubbing his nose and chuckling triumphantly. Something about him for a second reminded her of Martin, and the old feeling of giddiness swept over her again so violently that she had to clutch the door-strap. It hadn't been the intense emotions of relief and gratitude for his safety that had blacked her out this morning, but the tremendous effort it had taken to keep them hidden. After a sleepless night, she had got up this morning in the usual way and dressed in the kind of skirt and blazer jacket she normally wore to work. She had chatted in the lift to Mrs Da Silva about how long it took to get downtown these days; she had said hi to the doorman. She had gotten on the Metrobus (no problem with a seat today) and taken the familiar route down Connecticut Avenue, catching glimpses of Martin's face at the news-stands . . . and all the time she wanted to scream out, *this is my man — I'm the one who suffered most when they kidnapped him; I should be the one he comes back to!*

Instead, she had stepped off the bus at the Mall, holding tight her locked briefcase and patting down her skirt against the blustery breeze. She had walked up the steps of the Capitol and along to the committee room, politely greeting colleagues and giving distant smiles to others, wondering what they'd done to him, how scarred he would be, why he hadn't gotten in touch to keep the appointment he'd broken those eight days ago (even though he'd been back less than twenty-four hours) . . .

And Jack Traill — how much did he know? Exploring, she said, 'Jack, what is it that bugs you so about the CIA?'

Traill gave her a quizzical look. 'Any special reason for asking that?' Before she could reply, he went on: 'I'll tell you something. America needs the best intelligence it can get. But it also needs to know what the hell is going on. Look at Iran. There were enough reports coming out of Iran that the Shah was going to fall. Did Congress get to hear of them? Did we hell. I said then we needed more accountability, but the Senate chickened out. We brought a 172-page charter bill to the floor, and we ended up with a four-page scrap of paper which reduces the oversight committees from eight to two and lets the CIA goof off any way it wants and tell us afterwards. If we're lucky.'

It was not exactly what she wanted to know, but there was no stopping the Senator from Rhode Island once he got on his favourite subject. His voice charged with urgency, he addressed her as if an entire public meeting had crammed into the back of the taxi-cab and needed to be convinced of his every word.

'Look at Martin Commoner,' he exclaimed. 'You might think that when the Deputy Director of the Central Intelligence Agency is kidnapped, the House Intelligence committee would be given a full run-through of the potential security risks. The President gets it. Not us. Not until I muscled in and found what we'd gotten ourselves into. I'm not blaming Commoner. He's a conscientious man, a fine public servant. But there's growing terrorist pressure on Americans abroad. Unless the Agency starts coming clean, I'm going to ask again for prior consultation of all covert operations, and I'm going to put the screws on till I get it. What's more —'

'Okay, lady?'

The cab had pulled up in front of Nancy's tall grey-white apartment block, and she never got to hear the rest of the fate in store for the CIA. Hardly pausing to draw breath, Traill scrambled out of the cab, his blue jacket rumpled and cigarette ash on his trousers, and came round to open the door her side.

'Let me get this,' she said, embarrassed, noticing the doorman staring at them inquisitively from outside the lobby.

'It's done,' said Traill. He took her arm solicitously and led her through the glass doors which were opened with a flourish for them.

'Are you okay now?' he asked.

'I'm fine now. Really.'

He frowned at her anxiously — like the bear in the old illustration, she thought with a nervous smile, frowning at the

155

beehive and wondering if it would get stung if it put its hand in for the honey.

'Do you want me to see you upstairs?' he asked her gravely.

'Jack, I'm really okay now. Really. Thanks a whole lot.'

Traill patted her awkwardly on the arm and lumbered out. She felt a sudden pity for him. There went a man with a wife he hardly saw since she'd refused to come to Washington with him; a man who had sublimated all his love into politics, and whose home life consisted of a toasted cheese sandwich in an empty apartment late at night while voices on the telephone wire talked at him about the decline in cotton sales and inflation hitting the tourist trade along Narragansett Bay.

But as she got into the lift, she reflected that, after all, it was Jack Traill's choice. Politics didn't tend to attract the most secure sort of men to start with: she'd had plenty of opportunity to confirm that. A politician could surround himself with a great warm family, have them photographed for the newspapers smiling up at him lovingly around the hearth, and still be a lonely inward man, haunted by the thought of failure. She would never marry one, she'd decided that long ago. It meant giving too much up, making too many sacrifices. That was the way the typical Washington marriage drifted towards the rocks; the reason why one in five of professional women here were either divorced or separated, and changed their shrink as often as their hairdresser.

She got out of the lift on the fifth floor and walked down the thickly-carpeted corridor towards her apartment. Martin was not like that. He was one of the sanest, best-balanced company men she had met in this company town. Okay, she teased him sometimes about being so straight and serious-minded and a bit pompous at times, but, God, if that was all there was to worry about . . .

She had her key out to open the door when she heard it: quite clearly, the sound of somebody putting down the telephone inside the apartment. So much for her worries. Martin hadn't wasted any time. Throwing open the door, with a little laugh of delight she said, 'Caught in the act!'

Then she froze.

There were three men in her living-room.

One of them, kneeling beside her upturned coffee-table, held a small object like a pencil-torch between his fingers. Next to

156

the telephone was a man in grey overalls carrying an electrician's bag. His mouth was open. The third man, youngish with a pasty, jowly face and sideburns, was standing in the bedroom doorway. He had his hand in the pocket of his dark blue overcoat.

'I'm sorry,' she said stupidly. 'I thought you were someone else.'

'Miss Koscinski?' It was the man in the overcoat who spoke.

'Yes.'

'I'm Paul Shusterman. CIA.' The young man took his hand out of his overcoat and flipped open an ID, unreadable from where she was standing. 'Will you please step inside and close the door?'

After some hesitation, she did so. Shusterman recovered his composure and came across the room to her with a warm smile, holding his hand out in front of him like a politico across a roped enclosure.

'You must be wondering what we're doing here,' he said. His palm was clammy, and his smile twitched as if it didn't belong.

'Right now, I'm wondering where your search warrant is,' she told him.

'I appreciate your concern —'

'Mr Shusterman, I'm not concerned. I'm mad. What gives you the right to come snooping — I mean snooping — into my home?'

'I can explain.'

'Please. Explain.'

'If you'll let me. I work in an area with Mr Hemming —'

'You amaze me.'

'And Larry and Bob here are carrying out a routine sweep of your apartment to check for any surveillance appliances that may have been implanted. Uh — Larry? Bob? This is Miss Koscinski. Nancy, isn't it?'

The two men behind Shusterman grinnned sheepishly. The one in overalls raised his hand and said, 'Hi, Nance.'

She came across the room and planted herself next to the upturned coffee table, breathless and a little flushed. Her heart had stopped pounding: she was starting to think clearly again. Gripping her purse she said, 'So that's what Larry and Bob are doing?'

'That's right.'

She pointed to the one on the carpet, who by now had palmed the pencil-torch. 'Okay, so why is he about to put a bug into my table? I mean, are you guys for real? What kind of greenassed kid do you take me for? You aren't sweeping my apartment. You're bugging it.'

Shusterman sighed and shook his head. A mask of bureaucratic impassivity had come down over his countenance: she would tear it off if she had to claw his face open.

'I'm a lawyer,' she exclaimed. 'You know how many of my rights you creeps are violating? Maybe you got the wrong apartment block — Watergate is down the hill.'

The man in overalls whistled. 'This dame's got a sensayuma,' he observed, picking his nose vigorously.

Shusterman came and touched her elbow. He said, 'Let's go next door and talk.'

It was like a replay of Hemming. He sat stolidly at the kitchen table; she made herself coffee. He talked about national security and protecting the interests of the United States. She listened.

After a minute she said, 'I understand what you're saying. What I resent, *really*, is your underhand secrecy. Why didn't you come clean at the start? If you didn't trust me enough to ask me before tapping my 'phone, it means you still don't trust me. You could be full of shit.'

Shusterman had his confident smile back. 'Nancy — Miss Koscinski — you have a romantic view of intelligence. It has nothing to do with trust. It has to do with expediency. If you hadn't come back early, we could have been out of here without needing to trust anybody. Even you.'

She shrugged. 'Okay, I'll cooperate. On one condition.'

'What's that?'

'I want written confirmation why and for how long you're bugging my 'phone.'

'I'll get on to it right away.' Shusterman beamed with sincerity. 'Like I said, it's not you we're interested in. It's anybody who might try and get at you because of Martin. Any more questions?'

'Yes. Can I have my apartment back now, please?'

Shusterman got up, bulky in his dark-blue overcoat. She followed him into the living-room. The other men had gone. Her table was back on its feet, with the fan box on it. She gave it a wide berth, as though it had power to hurt her. At the door, he turned to her and put out a podgy hand.

'I really appreciate your collaboration, Nancy.'

'Goodbye Mr Shusterman,' she said, and shut the door.

She felt so tired, suddenly, that she could hardly stand up. Too many sleepless nights. She couldn't be bothered to make herself a meal. She went into the bathroom and opened the mirror-cabinet. The sleeping pills were there . . . but no, she had work to do. So much work to do. It was sweet of Jack Traill to tell her to take a rest, but really, he couldn't cope without her briefings. He'd be cut down, like a general who's outrun his troops. Custer, alone against the Indians.

She wandered back into the living-room, yawning and rubbing her face. It didn't welcome her; it wasn't her room any longer. It had been taken over by listeners, hiding under the table, crouching in the potted plants, winking at her from behind the pictures on the walls. She could switch the television on. But it would mean bringing Martin into the room again — Martin driving away from his house pursued by reporters, Martin returning to his house pursued by reporters, Martin standing on his front steps as the TV cameras closed in, looking pale and impersonal, sharing her with a million viewers. No, she was too tired to cope with that.

In the end, she went into her bedroom and pulled down the bamboo blind. In the shady darkness she lay back on the pillow and switched a small spotlight on to the Japanese silkscreen painting on the wall, her most treasured possession.

It was of an old and weary peasant, bent almost double under the weight of the bundle on his back. Above him towered the craggy, emerald and precipitous mountain, up which he would have to bear his heavy load. With her eyes, Nancy traced his path as it corkscrewed upwards. Every now and then she would encounter the peasant on his journey, his figure diminishing in size but straighter-backed and brisker as he marched on through the wisps of white cloud. At the end of his long journey he emerged for the last time: no longer bent double under his burden, but sitting in a tree-shaded pavilion on the topmost promontory of rock, looking up from a scroll and peacefully contemplating a skein of wild geese which flew beneath him and disappeared into the pale of the sky.

Peacefully, she fell asleep.

TUESDAY

Martin lay awake most of the night. He turned like a man being grilled on a spit, alternately tossing off the blanket and pulling it over him as his body chilled. At about four in the morning his eyes fixed themselves on the shadows on the wall cast by the moonlight coming through the window. Every now and then a gust of wind would bring into view a pair of black knives beckoning him and pincering together above the window frame.

He got out of bed and closed the shutters. After that, he slept dreamlessly for several hours, half-awaking to a faint persistent tapping which sounded to him, as he opened his eyes in the dark, like the tapping of rescuers. He got up, stumbled to the window bare-footed across the wooden floorboards, and opened the shutters wide. The sun burst in, and the woodpecker who had been tapping on the bright aspen branch outside the balcony flew up and over the gable.

He laughed aloud with relief, and looked back at the big double bed. Barbara was still asleep; he must have kept her awake all night with his feverishness. Quietly, he slipped the door-catch and went out on the balcony.

Potter's Key — an old hunting lodge, the helicopter pilot had called it — stood at the head of a valley between two high ridges of the Catoctins. The Agency owned a lot of real estate, from townhouses in New York to a cabin in the Alleghenies he'd once gone hunting from. As he might have expected, it had chosen this safe house carefully. There was no road access to it from the valley floor. Beyond the lawn, with the helicopter pad off to one side, there was a long swathe of woodland, and what looked like a farm in the far distance. Following the balcony round to the other side, he could see the dirt track that led to the house cross a bridge over the stream that bordered the property to the north and west and then wound up through the trees, presumably to come out on one of the small roads that led to the Baltimore-Hagerstown highway over the ridge.

The intoxicating air and the scenery were making him giddy: he wasn't used to this openness. He went back into the bedroom. Barbara, still sleeping, had turned towards the light, and thrown one arm across his pillow. It was something she used to do in the old days, when they were first married and slept in the same bed together. The thought of it filled him with affection. He used to bring her hot coffee and watch her come alive with luxurious slowness, yawning and stretching herself out, dabbing her blonde hair off her face. When there had been time, he would get back into bed beside her, and let the hand that had been outstretched on his pillow lazily run itself over him and explore him bit by bit until it found what it was looking for. Those mornings he had been late into work; back then, it hadn't seemed to matter.

Today he would make coffee and bring it up to her in bed again. Shrugging on a bathrobe, he went downstairs and found his way to the well-stocked kitchen. There was a note on the table from the caretaker who lived down the valley. His wife had called earlier in the morning and left fresh milk and a basket of fresh eggs. Martin put them in the fridge and ground the coffee beans.

He said aloud, 'I'm going to like this place.'

Waiting for the water to boil, he switched on the small TV set on a stool in the corner. An interview was in progress on CBS news. It was a man he recognised, a big bear-like man with a large nose and shiny grey hair, sitting in his office with the Stars and Stripes on a kind of umbrella-stand in the background. James Traill. And he was talking about the CIA.

'. . . in timely fashion,' he was explaining to the camera. 'That is the law of the land, that the CIA should inform Congress *in timely fashion* after a covert operation just why it needed to do it covertly. My impression is that CIA time is a whole lot slower than what the rest of us use.'

'Senator,' came the interviewer's voice, 'can you tell us, sir, whether this request of yours has any connection with the, uh, kidnapping of Martin Commoner, the Deputy Director?'

Martin switched off the water. In the silence, Traill gave his practised smile. 'Let me say that, like everyone else, I have nothing but sympathy for the ordeal Mr Commoner has gone through, and admiration for his fortitude. It says a great deal about him that he came through this ordeal unscathed.'

'And so?'

'I repeat. I'm not concerned that the CIA should have a boom-and-bang philosophy. I'm saying that, if you carry a gun, it shouldn't have a silencer so effective that your own friends don't know you're protecting them. One day they might get hurt.'

Martin lifted his finger in a rude gesture at the screen. Traill vanished, and was replaced by the TV reporter standing palely on the steps of the Capitol.

'Rhode Island Senator James Traill,' he said, 'who this morning formally requested the Director of the Central Intelligence Agency to appear before the Senate Oversight Committee on US Intelligence —'

'Damn!' Martin turned off the TV, and swore again at the grey space where Traill had been. 'Interfering sonofabitch!'

'What's the matter?' Barbara, in house-gown and slippers, was in the doorway, her eyes frightened, blinking back sleep.

He looked at her, frowning. 'I thought you were out for the count.'

'I heard voices.'

'It's the News. The General's getting it in the neck again from some liberal Senator.'

'Traill?'

'That's right.' he hesitated. 'I was just making coffee for you, Babs. I was going to bring it up.'

'I'll have it down here. Thanks. Well, what do you think?'

'I think he's got a hell of a nerve, summoning the Director like an —'

'I mean, here. Potter's Key. Isn't it smart? It's so much smarter than I thought it was going to be.' She went over to the kitchen door, her slippers smacking on the flagstones. Opening it, she let in the smell of warm earth. Miles away a dog barked, the sound carrying on the still air.

'It's lovely,' he agreed, grudgingly.

'There's a patch of wild strawberries. I'll pick some for lunch. How would you like that, darling?'

'Lovely. I'd like to empty a plate of them over Traill.'

'Oh really —'

'You know, it's all gotten insane. Before Watergate, the House and Senate used to see their role as protecting the CIA. Defending it. The oversight committees used to refuse to let us tell them about sensitive missions. Now they lam into us every chance they get.'

'Not so much as they used to.'

'Traill does.'

He stared into the coffee. Barbara came back and put her arms round him. She kissed him on the mouth.

'I'm not picking strawberries for Traill,' she said.

'Right.' He carried the cups to the table, slopping coffee in the saucers. How had Traill known about BeeSting? There was something going on here that he ought to know about . . .

'Did I tell you about John's exhibition?' she asked him.

'Who?'

'John. Our son, remember? He's been arranging an exhibition for the University photographic society. Asking a whole lot of famous photographers, people like Weston and Uelsmann, to contribute a picture in which they've found something unexpected or strange, something they didn't mean to photograph.'

'Hoosman?'

'Uelsman. And lots of others, Callahan, Avedon.'

'It sounds fun.'

'Darling, I thought I'd ask John to come and have lunch here. On Sunday. Seeing that you missed him yesterday. I know he'd love to see you.'

'That's fine.' He noticed her watching him with a bright attentive expression and took her hand absent-mindedly. 'You'll be okay.' he said.

'I'm sorry?'

'There's nothing for you to worry about. You can relax. How's the Library job? And the Center. Tell me about the Center. Have you got all the money yet?'

'Oh, I meant to tell you. I'm having a barbecue for it in the garden. Tuesday week. Judy says we're only 4000 shy of our Christmas target of 28,000 dollars, and I figure that with three barbecues at forty dollars a plate — myself and Laura Naderson and one other — we should lick it. That's what Judy says.'

'Very good. No, I mean it.'

'Well it *is* good, actually. It means we get the Evening Program sorted out, and a music teacher two hours a week.'

'I thought the kids were autistic?'

'That's right. It doesn't mean they're deaf. It means they have problems in communicating. They're loners, out of contact with the real world, they can't break through. Any *shared* activity — music, or dancing, or art classes — it's a way of helping them.'

'Oh I see.' *Out of contact.* He stared past her, out through the open door. 'Come on Babs, let's go and survey our property,' he said.

'Don't you want to put shoes on?'

'No. I want to feel the earth under my feet. Come on.'

He took his wife by the hand and led her out into the garden. The grass was already warm. He wanted to take off his bathrobe and roll naked in it, like a colt, listening to the birds sing. But Barbara might take one look at this middle-aged man rolling naked in the grass and go call the kidnap doctor. He contented himself with breathing deeply and waving his arms at the blue sky like a windmill.

'Good exercise,' he panted.

Barbara was already kneeling under the magnolia tree, testing the second-crop wild strawberries. 'You know, I think we should plant a magnolia in the garden,' she called. 'I think the *fraises de bois* like them.'

'You just want something that blossoms before the people next door,' he called back. 'You want to be right up in front there when spring comes!'

'That's a cheap shot.' She brushed a greenfly off her nose and grinned at him. He liked her with her hair down; it made her younger-looking. And the sway of her breasts as she picked the strawberries, and her white ankle half out of its slipper. In a few minutes she would go upstairs, and come down a different woman, with smart new sandals, and a smart shirt tucked into her trousers and buttoned up to wherever smart women were buttoning their summer shirts this year.

Keeping a straight face, he took off his bathrobe and rolled naked in the grass, feeling it crackle beneath him. Shading his eyes from the sun, he looked up to see Barbara standing over him with a big handful of strawberries.

'Anything I can do for you?' she asked.

'I've got an ant biting my ass,' he said. 'Improve on that.'

164

She knelt and gave him a strawberry. It tasted sweet and sharp. He drew her down beside him. She clutched her housegown and looked at him anxiously. 'Shall I get a pillow?'

'No. I just want to talk. It feels good, that's all. I started to think I'd never see the sun again.'

Holding her hand, but not looking into her face, he told her about the kidnap. When he came to the part where Ishmael attacked him with a knife, he grew cold and pulled the bathrobe over his chest. Strangely enough it was all more comprehensible to him out here than it had been in the DCI's office, as though there was a curative magic in the retelling of it. It was only when Barbara, with tears in her eyes, ran her hand over the bump on his head, and he brushed her hand away impatiently, that he realised he hadn't told the story to her at all, but to himself. She only understood the physical hurt of his kidnapping. For him, the story had a deeper significance, and he would go on living with it, like the Mariner's albatross, until it was ready to let him go.

Later, they had a lunch of cheese and peaches on the terrace, looking out over the valley below. After it was over he sat on for an hour or more, gazing out. The sky clouded over thunderously. In shadow, the valley looked quite different: smaller and somehow narrower, more enclosed, as if the two high ridges of the Catoctins were bending towards each other like trees over a long dark road.

Twenty-four hours ago, William had thought himself in reach of bringing the investigation to an end. Flying down to Swansea Airport, he had a vision of Detective Chief Inspector William Pomfret standing to attention while the Queen's Police Medal was pinned to his chest.

Swansea was where Jack Jones lived, the father of the girl they were hunting for. It had taken Mrs Gwynneth Jones, a sweet-faced, birdlike old woman sitting in a wheelchair beside her hospital bed, some time to collect her thoughts about her granddaughter Margaret. She had gone off on a camping holiday — no not Margaret, but her three American friends . . .

'Where did they go, love, can you remember?'

'Oh. Didn't I tell you? I got a letter from Jack, just this

morning.' She rummaged among the Get Well cards on her bed-side table, and then in a small black plastic handbag. 'Such a good girl to go all the way to Swansea to see her dad. She took three friends with her too. They were off on a hiking holiday, did I tell you? But not Margaret, you know. Margaret's got my house to look after. Margaret wouldn't leave without telling me.' Her face crumpled. 'She's not been a bad girl, officer? Tell me she's not done anything wrong?'

Before William was out of the hospital door, an alert had been put out to the South Wales Constabulary and to the port authorities and immigration officials in Swansea, Milford Haven, Fishguard and Holyhead. By the time he arrived in Swansea, police and CID had searched Jack Jones's small terrace house from top to bottom. There was no sign of American hitch-hikers, no sign of Margaret and no sign of her father.

Most of that day, they were one step behind him. Jack Jones collected his unemployment benefit. He paid a visit to the labour exchange. He attended a choir practice at the local Baptist church. He called in at a pub, not his local, for a couple of quiet drinks. By the time he was picked up for questioning, walking soberly home, it was already dark, and William could no longer feel the imprint of the medal on his chest. What Mr Jones had to tell him — that Margaret and the three Americans carrying rucksacks had arrived mid-morning Sunday and stopped only for coffee and a late breakfast — made him no happier.

When William got back to the Yard on Tuesday morning, the confirmation he dreaded was beginning to come through. On Sunday, a party of hitch-hikers with rucksacks, three men and a girl, had bought Sealink tickets at Fishguard to cross over to Ireland. From Rosslare they had bought train tickets to Limerick. From Limerick, as William knew, it was fairly quick bus ride to Shannon Airport.

He was about to get through to the Garda in Ireland when a sergeant brought in off the telex the news he'd been expecting. The same party of four campers had gone through customs and immigration at the airport two days ago, at 4.30 in the after-noon. They had boarded a TWA flight to Boston, Massa-chusetts — which meant that they had nearly forty-eight hours in North America to make themselves scarce.

William swore, softly and very fast. It was over to the FBI

now. But the FBI might not have it all their own way. He noticed the names in which the four air tickets were booked: Margaret Jones was there, but not Jonathan Bisley. That meant that Bisley at least, and maybe the other two men as well, had somehow managed to get themselves false passports.

Nutters, he had called them. Now he wasn't so sure. Maybe Vanderbyle had been right all along. He picked up the phone and called through to Johnny Wax at his home in Denham.

'Johnny? Our four birds have flown. Back to the Land of the Free. If I can clear it, I'm going after them.'

When the storm broke in the mid-afternoon, Barbara came out on to the terrace. Martin was watching the crows alighting in the poplar beside the stream. 'I'm okay,' he said, but let himself be persuaded to go rest in bed.

The house was well stocked with shelves of tattered detective stories, which the Agency must have bought in a job-lot to keep the minds of its operators supple. Martin found a Travis McGee novel he hadn't read; but it didn't amuse him. He found scenes of quite mild violence difficult to read, and threw the book aside.

When Barbara came up, the sky had cleared and he was propped up on the pillow, staring out of the window at the distant hills. They'd had a whisky still up there in the woods in Prohibition days, so his father had told him. It was still there, as a State tourist attraction, the moonshine doctored to make it undrinkable.

'From the top of that ridge you can see right over to Hagerstown,' he said.

'Of course, I forgot you were a local kid.'

'I wasn't what you'd call a country boy. Pa used to take Richard and me fishing, and I'd spend the whole time sitting against a tree with my nose in a book, wondering when we could start on the meat-paste sandwiches.'

'It was in your genes, darling: son and grandson of a lawyer, what do you expect?'

'My brother escaped it. Mind you, we both still ended up in 'Nam.'

'Him fighting, darling. You still reading.'

167

Grinning, he drank the orange juice she had brought him. She leaned over him, brushing back his hair.

'I think we should stay here longer, darling. I'm definite. Four days isn't enough.'

'Sorry, Babs. You don't appreciate the workload I've got. Papers, decisions, committee meetings . . . Jesus! Another few days and it would be out of control!' He swung his legs out of bed and began massaging them vigorously at the thought of all that had to be done. 'I'm going fishing,' he announced. 'The rain will have brought the fish up. We'll have trout for dinner!'

Martin came back at eight with a 14-inch trout and a contented smile. Barbara had set the table in the dining-room with candlesticks she had found in the cellar and a bowl of wild flowers. Over the grilled trout and white wine, she talked at him about memories of New York, and dinners at Pierre's and the Café Argenteuil. With a creeping irritation he saw that she had decided that the past was the safest territory for both of them; but he joined in nevertheless, reminding her of other things, things he hadn't, thank God, put in his much-publicised letter — a time once in the elevator going up in Bloomingdales and getting stuck between floors, and another time at the Met.

But he felt a formality in the air, a distance between them as though there was a stranger at the meal-table, and he knew that she sensed it too.

'Did you get through to Feinstein today?' he asked.

'No, but I got her answering machine. That doesn't talk back either.'

There was a silence. He said abruptly, 'John's coming for lunch tomorrow.'

She looked at him in astonishment. 'Now you tell me!'

'Sorry. I forgot. He's coming in by Agency helicopter at mid-day. I fixed it with the General this morning.'

'Did you check with John first?'

'No. He can damn well cancel his other appointments.'

Barbara shrugged and smiled. She said, 'I'm worried about him, all the same.'

'Why?'

'He's so . . . I don't know . . . *unconcerned*. He doesn't seem to care about anything.'

Martin was playing with a fruit knife, balancing it in the palm of his hand so that the candlelight shivered along the steel blade. 'Perhaps it's us he doesn't care about,' he said.

'I'm serious. He's got a good brain but he isn't using it. If he wants to drop out, that's his business. But this isn't the sixties. Every kid on campus needs a job nowadays. It's smart to have ambition again, like it used to be.' Barbara's voice softened. 'Darling, why don't you speak to him tomorrow. Get him to sort himself out a bit?'

'If that's what you really want, Babs.' He let the knife topple from his hand on to the cloth where it lay in the shadow. What did he know of his son any more? John was a stranger to him. He'd had more contact with Ishmael in one week than he'd had with John in years. They were all out of reach, the people around him, like Barbara's autistic children.

The wind rustled in the dark. Barbara said, 'That was what I loved about our house in Spring Valley. The trees and the wind.'

'Babs, it was you who wanted to go live in Georgetown. As I recall, you'd been reading the Washington Dossier real-estate column and you decided that Spring Valley made the wrong kind of statement about our lives.'

'It was where we were living in Spring Valley,' she corrected him, ignoring the sarcasm. She pulled the trolley up to pour the coffee. 'Too suburban. We both needed a higher profile. You said so yourself at the time.'

'Did I? I hardly think so, Babs. It's not my language.'

'Maybe you've changed.' She pushed a cup of coffee over to him. 'You've got where you want to get to. I'm still fund-raising.'

'Meaning what?'

'Meaning I need to keep in touch with people,' she said in a shocked voice. 'I couldn't do voluntary work stuck out the far end of MacArthur Boulevard!'

'Oh.'

'Which reminds me,' she went on, changing the subject. 'There's a party at the end of next week I'd really like you to come to. A very small one. The Gershweiners are throwing it for Jerry DiSenzio. He's giving up his political column at Christmas.'

'Jerry is?'

'Yes. He's taking over a chat show for NBC. The

Gershweiners rang the day you got back: Jerry wants you to be his first guest.'

'Jerry DiSenzio wants me to appear on his chat show?'

'Yes. Now that you're such a celebrity, darling. Not to talk about . . . about anything, of course —'

'Just to — *chat* — right?'

Martin chuckled. He picked up the fruit knife again and speared a peach from the fruit bowl. He held it up on the knife so the juice ran yellowly down the blade, and went on chuckling. 'What shall I *chat* about, Babs? Washington house prices? Dinner at Pierre's? The problems of an only son who can't settle down? Us and our marriage?'

'What's so funny about us?'

He gazed at her, trying to bring her into focus, and then reached out and touched her hand. 'I don't know,' he said, shaking his head. 'I really don't know. But I think it's time I went to bed.'

It was a long time before she followed him. He heard the terrace door open and close, and the creak of the rocking-chair on the wooden boards. He must have dozed off, because when he opened his eyes Barbara was in her nightdress getting into bed beside him.

He took her hand. Her pale pink nails were filed almost down to the quick. 'It must have been rough,' he said, in a kind of apology.

She lifted his arm over her shoulders and rested her head against him. Instead of the usual whiff of a scent by Halston or Gres, he fancied he could smell the sun on her, an earthy attractive smell of warm skin. Without looking up at him, she began talking in a low voice.

'You know what happens. You must have done it too. I just lost hold on things. I didn't know who I was any longer. Mrs Martin Commoner — who's she? The wife of a man who isn't there? I started to wonder if you'd ever been there — I mean, except as a kind of landlord who comes in the evening and pays all the bills and goes visiting with you at weekends. And then I'd start counting all the times I'd accused you of getting home late, and still being someplace else when you got here; and I'd start thinking it was my fault you'd been kidnapped, and that I'd driven you out, you know?'

'Oh, Babs.'

'And then — oh God, the old traumas. About not knowing what anything was for, or where I was heading, except around in circles. It was okay in the daytime. But eight hours of darkness is a long time to go between drinks.'

'Did you try Geoff Maclaren?'

'Geoff was out of town.'

'What about Ms Feinstein?'

'I got her on the phone. I couldn't leave the house. Besides, this was her first kidnap. I got the impression analysis hadn't prepared her with the correct response.'

Martin nodded at the glass of orange on the bedside table. 'All this is why you're washing out your system with fruit juices?'

'Some well-wisher sent over a litre of Glenfiddich malt whisky. It gets you from A to B. That was all I asked.'

'Did Max bring it?'

'It just arrived.' She shuddered involuntarily and looked up at him now. 'Tell me about Max Hemming. I'm curious.'

Martin shrugged. 'There's not much to tell. His profession is to know more about people than they know about him. What did he tell you about me?'

'Nothing much.'

'He's very cautious, very careful; you know, the kind of guy who sucks cough pastilles for breath fresheners. The sort who always pees at the edge of the lavatory pan because it makes less noise. He's unmarried; he wears eggshell suits; he's got an apartment on the Hill, in one of those bay-fronted respectable houses behind the Supreme Court . . . what else can I tell you? He drives a Ford Mercury, he eats fast food, and he gets his hair shorn off by the Agency barbershop in the Langley basement. He's the functional, dedicated type: the sort we need to keep the wild men under control.'

The last light faded. A frog was croaking from the stream below the tennis court. Barbara said drowsily, 'You don't like him.'

'I respect him. He's got balls.'

'That's nice . . .'

'What?'

'Where your hand is.' After a moment she murmured, 'Why did we ever move apart?'

'If you mean the beds,' he said, teasing her, 'it comes back to the hours I keep.'

'Don't take your hand away.'

They lay in silence for a few minutes, watching the darkness thicken in the high-ceilinged room. Barbara lay curved into his side like a small child. He felt the soft pressure of her breast as she breathed, and thought she was asleep; but then she said clearly, 'I wish we could stay here longer. I wish it was always like this.'

'So do I.'

'I don't think we would be like the Nadersons, do you?'

The Nadersons were like several other of their Washington friends. While they were both working hard to make money, their marriage had gone well. Only when they decided on a more relaxed lifestyle did they have time to discover that they had nothing to say to each other.

'We have much more in common than the Nadersons,' said Martin.

Another silence followed. Barbara's hand slipped downwards. Martin felt himself suddenly stiffen, as if he'd taken a dose of Spanish fly. Pulling back the sheet, he began making love to her, not moderately and slowly as their custom was but with rough thrusts, passionately as a lover, while with tightly-shut eyes he felt for her open mouth, pressing his own down on it and stifling her gasps of pain and triumph.

Then he rolled off her, and lay with his eyes open, not hearing what she was saying to him but staring at the window, and wondering how long before the moon broke through and set the black knives dancing on the wall.

WEDNESDAY

For the first time in ten days, Martin woke gently and peacefully. Leaving Barbara to sleep, he got out of bed and massaged his ankles vigorously. The swelling and soreness was almost gone, so he put on his running shoes and shorts and went for a gentle jog, as he did most mornings in the city.

Three times around Potter's Key was all he could manage. Limping back to the kitchen, he found Barbara making coffee and toast.

'I'm as weak as a rained-on bee,' he said, slumping into a chair.

'You can't expect to be back to normal.'

He glanced at her. Barbara's blonde hair hung loose around her face, giving her a girlish look; but there was a tiredness and redness about her eyes. He wondered if she had been crying, and was suddenly irritated with her for no reason at all.

She brought him coffee. 'Can you remember how to do an old-fashioned barbecue?' she asked.

'You mean, rubbing two sticks together?'

'Not that bad. I've found a couple of firelighters. John's bringing the charcoal.'

'Then what's the problem?'

A quick little smile. 'There isn't any problem.'

'Good.' He gulped his coffee and went upstairs to shower, feeling the vague irritation prickling him like a cold in the head. The problem was, he was surrounded by people with silly smiles on their faces. What he needed was some straight talking; somebody who punched back.

He stayed upstairs, prowling round the house until, much later, he heard the throbbing vibration of the Agency helicopter bringing in his son. From the balcony, he watched the lanky, straw-haired figure shamble across the pad, bending under the rotor blades. Barbara came up to embrace him, throwing her arms round him perhaps so that she could whisper words of warning about Martin in his ear. Then she went on to speak to the helicopter pilot, who had furnished himself with a picnic lunch to eat by the stream.

John looked up. Immediately, Martin left the balcony and went downstairs. He found them on the terrace, waiting for him.

John awkwardly patted him on the shoulder. 'Hi, Dad. What's it like to be a hero?'

'What's it like to be a half-wit?'

'You've lost weight.'

'That's right. And my hair's gone white and my nails have fallen out. So what else is new?'

They grinned at each other affectionately. 'How's Linda?' Martin asked.

'She's okay.'

'They've split up,' Barbara put in.

'*No, Ma!*' John's amiable face screwed up in exasperation. 'It's okay. We're in our own lives, that's all. She's got a lot of things to work out right now.' He looked at Martin and shrugged, as if to say how tiresome it was that mothers had to have things spelled out for them.

Martin was still grinning. 'Did you remember the charcoal?'

'It's in the chopper.'

'Okay, haul it over. Let's get started.'

For the barbecue Martin had chosen a small brick patio beside the terrace, sheltered from the wind that came funnelling down the valley. One of the tripod legs was broken, so they hunted around and lugged out two breeze-blocks from the garage to support the grilling pan.

'I should have brought this out yesterday,' said Martin. 'I caught a 15-inch trout, did Barbara tell you?'

His son feigned amazement. 'Hot shit! Another two weeks out here and you'll be trapping bear and making snow boots.'

'Okay, wiseguy. You're not such a great handyman. I'd be surprised if you can tell one end of a gun from the other.'

'We don't use them in my line of work, Dad,' said John with a smile.

Martin prodded the charcoal with a twig, thinking how to recover lost ground. 'Talking of work, how are you making out?' he asked.

John's long face lit up. He pushed his unruly yellow locks up his forehead, and his Adam's apple bobbed up and down. 'Terrific. Did Ma tell you about the exhibition?'

'The photographs?'

'Yup. It's going to be a sell-out. The *Post* has got a piece in today, I brought it for you to see. We've really attracted some big names, you know? Brett Weston sent us one of a sunset he took at Point Reyes, and there's a little spot way out in the ocean which in the enlargement you can see it's a head. And John Vernon in the Art Department — really gruesome — he was driving along and took a picture of this car, an old Buick, that had skidded off the road. And when he developed it, what he had taken as shadows turned out to be legs sticking out from underneath. Weird.'

Martin remembered how the guerrillas had got Solowitz in Buenos Aires. A peaceful Sunday morning; a man washing his car on the other side of the street, casually reaching into the driver's seat for the gun. 'People don't notice things,' he said.

John cleared his throat. 'Did you notice anything?' he asked awkwardly. 'I mean, when they kidnapped you?'

Martin shook his head. 'Just an icecream van. A girl in a blue dress holding an icecream. And the Park Warden pointing a pistol at my head.'

John seemed to be examining his tennis shoe. He picked at a bit of loose rubber on the sole.

'Did they . . . hurt you much?'

'Nope.'

'It must have been pretty scary?'

'Yes.'

'When people asked me what you'd been doing, I —'

'Who?'

'What?'

'Who asked you about me?'

'Jesus, Dad. Friends of mine, okay? People who knew you were my father.'

Martin nodded, lowering his eyes to the charcoal.

'So I said you were engaged on a high-level diplomatic peace mission. It worked a dream. Now they all think you're a cross between James Bond and Averell Harriman. Ain't that a joke?'

John's eyes were pleading. Martin stared at him, unable to speak. He saw the pride and the fear in his face, and understood, for the first time, just how much his son needed to believe in him. This was what Ishmael must have felt about his own father: the more troubled he was by what his father did, the more fiercely he would be impelled to defend him.

'Dad?'

Martin shook his head. 'There's no need . . .' he began.

'No need for what?'

'I think . . . I think we're ready to eat. I'll go get the steaks.'

He stood up. At that moment Barbara came out on to the terrace carrying a plateful of red steaks which she had marinaded in barbecue sauce.

'Who's for lunch?' she cried.

'Hey!' John raised his hand.

'The franks are inside.'

'I'll get them,' said Martin. 'John, why don't you lend a hand with the salad.'

'It's done,' Barbara said.

'Okay, I'll fix the drinks. Beer? John?'

'A Coke. Please.'

Martin was already inside the terrace door. Rubbing his head, he walked quickly through the house and up the stairs to the bedroom, where he lay on the bed with his hands over his face. His thoughts were confused; he could not fathom what was wrong with him. The people who had done this to him: they were John's age. Whenever he looked at John, he saw a judgement in his eyes. But why? What had he to be ashamed of? Nothing. Nothing at all. What they said to him in the tent — was it his fault? Was he missing something? From below he heard his wife and son accusing him. In Ishmael's voice: *David Bisley trusted you. He was really loyal to you, Commoner. He said you were his buddy. He said you were one of the only good guys at the top.*

'Martin!'

It was Barbara, from the kitchen. He took his hands away from his face, scowling at his feebleness. Nobody had the right to judge him; youngsters least of all. He went downstairs and poured himself a scotch with a steady hand, and took a long drink of it before going out into the sun.

Waving a spatula, John was discussing one of his teachers in a loud voice. 'It's bullshit,' he exclaimed, without looking at Barbara. 'The man's a piss-artist.'

'Who's that?'

'You know him, Dad. Our celebrated Professor of International Politics, no less. He's set us a paper to argue the case that, I quote, "The ultimate practical and moral test of political behaviour is not the ends sought, or the means used, but the consequences that result directly from the action."' He shrugged. 'I mean, you know —'

'What's wrong with that?'

John let his jaw drop. 'Well if you can't see . . . I mean he's saying, go ahead, murder this guy, if it gives you credit on the bottom line. If the consequence works out for you, get there any way you like! It might justify his own foreign policy, in Vietnam and Latin America, but to me it stinks.'

Martin shook his head. 'I think you've got him wrong. That's not what he's saying at all. He's suggesting that even if you do something for the right reasons — like, say, saving the Chileans from Marxism — if the direct consequence is murder, torture and repression then your action is bad on all counts.'

He took the spatula from his son and began turning over the steaks. They were sizzling and giving off a delicious smell. 'People in college are always talking about the means to an end as if it was that simple,' he said with an edge in his voice. 'The fact is, you can't look that far ahead. Everything you do in dealing with foreign governments has to be one step at a time, in case the consequences get out of control.'

John paced up and down beside the barbecue. 'Is that the way we behaved in Vietnam? In Chile?'

'I'm not defending —'

'And what about General Videla in Argentina? Jailing and killing thousands of left-wingers had the consequence he wanted: it kept the opposition quiet. According to you, that means he passes the practical and moral test of political behaviour, right?'

John was deliberately baiting him on his home territory; Martin liked the chutzpah of it. 'You're mixing up the ends and the consequences,' he explained. 'The *end* might have been to keep the opposition quiet; the *consequence* is the disappearance of thousands of innocent people. Videla might have called that good; I can't speak for him. *We* would call it unacceptable. Babs, what's your opinion? I think the steaks are ready.'

They ate with their plates on their laps; Martin and Barbara sitting on the end of the terrace, John on the grass resting his back against an old wooden water-butt. The CIA pilot had finished his meal and was sun-bathing on the grass beyond the tennis court.

Looking up, John said with his mouth full, 'Okay, so what are you not defending?'

'I'm sorry?'

'About Vietnam and Chile?'

Martin thought for a moment. 'If you mean the Agency,' he said, 'I guess you're right, we misjudged the consequences. We're not diplomats, like State. We don't have the time to sort out all the conflicting interests over negotiations in luxury hotels. Intelligence is war by another means, and for us the war has already started. Us and them. Right and wrong, no half measures. And sometimes — *sometimes* — that's meant the ends have blinded us to the consequences.'

John got up and carried his plate over to the terrace where Martin was sitting. He screwed up his face in agitation and pushed his yellow hair back over his forehead. It was the same gesture Ishmael had.

'Are you seriously trying to tell me that that's what life's about? Dad? That it boils down to a straight fight between us and the Commies? I mean, do you seriously believe that? Is that what you do with your life?'

'John!' Barbara cut in sharply, but Martin hardly heard her. He heard the naive astonishment in his son's voice, and he fancied he heard pain and disappointment there too, and it filled him with a sudden anguish.

'I spent the last week hog-tied in a tent having to listen to people like you', he growled. 'It's because we keep the peace that you're free to hold all your half-baked notions of moral justice.'

'Yeah, sure, but —'

'Just because the guns aren't firing and the bombs aren't coming down doesn't make it any less real. There are still casualties. Human lives get wasted.'

'Sure —'

'It may seem like a game to you. Like looking at photographs

178

of something that shouldn't be there. But by God it's real to me.'

Martin bit his lip to stop himself ranting on. What was wrong with him? It wasn't what he'd meant to say at all, if John hadn't riled him. John had gone red in the face, and his Adam's apple was moving rapidly up and down. He grinned lopsidedly, and gave his father a mock salute.

'Sorry sir!'

Martin disliked himself. 'Forget it,' he said. 'I'm a bit strung out, Babs will tell you. Listen, why don't you and I go for a walk down the stream? I'll take you round my domain, eh?'

He stood up. John laughed and backed away. 'I'd love to, but I need to go. I've got about eighteen famous photographers ringing me from all across the States this evening, you know? Great lunch, Ma.'

He bent awkwardly like a flightless bird and gave her a peck on the cheek. Barbara gazed at him with a worried frown.

'Is there anything you want?' she asked.

'Nope. Y'all make sure you come to my exhibition, okay? Bye, Dad. Take care now.'

With that, he ambled off towards the chopper, calling to attract the pilot's attention. A moment later he was back, with Tuesday's *Washington Post* which he offloaded on the rocking-chair.

'It's a family issue,' he called out. 'Don't forget I'm in it too!'

'What's he mean?' Martin asked, as the helicopter whirred into life, rattling the lunch plates.

Barbara shook her head and gathered up the remains of the food. At the door into the kitchen she said, 'Looks like you frightened him off.'

'He had to go back anyway.'

'I think you could have been nicer to him.' She went through, and her voice floated out from the kitchen. 'You know this damn dishwasher has died on me?'

Martin didn't answer. He was staring at the front page of yesterday's *Post*. Looking up at him was a photograph of his wife. Below it the caption read, 'INSIDE: *Mrs Martin Commoner Talks About Life with A CIA Boss*' . . .

'*Barbara!*'

His fingers shaking, he turned the pages hurriedly. The interview with his wife took up nearly half a page, next to an announcement by a jeans manufacturer of a prize for the best bottom in the District of Columbia. Under a headline, 'The Man I Love', it carried an extract from the letter he had sent her from captivity:

> *Remember me for all the good times we had together. The day Harpers took your first article and we borrowed Bob's boat and went sailing in Long Island sound ... We have shared so many memories together, don't let them fade.*

Disbelieving, Martin read on. The interviewer, a woman, was putting intimate questions to Barbara about their private life. *How did you feel when he was kidnapped? Did you have anyone to turn to? Is it easy being married to a top man in the CIA? Does he confide in you? What is your recipe for a happy marriage?*

And Barbara hadn't kicked this woman out of the house or reported her to the police. On the contrary, she had answered every question, as frankly as if she was talking in confidence to a close friend!

She had been 'devastated' by his kidnap, he read with prickling horror. She had been terrified that he would be brave and refuse to tell them what they wanted to know. She had experienced 'much pain', and switched from moods of resenting her husband for making her suffer to 'tears of guilt' for being 'so selfish'. His farewell letter had been given her by the CIA and described as a softening-up tactic by the kidnappers, but she knew at once it was genuine by the love and heartache in it. After reading it, she had gone to her bedroom and cried for three hours. She had felt closer to him at that time than she'd ever been — 'a kind of union of our souls'.

It was 'challenging, sometimes frustrating' being married to Martin, like it would be to any senior government official who worked twenty-four hours a day. But she had always taken the attitude that 'marriage is a job to be worked at like any other', with the burden as well as the joys to share, and that was her idea of how a happy marriage should be ...

Martin had dropped into the rocking-chair. He looked up to see Barbara standing with a dishrag, reading over his shoulder.

'I meant to tell you,' she said.

'You ... you ...' He was choking with anger and bewilderment. 'How could you do this to me?'

'Darling, it wasn't me. I didn't give them the letter. Your people made it public, I told you so. They said it would create sympathy.'

'Sympathy!' He was beside himself. 'And does this create sympathy? Exposing our lives like ... like some peekaboo machine? Jesus, Barbara! Why didn't you take your clothes off for *Playboy* while you were about it? Or sell your fantasies to the *National Enquirer!*'

'Shut up!' Barbara's mouth was trembling; there were tears in her eyes. 'I'm not your son, you can't bully me like that. I was told to do that interview. I did it to show I was standing by you. If you can't see that, you're a damn stupid pig-headed blind idiot!'

He got up and faced her, crumpling the page in his hand. 'It's my life too, you didn't think of that. What *were* you thinking of? I've just been through the worst experience of my life. Drugged, humiliated. I come back to recover my self-respect, get some peace and privacy, and here you are hanging me up in public view like washing on a line.'

He flung the paper on the ground. Barbara knelt and picked it up, the tears coursing down her cheeks.

'It wasn't my idea,' she said in a low voice.

'Who was it? Judy Gelb? I can just imagine —'

'Someone from the Agency. I don't know who. They rang up and said someone from the *Post* was coming round and if this interview appeared in the English papers it might influence the people who had taken you.'

'No. Not the Agency. No-one at Langley would stoop to that.'

'Someone did — and why not? They might have let you go, that was all that mattered. I think you're being bloody unreasonable —'

'It was someone else. A con trick. Why didn't you check with Max? You had a line to him. Or were you too busy getting your hair done for the photograph? You know how I feel about publicity. I just don't understand you, Babs. I don't understand.'

He went past her into the house. She came after him and took his arm. He pushed her away.

'Leave me alone.'

'Martin,' she pleaded.

'Please. Leave me alone.'

181

He walked through the house rapidly, in no partiuclar direction. The thought of the newspaper story went with him, like a stain on his underwear. Going into the hall he noticed the gun on the rack. He took it up and loaded it. Then leaving the house the front way, so as to avoid Barbara, he strode off down the garden and into the wood, taking the route he had planned to take with John after the barbecue.

It was cool in the shade. The wood smelled of autumn, even though the green leaves on the trees were pretending that decay hadn't set in. A rabbit shot out from under his feet and sprinted away into the gloom. He fired at it and missed. From the house he heard Barbara call his name, and smiled bitterly. He knew what she was imagining. That would have given the *Washington Post* something to write about.

He walked on for a while, crossing the stream at the stepping-stones he had come to when he was fishing the day before. It was incredible that she could suppose that the Agency had encouraged her to give that interview. It went right across all established practice; it broke all the rules. But who would have made that phone call? Surely it wasn't the kind of ruse a journalist would have the nerve to try. Not even Jerry DiSenzio.

He recalled what Hemming had said in the Director's office. *A political connection. Someone in Washington who wants to give the CIA a bad name.* At the same instant he thought of James Traill in his office, smiling at the camera and mouthing his prejudices about the Agency.

Traill.

It was absurd. He was a respected Senator (respected by some). The Agency had dug into his past when he'd first raised his head on the Church committee, and they'd found nothing to dump on him. But Traill had been tipped off. And he had the motivation. He'd been fighting for years to get tougher oversight on CIA operations. Any ammunition would serve where he was concerned. Operations that went wrong. Personal failings . . .

Nancy?

He stopped for a moment, kicking idly at a green fungus that spread over the stump of a tree. All these thoughts of conspiracy! It was what he had come out in the fresh air to clear his mind of. It wasn't the kind of reasoning that the General would let pass. 'Circumstantial evidence!' he would bark. 'I don't want suppositions, Martin, I want the facts!'

But a remark of Ishmael's (it had made no sense at the time) came back now to haunt him — *How do you think we'd have got you here if it wasn't for them?*

Trust. It was all a matter of trust. Start losing trust in people and you were in a morass. No landmark in sight and no way of knowing which way to get back on to firm ground. For the hundredth time since Martin had arrived in Potter's Key he thought back to what the DCI had said about BeeSting. The Israelis had trusted him. Mutual trust, that was the whole reason BeeSting had gone ahead. Remove that trust and — what? Everything fractured . . . distorted . . . like a face seen through a splintered pane of glass.

He trudged through the dry undergrowth until he came to a barbed-wire fence which blocked his path. Unslinging his gun he pushed it through and crawled after it. This had to be national parkland, he thought, and almost at once had it confirmed by coming to a well-cleared path up the hill.

Bisley must have felt that way. Seeing the faces of his friends, the people he needed to trust, distorted out of true by suspicion. Trust was intangible. You could never be sure of it once you had stopped taking it for granted. Even in your family, in your own son, you could not be sure of it.

Maybe Bisley had worked all this out for himself a long time ago, and that was why he had offered Mitchum his loyalty. He was breaking the rules of course. In the CIA you played by the rules or not at all. But what if Bisley, as a street man, understood something about loyalty which the rest of them, blundering on about treason and lawbreaking, had utterly ignored? That if you weren't loyal to your friends and loved ones you couldn't be sure of being loyal to anything else? He'd preached at John just now, but the fact was that he, Martin, had never faced the ultimate moral test over Bisley. The ends and means might have been honourable, but the consequence was a suicide. His gun over his shoulder (illegal up here, but what the hell), he came out on a spur where the ground dropped away sharply through the thick trees towards the valley floor. From here there was a good view of Potter's Key, the only house in sight, standing foursquare in its clearing of lawns with the tennis court on the left and the track snaking away up the top of the valley. Shading his eyes he could even make out the rocking-chair on the terrace. Of Barbara there was no sign.

The wind blew smells of pine from the hillside. It was obviously a popular vantage point: in the neat wooden trash basket beside the path he noticed discarded wrappings of rolls of ciné-film. But the view didn't soothe him. He had no desire to encounter any passers-by. He set off down the way he came.

By the time he got back, the late afternoon sun was lipping the edge of the brick patio where the barbecue pan still lay. The house seemed deserted; Barbara did not answer when he called her name from the terrace. He went upstairs, finally, and found her lying on the bed with a cold compress over her eyes. He sat beside her.

'Babs, I'm sorry about this afternoon.'

'That's okay.'

'I guess I need your help to get over this. More than I'd figured.'

'Uh-huh.'

'It's odd . . . living on your nerve-ends . . . how you start suspecting things.'

Barbara made a restless movement with her hand. 'Please don't talk to me. I've got a headache.'

Her hand fell back on the blanket. Martin sat in silence for a few minutes. Then he got up quietly and went downstairs.

When Barbara came down later that evening, Martin was in the kitchen, a three-quarters-empty bottle of Scotch beside him, watching a soap opera on the portable TV.

'I want to get back in time for a lunch tomorrow,' he said, thinking about Nancy.

'What do you want to eat?'

'Did you hear what I said?'

'I heard you. Is an omelette all right? I don't feel like cooking, much.'

'That's fine by me.'

He got up to turn off the television. With her back to him, cracking eggs, she said, 'Get me a Scotch and water will you? Make it a large one.'

She had a second whisky before dinner, and another couple with the food. They ate mostly in silence.

'Babs, I've told you I'm sorry,' he said as he poured her fifth drink.

She said in a muffled voice, 'You fired that gun on purpose. You wanted me to think you'd killed yourself.'

'That's ridiculous. I went hunting, like I did yesterday. You're being paranoid.'

She flushed. 'You're not the only one living on your nerve-ends. How do you expect me to feel? First you drive our son away —'

'That's not true . . .'

'And then you start on me. Now you decide we're going home early. What is it? Aren't I good enough for you? Is there someone else you want to hold your hand?'

She was shrilling at him, trying to hurt him. He cut himself off from her disappointment. 'You've had too much to drink,' he said.

'Is that all you've got to say?'

'Yes.'

He pushed his chair away from the table. Barbara stood up and threw her glass of whisky in his face. Then she burst into tears and rushed out of the room.

He did not follow her upstairs. He read for a couple of hours on a sofa in the living-room, and then lay down on it and closed his eyes. A surge of weariness scattered his unhappy thoughts and left a blankness, into which he fell asleep.

THURSDAY

Martin slept deeply until dawn. When he woke, he looked into Barbara's face and thought for a moment that they were in bed together. In her nightdress, with a shawl over her shoulders, she was lying on a pile of cushions beside the sofa with her head resting back against the arm.

She could not have dyed her hair for some time: he could see strands of grey among the blonde. She had given him the best part of her life, it occurred to him. She had waited for him in Washington when he went out to Saigon. She had followed him out to Buenos Aires. They had been through a lot together — the death of one child and bringing up of another. You didn't throw all that away for a splash of whisky.

He lifted her hand off the sofa and held it in his.

Barbara opened her eyes, which were still red from weeping, and frowned at him slightly as if she was trying to read his thoughts. Then, without speaking, she laid her head on his chest and closed her eyes again.

They lay like that for another hour or so. Then Martin heard steps on the driveway and, a moment or two later, the back door quietly opening. Lifting Barbara's head, he eased himself off the sofa, put on his shoes and went out to the kitchen.

It was a youngish woman, with mousy brown hair tightly bunched under a headscarf and big round tortoiseshell glasses. When she saw Martin she gasped and nearly dropped the milk she was carrying. 'Oh boy, I didn't expect to see *you*,' she said.

Martin shook her hand. 'Hallo. I'm Martin Commoner.'

'Of course you are,' she said, smiling and revealing buck teeth. 'You're in all the papers!'

'Ah. Well, we really appreciate your groceries. Can I make a contribution?'

'No problem. They're paid for. Hey, you're really a hero! I'd have brought down some of our home-cured ham if I'd known.'

'I'm not a hero, ma'am. Just a survivor. Thanks all the same.'

After she had gone, Martin poured himself an orange juice and checked his watch. 8.00 on a Thursday morning. He should be at work right now. He felt superstitiously that the sooner he could immerse himself in his job, the quicker he would sink below the public horizon and become normal again. Not pausing to make himself a proper breakfast, he hurried out to the phone in the hall. He had his lawyer to ring, Nancy's secretary to confirm lunch, Geoff Maclaren to call if he was back, and Betty at the office to arrange for the helicopter.

He was on the phone for the next hour. At some point Barbara brought him coffee; he thanked her with a glance. Geoff Maclaren, whom he'd finally tracked down at the Georgetown Center, was explaining that Kathy his little girl had the day off and he was taking her to Washington Zoo. Martin arranged to meet him there at 2.30.

'Our delivery girl tells me I'm in the papers,' he went on to Maclaren with a note of anxiety in his voice.

'Just a couple of paragraphs, floating the idea of a ransom demand.'

'Ransom demand? There wasn't a ransom demand!'

'You might be more interested in something that's just come in. Libya and Pakistan have just signed a mutual defence pact, under the umbrella of the Moslem Alliance.'

'What!'

'It's not public yet, but I thought you'd like to hear. The worst thing is, as far as we can tell here, it gives the Libyans access to the Pakistani bomb.'

Martin swiftly changed the subject. Geoff didn't know about BeeSting and he didn't want to compromise himself. But it occurred to him, as he put the phone down, that the Israelis would be getting desperate. And that was bad news for Peter Fisher.

He'd have to thrash it out with the General at dinner. Things were moving fast, too fast for his liking. He'd had his rest-cure. He was ready for some action.

* * *

Squinting in the bright sunlight, William Pomfret looked at his watch. It said 5.00 in the afternoon. By the clock in the dashboard of the L.A. police Cadillac it was only 9 am. The Detective Chief Inspector adjusted his watch from London to Los Angeles time and yawned. 'Excuse me?' he said politely to his driver, a handsome black detective who in the shade thrown by his peaked cap looked like Sidney Poitier and, for all William knew about this city of showbusiness, might well have been.

'I was saying if you'd come into Long Beach airport, you'd have flown over your famous old ship the Queen Mary.'

'Uh-huh.'

'Sure. You'd have come in over the Queen Mary. But not for long. She's getting towed away. Now see there?'

They were driving past a giant hoarding with the words 'Paradise Island', on which the snout of an airliner nosed towards two bikini-ed girls sunning on a palm-fringed beach.

'Very nice,' said William.

'No, the sidewalk. Last week I picked up the victim of a shooting on the sidewalk there. When I went up to him he said, "Don't touch me, man. I'm clean." Clean? Huh! He had four bullet holes in him. He was bleeding like a pig.'

'Did he pull through?'

Poitier shrugged. 'Some do, some don't.' In a city in which up to ten homicides were reported every day, it was obviously only the zany or offbeat angles on crime which caught his attention any longer. As if reading William's mind, he went on, 'We're like the airlines. If you run a shuttle service you don't have time to worry about your passengers either end.'

'I guess not,' said William. He pressed a button, and his seat reclined with a luxurious sigh. It was just like on TV. He lay back. It had not been his idea to come straight out to California, where the trail was old — rather than to Massachusetts where the kidnappers had landed, or to Washington where Martin Commoner was and where Ishmael might be heading. But the FBI hunt was headquartered on Los Angeles, and without its invitation he could not have made this trip.

Poitier drove down a ramp into the semi-darkness. Going into the FBI building from the underground car-park was like stepping out of a hot bath into a freezer compartment. William, feeling the sweat grow cold on his face, followed the police driver down several brilliantly-lit corridors, past FBI agents, secretaries and filing-clerks, their collars buttoned up against the air-conditioning.

'We're heading for IS-2,' explained Poitier. 'That's domestic intelligence. Under President Carter it was down to two men and a dog, but it's picked up since then. Mr Krantz, he says it's almost back to what it was in Nixon's time.'

'Mr Krantz?'

'Yeah. He's your contact. He runs Screwball Alley.' Seeing that William looked none the wiser, he amplified. 'Mr Krantz runs all the domestic security cases that isn't commie-socialistic in definition. It's mostly Hispanics, but we get a few screwballs like yours shooting their feet.'

Mr Krantz, as it turned out, was not to be found in Screwball Alley after all. His assistant, a small nervous man with round black glasses balancing on a button nose, directed them to the basement where Mr Krantz was testing out some audio-visual equipment that had just come in.

From the respect which everybody seemed to have for his contact, and the two macabre anecdotes which Poitier dispensed on the way down, William assumed he would be meeting a cross between Vanderbyle and Charlton Heston. But when Poitier softly opened the door into the darkened basement room, all William could see was a shapeless mass, culminating about four feet off the ground in rolls of fat, upon which sat an enormous head with two little ears sticking out at right angles. The head was silhouetted in the flickering light of a large video screen, from which came a low babble of voices.

Poitier stepped in the doorway. There was a loud crack and a scream. The lights went up. What they had seen was the crouching bulk of a very fat detective who, when he stood up, towered at least five inches over William. His head was scarcely more attractive from the front than from the back. His features bulged up in the middle of his face as if they had been squeezed there from the sides: a small dimpled chin, pouting lips and a puffy red nose that looked as if it had been pushed on as an afterthought. Only the small grey eyes, deepset and glinting, gave his face intelligence and humour.

William was introduced by Poitier, who at once removed himself. The fat man shook his hand.

'Allen Krantz, call me AK. You did a great job,' he said without enthusiasm. 'Has the CIA given you a medal yet?'

189

'Not so as I've noticed.'

'Well you should. You saved those assholes a lot of embarrassment. They couldn't locate the hump on a camel. Take a chair, Mr Pomfret. Let's talk about this.'

William was getting frayed at the edges. He hadn't rested on the plane; he was tired and dirty. But he needed the FBI more than they needed him. He sat down.

Krantz lowered himself on to a bench beside him. 'The CIA looks after its own,' he said, scrutinising him. 'They don't mess with the Feds and we don't mess with them. So how come they sent you to us?'

'They didn't. Johnny Wax did. I'm not here for the CIA, I'm here for the Yard. If the CIA had its way, I'd still be in London.'

William explained something of his relationship with Vanderbyle, watching Krantz's face brighten visibly. When he had finished, Krantz did not answer him directly. Instead he gestured at the audio-visual equipment around them and asked, 'Ever seen this stuff before?'

William shook his head.

'It's new training equipment. It's how we teach the rookies to hold on to their balls. Let me show you, Inspector.'

William wanted to say that he hadn't come 8000 miles to play charades, but he bit it back. Half-amused, he allowed Krantz to put headphones over his ears and a laser gun in his hand and guide him to a firing position about 50 feet away from the video screen at the end of the room. 'I'm gonna talk you through this,' came Krantz's voice through the headphones. 'The gun you're holding —'

'It's heavier than the British police issue —'

'It's the same weight and grip as the Magnums we use here. Now, as I switch the lights off you'll see the picture come up, and you're on a desert road about to overtake a speeding car which may contain a couple of bank robbers.'

Hardly pausing for breath, Krantz took William through an elaborate stop-and search routine, followed by a car chase and a gun battle in derelict mine workings. It went on too long for Krantz's comfort. Instead of aiming for the head and upper torso, as the LA police cadets were allowed to do, William bided his time, finally disarming one gangster and shooting two tyres out on the car in which the other one was trying to make his escape.

When the lights went up, Krantz rubbed his nose and sighed, 'If we taught our rookies that way we'd never get them through the Academy.'

William said, 'If we *didn't* teach ours that way we'd have everybody baying for our blood.'

At that, Krantz finally rumbled a laugh. 'Here, we tell 'em, if you want to be loved, go join the ambulance brigade. Let's go upstairs, I might have a couple ideas we should work on. Things you ought to know.'

The Angler's Inn, where he'd arranged to meet Nancy, was about six miles out west along the Washington Memorial Parkway. Martin saw Barbara off in the Agency limousine, then hailed a cab from the Observatory Pad.

All the way there, he thought over what Geoff Maclaren had said about the Moslem Alliance. Not until the cab pulled in to the car-park beside the Angler's Inn did he realise with a shock that he was about to complete the journey he'd set out on ten days earlier. Even the building itself, with its stone walls, gables and fat chimney-stack, looked like the kind of English hotel Nancy would have gone to. He stood in the car-park for a moment, looking at the white metal tables and chairs in the courtyard, trying to collect his emotions. But he didn't know what he felt, except that somehow the sexual excitement Nancy always aroused in him was missing. He wanted to see her; he longed to see her — but another part of him told him he was going in to meet a stranger.

Head bowed, he picked his way between the chattering couples in the yard. Inside the fake-antique lounge, he stood motionless at the corner of the bar for a moment, accustoming his eyes to the dim light.

He saw her then. She was sitting upright on the edge of a badly-stuffed sofa, staring into the fireplace, smoking a cigarette. The candles in the hurricane lamp on the table lit up her strong cheekbones and the curve of her jaw, and put highlights in her dark hair. She was wearing a quilted blue skirt and a pink high-necked blouse, and a navy jacket waiting to slip off her shoulders. For a moment Martin forgot everything except the sight of her, and stood for a moment longer, drinking it in. He had been in town for four whole days without being with her: that was the only unpardonable crime.

He went up to her, and blew out the candle.

Glancing up at him with an ironic smile which trembled at the corners, she said, 'Hello Martin. Are you trying to tell me something?'

'Only that I don't need the light to see how beautiful you are.'

'Or that you operate better in the dark.'

Grinning, he sat down beside her and raised her hand to his lips. 'Hello Nancy.'

She smiled again and looked away. 'This place is such a sham,' she said. 'Look at those copper tea-kettles. Circa 1970 I should think.' She stood up. 'What do you say we get something to eat?'

The dining-room, up the spiral ship's stairs, was relatively empty. They chose a corner table. Nancy sat with her back to the wall. She leaned over and put her hand on his. Martin felt how cold it was.

'I thought you weren't coming back,' she said.

He divined her meaning. 'I'm here now.' Seeing the tears in her eyes he added, 'You know, I'm so sorry I landed you in all this mess —'

'Oh!' She was smiling and crying at the same time. 'You're pretty dumb for a superspook, you know that? I don't care about all that. It's you. It's you I care about. You.'

He squeezed her hand. There was a lump in his throat. Before he could speak, a waitress came up to them with two large menus. 'Hi, how are you today,' she said flatly, and left.

'So?' asked Nancy, looking at him.

'So what?'

'So how are you?'

'Me? I haven't felt so good in weeks.'

'After what you've been through, that's not a compliment,' she said reprovingly. 'What are you looking at?'

'I'm looking at you. Who needs a menu?'

'Very funny.' She made a wry face. 'Do you think I've changed?'

'Put the menu down so I can see. Your hair is longer.'

'No it's not.'

'And didn't your eyes use to be green?'

'Oh God.'

192

'Also, I hear you're chairing committee meetings. You have that kind of important look about you. Like Meryl Streep in that film about Washington, serious with responsibilities —'

'You want to have lunch with me?'

'Okay, I take it back. Peace. Peace and love. What are you having?'

'Anything but fish. This Angler's Inn makes me feel seasick. How about a caesar salad?'

'You know what I like about you?'

'No. Tell me.'

'Everything.'

As they ate, the restaurant began to fill up. He glanced at her. Her dark head was turned slightly. Her chin was resting on her hand and she was looking down her nose at him through half-closed eyes. Her tip-tilted face had an inquisitive, ironic expression which made him smile.

'It's been a long time,' he said apologetically.

'Don't worry. It's the same at Christmas.'

'What did you think when I never turned up?'

'I *thought* . . . I thought I hadn't divorced Stefan in New York and moved to Washington just to trail halfway round the world after a man who's just as inconsiderate. That was before the phone rang.'

'Right. And back here? What's been going on?'

'Oh, I chaired committees. Got important.'

'Seriously.'

'Well. Let's see. I attended meetings of the Capitol Hill Women's Political Caucus. I went to my Book Group with Elise and May and Laura Cohen and Betty Schaefer. Last week we were at Laura's, discussing *Pride and Prejudice* from a feminist viewpoint.'

'Oh Jesus.'

Nancy tapped her cigarette and said, colouring slightly, 'I had to leave early because Laura was going on about you and how awful it was. I went home and rearranged all my furniture. Isn't that dumb?'

Martin took her hand, lifting her fingers, noticing how her nails still looked ragged although she'd filed them. She only wore one ring, which Stefan had given her before they were married. She never wore a lot of jewellery, like Barbara did. It got in her way, she'd told him once. Like high heels — you

, couldn't wear high heels if you wanted to keep up with the men down the corridors. He'd thought of her saying that when he'd seen Esther in her running shoes.

Nancy pulled her hand away. 'I need a manicure, if that's what you're thinking.'

'No. I was wondering if you'd moved the old Japanese peasant in the bedroom.'

She shook her head.

'Or the bed? You didn't throw the bed out?'

She fluttered her eyelashes outrageously at him. 'Mister, you're pretty horny for a kidnap victim.'

He grinned. 'I just like to know what's changed while I've been away.'

'I changed the sheets.'

'You did?' He couldn't wipe the grin off his face.

'And I bought a new comforter.'

'I'd love to see it.'

'It's pink, with streaks of white in it.'

'Can I come and take a look at it?'

Her eyes opened wide in mock innocence. 'What, now?'

'Yes. Or no, I mean.' Martin sighed. He wanted to forget everything that had happened to him. But events were taking over. He was tied to them, like Prometheus chained to the rock.

'Give me twenty-four hours,' he said.

Nancy dropped him off on Macarthur Boulevard. In high spirits, Martin took a taxi to the Zoo past the Cathedral, directing the cab driver along the valley road from which he could look up at Nancy's apartment building close by Connecticut Avenue. He thought with affection about the man he was going to meet. Geoff Maclaren had joined the Agency in the same year as Martin, and they had immediately struck up a friendship based on the mutual feeling that they were smarter than the rest of their intake. This conceit must have communicated itself to their mentors, because within eighteen months they were separated. Except for brief interludes, Martin saw nothing of him for the next eleven years.

Both of them had luck with promotions, and Geoff Maclaren would have been a strong contender for the job Martin was in if there hadn't been a messy relationship with a married woman while he was Chief of Station in Paris. Maclaren, characteristically, had admitted everything (most of Martin's colleagues would have dissembled their way out of it), and he had been brought straight back to Langley to head a team working on operational strategy.

In this rôle, less than a year ago, he had pulled off the biggest intelligence coup of his career. He had gone down to Fort Chaffee, Texas, where the Government was still holding several hundreds of the Cuban riff-raff sent across with Castro's blessing during the Carter administration, and selected twenty of the loudest malcontents. He flew them to a secret training camp in Florida, where they were told they were going to be trained as guerrillas to take part in an invasion of Cuba. When Maclaren was ready, they were made to believe the invasion was beginning. They were given Cuban weapons, Cuban battledress and false passports for cover, and flown south by night on a long journey in an unmarked plane to a landing strip in the jungle. There they followed Maclaren's instructions to go east with their heavy load of weapons and make contact with the main invading force, codename M-19.

Several days later, Colombia officially suspended diplomatic relations with Cuba, claiming that Castro had brazenly intervened in its internal affairs by sending weapons and advisers to its left-wing terrorist movement M-19. The Cubans, who had no way of proving they hadn't flown from Havana, exchanged an American jail for a Colombian one — until the CIA, through intermediaries, could pull them out.

Officially, Maclaren had now left the Agency and was based at the Georgetown Center for Strategic and International Studies. Unofficially he was still a useful contributor at Langley policy meetings and had kept his security access to the personal CIA files in the basement. More than that, he was one of the few people now who could really be trusted . . .

It was a warm bright afternoon and the Zoo was quite crowded. That suited him. Martin strolled up the path past the restaurant and the Giant Panda House with its 'Out of Order' sign, and finally ran them to ground in the Hippo House, a large gloomy building with rubber plants and a tiled floor. Kathy, sucking her ribboned pigtail, was staring at a baby hippo dozing under a hosepipe shower. In the next cubicle, another hippo floated half-submerged and motionless like a lump of sewage in a pool of murky water.

Maclaren took his arm. 'I bet you didn't know,' he declared, 'that this Zoo has had amazing success with pygmy hippos? That it's bred more pygmy hippos than any other Zoo in the world? Isn't that so, Kathy?'

'Yes.' The little girl turned an attractively freckled face to Martin, and shook his hand. 'We had lunch in the Cathedral Luncheonette,' she announced.

They walked out slowly, loitering so that Kathy could inspect the two fat Nile hippos at the end. Maclaren chatted easily. He seemed to Martin to be the first natural person he'd met since getting home from England.

'How's Barbara?' Maclaren asked.

'She's got a new job. She's helping out at the Dahlgren Medical Library three days a week.'

'Yes, but —'

'Oh well, you know. She's pretty hyped-up. My fault, probably. I mean . . . I think we both are,' he concluded lamely.

Kathy was scampering ahead of them. Maclaren asked quietly, 'Is Nancy an issue?'

'With Barbara? No. No reason why she should be. We go our own ways, we always have.'

'Good. So blackmail's a non-starter.'

'Blackmail? What are you talking about?'

Maclaren coloured slightly, one of the penalties of his pale complexion. 'Martin, you know how the Russians operate. Any handle they can find —'

'The Russians! *The Russians!*' His exasperated cry made an old lady who was passing look fearfully over her shoulder, and provoked a wail from a nearby baby carriage. 'I tell you, Geoff, the KGB has nothing to do with this. If anything, I was framed from here. And I intend to find out who by. I've got enough enemies.'

'Who, for example?'

'The Agency has its enemies in Congress.'

'Granted.'

'Senator Traill, for one. He would have known I was in England.'

'Jim Traill?'

Maclaren said no more, but his tone had been of incredulity. Martin felt a twinge of impatience.

'I know it's hard to take, Geoff. God knows. I've spent the last four days coming to terms with it. But I don't like coincidences. I brood on them. And Max is right. Bisley's son and those other freaks couldn't have pulled this by themselves. There's a high-level involvement here; maybe more than one; maybe using Jonathan Bisley as a sleeper. Geoff, I want you to help me nail 'em.'

Maclaren looked at him hard for a moment without speaking. Then he said, 'Are you sure?'

'I know what I'm doing.'

They were in the Monkey House. It echoed with the screams of apes and the sound of children's voices. Kathy was staring through the glass windows at the barred cage of M'Wasi, a gorilla on loan from the Bronx Zoo. While small birds pecked at its yellow droppings, the animal itself was hunched in a small cubicle halfway up the back wall, its head turned longingly to the window, sniffing the fresh air. Martin looked at it and shook his head in sympathy.

'Do me a favour,' he said. 'Look out David Bisley's file, you've got the clearances. I want to know who his contacts were at Langley. And I want to know whether surveillance was ever put on his son.'

Maclaren nodded silently. Kathy came running up to them.

'Daddy, can we go see the elephants now?'

'You know what they say about elephants.' Her father grinned at Martin. 'Hell, I've forgotten.'

Martin left them at the Elephant House and drove back home down Rock Creek Parkway. His parking space was occupied; he had to park across the street. As he hurried across the road, three reporters and a photographer came out from nowhere. One of the reporters thrust a microphone at his face.

'NPR, Mr Commoner. Can you tell us if your kidnappers have been captured yet?'

'I don't believe so.'

'What did they do to you, sir?'

'No comment.'

'Have you recovered completely?'

'How do I look to you guys?'

'Just fine, sir. Was a ransom paid for you?'

'No comment.'

'Are you back at your desk now, Mr Commoner?'

'No comment. That's all I have to say. Watch out for your fingers.' Martin slammed the front door on the microphones and camera. Barbara had fallen asleep watching TV. Without disturbing her, he went upstairs to change.

There was no problem with clearances this time. A car came for Martin at the stroke of 7 pm, and took him straight to the underground garage at Langley. He was joined in the elevator by the CIA driver, who accompanied him as far as the DCI's outer office on the seventh floor.

The smile Mrs Lomax turned on was almost effusive, compared to the wintry reception she had given him on Monday. 'They're in the French Room,' she said, ushering him through like a visitor.

The panelled and luxurious French Room could hold eighteen or twenty dinner guests. Martin was relieved to find only four people waiting there for him: the General himself, Max Hemming, Vince Addams and a younger man whom Martin recognised as Paul Shusterman, Max's new deputy.

After a moment's dead silence, everybody started talking at once, shaking his hand and clapping him on the back, each with a prepared greeting. The DCI opened a bottle of pink champagne and handed Martin the first glass.

'You've sure as hell got your colour back,' he exclaimed. 'How was the fishing?'

'I landed a 16-inch trout.' He coughed.

'You caught a trout? That's good. And how's Barbara?'

'She's borne up very well. But she's still under strain. She's had a tough time.'

'She's a wonderful woman, Barbara. A real sweetie. Max, you don't know what you're missing.'

Max Hemming flashed his boyish smile. 'Women like that don't grow on trees,' he declared.

'I should hope they don't!' said the General with a bark of laughter, in which Addams and Shusterman joined. 'I see they're bringing the chow in,' he added, using one of his favourite expressions. 'Let's go eat, gentlemen.'

They sat down to dinner by the light of artificial candles — a precaution against discolouration of the specially-designed plaster ceiling. There was a note of forced conviviality about it all which Martin recognised in the frequent short silences before the DCI turned the conversation to the Washington Redskins or Vince Addams launched into a scurrilous account of a private party at the town house of one of the royal Saudi princess in Riyadh.

It was the first Martin had seen of Addams since his abduction (as he now preferred to call it). His face was as puffy as ever, and there were dark rings under his eyes. Martin wondered if he had an opium supply. It would not have surprised him. He knew several Arabists who'd taken that route, and Addams was the type to go native. As a field agent he had been in his element, mixing with the rabble and picking up tips. He should never have been brought in to head up Martin's old desk: administration made him restless and aggressive, boorish too. It was said that Addams drank heavily and beat up his wife; he could well believe it.

His steak was too rare. Since the abduction he had developed an aversion to red meat. He took a sip of the fruit juice and waited impatiently for the General to finish his baseball story and get to the point. It was typical of the DCI to bide his time. For all his soldierly directness he was an expert at hedging his bets — listening to advice and letting things happen without appearing to steer them the way he wanted. He liked to call himself a trimmer, after one of his heroes, the seventeenth-century British statesman Lord Halifax, who preferred retreat to failure and believed that the highest good sense came in knowing when to leave things alone.

But the General was now ready to discard the Trimmer's mantle. After a blistering condemnation of the Redskins' latest defeat, he turned to Martin without pausing and said, 'Talking of robbery, I guess you know we've let it get out it could have been a ransom kidnapping?'

'Yes.'

'How do you feel about that?'

It was Max speaking this time. A typical counter-intelligence question. Martin glanced up and saw three faces turned in his direction.

'I appreciate we're stalling on all fronts until Ishmael and the others are caught,' he said carefully. 'The ransom idea is as good a blind as any. But you say Jerusalem want proof, and my feeling is we've got all the proof they need. We know Bisley's son was involved, and there's a sound motive there. We know about the girl.' He paused. 'Why don't I go talk to the Defence Minister? I can convince him —'

Addams was shaking his head violently. The DCI acknowledged him and broke in. 'It's too high-risk, Martin. The Israelis have got us over a barrel. They won't budge until they're a hundred per cent certain and then some.'

'What about BeeSting? The Israelis aren't going to hold on much longer, especially now. Damn it, General,' Martin pushed his plate away, holding on to his temper. 'Maybe I shouldn't be saying this, but I think we've got to take the ball and run with it. Up to the Bay of Pigs, this outfit used to take risks, play for high stakes, in the belief there was something worth fighting for. It seems to me the game's the same but we've lost our instinct for it. We hang back. We get tied up in the politics. You know it never used to be this way.'

His appeal struck home. He could see the DCI wavering. But before he could reply, Max Hemming cleared his throat.

'The tests . . .' he murmured.

Martin glanced at him. 'What tests?'

'The usual ones.' Max grimaced. 'Martin I'm really sorry, I know how you feel, but it's procedure. I think you'll agree we can't break the Agency rules. Even for the DDO.'

'You mean you want to check my story on the polygraph?' Martin smiled grimly.

'Just routine questions. Tomorrow, 1 pm, we'll go over the ground with you. You'd be surprised how much amylobarbitone can make you forget! Isn't that right, Paul?'

Shusterman, reddening at having to venture an opinion in such august company, nodded. 'The truth drugs professionals use have worse effects still,' he said slyly.

Martin's throat was dry. He poured more fruit juice and drank it, spilling a few drops on his chin. He looked at the General, who nodded, frowning at the tablecloth.

'Let's wait on that, Martin,' the DCI said gruffly. 'It's worse to fail than to appear to hesitate, as Kennedy used to say. Let's stall a bit longer.'

A brief silence hallowed this decision. Mrs Lomax, who always waited at table when it was one of the DCI's confidential dinners, cleared the plates and brought in the coffee. Martin thought about something he'd been told during training when he'd first joined the CIA — 'It's a family you're coming to, and family rows are the toughest. The analysts want one thing, the spy-runners want another and the political operators something else. If you want to get places, you have to tussle for your point of view all along the line.'

Loudly, Addams broke in on his thoughts. 'Martin, how about these guys? Did they really quote scripture at you?'

'Yes. That was their method. Ishmael was the one —'

'Are you talking 'bout Jonathan Bisley?'

'The same. When I think of him it's as Ishmael. He was the one used as the voice of conscience. The other two, Luke and Zed, preached salvation at me, you know the kind of thing. "What shall it profit a man if he gain the whole world and lose his own soul?"'

In the momentary silence, Addams chuckled uneasily. 'Nice kids. What about the girl?'

'She didn't talk about anything much.'

'Hah,' said Max Hemming suddenly. He took a small pill-box out of his jacket pocket, unscrewed the top and dropped two sugar-substitute tablets into his coffee. 'In your letter to your wife,' he said, blinking rapidly, 'you talk about agents being often betrayed.'

'The agents of freedom, Max.'

'Whose betrayal did you have in mind? Your own?'

'No. I meant it generally. I was talking in generalities.'

'I can appreciate that.' Max nodded. 'By then you must have been feeling pretty sore at not being rescued.'

Martin paused, looking at the Counter-Intelligence head. He knew the way his protégé's mind worked, how he persisted when the pattern eluded him. He wasn't going to fall for that, he wasn't going to admit to thinking his colleagues could have betrayed him.

'I wrote that letter expecting to be killed,' he said in an even voice. 'It was a private letter to my wife, to raise her spirits, give her strength —'

'Oh, sure, I —'

'It was not written to be publicised. Nor to be an exhibit in a court of law.'

Max raised his hand with an apologetic smile.

The DCI interrupted. 'It wasn't my idea to release your letter,' he said. 'But Max is right, it might have done some good.'

There was an awkward silence. The General cleared his

201

throat. 'What bugs me is this,' he said, glaring round the table. 'These sons-of-bitches mounted a damn fine operation to kidnap Martin. Then they turn out to be religious wierdos who want to save his soul. Now I don't care for coincidences. I brood on them. And the fact is, they picked Martin up when we were fully extended on BeeSting, one of the most critical operations we've ever handled. What's the connection?'

They all looked at Martin (Addams with a half-smile on his face). Martin felt himself darkening with anger. What were they trying to get him to say? That he was the spy? That he'd set himself up? The absurdity of it appalled and amused him at the same time. Shusterman was gawping at him as if he was some sort of agent from the KGB. He was probably getting ready to use a Psychological Stress Evaluator on the tape-recording of this question-and-answer session. That was why the General had served only soft drinks and fruit juice with the dinner . . .

'General, your guess is as good as mine,' he said with a casual air. 'Maybe Peter Fisher can shed some light on it, when they let him go. Max, if I've been framed, if there's any question of that, you'd better find the bastard that did it.'

Hemming nodded. 'Leave it to me. There's one other thing —'

'Excuse me, Max.' It was the DCI interrupting again, all sweetness and light. 'Let's take a raincheck. This was a welcome-home dinner, remember? Martin, I just want to say I think you've come through like a pro. I'm sure I speak for everybody here when I say you've been an example to all of us.'

Hemming raised his Perrier water in salute. Addams muttered indistinctly and coughed. Shusterman said nothing.

'Thank you,' said Martin. 'I'll tell you something,' he added as they got up from the table. 'I read a book once called Optimism. I remembered it in the tent. The scientist was testing theories about death. He placed rats in large containers of water and made them swim until they drowned. The wild rats last only three or four minutes; they die of despair. The laboratory rats on average take between sixty and eighty hours before they sink to the bottom; they're used to laboratory ways and hope makes them go on swimming.' He stopped and looked round at them. 'I figure we're all laboratory rats here,' he said.

Mrs Lomax had gone home. On the way out, Martin took Max

Hemming by the elbow and steered him into a quiet corner of the anteroom.

'Max, you asked me on Sunday about a political connection. Someone with a grudge against me or against the CIA.'

'Right.'

'There is someone. Jim Traill.'

'The Senator?' Max looked at him curiously. A smile began to spread across his face.

'No. I'm serious. Traill's got an obsession about this place. He'd go to any lengths to get prior oversight through Congress. And if BeeSting explodes in our face, he's got what he's after. There's something else. Nancy Koscinski.' Martin swallowed. This part came painfully. 'Traill will have known that Nancy was in England.'

Hemming nodded. 'Does he ask her questions about you?'

'Not that I know of. But he's no fool. He can put one and one together to make two.'

Hemming blinked and looked away. 'A pity about Miss Koscinski,' he said reflectively.

'Why?'

'I mean, her being in England, it distorts the pattern. It's . . . untidy.'

'Love affairs often are,' said Martin with a grin. 'See you Saturday.'

Leaving Max to finish up with the General, he went into the corridor and buzzed for the elevator. He was still smiling to himself. How . . . *Californian* Max Hemming was. He was head of Counter-Intelligence; he had the best mind of the lot of them; but there was a rawness about him, a kind of innocence which was almost dangerous. He was pristine, in the way of many people, especially from the far West, who saw such bounty and opportunity all around that they felt they had no need of the past and the cautions of the past. Every morning they discarded the past like an old skin and faced the future as if born for the first time, with no more sense of morality or history than they could pick up in the twenty-four hours before it was time to start again. It was this simplicity that had given Max his ruthlessness. Martin used to envy it; now he was not so sure.

The elevator arrived. There was a man standing in it. With a start of surprise Martin recognised his driver, who nodded briskly as if he had been waiting for him. He stepped in with his chaperone. The elevator door closed behind him.

At a press conference in Islamabad, the Soviet Foreign Minister praised the Moslem Alliance and warned of the dangers of American military imperialism in Pakistan. In Washington, the President took the salute at a march-past of disabled veterans from Vietnam. Here in LA, Louella Markovitch, socialite wife of the film magnate's son, had been mugged and shot as she left a beauty competition for toy dogs which was being held in aid of the American Red Cross.

William tried a couple of other channels, then switched the thing off. For some minutes, he sat in his pyjamas at the end of the bed staring out through the mesh curtains at the purplish glow from the neon *Vacancies* sign hanging the other side of the invisible swimming-pool. In another 90 minutes it would be dawn in England. He had to get to sleep before his brain alerted itself to keep him wakeful. But this city, this country, delighted and appalled him too much for sleep. It seemed to have no secrets. Everything was out in the open ... the violence, the riches ... there was no cover. It was like *High Noon*: the crime was in full view and the detective had no choice but to go out on the streets of America after it, hoping he packed more ammunition.

Krantz had taken him up to IS-2 and filled him in on what they had. It didn't add up to much. William was again made to understand that there wasn't any love lost between the FBI and the CIA. As Krantz growled, scratching the hairs on his chest, the spooks were still trying to rustle his cattle, as they had been for years. Domestic intelligence-gathering was a job for the FBI: the CIA had the whole of the rest of the world to play in; that was what they were set up to do, and the sooner they returned to it, the quicker they'd get help from the Feds when one of their golden boys went missing.

As it was, there was little Krantz could tell William that he didn't know already. The FBI had pulled in their West Coast informers from Mendocino down to San Diego. Jonathan Bisley's surviving relations had been questioned — a couple of cousins and an uncle in Boston — and they had drawn a blank.

204

They knew everything about him and nothing. They had his birth and school records. They knew his Social Security number and his driver's licence (New Jersey, expired). They knew his height (five foot eight), his last recorded weight (150 pounds), the colour of his eyes (brown) and of his hair (black, frizzy). They had information on his bank account and on his last recorded bank transaction, a transfer of funds to Britain one week before the kidnap of Martin Commoner. But on the kind of things the Detective Chief Inspector needed to know — whether he swaggered or sloped, the sort of clothes he wore, whether he spoke with a lisp or an accent, the hobbies he had and the obsessions — in fact what made Jonathan Bisley into a human being — the Feds were silent, and not a little condescending.

Krantz's researchers had unearthed an old photo of him. That at least was a bonus. William picked it up off the TV console, and felt a fleeting pang of nostalgia for the marmalade jar on Jenny's kitchen table. It was from his old class-book, and it showed Jonathan Bisley in his graduation-day costume, staring proudly out with a slight superior smile twisting the corner of his lips. In one hand, with disarming vanity, he held his spectacles. On his black suit he had pinned a lapel badge with the message, 'I Love America', picked out in a pattern of stars.

William had a photograph of Esther too, but it told him little. It was more recent than Bisley's, perhaps three years old. But in his experience, posed photographs of women gave almost nothing away. Women had the gift of being able to change their appearance and personality much more radically than men, and in the picture he had been given by her mother she was evidently Margaret Jones still, no apparent relation to Esther, made up to the nines and with a bored smile on her face, playing the child of the family.

But Esther was his only lead. Krantz had done some checking, and was able to confirm that as Margaret Jones she had attended at least three semesters, maybe more, at the University of California, Santa Cruz, in 1980. This meant that there were still people in Santa Cruz who remembered her. An agent from the San Francisco office had tracked one down.

Krantz gave him this information grudgingly, as if he had no interest in it. But when William announced his intention to fly up there the following day, the FBI man had clasped his hands across his belly and scowled at him.

'You're fresh out of England, you don't know your way around.'

'I want Bisley. I don't have that much time.'

'There are two people working on Commoner in the field office up there right now. And one of them's off sick.' Krantz unclasped his hands. 'I'll drive you up myself,' he said, his small eyes darting to watch William's reaction. 'I'll send a car round to the motel at ten, Mr Pomfret, if that's okay. Right now I think you could use twelve hours' sleep.'

As so he could. But not yet. Getting to his feet, he went over to the bedside tea-kettle and plugged it into the socket as the instructions explained. Then he sat down at the dressing-table and studied one of the motel's guest postcards, a night view of the neon-lit *Vacancies* sign with the swimming-pool glowing in the background. Turning it over he began to write.

'*Darling, a pc from the City of Dreams,*' he scribbled in his neat, small hand. '*Had a lousy flight on British Airways, food better than usual. LA stifling but v. quiet — nobody walks the streets. My boil has gone down, but may have another one coming up. Off to San Francisco tomorrow, hope for sun, will write from there. Miss you and have to make do with a plastic teamaker. XXX to kids, Love Wm.*'

The tea was ready. On his way over he picked up the photograph of Jonathan Bisley. He was about to put it on the table, but he was struck again by the expression of pride, of desperate pride, in the tensed-up figure, and sat on the bed gazing at it for a long time while the tea-kettle bubbled and hissed behind him. Ishmael, he had called himself. Ishmael, the outsider, the cast out from God. Looking at him, William knew he would strike again. He had nothing to lose; nothing to repent.

FRIDAY

The phone went all morning. First Barbara answered it, telling callers that Martin was asleep. Then at 9.00 sharp, as punctual as always, Betty his office secretary turned up on the doorstep, bringing the private mail that had collected for Martin in his absence.

Martin was in his study, at the cherrywood desk which Barbara had bought for him in New Hampshire after they were married. Despite the sun outside he had kept the blinds down, and put the desk-lamp on. 'Betty, thank God,' he said. 'You can take some of the heat off Barbara. She's been parrying half the goddamn newspapers in America, plus the *Washingtonian*, National Public Radio and a TV crew from England. Plus I've had four literary agents and a film agent from Hollywood asking for rights in the story.'

'I'm not in the least surprised.' Betty stepped briskly across the room, clutching her mail and notepad with one arm across her bosom in the way Martin knew so well. With her lined, ageless face and black hair set in a 'fifties wave, she looked as though she would never be surprised by anything. But when she dropped an advance copy of that week's *Time* magazine on his desk, she nevertheless did allow herself a smile.

Martin picked it up and swore very softly. On the cover it had an artist's impression of his face, blindfolded, and a diagonal strap-line which read bluntly U.S. SECURITY.

There was another photograph of him inside at the press conference, with Barbara and the General standing so close to him it looked as if he was being supported. The article below followed CIA guidelines to the letter, praising Martin in fulsome terms for his courage and endurance and giving a brief, approving account of his career. So far, so good. It then went on in a more critical spirit to examine other cases of CIA disappearances, kidnappings and unexplained deaths in recent years, from the death of Jack Paisley in 1978 through the CIA hostages tortured in Teheran to the disappearance and likely assassination of three CIA operatives in Greece three months ago. It then returned to Martin's case, concluding that if the Agency could not be trusted to carry out foreign intelligence safely, congressional oversight would become inevitable.

'Hogwash,' said Martin. He spun the magazine in the air so it landed face down on the carpet between them.

Betty bent with her knees together and rescued it. 'Are you going to send a letter?'

'Not yet.' There were more important things to do, things Betty shouldn't know about, like finding out who wrote that *Time* story and then tracing any contact links to Traill.

Breaking in on his thoughts, Betty put his mail on the desk in front of him. 'You're meant to be having lunch today with the editor of the *Strategic Review*,' she said. 'It was fixed up a month ago —'

'Cancel it.'

'And you're due to be giving that lecture at Aspen this weekend. On security developements in the Middle East.'

Martin rubbed his head and sighed. 'Have a chair, Betty,' he said. 'Let's sort out my life.'

It was nearly midday before they were through. Betty fielded several more telephone calls, explaining that Martin was in conference and could not be disturbed. Halfway through the morning Barbara put her head round the door to complain that she'd been bugged by a photographer taking pictures of her all the way from the car to the front door. Half an hour later she went out again, wearing dark glasses, to the weekly Intercultural Coffee Hour she helped run for the Office of International Programs at the University.

By the time Betty left, Martin had begun to feel he was getting back into control. As soon as the polygraph business was finished, he could climb back into the driving seat. His abductors would be caught; from what he heard, they had no money and no place to go. But somehow he could not bring himself to think about them in a hostile way. What did it really matter who they were or what they had wanted for him? They were the catalysts, that was how he saw them now: the shapers of an experience which had changed his life, made him realise that there was nothing he could take for granted, not the trustfulness of friends nor the loyalty of colleagues. You were on your own in this life. When it came down to it, you were on your own — an outsider.

But his aloneness made him all the more keenly aware of the forces ranged against him. Try as he may, he could not rid himself of the growing conviction that here in Washington there had been a conspiracy on his life, a conspiracy that was still active. The more he thought about it, the more agitated he became, until he had to get up and walk around the room. How could he run Traill to earth? Had Hemming followed up on him? It would be disastrous to confront the Senator too early. He must talk to Nancy . . .

The phone rang. Nancy? He picked it up. But it was one more journalist, Jerry DiSenzio, who had somehow gotten his private number.

'Keep off, Jerry. It's not for you; it's not political. It's a straightforward felony case, abduction and attempted murder.'

DiSenzio gave a braying laugh. 'In this city, everything is political, nothing is straightforward. My CIA sources tell me your clearances have been suspended. Is that right?'

'Bullshit. It's total lies.'

'Don't get mad at me, old buddy. I just write the news. The word is, you haven't got your red tabs back because you're not yet back on full operational capability.'

'What does that mean?'

'You tell me.'

Martin felt a moment's panic. 'Listen, Jerry. If there's a story here, I'll give you background on it soon as it breaks. That's a promise. Until then, you've got nothing to write about.'

'It's a deal. I'll hold you to that.'

Feeling more vulnerable than ever, Martin rang the Middle East desk at Langley. When Addams finally came to the phone, he could think of nothing to say to him. He blurted out, 'Is there any news from Jerusalem?'

'No.'

'What do the cables say about Peter Fisher?'

'Nothing.'

'C'mon, Vince. Open up a bit. What's going on down there?'

The Middle East head gave another non-committal answer. He would not be drawn on their dinner the night before, either. Coldly, Martin broke off the conversation. Anybody would think it wasn't a safe line he was phoning on. Either that, or Addams was in this too. He was ruthless enough. And a careerist, ambitious — it was no secret he wanted Martin's job.

It's no good thinking this way, he told himself. But he thought about it all the same. He thought about it all the way from Georgetown to Langley, chauffeured by a CIA driver who kept as close to him as a bodyguard. He had to explore every angle. He couldn't afford to reject any conspiracy theory, no matter how illogical. He had to consider, for example, the fact that Addams knew about BeeSting. He would have known, more surely even than Traill, the moment to strike.

How do you think we'd have got you here if it wasn't for them?

In the Agency's underground garage, they did not, this time, take the elevator, but went up a short flight of steps into a white antiseptic corridor. They walked for a hundred yards past flush doors with small printed name-plates, until they came to a door with no markings at all. This was the lie-detector room.

It was four years since Martin had been fluttered, as the test was called, and he told himself that his feelings of anxiety were no worse now than then. It was a five-yearly routine for every CIA operative and they all felt the same way about it, no matter how easy their consciences. Going to the dentist, some of them called it; others, going to the electric chair. They made jokes about it, right up to the moment they were strapped in; but jokes were not encouraged once the questioning started.

The small square room had a sanitised smell, as if it had just been unwrapped from polythene. Martin went in, and stopped in astonishment.

Larry Grueller was there, checking off questions on a yellow legal pad. One of the most brilliant psychoanalysts the Agency had ever employed for interrogations, Grueller had left Langley a few months ago. He had gone to work at a Midwestern University on a foolproof personality-assessment procedure, a project he had ironically dubbed, 'Fool's Gold'.

'Larry, what are you doing here?'

Grueller was wearing a grey scarf wrapped tightly around his neck. He squinted up at Martin through his thick glasses and shook his hand without any trace of hostility. 'Uh, I will be

210

putting the questions,' he said in his slow deep voice. 'Martin, I am sorry for this business —'

'Forget it. How's the ultimate questionnaire?'

'I have not yet squared the circle.'

'And, uh, your daughter, are you still training her to be a chess champion?'

'Bettina is beating me already. And you? You look well. Did you have a good breakfast?'

'Shouldn't you strap me in before asking questions?'

Grueller chuckled and Martin uncomfortably remembered what people said about the polygraph — the more jokes you made, the more you had to hide. He went into the sound-proofed box and sat in the chair, waiting for a white-coated technician to come and wire him up.

He was facing a blank wall made of one-way glass, behind which Grueller would be sitting looking at him. He had been on that other side, Grueller's side, often enough, looking through at the victims of the psychoanalyst's remorseless interrogation squirming like naked models in a peepshow. It was the innocent ones who flushed and stammered, who backed up on questions, contradicted themselves and sometimes broke down and cried. The guilty ones, the liars, were as cool as cucumber. They tended to answer questions quickly and confidently, smiling a lot — not to fool the interrogator, since they imagined they already had him fooled, but to calm and control the responses of their own body.

Grueller had once told him that, after years of experience, he had come to place more faith in his intuition than in the lie-detector machines. The cool, clever ones were the suckers, because they accepted to play the game on his terms and he could always beat them at it. Even hypnotised people and psychopathic liars could only beat the polygraph if it was being worked by someone who wasn't expert at it. The only agents who could buck the system were the ones who had been trained in how it worked and could fake a paranoid reaction to each question in turn, including the ones that were no danger to them.

The technician came in, with a deferential smirk, and took Martin's jacket. Grasping Martin's left wrist, he wrapped a rubber cuff around it. His right hand the technician fastened with springs palm-downwards to the arm of the chair. Around his chest he tied an inflated rubber tube, fastening it at the back. The ridged tube was to measure Martin's rate of breathing, the electrodes on the metal plate under his palm the rate of perspiration. A sensor in the rubber cuff measured his blood pressure. Wires ran from each of these instruments to three pens on a black box behind his chair, which would chart continuous lines on a sheet of rolling graph paper as soon as the interrogation started.

Martin stared straight ahead, keeping his breathing regular. Somewhere in the room beyond was another rolling chart attached to the Psychological Stress Evaluator, which would measure sub-audible micro-tremors in his voice, picking up the slightest hint of stress or anxiety such as telling a deliberate lie might provoke. To test it, Grueller would shortly slip him some outrageous question which would set up an exemplary stress pattern on the machine.

It was Max who enjoyed using the PSE. He had probably concealed it somewhere in the French Room at dinner two nights ago, which would account for those questions about betrayal. Come to think of it, Max was probably looking at him right now from behind that one-way glass . . .

He had a sudden paranoid vision of the entire dinner table crowding into the lie-detector room, invisible to him, to watch his reactions and comment to each other behind their hands. *Why did he say that? What's gotten in to him? What has he got to hide?* Addams would be pulling the General aside, reminding him of Kampiles and Barnett and whispering in his ear that as soon as you find one double agent in the CIA the odds are running in favour of finding another. Max would be standing a little apart, his arms judiciously folded, analysing, interpreting, targeting the flaws —

'Martin!'

'What?'

Grueller's voice. 'I said, are you ready?'

'Yes.'

'Very well. What is your name?'

'Martin Commoner.'

'Your age?'

'Forty-six.'

'What is your address?'

'3286 P Street, Washington DC 20007.'

'What is you job?'

'Deputy Director of Operations for the Central Intelligence Agency.'

'Where did you go to high school?'

'In Hagerstown, Maryland.'

'Did you masturbate at school?'

'Uh, I guess so.'

'Yes or no.'

'Yes.'

'Do you still masturbate?'

'Do I still . . .? No.'

That was a half-lie; an easy one to be allowed to give. The scribbling pens had the measure of him now. Larry could lay off him.

'Why did you join the CIA?'

'To serve my country.'

'Have you ever been subjected to blackmail?'

'No. Never.'

'Do the names Harry Abramson and Peter Draycott mean anything to you?'

'Yes. They were, are, radicals, left-wingers I guess. I met them working as a journalist on Daylight, before I joined the Agency.'

'Have you met them or had any personal contact with them since joining the CIA?'

'Not to the best of my recollection.'

'Have you met or had personal contact with any other communists, since joining the CIA?'

'Not to my knowledge. Not outside my professional work of keeping tabs on foreign nationals, attending Eastern bloc receptions, that kind of thing.'

'Did you employ Peter Fisher here?'

'Yes.'

'Did you employ David Bisley here?'

'I used him. I did not originally employ him.'

'Was David Bisley a communist?'

'He was suspected of being a traitor, maybe a KGB agent.'

'You said you had no contact with communists —'

'Bisley was not a communist, so far as we knew. Anyhow, we fired him.'

Martin shifted in his chair and coughed, to throw off the rhythm of the questioning. He shouldn't have snapped back that last answer, it sounded like he was getting rattled. He ought to know Larry Grueller's technique by now — asking a series of provoking, silly questions and then slipping in a really cunning one just as you were starting to underestimate him.

'I'm sorry, I didn't hear that last question,' he said.

'I asked you, when were you kidnapped?'

'At 4.30 pm, approximately, the Monday before last.'

'Who kidnapped you?'

'A group who identified themselves to me as the Family.'

'How did they know your movements?'

'It was in a local newspaper. That I would be at Leeds Castle.'

'How did they know your schedule?'

'I figured they waited for me.'

'Are you a KGB agent?'

'No, sir.'

'Who knew when you were leaving Leeds Castle?'

'I didn't know exactly myself.'

'Did Nancy Koscinski know?'

'I told her to expect me sometime in the afternoon.'

'Did you tell people here you were meeting Miss Koscinski?'

'They knew.'

'Could she have told your kidnappers?'

'Yes. But I am satisfied she did not.'

'Do you have a view on how they found out?'

'Like I say, they could have just waited for me.'

Grueller pursued this theme for several minutes, chasing down every detail on the kidnapping. Martin relaxed. This part was easy. He had been through it all with the police.

But then Grueller changed tack. 'Were you frightened when you were kidnapped?'

'Yes.'

'Did you urinate in your pants?'

'N-no.'

'You hesitate, why?'

'Later I was forced to . . . to do that. When I wasn't allowed to use the bathroom.'

'Did you feel humiliated?'

Martin paused. 'I suppose so.'

'Yes or no?'

'Yes.'

'Have you ever had a nervous breakdown?'

'No sir.'

'Do you feel afraid at the moment?'

'No.'

'Do you feel you are vulnerable?'

'Do I feel I am vulnerable? Yes.'

'Why?'

'Because everybody is vulnerable in this situation.'

'Are you vulnerable to blackmail?'

'I would say not.'

'What were your relations with your kidnappers?'

'How do you mean?'

'Were you intimate with them?'

'No, I was not!'

'Did you answer the questions they put to you?'

'I refused to answer any questions that might jeopardise the security of the United States and its agencies.'

'Which questions did you refuse to answer?'

Martin was silent. He could not think of any. They hadn't been that sort of questions — surely? He shook his head in puzzlement.

Grueller pressed him. 'Are you stating to us that you told your kidnappers everything they wanted to know?'

'They didn't want to know much. Yes, I mean. As far as I can recall I was asked no incriminating questions . . . that is, to which my answers would be —'

'Were you asked about BeeSting?'

Martin opened his mouth in surprise. Grueller should not have been accessed to that name. 'No!' he replied, shocked.

'Were you asked about high-level photographs?'

'No.'

'Were you asked about US missile bases in Oman?'

'No.'

'Did you reply that such missile bases existed?'

'No sir.'

'Are you aware that such missile bases exist?'

'I . . . I . . . can't answer that question.'

'Did you know about the use of Agent Orange by the US air forces in Cambodia in March 1970?'

'I read about it, yes.'

'Do you know that during the period of your interrogation the Soviet press agency put out details on these stories?'

'Yes.'

'Did you provide this information to your kidnappers?'

'No! No, I did not.'

The questions came on at him like a tattooist's needle, jabbing and withdrawing, circling for a new target and jabbing again, producing a pattern of answers to which only Larry Grueller held the design. Martin kept his nerve. He knew how Grueller worked. Grueller was famous for asking a question, ignoring the answer, and then later asking the same question as if he hadn't heard the first time.

That was okay. Martin knew his little tricks. He stared straight ahead, imagining he could see the motionless shadow of Max Hemming on the other side of the glass.

'Why did they let you go?'

'My guess is, they gave up on me.'

'Did they want you to escape?'

'I don't know.'

'Did they want you to come back to Washington? To spy for them?'

'No!'

'Did you kill David Bisley?'

'Hell, no.'

'Does his son think you killed him?'

'It's what he says.'

'Do you believe he thinks you killed David Bisley?'

'Yes.'

'Then why did he let you go?'

'I've told you. He tried to kill me. He was stopped.'

Martin thought of Ishmael with the knife. The tube around his chest was constricting him. He moved restlessly, wishing that his voice didn't ring so hollowly in the sound-proofed box.

'Do you approve of defectors, Mr Commoner?'

'No.'

'Are there to your knowledge any double agents in the CIA?'

'No.'

'Was David Bisley an agent of the KGB?'

'I don't know. I think . . .'

'Yes, Mr Commoner?'

'I think now he was not.'

'Has there ever been any high-level penetration of the CIA?'

'Not to my knowledge. Although I know Anatoli Golitsin claimed as much.'

'Did you express your belief, recently, that there was some person here attempting to compromise you?'

So Hemming was there. He replied carefully, 'Yes. But not necessarily within the CIA.'

'Are you an enemy agent?'

'No, I am not.'

'Has a foreign service ever tried to recruit you?'

'No sir.'

'Do you feel you have been misused by your country?'

'No.'

'Thank you, Mr Commoner.'

The technician unstrapped him. Martin sat back and let his muscles relax. He had no great desire to leave; he could have sat there answering Grueller's questions all day. Without intending it, a smile spread across his face as he contemplated the invisible Max Hemming on the other side. Max ought to be proud of his old boss. He had come through rather well.

Thinking vaguely of Haight-Ashbury days, William Pomfret had expected his FBI lead to Esther to be a bearded drop-out in sandals and frayed jeans. The contact did indeed have a beard, but it was a neat goatee in keeping with his smart pearl-grey suit and platinum cuff-links. A salesman of typewriter-cleaning materials, he talked about Esther with a distant amusement, as if he was having a hard time trying to convince himself that his earlier life had ever happened.

He had been majoring in English at Santa Cruz, two years ago. Esther had come in to a few of the classes. He was impressed by her long face, dark hair and greenish eyes, and her odd accent which he had taken at first to be Australian. After class once, when she got on her bicycle, he followed her at a distance in his car and tracked her back to a commune in the hills, out Branciforte way.

Driving straight up the hill out of Santa Cruz, they turned left before the entrance to the University and got out into open country. Krantz was spreading across two-thirds of the back seat, leaving William, who didn't think of himself as a small

217

man, to take up the other third. Krantz was talking about the Manson murders, and William could see the typewriter-cleaning salesman in the front seat getting nervous, the little droplets of sweat beading his neck under the short haircut.

'It's gone big-time now of course,' Krantz was saying. 'That's what's wiped out the wierdo cults. They've all upped and joined the Moral Majority, or the Evolutionists or suchlike. There's no afterlife in it for them — hah! No future. I mean, how many times can you be born again?'

The FBI driver nodded. 'No kidding. We used to hit the jackpot up in these hills. Sex murders, ritual murders — it wasn't always LA up front. There was a year when Santa Cruz had the highest homicide rate per capita in the US of A.'

'Turn left here,' said the salesman, swallowing.

'Pigs, they used to call us,' the FBI driver went on sombrely. 'Who in hell calls us pigs now? It's yes officer, no officer, three bags full officer, and they all come out of college in their smart grey suits and sniff coke and get into computer crime.'

'I think we're almost there,' came the salesman's hoarse voice next to him.

Krantz shifted to look at the Englishman, his gun butt pressing painfully into William's thigh. 'How do you want to play this, Bill? You want us to come up, look for some dope, while you're asking the questions? It opens their mouths.'

They had turned off the road and were bumping down a dirt track towards a meadow bordered by a stand of eucalyptus trees. William could hear voices and see the roofs of stout wooden cabins.

'Let me go in first, if you don't mind,' he said. 'Come after me in about ten minutes. You can put the screws on then, if they aren't talking.'

'Take a rod,' said Krantz, heaving at his holster.

'No thanks,' said William. 'I'll just keep saying Peace and Love until they put their tomahawks away.'

He walked up the track. The scene that confronted him reminded him of a package-holiday trip to India he had taken with Jenny once. A skinny barefoot blonde girl in cut-off jeans, clothes-pegs in her mouth, was hanging up washing on a line strung between two trees. A goat nearby, tethered to a stake, chomped noisily on the grass. Between two of the wooden houses (built of squared-off logs, frontier-style), there was a carefully-tended vegetable garden where a stocky dark-haired woman and a young boy were making small mounds of earth and planting seeds in them. Beyond, William could see a large patch of apparently wild undergrowth and tall grasses which probably concealed the marijuana crop, stretching down the hillside towards a small lake. Apart from an ancient Ford truck, the only sign of the technological age was a large notice stamped in black on orange metal saying, PRIVATE — KEEP OUT.

A dog barked. The blonde girl saw William and stood still.

'Hi there!' said William.

The girl made no response except to spit the clothes pegs out of her mouth. The goat took one look at William's dark blue suit and Fulham Rugby Club tie and retreated from him to the far end of its rope.

. 'A beautiful place you have here,' said William, aware of the impression he was making.

The girl looked at him suspiciously. She had small soft features and a slightly crooked nose which gave her face character. Snapping a clothes peg between her fingers she said, 'We don't need any insurance, mister.'

'I haven't come to sell you anything —'

'Private dick?'

'No, I'm from Scotland Yard.'

'Scotland?'

'Scotland Yard, in London, England. My name's William Pomfret. I've come to ask if you can help me.' He showed her Esther's photograph. 'Do you recognise her?'

The girl took the picture and looked at it without interest.

'Her name's Margaret Jones. You might have known her as Esther. She was here two years ago definitely. She may have lived here as recently as a year ago or eighteen months. Have you seen her?'

'Nope. Ann can tell you. She's been here three, four years. Ann!'

The stocky, dark girl who had been looking at them curiously came over from the vegetable patch, her hands in her dungaree pockets. She looked at the photograph and then at William.

'Why do you want to know?'

'She's mixed up with some people who might hurt her. Badly.'

'That figures.'

'What do you mean?'

Ann scowled. 'Esther was freaky, you know? That's why she had to go.'

'You chucked her out?'

'No, it was a democratic decision. I mean, she was sort of screwed up, you know? She thought this community was like the Garden of Eden or something and she could go round bare-ass naked, fucking for peace and love or whatever. Christ!'

'And that isn't your bag?' asked William, grasping at a dimly-remembered phrase.

Ann handed back the photograph. 'Are you for real?'

'I'm sorry?'

'We're not living in the 'sixties you know. This is a caring, relating community. We have rules. We don't trespass on each other's living space. Didn't you see that notice back there?'

A man's voice called gruffly from the nearer cabin. The flaxen-haired girl turned obediently and went inside. William took out his notebook.

'Did Esther go with anybody?'

'I told you, she went with everybody.'

'I mean when she left.'

The girl didn't answer at first. She turned away from William, her shoulders hunched and her hands deep in her dungarees, looking at the small boy who was kneeling by the flower beds making circles in the dirt with a stick. When William repeated the question, she shrugged.

'She took Luke away,' she said. 'She took Luke Purdy.'

'A big man, was he? With big hands? A round, moon face?'

The dark-haired girl turned back to him. Her mouth was tight and there were tears in her eyes. 'He was a *good* man,' she said violently. 'That's what she hated, his goodness. She fucked him up like she fucked up everything else around here. Jake was ours, Luke and me, and she'd have taken Jake as well.'

Running back to the vegetable garden she picked up Jake in her arms and smoothed his hair, as if comforting him for her own distress. Looking around, William saw Krantz and the driver coming up the track. He gestured for them to go back to the car. There would be no call for threats and bluster. The proper commiserating tone would unlock all the information he needed.

Even so, the girl couldn't pass on more than tantalising scraps of knowledge. It was the kind of frustration William had grown accustomed to in England, dealing with the shiftless, rootless generation of the young, who cut off all communication with their families and moved restlessly from place to place, changing jobs and cars and houses and leaving no forwarding address. In Krantz's words, as they drove the coast road back to San Francisco, they were the people who'd fallen off the side of the print-out, and weren't in any hurry to get back on.

The girl in the commune knew nothing about Luke's parents or where he had come from. He had driven up one day in an old truck with eighteen sacks of fertiliser in the back: that was the extent of his history. After more pressure from William, as gentle and persistent as the tapping of English rain, the girl remembered an aunt he used to talk about — perhaps the woman who had looked after him in childhood, she didn't know. Aunt Em, or M as it might be, she owned a caravan site near Pittsburgh. Or she used to.

Zed she remembered too, though not in connection with Esther. He had been a familiar sight at open-air gigs up and down the Pacific coast, until he'd discovered Jesus and dropped out of sight. A thin, hunted-looking man, he swung his guitar like Neil Diamond and sang in a husky voice amateurish songs of his own composing. He hailed from New Jersey, because that was how he had introduced one of his songs on the Santa Cruz campus. It was all she could tell William.

'How about he wanted to get famous,' suggested Krantz. 'Like Bruce Springsteen.'

'Bruce Springsteen?'

'Bruce Springsteen, he's from Jersey. Maybe Zed's after celebrity status the easy way, like that guy who shot John Lennon. Ten to one, he's writing a song about kidnapping a CIA chief for Jesus.'

'He can write about being in prison for Jesus,' said William shortly. 'Because that's where he's going to be.'

He spoke with more assurance than he felt. Nothing quickened for him out here in California. He'd found a trail all right, but it was an old one, a trail without a scent, which had lain undisturbed for months or years.

When Krantz told him in the San Francisco field office that they had located Emma Purdy, Luke's aunt, on a caravan site she ran in Clarion, Pennsylvania, he decided to make it his excuse to go east without further delay. Getting Krantz to wire ahead for him, William booked an afternoon flight to Pittsburgh.

The morning had been muggy and overcast. By the time Martin left CIA headquarters the sky had cleared and the sun was hot. Telling the driver to stop on M Street, he walked down Wisconsin to a car-rental place near the river. He took the smallest car they had, a Volkswagen Rabbit, and set off in the direction he'd taken the day before.

He drove fast, thinking about the polygraph test and checking off his answers one by one. When they'd unwired him he'd felt exhilarated, like a soldier who's come under fire and got through to the other side. Now as the exhilaration drained away, a sourer feeling replaced it, a mixture of all the resentments that had been building up since he'd come back.

The lie-detector was part of the game, of course, a necessary part, and there was the customary pleasure to be had in playing it skilfully. Probably he was imagining the note of antagonism that had run through Larry Grueller's questions. But allowing for all that, it was still almost incomprehensible that at the very moment when he ought to be taking charge of a highly sensitive covert operation which was in danger of auto-destructing, he should be shut up in a cubicle for two hours, fielding adversary questions on his rôle in the abduction.

It was over now. He could get back to doing the job he was paid for. Meanwhile, he had to find out from Nancy what was going on with Traill.

Six miles out of Washington, he left the Volkswagen in a lay-by and set off on foot down a narrow dirt track between the trees. It came out at a high green metal-frame bridge over the canal and the canal-path. He could hear the river itself, in spate, somewhere on the other side. Nancy had got there before him. Standing on the bridge, she was watching four middle-aged men in tracksuits jogging briskly along the path in the afternoon heat.

Slowly Martin climbed the steps.

Nancy squinted up at him. 'It took a lot out of you, didn't it,' she said suddenly.

'All my grey hairs, you mean? You told me you liked older men.'

'No, really. You look as though you could use a couple of weeks' sleep.' She lifted her hand and brushed his cheek. It was the first time she had touched him. 'Have they been dumping on you, at Langley?'

'Ah.' He gave a short laugh. 'Nowadays it's the victims who have to prove their innocence first.' Seeing her frown, he added quickly, 'That's a joke.'

In silence they crossed the bridge and went down another path through some bushes to the river itself. Across a thin ribbon of the Potomac, straight in front of them, was a narrow island hardly bigger than a sandbank on which stood an old green timber-framed boat-house surrounded by trees. Beside the path leading to it, and under a long green-roofed shed nearby, several ancient-looking canoes lay hull-upward on the grass.

Next to where they stood, a yellowing notice pinned to a tree leaning out over the water flapped in the breeze. Martin read out, '"Sycamore Island Canoe Club. Established 1889." Do you think we can get across?'

'There's a prohibition on swimming.'

He looked around. Nancy had sat down on a tree-stump on the bank and was staring into the fast-flowing water. She said, 'Martin?'

'Yes?'

'Do they think it's my fault?'

'Your fault?' He sat awkwardly on the grass beside her. 'Of course not. How could it be your fault?'

'Your friend Hemming talked about blackmail —'

'Oh, heck. Max is still living in the 'fifties. We're not a state secret, you and I. We've nothing to be ashamed about.'

'Do you really mean that?'

'Of course I do.'

He leaned back beside her with his arm resting on her lap, hearing the knocking of the water and the scuffing of invisible joggers on the canal path a few yards behind them. Casually he said, 'How's your Senator these days?'

Nancy's expression didn't change. 'Jim? Much the same. Living on Chesterfields and black coffee and not much else. He drives himself into the ground; I worry about him.'

So it was Jim, now. Not Senator Traill any longer. 'If he works that hard, I'm amazed he let you come to England,' he said.

'Oh no. He's hardest on himself. He told me to take time off, after I came back. But I needed to work. I couldn't have faced not doing anything.'

'Did he know . . . what you were going over for?'

'What was I going over for?'

'I mean, to see me.'

'He knew I was going to England.'

'You didn't tell him why?'

'Hey, what is this?' Nancy glanced at him. 'Of course I didn't tell him. It's none of his business. Why do you ask me?'

'No special reason.'

'Martin.' Her voice was reproving. 'There's always a reason with you.'

He stood up. Gazing at the timbered boat-house he said, 'If I could find a boat, we could row over.'

'I don't want to go over, thanks. I want you to tell me what all this is about.'

'Okay. Tell me one thing.' He turned to face her. 'Why does Traill want to cripple the CIA?'

'Oh, c'mon. We've talked about this. You think he's a lackey of the State Department. He's not. He's not anti-CIA. He just wants more accountability. It's a point of view.'

'He seemed to know a lot about our Pakistan operation.'

'What Pakistan operation?'

'BeeSting.'

To his relief, she looked genuinely puzzled. 'I don't know about that,' she said. 'I think he just wants to know why, when you were kidnapped, the committee wasn't given a run-through of the security risks. That's what he said to me.'

'What did he have in mind?'

'How should I know? I'm his legal assistant, not his security adviser. Do we have to talk about this now?'

Nancy had coloured with exasperation. She was in the clear: he was sure of it. But having started on Traill, he couldn't stop himself.

'I just have to know this,' he went on doggedly. 'Does he talk to you at all about the Agency? About his feelings for it?'

She shook her head. 'Not much. Nothing he doesn't say in public, like on Greece.'

'What did he say?'

224

'He said there are people in the Pentagon and the CIA who hate the Communist system so much, it leads them to behave as if democracy isn't strong enough to oppose it.'

'Is that all?'

'I guess he was right, huh?'

'Is that all he's said?'

He had risen on one knee, turning in towards her. She stood up abruptly, knocking his arm away. She slung her purse over her shoulder and stood facing away from him.

'Let's go,' she said. 'I want to go now.'

Martin followed her and took her hands. A muscle in his cheek was trembling uncontrollably. 'Please,' he said in a low voice. 'Nancy, there's something going on. I don't know what it is. There's somebody over here —'

'Jim?' She stared at him in anger. Her brown eyes were hard and bright, and her whole body was tense and quivering. For a moment, it was Esther standing in front of him.

'You think it's Jim?' she repeated. 'Jim wouldn't hurt a fly! Jesus, he's got enough enemies without you joining them. You know, he really admires you. He thinks you're one of the best things the CIA has going for it. And now you come on with this dumb business about him trying to frame you?' She pulled her hands away. Her eyes had tears in them. 'Is this why you had lunch with me?'

'Of course it isn't.'

'You brought me out here for this?'

'Nancy —'

She started away from him. He pulled her back. Tightly he held her to him, pressing his face against her hair.

'For God's sake, go easy on me,' he said. 'For God's sake. I need you badly now.'

He felt her relax a little; enough so that he could lift her head and kiss her mouth. She turned her head away, but not in anger.

'Let's go back,' she said.

They didn't talk much on the journey back to Connecticut Avenue. At the Devonshire, instead of driving up to the main entrance, Martin out of habit turned right down the short service road and parked outside the back entrance. The lobby was deserted. In silence they took the elevator up to Nancy's floor.

225

Inside the apartment he felt the same uneasy sense of things being subtly shifted and changed that had dogged him ever since he got off the plane. There was the same cosy mêlée of floor-cushions and pot plants and bamboo furniture; on the coffee table the same Japanese fan box with its brush painting of a sage grimly studying a dragonfly; the same familiar delicious smell of Nancy's perfume, mingled with the scent from the bunch of white lilies on the windowsill. And of course, she'd been moving things around: that would account for it.

To break the silence he said, 'Isn't that a new picture?'

'Yes. Not the real thing. Elise made a copy from a Japanese woodcut.'

'It's rather striking.'

'Oh, she's not bad. She's exhibited at the Kramer Gallery.'

'Should I know it?'

'Oh, no I shouldn't think so.' Nancy gave a nervous short laugh. 'It's the kind of place where you can get flapjacks and coffee downstairs.'

He stole a look at her. She was standing a few feet away from him, smoking a cigarette, her elbow cupped in her hand. She looked at him and looked away, tapping her ash into an ashtray hollowed out of sandalwood.

He said, with a smile, 'Agency people aren't supposed to know about art. It's regarded as a sign of latent homosexuality —'

'Which is blackmailable. I know. You told me once. I said I'd appear as your witness if you needed me, remember?'

'We can be pretty dumb about a lot of things. But we can apologise, too.'

Nancy nodded in acknowledgement, and came forward with a half-smile. 'So can legal assistants,' she said, putting her arms round his neck.

Kissing her, he drew her down on to the cushions by the telephone. Just as he was starting to look for the hook on her skirt, she shifted away from him, frowning.

'Not here,' she said. 'Not in the living-room.'

'Why ever not?'

'Let's go in the bedroom.'

'On that hard mattress you call a bed?'

'Come on.'

Grudgingly, he allowed himself to be tugged into the bedroom. Nancy left him there, shutting the living-room door behind her. Martin took his clothes off, and caught sight of himself in the closet mirror. He'd put a bit of weight back on since London, he noticed, though not as much as he would have expected. And his Potter's Key tan had already almost faded. Stepping over a pot plant, he hid himself under the pink-and-white duvet which covered the thin mattress on the floor.

There was a sudden burst of opera from the living-room. He raised himself on one elbow, puzzled. When Nancy came in from the bathroom, wearing her blue and yellow kimono, he said, 'Do we have to listen to Verdi? Isn't this something new?'

'The plants like it. It helps them grow.'

'You're kidding!'

She slipped off the kimono and slid in beside him. Throwing the duvet back so that he could see as well as touch her naked-ness, he pressed her body to him, feeling her firmness and compactness, her smoothness where Barbara was no longer smooth and firm.

'Nancy,' he murmured. 'My darling. How I thought about this!'

She kissed him hard then rolled over on to her back, smiling up at the white ceiling. 'A country walk and sex in the after-noon. Some career woman I am!'

'What would your boss say if he saw you now?'

'Poor old Jim. He could do with a really nice woman. The trouble is, he works so hard he frightens them all off.' She sighed and stroked Martin's brown hair, pulling out a couple of strands of grey. 'It's a shitty life being a woman in this town. All the interesting men work too hard. And the problem with the ones who *aren't* ambitious is you get bored with them. That's why over half the white-collar women in Washington are single. Like me.'

'Mm.'

'Besides, when do I ever get the chance to meet people?'

'My heart's bleeding. Feel it.'

'Oh, shove it!' She rolled over on him and tried to pinch him. He gripped her wrists, laughing. He loved her in this mood.

'It's okay for you,' she panted, pulling out of his grasp. 'You've got a family, and a bit on the side. We career women need security.' She was murmuring now. 'We need something we can hold on to and call our own.' She had found something she

227

could hold on to. It seemed to be getting harder all the time.

Grinning with pleasure, he slid his hand between her legs, and found her moist and ready for him. He entered her.

'Oh, yes,' she murmured, pressing her nails hard into his back, enough to draw blood if she hadn't filed them down.

My sweet lord.

He juddered in shock and recoiled from her. 'What did you say?'

It was Nancy lying there. She gazed at him in surprise. 'I didn't say anything.'

'I'm sorry. It's my fault. Let's start again.'

But he could not start again. He got up and pulled down the blinds, shutting out the whiteness. It made no difference; he was limp and useless. He knew why. The stitches had broken; his memory was bleeding back.

'Martin?'

'It's nothing.' He lay back and stared at the Japanese painting on the wall. A long way to go, to get back up the mountain.

Nancy raised herself and looked down at him. 'Is it to do with what you were saying before? About the victim having to prove his innocence?'

'No. I told you that was a joke, didn't I? Didn't you hear me, or what?'

She put out her hand and touched him. 'It's really not important. My love. It doesn't matter.'

Through clenched teeth he said, 'How do you know what's important. What do you know about it?'

She made no answer then, but turned away from him and curled up on her side as if she had been wounded.

There was silence, except for the sound of Othello dying in the next room. After a minute, Martin said, 'I never told you she looked like you.'

There was no reply. In a low voice, Martin began to talk about Esther. For the first time, he talked about his sexual humiliation: how Esther had danced in front of him to the music of 'My Sweet Lord' on the tape cassette; about her long slender feet like Nancy's, and the way her breasts had moved to the music; about how she had taken her skirt off and caressed herself in front of him and how ... he couldn't help himself ... and she had taken him in her mouth.

228

Nancy turned back to him. He put out his hand to hold her away so that she wouldn't look at his face. He had to tell her the rest, about the others watching and laughing. But it didn't matter any more. Spasms of pleasure jerked through him. Nancy was above him. He was inside her. Reaching out blindly, his hands circled her hips and he lifted his body into her, feeling the wonderful warm release. He opened his eyes. Nancy was smiling down at him. Her naked body was flushed, shell-pink and white as the duvet which floated around her in waves.

'Did I ever tell you what I like about you?' he asked her.

'Everything.'

'And then some,' he said, and shared in her laughter.

What were your relations with your kidnappers?

How do you mean?

Were you intimate with them?

No, I was not!

. . .

Were you asked about BeeSting?

No!

. . .

Did you know about the use of Agent Orange by the US air force in Cambodia in March 1970?

I've read about it, yes.

Did you know that during the period of your interrogation the Soviet press agency put out details on these two stories?

Yes.

Did you provide this information to your kidnappers?

No! I did not.

The General leaned across the table and turned off the tape recorder. He looked up from under bushy eyebrows at the four men standing opposite him. In their dark suits and conservative ties, they looked like a quorum from the local Lions — Addams flushed and aggressive, Vanderbyle with a puzzled frown on his face, Max Hemming expressionless and his assistant Shusterman smiling in a kneejerk reaction to the Director's glance.

'Is that all?' asked the DCI. 'Are you telling me that's *proof*?'

There was momentary consternation on the other side of the table. Hemming raised his head before the others could speak.

'With respect, I am not advancing theories,' he said evenly. 'I'm merely evidencing a congruity of polygraph readings. We know Martin Commoner lied on the early question about masturbation —'

'I'd have done the same myself.'

'Of course. It was a test question. But he evidenced similar stress patterns, you will notice, on the intimacy question —'

'Max, are you suggesting Martin screwed around? With a head wound, his hands tied, and doped with barbiurates?'

Hemming looked at Vanderbyle. The tall ginger-haired man gazed at the table, not meeting the General's eye. 'The police found traces of semen on the airbed, sir,' he said.

This time the twinge of backache went all the way up the DCI's spine and clutched his neck. He reached behind him for a chair and sat down.

'I don't understand that,' he said.

Hemming ignored Vince Addams who was shaking his head. He continued, in his methodical manner, giving a cough to attract the General's attention.

'There's a higher doubt factor on the BeeSting/Agent Orange question. The voice stress is similar. So is the heightened breathing rate. We now have to ask ourselves why, if Martin Commoner was lying on these substantive questions, does the polygraph register negatively on him being an agent of the KGB and/or working for a foreign intelligence agency. May I answer that?'

The DCI waved him on impatiently.

'Okay. I've been through the files, there's no evidence of special counter-training. But there would have been time, just the right amount of time, for Commoner to have been hypno-programmed against lie-detection equipment.'

Addams butted in. 'You mean, he'd consciously believe what he was saying? Believe he was innocent?'

'That's right. We've already established that if someone in Martin Commoner's position chose to defect, a violent mock-kidnap would be a perfectly logical scenario; an ideal cover for returning to his previous duties. Also, as I said to you last week, Director, Commoner is a highly experienced operator. He could use that experience to mislead the polygraph. I agree it's not conclusive. But there's one other point to bear in mind. You heard the Kremlin number two yesterday in Karachi, talking about US military imperialism in the area. Three leaks — Oman, Greece and Agent Orange — could be bad luck. A fourth — if I'm right and the Soviets have got wind of BeeSting — is too much of a coincidence.'

There was a long silence after this. The General sat motionless in the chair, his head hunched low between his shoulder-blades like an old man.

Addams broke into his thoughts. 'What about Nancy Koscinski?' he demanded. 'If Commoner can deceive his wife over all this time, he sure as hell can deceive us. I mean, he should be pretty good by now at —'

'That's enough!' The General cut across him, scowling. He got to his feet and stomped over to the window. The late afternoon sky had clouded over, trapping the heat. There would be an electric storm tonight. In the room he could sense it, even though the plate glass.

'What we need is facts,' he went on, feeling for his pipe and clamping his fingers round its comforting familiar shape. 'What you're implying about Martin, let's face it, would be the biggest disaster ever to hit the CIA. It would shake down a lot of people, including some of us standing here. So what I say is, if you're going to destroy Martin, don't do it with suppositions and innuendoes. Do it with facts.'

He turned back from the window, his pipe swivelling at the four men standing in a half-circle round the table. It stopped, pointing at Addams. 'Defects of character are damned hard to isolate,' said the DCI. 'Harder still to act on.'

Blinking behind his spectacles, Hemming responded. 'We hung that on Bisley. We were right then.'

'Martin isn't Bisley.'

In the pause while the General filled his pipe, Vanderbyle cleared his throat, his Adams apple bobbing nervously. 'About the kidnappers, sir.'

'Yes?'

'We know that the leader, Jonathan Bisley, must have used a false passport. That, and the safe-house Esther provided . . . there's a sophisticated support apparatus there. It's a Carlos Ramirez hall-mark to use young women as safe-house keepers. I don't think we should discount the terrorist option.'

The DCI shook his head. 'Go play with it if you want. I think it's highly problematical. What I need is facts. I want the goddam kidnappers. They're here now, could be right on our doorstep. What you do is haul ass and find them. Then we can give Jerusalem the green light, and bring Fisher home. Talk to Martin again if you want. Do what you have to. Just bring me Bisley and his little friends. That's all I'm asking. Find them.'

William's plane was delayed by fog. By the time the Detective Chief Inspector landed in Pittsburgh, it was already dark. It was also cold, with a chill gusty wind that buffeted Sergeant Oestricher's car every time it nosed to the top of one of Pittsburgh's steep hills.

'You been talkin' to Mr Krantz,' remarked the Sergeant, his jaws working on a piece of gum.

'In Los Angeles, yes.'

'Is it true they're switching police target practice to video machines?'

'It could be. He was testing one of them out when I got there.'

'California.' Oestricher shook his head disgustedly. 'Space Invaders ain't the half of it.'

'Where are we headed?'

'Where we headed? Clarion. It's an old township 'bout thirty, forty miles from here on the edge of the hills. Bear country. We got the Purdy trailer camp under surveillance. It's the other side of Interstate 80. Big place.'

'Has it been checked out?'

'I guess so.'

William felt a keen sense of disappointment. Since Santa Cruz he had had a hunch, almost a physical feeling between the shoulderblades, about the caravan site in Pennsylvania. Luke's aunt was the only firm lead he had. It was exactly the kind of place a group of young frightened people might have gone to ground. But if there had been any news, wouldn't Krantz surely have heard, and got a message to him at the airport?

'You know something?' asked Oestricher, chewing.

'What?'

'FBI has a collection of one hundred seventy-five million fingerprint cards? Stacked up, that's eighteen times the height of the Empire State Building?'

'Uh-huh.'

William spoke very little for the rest of the journey, replying shortly to Oestricher's anecdotes and his questions about London, England. Before long, they crossed the Interstate and drove the few remaining miles to Clarion.

It was a solid-looking American town of neat wooden houses around the usual garish main street of realtors, restaurants and motels. Inside the police station there was an atmosphere of sourness and tension. William was ushered straight through to the Sheriff's office. A wizened little man with a nut-brown face and a broad moustache that looked too heavy for his wrinkled features stood up courteously and introduced himself.

'You been to Clarion before?' he asked.

'I'm afraid not.'

'We got our own way of doin' things in Clarion. Ain't that right, Mr Mire?'

The man who stepped forward, tall, in a loosely-fitting dark blue suit, had FBI written all over him. Like William he had lost a lot of hair, the sign of a conscientious policeman.

'My name's Meyer,' he said. 'I'm running the FBI operation here. Under the Sheriff's guidance, of course.' Here he shot a sarcastic glance at the Sheriff, who had taken up a paper-knife and was cleaning his nails with it.

William interrupted. 'Have you checked out the caravan site?'

'Not so far.'

'You *haven't*?'

'We've had, uh, a little local difficulty.' Meyer glanced at the Sheriff again. 'A communications problem between us and the Sheriff here. Seems he didn't know we were coming in.'

So William's journey hadn't been wasted. His instinct hadn't after all been proved wrong — not yet. He couldn't help rubbing his hands.

'Is there any news?' he asked hungrily.

Meyer shrugged. 'According to the Sheriff here, some youngsters answering to the right description have been seen around. Howso, we'll find out tomorrow morning.'

William frowned. 'Why not tonight?'

Meyer shrugged again and waved at the Sheriff. The local man spoke slowly without looking up.

'A dawn raid. Yes sir. Catch'em with their pants down.'

Meyer amplified. 'One of the Sheriff's squad cars is out of action.'

233

'Why do we need squad cars? Hell, all I need is two armed policemen and I'd go in right away. No fuss, no noise. Isn't that the way to do it?'

The Sheriff remained unperturbed. He put the paper-knife down and strolled across to the Englishman.

'We got our own way of doin' things in Clarion, yes sir,' he said, reaching up and slapping William on the shoulder. 'We don't stint for nothin'. We'll go in at dawn with back-up squad cars and we'll have those sons of bitches runnin' aroun' with their pants down round their ankles. Now how about you catch some sleep, and I'll take you along for the ride tomorrow, eh?'

William was suddenly too tired to argue. Hungry too: he hadn't eaten since lunch on the plane. After Vanderbyle and Knight, he knew a power play when he saw one. The Sheriff had plainly decided to teach FBI a lesson: there was no point in him interfering.

Meyer had fixed him up a room in the Sunrise Motel down the street. After arranging a 4.00 am call, William went into a cafe called the Niterie, across the street. Oestricher was there. Oestricher had seen him. Oestricher had pulled out a chair. Reluctantly, William sat down, opposite a large T-bone steak which Oestricher had doused in sauce from a red and green plastic tomato.

As the steak got steadily smaller, and Oestricher regaled him with more episodes from the FBI story, William started to perspire. It could have been the pounding disco music on the jukebox, or the harsh cafe light reflecting off the shiny surfaces of formica and aluminium, or Oestricher's T-bone steak — but it was none of these. In his bones, in every part of him, William knew that the people he had been searching for, the kidnappers of Commoner, were at this moment sitting in a trailer, hardly more than a mile away, planning their next move. If he didn't get there soon —

'Your order? Sir? Can I take your order now?

William looked up at the waitress. A mood of black depression had settled on him, affecting even his appetite.

'I'll have an omelette,' he said. 'Plain. Nothing on the side.'

The man in the shiny raincoat was the last to get off the bus. He

234

had no luggage of any description, but he looked around him at the terminal, adjusting his spectacles with an air of uncertainty, as if he'd never been in Pittsburgh before. Then he set off with a determined stride, heading for the city centre.

The gusts of winds blowing up the black streets had enough cold in them to take the breath away. But the man didn't seem to feel the cold, although all he wore underneath his raincoat was a dirty white T-shirt and a pair of frayed blue jeans. He walked quickly into downtown Pittsburgh, his hands deep in his pockets and his large head thrust forward.

In the deserted streets off Liberty Avenue, his manner changed. He slowed down to a loiter and began to look carefully at the parked cars, only quickening his pace when he heard footsteps on the sidewalk. Eventually he found what he was looking for: a narrow alley with windowless walls on either side, and a shabby green Maverick parked halfway down.

He forced open the door-catch with a pocket-knife and released the hood. Hurriedly, with fumbling hands, he got the car started, crashed the gear out of neutral and drove away. According to the dial, the tank was full.

Which was nearly enough to take the man in the shiny raincoat to his destination.

Martin drove back slowly from Nancy's flat, checking repeatedly in his rear mirror. Parking outside the house, he was inside the front door before the two newspapermen waiting across the street could intercept him.

Barbara was not back. The house was empty. He took off his coat and went slowly up the wooden stairs. On the wall there were the signed photographs he'd collected over a twenty-year career. Barbara had hung them in order, the handshakes getting warmer and the signed notes more cordial as the years went by — Martin in the DCI's office, Martin at some presentation to an old White House hand, Martin with the President on the White House lawn (signed with a flourish, *All Good Wishes*) — only his smile, as he looked at them, was always the same smile, remote and a little smug, as if he'd seen the steps in front of him and was sure of his footing.

Not any longer.

The telephone was ringing. He went into the bedroom to answer it. Barbara said something to him in a sharp voice.

'Where are you?' he asked.

'John's preview, where do you think? Martin, you *promised* him.'

'I'll be right over.'

'It's no good, it's almost closing time. You can pick me up anyway.'

'Where is it?'

'You know the Arts School. It's —'

There was a click, as though the downstairs receiver had been replaced, and Barbara was cut off. Frowning, Martin tapped the exchange, and then tried dialling the operator. The line was dead, as if the cable had been cut.

John had left by the time Martin got to the Art School. He walked quickly round the exhibition, glancing not so much at the pictures — he was uninterested in arty photographs; photographs were for purposes of record — as at the general layout and the care John had taken with the captions and attributions. There were still gaggles of students around, with fuzzy heads and purple silk trousers; and someone was chanting on a tape of old rock music, '*Break on through to the other side*'. The words disturbed him. He sniffed the air suspiciously and strolled on with his hands clasped behind his back.

Going over to the car with Barbara, he said, 'If John took as much trouble over his classes he could be really good.'

'There are other things in life beside good grades.'

'You want him to do well, don't you? You said so in Potter's Key.'

'Yes. But I don't want him spending his life thinking that work, work, work is all that matters, and success equals getting to the top.'

'I don't think that either.'

'Don't you?'

She got into the car, slamming the door, and threw her purse on the back seat. Her face was flushed and she was fiddling nervously with a strand of blonde hair that had come loose from her coiffure. He wondered how much she'd had to drink.

'Let's not quarrel,' he said quietly.

'I'm not quarrelling. I'm not quarrelling. I just want John to be

236

able to keep things in perspective. You've got to accept he doesn't need you as an example any more.'

It was beginning to rain. Barbara did not put the window up; she watched the droplets splash on her long-sleeved blouse. 'Anyhow, you won't be seeing much of him this vacation,' she added. 'He just told me he's going to advertise as a bartender at private parties this winter. He's going to put ads in the *Uptown Citizen*.'

'Good for him. It's time he earned some dollars for himself.'

'Is that all you can say? Time he earned some money! That's why he's doing it: it's not to earn money, it's because we're pressurising him, pushing him out of the house!'

'Oh, Babs. Come on. I haven't even bought him another car.'

'It's true!' Looking at the little scudding raindrops on the window, her eyes filled with tears. 'I don't think you ever wanted children,' she said, 'Edward *or* John. I don't think you like them. You'd have preferred a childless marriage, with a professional type. The type of woman who thinks that careers and getting ahead are all that matter because that's the kind of ambitious bitch she is. Well, you've got half the working women in Washington to choose from.'

They drove the rest of the distance in silence, except for the wipers washing the rain away.

The house was dark when they got in. Martin pushed the hall switch. Nothing happened. He remembered the telephone going dead, and hesitated.

Barbara pulled at his arm. 'We'd better get the police.'

'No. It's okay. You wait here. I'll go to the kitchen, get the flashlight.'

Treading softly down the hall, he checked the door leading down to the cellar. It was locked. The kitchen door was ajar. He kicked it open: in the evening light from the garden he could see that the kitchen was empty. He collected the flashlight and went back.

'It must be the fuses,' he said. Any other time he would have believed himself.

He went to the foot of the stairs and called up. 'John!' There was no reply. For a moment he stood undecided. He thought of the handgun he'd been issued in Saigon. That was no use; it was in the drawer up in the bedroom. But there was his hunting-rifle in the cellar ...

He loaded it and trod quietly up the stairs. There was no-one in any of the rooms. There was no sign that anything had been taken, not even Barbara's jewel-cases.

Downstairs, Barbara was on the 'phone to the police. That puzzled him some more. A couple of hours ago the line had been dead. Either there was an electrical fault, or someone was tapping his telephone. Holding the flashlight he went back down into the cellar.

The fuse box was ajar. The main fuse was switched off. Had he done it? The worst of it was, he couldn't remember. Switching it on, he heard voices upstairs. When he went up he found Barbara standing alone in the living room. She was holding Edward's photograph. When he came in, she put it back on the table.

'That was John,' she said in a tired voice. 'He was just getting some stuff. He's gone to spend the night with a friend.'

SATURDAY

William woke with a start to see the squad car beacons flashing through the Motel window. He had slept through the alarm: it was 5.15 am. Shuddering awake, he pulled on his overcoat, laced up his shoes and stumbled into the cold night air.

The door of the squad car opened. He slumped inside. Oestricher was in the back seat, flanked by a couple of large policemen carrying the standard equipment of revolver, ammunition, nightstick, mace and handcuffs strapped to their belts, a second pistol concealed in shoulder-holsters under their jackets and, for all William knew, a throwing-knife inside their shiny boots.

'Hi there!' said Oestricher.

William grunted. The car had tagged on the back of a convoy of four squad cars blazing down the Pittsburgh road. As they came to the filter road up to the Interstate, the lead car swung left on screeching tyres through a gate in the wooden fence into the caravan park. The other cars, their sirens all wailing, peeled off in formation after it like a stunt team and skidded to a halt in front of the office buildings.

As police with drawn guns pounded on the main office door, lights began to go on inside the parked trailers, adding to the dim illumination of the light-bulbs strung above the camp on long cables like Christmas lights. Meyer was already running towards the offices. Oestricher started after him, shouting at William to follow. Instead, William got out of the car and waited, standing in the flashing red-and-white glare while the unattended sirens went on wailing.

The office door had opened. A stout woman in a towelling robe had come out on to the step, and was listening to Meyer speak urgently. She nodded and said something, then raised her arm and pointed across the caravan park.

William followed the direction of her arm. As he watched, an engine roared to life. Less than a hundred yards away, in the nearest line of parked vehicles, a battered old Chevrolet Impala towing a small trailer rocketed forward and made straight for where William was standing.

William had time to shout at Oestricher and jump for his life. The Impala slowed at the last moment — William caught a glimpse of a man with a thin moustache and the frightened face of a girl in the rear seat — hit the squad car a glancing blow and forced it out of its path to the gate.

There came a fusillade of shots from the Clarion police, running back from the office. The Impala slowed again and stopped in the driveway. As bullets tore into the trailer, William, ducking by the squad car, heard the sounds of breaking glass and splintering wood, and a scream of pain.

'Let's go get them!' a voice shouted.

The two lead squad cars reversed on the slippery grass and drove down to the gate. At the same moment, the Impala accelerated away, leaving the trailer resting on its tow-bar and blocking the exit. One of the squad cars rammed it, but only succeeded in wedging it against the solid wooden fence. Once again the police opened fire at the escaping Impala, spraying bullets wildly down the road. But it had headed up the slip road and vanished in the early-morning mist before they could get out to follow it.

Slowly, William walked up to the caravan office. Meyer's sick face showed he felt the same way: the operation had been a cock-up from start to finish. If they'd been able to go in quietly, the way William wanted, by now they'd have had the handcuffs on the kidnappers of Martin Commoner.

Mrs Purdy, Luke's aunt, was on the verge of hysterics. William calmed her down, with Meyer's assistance, and got her to talk about the fugitives. Luke had arrived three days ago with the other three, driving the Impala. She had rented them a trailer. After that she had seen little of them, except for Luke who had come across and helped around the place ('a real nice kid, always been a real nice kid, you gotta believe me, he wouldn't hurt a dumb animal'). He had talked to her about moving on, but never gave a destination. *Movin' is all*, he'd told her. *You go through this life carryin' a weight of sins, and if you stop, they multiply.*

The thought of Luke's Christian charity made the tears come to Mrs Purdy's eyes again. She wiped them with a corner of the towelling robe, and looked at them with hostility.

'Mrs Purdy —' William began.

'I've nothin' more —'

'Not Luke. About the others. I only saw three people in that getaway car. I saw the girl, Esther. And the one with the moustache, Zed. And another. Was that Luke? Or is he hiding here? If he is, you know we'll find him.'

It took a little time, but they got it out of her in the end. It was the one with the fuzzy hair and glasses who hadn't been with them. She didn't know he was Ishmael; she called him 'the wild one'. There had been a quarrel, that was all she knew. Ishmael had gone away and left them, saying he had unfinished business in Washington. Luke had come round to her in great distress. They were God-fearing Christians, he kept saying. God had given them a message and they obeyed. The wild one, he didn't listen to God any longer. He refused to hear God's message. There was no forgiveness in his heart.

'When did he go?' Meyer asked.

''Bout this time yesterday. Stealing away like a thief in the night. I'll kill him if he comes back.'

William cocked his head. 'Why?'

'Why?' Mrs Purdy scowled at them indignantly. 'He stole my gun. That's why.'

The sky was already light when the man awoke. Cursing and shivering, he unrolled the raincoat, which he had used as a pillow, and clasped it around his thin body for a minute before clambering into the driver's seat. As he backed out on to the road, he saw he had left the gun in full view on the seat behind. Grabbing for it, he stuffed it into his coat pocket.

It had been a long drive from Pittsburgh on minor roads through the Appalachian mountains. The last town he'd passed through was Shepherdsville, which put him close to the Maryland border. He was pale, as if he hadn't eaten in a long while, but it was gas stations not truck-stops that he studied carefully as he rode by.

The fourth one he went past was still closed like the others, but there was the sound of an engine revving up in the garage round the side. The man hesitated. He looked down the empty street. Then he drove back and got out of the car.

There was an old man in mechanic's overalls inside the garage, polishing the window of a glossy brown limousine, a Chevrolet. The man in the raincoat smiled. He went in, closing the garage doors behind him.

Two minutes passed. The doors opened, and a moment later the brown Chevrolet was driven out of the garage. The man in the raincoat — no longer so shiny, with a dark stain down one side — got out and backed the Maverick in to where the Chevy had been standing. Hurriedly, looking over his shoulder, he opened the trunk and, with a great effort, hauled into it the heavy and cumbersome body. Then, not waiting to put down the lid, he ran out to the Chevy and drove away.

He crossed the state line into Maryland. Not much further on, he passed an access sign to Interstate 70 South. Washington was less than thirty miles away. For the twentieth time he reached into his pocket for a grubby piece of paper and checked the address he had been given right at the beginning, before he travelled to London to get Martin Commoner.

He put his foot down on the accelerator. There was no uncertainty now, no hesitation on the pale face. He looked like a man who knew exactly where he was going; a man who had it all planned.

Mid-morning, William was still in the Sheriff's office in Clarion, waiting for Langley to call him back. He had already spoken to Krantz in Los Angeles and got the reaction he expected. Martin Commoner's life was now in real danger, that much was plain. But the CIA had the ultimate responsibility. It might well decide to take Commoner's protection into its own hands.

The phone rang, and was passed to him. It was the Langley switchboard. William identified himself for the second time, and asked to speak to Vanderbyle.

'That's the Office of Security,' said the girl.

There was a long pause. The voice which eventually came on the 'phone was soft and devoid of emphasis, as if its owner had taken speech lessons.

'Inspector Pomfret?'

'Yes.'

'You have some information for us?'

'Who are you?'

'Let's forget about that —'

'I asked to speak to Mr Vanderbyle. I'll hold on.'

'That won't be necessary. You've been put on to us from his office. We're dealing directly with the matter in question, and we know all about you.'

William hesitated. There was no point in waiting any longer. He described what had happened that morning. The man at the other end listened in silence. At the end, William demanded to know if he had the authority to order round-the-clock protection for the Deputy Director.

The polite, neutral voice replied, 'Thank you, Inspector. You can leave this one with us. You can be sure we will take immediate steps to do everything that's necessary. Goodbye.'

The line went dead. William shrugged, and replaced the receiver. The eyes of Meyer and the Sheriff were on him.

'Looks like it's out of our hands,' he said.

When the call had come through at 8 am on the private 'phone by his bed, Martin had exercised his prerogative to demand confirmation from the Director himself. A few minutes later, the General had come on the 'phone. Embarrasssed, obviously upset by his Deputy's anger, he nevertheless upheld the request from Counter-Intelligence. He would 'appreciate it' if Martin would come into Langley later in the morning for further questioning 'to clear up one or two points' arising out of the lie-detector test.

Martin dressed and had a leisurely breakfast of coffee and toast. He had a squash game arranged with Geoff Maclaren at the Arlington Y; he was damned if he was going to cancel it. What's more, he'd go in his own car: he'd had enough of being driven around like a felon escorted to the court-house door. Gathering up his squash things, he opened the front door and stepped outside.

A car started up its engine and moved down the street towards him, slowly. So they had a driver waiting for him: they were efficient bastards at the Agency, he'd give them that. Shaking his head and waving the car away, he got into the Volvo and set off for the tennis club.

The other car, a shabby brown Chevrolet, followed. Martin considered stopping and giving the driver a piece of his mind. But it was beneath contempt, this surveillance. Since he habitually varied his route across the river, he had no difficulty in shaking off his chaperone before he got into Arlington. But it angered him that the Agency should have descended to this. There might have been a casual arrogance about the CIA before the Watergate era, but the old-timers had at least respected the notion of honour among thieves. The new breed, the kind of people that Max Hemming ran, seemed devoid of the respect and tolerance for each other that any enclosed community needed if it was going to operate as a team.

It was too late for one man to change the way things were heading. Twenty years ago, when he'd joined, the Agency was attracting men and women who saw it as a career for life. They had principles, beliefs; they believed in the idea of serving your country. That had gone. Nowadays the Agency was a profession like any other, with a code of conduct based on what you could get away with. It was an Employment Opportunity for graduates from minor Catholic universities and the redneck colleges where the Moral Majority held sway. Knucklewalkers, Geoff Maclaren called them: they did a quick stint at the School of Foreign Service to get their world geography right, and then went in punching.

Perhaps that was what was needed. Perhaps he had lived by the rules for too long. *It's all ancient history, Dad.* He could see John's lopsided grin, hear him summing up his doubts with the easy callousness of the young for whom the past is too short to insist on being reckoned with. But the past mattered.

He turned off the Memorial Parkway up Spout Run, checking in the rear-view mirror that he'd shaken off his tail. The Arlington Y (their usual, the St Albans, was closed for repairs), was on Kirkwood Drive, a box-like brick building attached to a long white barn which housed five indoor tennis courts. Martin found Geoff Maclaren already changed and waiting for him.

244

The game was a hard one. Twenty minutes into it, Martin was forcing himself to reach the ball. By the time it was over, he was dizzy with exhaustion. Chest heaving, he sat for a full minute on the changing-bench unable to speak or even towel himself down.

When he got his breath back he grunted, 'You made it easy for me.'

Maclaren laughed. 'You never let anyone make it easy for you, Martin.'

They changed, and went up to the lounge overlooking the tennis courts. Collecting soft drinks, they went further down past the bar and sat in pine chairs in a small alcove, glass-walled on three sides. The high-pitched buzz from the nearby Candy-Shop vending machine was enough to keep their conversation private, but Maclaren put his towel over the table phone before he started talking.

'I did what you asked,' he said without preamble. 'I checked on the Bisley file. No joy, I'm afraid. It's been checked out, to Max Hemming no less.'

'God damn.'

'What I did manage to do was to talk to an ex-CI man, one of the ones who got purged. He knew the Bisley case. He says he clearly remembers informal surveillance being put on the son, Jonathan Bisley.'

'And?'

'It was lifted. Quite soon afterwards — but then, we were cutting down a lot on who we kept track of round about that time. After which, Jonathan Bisley disappears from view. Until he came back from Ireland on his false passport, that is.'

Martin nodded. 'It all fits.'

'With what?'

'What I told you, Geoff. Someone's out to get me.'

This time Maclaren did not favour him with a polite incredulous smile as he had done at the Zoo. Instead he nodded seriously. 'You really think so, don't you?'

'Everybody's terrified of me. I walk into Langley and it's like a morgue. Low voices. Polite smiles. People shying away like frightened horses. I tell you, I'm a pariah. I'm being treated like a case of terminal leprosy.' He picked the Coke up and put it down again without drinking. 'It's getting to me, you know that? You said downstairs I wasn't sweating. Hell, I was sweating so much last night I had to get up in the middle of the night to change the sheets!'

He had raised his voice. Out of habit he glanced over his shoulder. The lounge was empty. Maclaren was watching him, his grey eyes taking in every movement he made. Maclaren was a loyal friend, but there was a limit. The Agency had to come first. If it looked like he was slipping, his friends, people like Geoff, would cut themselves loose and let him take the rap. *Public confidence has to be maintained* — that was the formula; he'd used it himself before now.

'What do you think I should do, Geoff?' he appealed.

'I don't know. But I'll tell you this. Whoever's behind it knew when to choose his moment. Your kidnap blocked the tubes. The Israelis are freaking out. The DCI spent half of yesterday in conference with the President. If anybody set you up, they must be laughing their heads off.'

Martin shrugged. 'I offered to go see the Israelis. I offered to speak to Karp, their ambassador here. No dice. I suppose they think . . .' his voice trailed away as he saw Maclaren's expression. He went on in a low voice, 'I guess you all think the same thing.'

'No. Not me. I believe you. I'm behind you 1000 per cent.' Maclaren scowled into his glass. His face had fallen into lines of age and disappointment. 'But you know how it is. Once the witch-hunt starts, you can't call it off until it's drawn blood. And it's been open season on all of us for a long time now.'

Martin stood up. He was not finished yet. 'Thanks for your help, Geoff.'

'Hey. Wait.'

'I'll see you around.'

Driving the short distance to Langley, Martin remembered what a man who had worked with him for years on the Middle East desk had said to him shortly before the last DCI had given him the push: *When your wife leaves you, you can learn to live with it. When your colleagues leave you, that's when you really feel like an outcast.* Maybe that was the kind of thought that went through Bisley's mind before he left the hill-cabin with the shotgun. An Ishmael. He was beginning to feel that way himself.

'*I'm behind you 1000 per cent.*' Very warming. As far as Martin could remember, that was what McGovern had said to Senator

Eagleton before dropping him as the Vice-Presidential candidate. Perhaps Geoff knew that. He certainly knew a whole lot of things that had not been made public. Like the fact that Ishmael came in on a false passport . . .

At the main entrance he drew up behind a cream-coloured Lincoln. Then he remembered: he didn't have his clearances. When the gate opened for the Lincoln he went through on its tail, paying no attention to the shouts of the Marine guards. Finding his own parking space taken, he left the Volvo outside the front entrance to the CIA and went inside.

There was no doctor waiting this time; just two grey-suited guards, who walked him in silence down several long corridors to a carpeted foyer, where a mahogany elevator took them up to an unnumbered floor. The room they ushered him into Martin knew as the Miscellaneous Projects Office, a place normally reserved for business so confidential that it had to be kept apart from everything else that happened in the building. Debriefings and interrogations, for example. Bisley had been questioned up here.

A surprisingly spacious room, with a slanting roof, it contained a closet, a long table and six chairs; no other furniture. Grueller was there. So was Hemming and his plump sidekick Shusterman. And somebody he hadn't expected, Vanderbyle from the Office of Security. Addams was absent.

He took the chair that was offered him. 'Gentlemen, this had better be a purposive meeting,' he said coldly.

Max Hemming nodded. 'I'm really sorry we have to go on,' he said, squaring off papers on the table in front of him. His face was flushed, and he was taking sips of water: he had most likely just come up from jogging round the track in the basement. Martin recalled that the one piece of ornament in Hemming's office was a prize he'd won for a long-distance track event at Berkeley — a silver-mounted pen-holder inscribed, *mens sana in corpore sano*. A Sound Mind In A Sound Body. Max took good care of himself.

Larry Grueller went first. Turning on Martin an apologetic smile, his eyes opaque behind his fat glasses, he came in at a disconcerting angle.

'That poem by Robert Frost, "An Importer", do you know it?'

'I can't recall —'

'It finishes, "Teach your grandmother egg suction"!' He gave a

247

little laugh, which the others did not echo. 'That is my feeling about telling you what you know already. That nobody is 100 per cent on the lie-detector, everyone has a little nervousness, there are every time . . . *discrepancies*. And such things. And since you are in a profession to be disturbed by loose ends —'

'Let's get on with it, Larry. I have a busy schedule.'

Grueller blinked. 'So. Let me see.' He studied a computer print-out, holding it up in front of him short-sightedly. 'You have an anxiety problem on masturbation. I understand that. No trouble. To go on. There is a jump in blood pressure at the question on Agent Orange. Agent Orange. I asked if you provided this information to your alleged kidnappers. You gave an . . . emphatic reply.'

'I can explain that. I was getting impatient. It was the third time you'd asked me the same question.'

'And just before that,' Grueller looked up, 'when you denied that your kidnappers had asked about BeeSting —'

'Sure. I was disturbed you had been given that name.'

'I expected you would say that.' Grueller, smiling, glanced at Hemming who remained impassive. He went back to peering at the print-out. 'Now to another moment of drama. Ah! Here we are. You appeared to be upset on my line of questioning about David Bisley. Do you feel guilt when talking about the agent Bisley?'

'Guilty?' Martin hesitated. 'Not guilty. No. I sometimes wonder if we gave him a fair run for his money.'

'On this question of Bisley being a communist. A good deal of tension you register.'

'I wasn't coming across to you. I wanted to make the point that Bisley's communism was not the main issue. It was the question of his supposed treachery.'

'*Supposed* treachery?' A soft, small voice. It was Hemming who had spoken.

Martin turned in his chair. 'Okay, we fired him. I think we took the right decision. However, as you know Max, we never got direct evidence.'

'The documents in his room? The air ticket to Beirut?'

'That was circumstantial.'

'You were sure at the time. Did his son help you change your mind?

'Are you kidding? I told you, Ishmael tried to kill me. I don't take advice from people who reason with knives.'

After a pause, Grueller said, 'If I can turn to another matter —'

'Can I say something?' It was Vanderbyle who had abruptly spoken.

'Please.'

'Mr Commoner, I'm no psychiatrist. I deal in known facts. I've read the transcript of your comments, forget about stress patterns, and you say you've been compromised. Now the KGB never managed to penetrate us during the so-called open-house years under Carter. What makes you think they have penetrated now?'

Martin sighed. 'I never said they had. I said there had been an attempt to discredit me. It is clear to me that the KGB are one of the organisations with a strong interest in doing this.'

'But you've stated your alleged kidnappers were nothing to do with the KGB.'

'I have not said that. What I think is they were made use of. Exploited. I think they were catspaws. Not necessarily of the KGB.'

Hemming lifted his eyebrows. 'What other organisations have you got in mind?'

'In the light of current operations abroad, which I shall not specify, I would say Islamic groups. And allies of Islam, of which we have some in this building.'

There was a silence. Grueller looked at Max Hemming. Nobody wanted names. They wanted Vince Addams left out of it. That was interesting.

Grueller coughed. He tugged anxiously at the woollen scarf round his neck. 'I'd like to open up this whole matter of your, uh, relations with the alleged kidnappers,' he said heavily. 'Yesterday you tell me you had no relations of an intimate nature with them. Now —'

He paused and looked up. Behind Martin the door had opened quietly. One of Martin's guards hastened across the room and handed a folded message to the Counter-Intelligence chief. Hemming scanned it, and glanced sharply at Martin. His face had paled.

'Please carry on,' he said, getting up unsteadily and knocking his chair over with a loud clatter. 'Pardon me. I'll be right back.'

He went out, with the guard following him. Shusterman

stood up uncertainly, like a dog expecting to follow its master, and then resumed his seat. Martin frowned. Whatever the message had been, it was not in his interest to have Hemming out of the room. It meant that an element of restraint was missing. Shusterman and Vanderbyle were unknown quantities to him: probably weak but you could never be sure.

'No personal contact, that's right,' he said to Grueller.

'Is that true?'

'Of course it is.'

'What about this girl you refer to as Esther.'

'What about her?'

'Did she make advances to you?'

'What?'

'Did she make advances to you? Did you respond to them?'

The realisation hit Martin with a dreadful certainty, as if he had known it all along. He had been betrayed. Nancy had betrayed him. CI had bugged her bedroom. The people facing him had listened in to them making love and had heard the whole sordid humiliating story from his own lips.

He felt himself reddening with violent anger. *He must not lose control.* He wanted to lean across the table and take Shusterman's fat neck between his thumbs and squeeze. Instead he locked his hands together round his knee, and spoke forcefully to cover the gruffness in his voice.

'She did make advances to me. I did not respond to them.'

Shusterman leaned forward. 'Could you tell us in your own words what took place?'

Martin ignored him. He replied to Grueller. 'Esther put some music on a cassette player and removed her clothes. My hands and feet were tied. She attempted to arouse me —'

'How?'

'However she could.'

'Did she use fellatio?'

The knuckles of Martin's clasped hands were white. 'She would have tried to,' he said. 'The other three appeared and she left me alone. That's all there was to it.'

Vanderbyle raised his pencil, like the classroom swot. 'There was semen on the carpet.'

'She had it off with one of them, the one called Zed. On the carpet in front of the tent. Anything else?'

Grueller coughed, genteelly putting the end of the scarf in front of his mouth. 'Martin, why didn't you tell us this?'

'What was there to tell? No intimacy was involved, on my part. The incident was irrelevant and superfluous.'

'Is that for you to judge?'

'It was an attempt to weaken my defences. It failed.'

'How many other incidents have you consciously and deliberately passed over in the statements you've made?'

'None.'

'Why this one? Are you ashamed of yourself?'

'No I'm not. Dammit, I've told you why.'

As Grueller spread out his podgy palms, Max Hemming suddenly took his place on the other side of the table. Martin hadn't seen him enter. He seemed to have heard everything that had been said. Wrinkling his pale forehead he began at once, 'You appreciate we are here to get to the truth. For example, the exact time you left Leeds Castle.'

'What?'

'The time.' Vanderbyle had picked up from Hemming; the voices coming at him from all directions now. 'You said on the polygraph you hadn't known when you'd leave the Castle.'

'That's right.'

'But you'd already told Nancy Koscinski a precise time — 4.30 that afternoon.'

They were all over him, biting, clawing, scratching, trying to get him down. Looking at them he saw Ishmael, four Ishmaels, baying for his blood.

Shusterman was the next to spring. 'Who else knew when you were leaving the Castle?'

'Whichever of you tapped my London phone.'

'Seriously.'

'I am being serious.' He snarled at them. 'You spooks should know. You spend your time bugging all my conversations, and running the tapes backwards and forwards, jacking off at the best bits. Nancy and me yesterday, you must have got a buzz out of that.'

Shusterman looked puzzled. 'Nancy and you?'

'Don't come smart with me, Shusterman. You had to dredge deep for this shit you're throwing at me.'

Hemming interrupted, looking at his watch. 'We're straying from the point,' he said, smiling calmly. 'I feel confident we can clear this whole matter up very easily. With your permission, Martin, I'd like to run a semen test.'

'A semen test? On me?'

'I've cleared it with the DCI. It won't take ten minutes.'

He stared at them. He couldn't believe what he was hearing. Who was it they were talking to? What was happening to him? Control. *Control.* If he lashed out now, it would sound like paranoia and they'd have all the excuses they needed. He got to his feet and jerked his head at them, speechless for a moment.

'So you think I've told you a pack of lies!' he said when he found his voice. 'You don't trust me; you don't trust your own bugging equipment; you don't trust a goddamn thing. Well, you can wipe that smile off your face, Max. I've got news for you. I don't live that way. And I'm not about to change to fit in with sons of bitches like you. I'll be at home if you want me. I can find my own way out.'

At the door, he heard Grueller call his name. He turned, blinking back tears of rage. 'I'll say this, Larry, and it's not goddamned self-pity. You asked me yesterday if I thought I'd been misused by my country. I said no. I'm changing that no to yes.'

He slammed the door, and strode away blindly down the corridor.

Nobody made any attempt to stop him. Outside the main entrance his car had not been moved. Switching on the ignition, he half-hoped it had been wired to plastic explosive so that he could blow the whole fucking building into the air like a pack of cards, a pack of knaves with him the joker in the pack.

It was midday. He turned on the car radio, to try and calm himself down, but they were talking about war in the Middle East and he switched it off again. What did they know of war, these media people who talked about defence postures and nuclear weaponry ratios? The real wars had all been fought out before the battles began: the secret wars, the wars of intelligence. He himself was in the middle of one now. The problem was, he didn't know who he was fighting.

He drove into Rosslyn and stopped for gas on the Lee Highway. The pump attendant, a stocky black with a fuzz of grey beard on his cheeks, filled the tank then leaned in the window and solemnly shook Martin by the hand.

'My name is Franklin Jones, Mr Commoner,' he said gravely.

252

'I just want you to know how proud of you we are for hanging in there.'

'Well, I thank you, sir.'

'It's been my privilege to fill you up. Have a good day now.'

Martin drove away, his fists bunched on the wheel. There was a man who had read about him in *Time* or *People* or one of a hundred journals and who felt the way most people might be expected to feel about a Government servant who had been beaten and drugged and held prisoner and yet went on defending his country. Apparently they were all misguided, all wrong. Apparently contempt and bitterness and suspicion were the correct way to feel about someone like him. He had been betrayed by the ones he loved, and treated as a pariah by those he worked with. That seemed to be the price of being a hero in this town. Go out on a limb for people: they'll thank you and chop the branch off.

His enemies hadn't had the guts to show themselves yet. Well he'd smoke them out. Then he'd counter-attack. He'd use Jerry DiSenzio if he had to. He'd make Hemming and the General put their cards on the table. If they thought they could put him out to pasture, force him to resign, they didn't know who they were dealing with. He wasn't past it yet. He wasn't ready to slip into his golden years, mowing the lawn, training the ivy and playing a pit-pat game of tennis doubles before the happy hour. He'd seen what it was to join the penumbral ranks of retired CIA operatives, each with his own little horde of closely-guarded secrets which grew fewer and more trivial as the years passed.

He gunned the car through Georgetown's lunchtime traffic, and turned up 33rd Street with skidding tyres. Winners and losers. The CIA was like everything else in America, divided into winners and losers. What made the difference? He used to think it was talent; now he knew better. The way to lose was to trust people, treat them as your loyal friends. The way to win was to treat everybody as your enemy. Trust was out. The stakes were too high for trust. As Hemming used to quote, 'This is no gentleman's club and I am no gentleman.'

He double-parked and ran into the house, slamming the door so fiercely that the silver tray rattled on the old desk in the hall. Barbara was in the kitchen. She called through to him.

'Is that you, Martin?'

'Were you expecting someone else?'

'John's coming in for lunch.'

He put his head round the door. Her hair tied back in a bun and a bright blue apron round her waist, Barbara was slicing squash with a knife and putting the slices in a liquidiser. She gave him a tight-lipped smile and picked up her cigarette.

'I wasn't expecting you.'

'Did Max Hemming bring anyone with him when he came to talk to you?'

'What?'

He repeated the question. Barbara shook her head doubtfully.

'I don't think so.'

'Then it must have been that weekend.'

Shutting the door on her question, he ran upstairs. Clever, really, to have sent them away to Potter's Key for health reasons. They'd wanted him out of the house so that they could infiltrate it with their electronic ears and eyes.

The bedroom, that's what they would make for first. Running in, he pulled off the sheets and coverlets and dragged the mattresses on to the floor. With maniacal energy he wrestled the two bed-frames on to their sides and unscrewed the legs and headboards. He ran his fingers over the headboards, feeling for abrasions in the wooden skin. They were clean; so were the legs.

Barbara was calling him from downstairs. He paid her no attention: he was doing the same to the chairs and the bedside table and the mirror and drawers on the dressing-table in the corner. The loose-weave curtains were safe: any bugs could have been laundered out of those. But the door of the pine closet had to come off its hinges, and the backs off the Ben Shahn painting and the wedding photograph, digging with his penknife behind the kiss. After that, there was nothing for it but to rip the cushions and the mattresses and hunt inside with his hand.

There was a scream from the doorway. Barbara was standing there, her hands up to her face. There was green slime on them from the liquidiser.

'You've got to watch what you're saying around here,' he said.

'What are you *doing*!' she screamed.

'It's got to be done.' He surveyed his handywork, panting and red in the face, crestfallen like a burglar who has found nothing to steal.

Something caught his attention. The child's sampler above his bed — how could he have missed that?

Be with me Lord this night I pray . . .

He snatched if off the wall. Steadying it against his knee, he ripped off the plyboard backing, looking for that sliver of metal, the size of a nickel, which would have passed on every sound made on and around the beds to a receiver in an Agency car outside.

There was nothing there. He threw the sampler away.

Pushing past his wife, he went into the study and searched with the same thoroughness. He spent thirty minutes taking his desk apart and checking everything on it. He unscrewed the light switch on his desk lamp; he took the calendar off the wall and felt with his fingers for any thickening in the glossy art paper. Throwing a shelf of books on the floor he tested their covers one by one in the same way and ran the penknife between the spine and the binding.

The living-room was the only room left to try. Frustration fuelling his rage, he went downstairs and started on it with the knife. He heard Barbara sobbing in the kitchen. He wanted to go in to her, but first he had to find proof, the proof he needed.

Halfway through, the telephone went. He picked it up. The blood was throbbing in his head so he could hardly hear the voice at the other end.

'Who is this?' he snapped.

'It's Jerry, Mr Commoner. Jerry DiSenzio. Listen, I really want to talk to you.'

'Oh yeah?'

'I think there are things you really want to say openly, Martin. I can say them for you.'

'I may have a story for you,' Martin said loudly, so the bugs could pick him up. 'I'm going to call it "The Rewards Of Loyalty", how about that?'

'Terrific! I'll —'

'Hold the front page. I'll call you back.'

With a flourish he replaced the receiver. That should give Hemming and Shusterman something to think about. That would test their reactions. He looked up to see John coming towards him as if to restrain him. He held up the knife in a manner which must have appeared menacing, because the boy backed away.

'I'm not done yet,' he said.

'For Chrissake, Dad! No-one's been here.'

'Go get your lunch. I'll tell you afterwards.'

Books lay in a tattered heap. Chairs and tables were upended. Bits of stuffing and feathers from the ripped sofa and cushions lifted a fine dust into the air which made him sneeze. Even the fruit in the fruit-bowl he had cut up into little pieces in case something had been inserted. Nothing had.

Nobody had called, John had said. Well, people didn't have to call to get into the house. Only yesterday they'd cut his fuses. Aching all over, his dark suit and his hair grey with dust, he went out to the kitchen. Barbara was dialling a number. When she saw him, she put down the 'phone.

'Go ahead, call the cops,' Martin said hoarsely. He poured himself a cup of water. 'Tell me this first. Did anyone send anything to the house while I was away? Anything bulkier than a letter?'

'I don't know what you're looking for.'

'Please.'

Barbara flapped her hands at him. 'How do you expect me to remember everything that came in? Groceries. Laundry. Flowers — they were thrown out long ago. A couple of review books. The whisky to celebrate your coming back. A few magazines —'

'Whisky?'

'I told you about it. The Glenfiddich. On the sideboard.'

He strode back to the living-room. The whisky was standing there, three-quarters empty. He picked it up and looked at it closely. He could see nothing in the glass. He began to pick the label off, but it was well fixed and his nails were bitten down. He looked round for the knife, and couldn't see it. In a fury, he swung back and hurled the bottle into the fireplace, smashing it in pieces. There was nothing under the label. He picked up the top which had rolled aside. It felt heavier than it should. Looking at it closely, he saw tiny holes bored round the serrated edge. He found the knife and cut around the top from the inside.

The false top peeled away.

When John came in, Martin was holding up the micro-bug like a jewel to the light.

'The first thing you learn in my business,' he said without

turning his head. 'Never accept candy from a stranger.'

There was one more visit to make yet. Leaving his home in a shambles behind him, he hurried into the street. Standing by his car was a policeman, writing him out a ticket for being double-parked.

For the first time that day, Martin threw his head back and laughed out loud.

As soon as William Pomfret got back to the FBI office in Pittsburgh, he was called to the phone. He swallowed a mouthful of cheeseburger and dill pickle (it was midday and he'd had nothing to eat since an early breakfast) and took the call at the front desk.

'Bill? AK here. You must be pretty darn pleased with yourself.'

'Where are you?'

'Washington. Capital of the East. I took a red-eye from LA. The big chiefs here want to know if you're gonna be pressing for extradition of the girl.'

'When we find her, yes.'

'How's that? Shit, don't they tell you anything up there? Your three little chicks are sitting pretty behind bars, up on the New York border. Meyer's with them now. They turned themselves in, 'bout an hour ago.'

William drew a long deep breath, and let it out slowly. 'Have they talked?'

'I don't know. Meyer's got the details, give him a call. He's at the police station in Warren. Warren, Pennsylvania.'

'What about Jonathan Bisley?'

'Yeah, well, he's a problem.'

'What do you mean?'

Krantz's breathing, normally heavy, became stertorous. 'That's why I'm here,' he growled. 'CIA is saying it's a security matter, they want to handle it from here on in. We're saying it's a federal matter, an American subject on American soil. I'm damned if those assholes are going to walk off with this one under my nose.'

'So what's happening?'

'Fuck all is happening. It's being *negotiated*.'

257

'But he's going after Commoner. He's got a gun.'

'I figure the spooks have Commoner under wraps. According to my CIA liaison Commoner went in to Langley this morning. Bisley can't do much to him there.'

William was about to point out that Bisley had got to Commoner at Leeds Castle without much trouble. Instead he said simply, 'AK? Do me a favour.'

'What is it?'

'I need to speak to Vanderbyle. I rang him this morning and was switched away to someone else. Can you get your CIA liaison on to it? Tell him it's urgent. I'll be by the 'phone here until I hear something.'

'It could take a couple of hours.'

'I'll wait.'

William waited. He finished his lunch. He made tea for himself. He wrote a postcard to Jennifer. He read the *Pittsburgh Chronicle* and the *Police Gazette*. He found out where the town of Warren was, north of the Allegheny National Forest, and called up Meyer.

He didn't need to check his photographs to know who Meyer was talking about. It was Martin's kidnappers: there was no doubt in his mind. They refused to recognise their real names; they called each other Esther, Luke and Zed. So far, they had answered every question put to them by the interrogating officers with quotations from the Bible that referred to the sins of men and the wrath of God. Since they had committed no felony on American soil (the car had been lent to Luke by Mrs Purdy), no charges would be laid against them until a formal identification had been made by Commoner.

Esther and Luke were at the police station. Zed was in the Warren State Hospital, north of town. A bullet had torn through his shoulder as they escaped from the caravan park. They had gone on as long as they could, dodging two police blockades and taking back roads through the forest; but Zed was losing blood. They carried him to the hospital and sat quietly in the waiting room, hands folded, eyes closed, lips moving, until the police came and took them away.

'We need you up here,' said Meyer. 'There's no point in flying them down until this, uh, Zed is fit to travel.'

'What about Commoner?'

'CIA is flying him up here.'

'What — now?'

'As soon as they can. They're getting their act together.'

'About time,' said William.

Another hour passed. It was a hot afternoon, as hot as Los Angeles. The office windows were open on the booming clatter of Pittsburgh traffic. The Feds around him, in white shirtsleeves, typed on word processors or stood chatting quietly in the corridor. William sweated. He didn't like Vanderbyle any more than Vanderbyle liked him. But there was nobody else in the CIA he could talk to now.

Krantz called back to say that liaison was still trying to contact Vanderbyle. 'Here's something else. Our friend Jonathan Bisley passed through Pittsburgh yesterday.'

'How do you know?'

'He stole a green Maverick. An alert went out, and it was found abandoned early this morning in a locked-up Texaco station off Interstate 70, about thirty miles north of Washington.'

'So —'

'That's not all. We think he headed on south in a brown Chevrolet. It belonged to an old guy, a mechanic, who used to work late in the body shop. We found him stuffed in the trunk of the Maverick. Hit on the head with the gun and tied up. He's given us a description.'

'Oh yes?' It was what had happened to Arthur Norman and the Park Warden at Leeds Castle. 'Surely you can get him now,' he said with anger in his voice. 'To hell with the CIA.'

'Yup. We've taken the wraps off. If that Chevy's in Washington, we'll find it in no time.'

'And Commoner?'

Krantz grunted, 'Commoner's not our concern. He's got the CIA to look after him.'

It was futile to argue the point. William didn't try. It was Vanderbyle he had to talk to. Bisley could have been in Washington for twelve hours now. With just one single purpose in mind.

It was three o'clock when the call came. He snatched up the 'phone. Vanderbyle's voice seemed to be coming at him from a long way away, calm, drawling and faintly sarcastic.

'How are you making out with the Feds?'

'Just fine. Look, I'm afraid I have to ask for your help.'

'You need *my* help?'

'I want to know who is responsible for protecting Martin Commoner.'

'We are.'

'Your office is? Then I want to know if you've acted on my request that he be given personal bodyguards twenty-four hours a day.'

'I don't know what you're talking about. I have no authorisation to give him that. This is America, Inspector, not a police state.'

William flushed with anger. 'If you don't protect your public servants, it could get that way. He's in extreme danger, I thought I made that clear. Jonathan Bisley is in Washington. He's done a violent assault once in the last twenty-four hours. Now he's after Commoner. With a gun.'

There was a silence at the other end of the line. When Vanderbyle spoke again, the drawl was gone.

'Who told you this?'

William described what had happened at Clarion and at the Texaco station. Before he could finish, Vanderbyle had interrupted him.

'Why didn't you make your request to me?'

'I tried to. I was put on to someone else. He wouldn't give me his name. He said he was dealing with the matter, and steps would be taken to do everything necessary.'

'Is that all he said?'

'That's all he said to me.'

'What do you mean?'

'The police and FBI have instructions from you to keep away from Commoner. They had the same instructions about Bisley until he started killing.'

There was another, longer pause. William could visualise Vanderbyle sitting in his clean air-conditioned office somewhere in the heart of CIA headquarters, his blue eyes abstracted, fingering his string tie in bafflement. A man who wasn't at the centre any more. He pressed home his advantage with a request. 'If Commoner is in the building, I'd like a word with him.'

'That's not possible. He left here at 12.00 this morning and went home. I think you'd best leave this one to me.'

'Does he get full protection from you or doesn't he?'

Vanderbyle hesitated. A minute ago, more than likely, he would have told William to go to hell. Now he sounded uncertain, insecure.

'He does,' he said finally. 'As soon as I can get to him. What about you? Are you staying on this line?'

'If you want me to.'

'Good. Stick around, Inspector. Just a couple of hours or so. I need to talk to somebody. I'll call you back.'

'What's your num —'

But Vanderbyle had put the 'phone down. William got up and went to the window. He felt restless, angry with himself for agreeing to stay on. He liked to be in the front line: it was where he came alive; it was the way he'd led the kidnap investigation. But here he was, stranded midway between Warren and Washington where the action was. Midway between the FBI and the CIA, come to that, used by both and trusted by neither. Vanderbyle wasn't the only one not at the centre of things. Nobody was at the centre; nobody ever was; they all pretended to be.

He scowled down at the street. The hot sidewalks were crowded with people shopping, people carrying messages, getting out of cars. It would be so easy for a nondescript like Bisley to lose himself in the crowd, as he jostled towards his destination. Especially with a little help from his friends . . .

Probably he was getting paranoid. Commoner must be feeling secure and well protected or he would have been out of Washington by now, lying low until all the kidnappers were caught. So why should William worry? Commoner was none of his business. Intelligence services played games; games were their stock-in-trade: he'd learned that years ago, watching Knight smoothly manoeuvring, trading for information with only passing interest in its market value. No doubt there was a plausible explanation for all this. Somebody in the CIA was having a game with Martin Commoner — perhaps using him as a bait to draw in Jonathan Bisley.

But bait had to be swallowed before the hook could be taken.

He blinked wearily. Across the street was a cafe. His imagination was getting fevered: he could use a long cold drink.

* * *

Martin Commoner crossed Rock Creek on his way up Connecticut. The cop had cancelled the parking ticket when he'd recognised Martin from the newspapers: that and the pump attendant were the only good things that had happened all day. Unless you counted finding the micro-bug. Like a prisoner finally sentenced, he felt better for finding out the worst: it allowed him to make his dispositions.

Ishmael's father must have made his dispositions very carefully. From what he could remember, David Bisley had put all his worldly affairs in order, with the precision of someone covering his tracks. How many letters had he written, how many household bills had he paid, how many people had he talked to in a normal voice over the telephone, before going up to that cabin and walking out into the wilderness with a gun? Only in his dying had he failed to cover his tracks. If he had succeeded, all this might never have happened.

There was a traffic tie-up up as far as Cathedral Avenue. He banged the wheel in frustration. Looking in his mirror he saw that his tail had found him again — the shabby brown Chevrolet he'd lost that morning, the sun glinting off its dusty windscreen.

It was odd that Bisley should have loused up like that, at the very end. Unless it was the last and carefullest of his dispositions. He'd trained Ishmael to hunt. Had he let him track him deliberately to the place of his suicide? Had he even talked to his son before putting the gun to his head? It was the kind of bitterness, of vengefulness, which Martin would have dismissed once as the act of a madman.

He understood it better now. He would be capable of doing the same.

His dispositions would not be like Bisley's. He was a fighter, a survivor. And he had right on his side. Whoever was attacking him was attacking the security of the United States. They had imperilled BeeSting. They had leaked stories to the Russians (how could they say it was *him*?). They had undermined relations between the U.S. and Israel. They had set the whole Agency against him, or else riddled it with so many traitors, so many enemies . . .

He shook his head in anguish. This was what a lifetime in intelligence did to the mind: straight well-ordered corridors became a labyrinth of twisting tunnels the moment something went wrong. Nancy could have been lying about Traill. He'd soon find out, he had the key to her apartment. If she'd connived to have it bugged, and not told him, he could assume she'd deceived him from the start. She could be Traill's mistress. Traill could have turned her, to spy on him. He would have used Martin because he was there, because he could frame him without fear of compromise. He'd have needed inside help, of course. Maybe Addams. Maybe one of the others.

He'd been made a sucker.

He turned left off Connecticut before the bridge, and sharply right again along the service road for the Devonshire. On his right, the ground dropped away steeply through the trees to the valley road he'd taken to the Zoo after that innocent lunch at the Angler's Inn. From her kitchen window in the big apartment block, Nancy had a view across the narrow wooded valley, with the roof of the old Chinese Embassy poking up through the trees and the great grey Cathedral beyond. Down on the service road, where Martin parked beside a delivery van, the trees shielded him from prying eyes.

He slammed the car door, skirted the circular flowerbed and ran up the flight of steps to the back entrance. There was no sign of the brown Chevy. Punching the elevator button he rode up to Nancy's floor, twisting her key in his pocket. He unlocked her door and gently opened it.

Nancy was sitting in a bamboo chair by the window. Her face, when she looked up, broke into a wide smile of delight. She stood up, letting the papers on her lap slip to the carpet, and came towards him with a skip of pleasure, tucking her brown shirt into her cotton slacks.

'Martin! How did you know I was —' She stopped, seeing his expression. 'What's wrong? What's happened?'

He kicked the door shut behind him. 'You know what's wrong.'

She looked at him dumbly. Or playing dumb.

Trying to keep calm, his voice came out in a croak. 'Why did you do it, Nancy? Why doublecross me? Why?'

She shook her head, fear widening her eyes. 'I don't understand —'

'Who put you up to it? Traill?' He advanced on her, his voice rising to a shout. 'Did *he* have the bugs put in? So you could

263

bring me up here and pump me for information when we were through with making love?'

'Oh!' She put out a hand to steady herself, the colour draining from her cheeks. 'You're so wrong!'

'Am I? We'll see how wrong I am.' He strode grimly towards the bedroom, his fingers closing over the knife in his pocket. Nancy got in front of him and put her arms out to stop him.

'No! Wait. I can show you. They tapped the 'phone. I came in while they were doing it, your people, the CIA. Look!'

She rushed to the telephone and picked it up, in her eagerness almost knocking over the vase of cut flowers. Martin took it from her. With his penknife he began unscrewing the back.

'That's why I didn't ring you,' she told him, a little breathless. 'That's why I left a message. I wasn't having that man Shuster-man listen to us. Martin?'

He fumbled at the screws in a mechanical way, knowing and not caring to know what he would find inside.

'They told me it was security,' she said in pleading tones. 'They said your life was in danger and I wasn't to involve you. The more you knew, the more danger you were in.'

The tip of his penknife broke. Martin lifted the 'phone in the air with both hands and smashed it down on the carpet.

'You think I'm a damned idiot!' he exclaimed, trembling with anger. 'Even now, even after this.'

'What?'

'They're in the bedroom too. Don't try and kid me, I know they are. That's the reason you took me in.'

Without listening to her, he flung open the bedroom door. It was just as he'd left it yesterday. The plants, the mattress on the floor, the pink-and-white duvet she'd thrown back to straddle him . . . he fancied he could still smell their lovemaking in the air.

Blindly, with tears in his eyes, he slashed at the duvet, tearing it apart with a ripping noise. It was futile to rummage through the synthetic stuff inside: he concentrated on the area round the zip. Then he turned his attention to the 'phone beside the bed.

Nothing. The bastards must have know he'd look there anyway. As Nancy watched, turned to stone in the doorway, he seized the nearest pot plant, a dark green yucca, and dug out soil round its roots with a knife. On the other side of the bed was a

264

tall grey-green ivy growing up a bamboo cane. Grasping it, he snapped the cane and ran his fingers through the thick leafage.

A small green object, like a heavy button, fell on to the mattress. He picked it up, and put it in Nancy's outstretched hand.

'You lied to me,' he said harshly. 'You lied.'

She was staring at the micro-bug as if hypnotised by it. He was mad now. He wanted to beat her head against the wall. to hurt her, so she would know what she'd done to him. He knocked the button out of her hand so it went spinning across the room.

'Tell me you lied about Traill!'

'No!'

He pushed past her. He didn't want to know any more. It made him sick, being up here. He needed to get out into the open air. She came after him, crying out.

'Jim had nothing to do with it. Martin, listen! It has to be one of your people who's doing this. Martin. Look at me!'

They were in the corridor now. A door opened, a peering wrinkled face over a metal chain.

'Martin!'

He ran down the stairs, taking them two at a time. He had to get away, from her, from all of them. The bastards. Sons of bitches. The people he'd worked with all his life. They were crawling all over him. Consuming him. He really was going mad. He had to get away while there was still time.

At the foot of the stairs he lost his bearing and had to cast around for a moment. The glass door was at the end of the lobby — he saw blue sky, green woods.

Nancy had caught up with him. She was tugging at his arm.

'Martin, please! Listen to me. Listen.'

She held on to him all the way to the door, and out to the top of the steps. 'I love you,' she said, weeping, furious.

'Let me go.'

Whoever had done this to him had destroyed love as well. They had blackened everything he had ever believed in, including the people he had trusted. The General. Hemming. Maclaren, Nancy. Even Barbara, for God's sake. He started down the steps.

'Hi there, old buddy!'

It came out of the thin air, a reedy voice, as familiar as the voice of conscience. The brown Chevy had found him. Frozen in an old memory, he watched the door open and a man get out. A slight man with rimless spectacles and an over-large head tufted with fuzzy black hair.

Ishmael.

Purposefully, taking his time, Jonathan Bisley came round the flowerbed and began to walk up the steps. There was a handgun stuffed awkwardly in his belt. He did not look down at it.

'I want to talk to you,' he said, stopping halfway up. 'About my father.'

Martin stared at him. He felt Nancy's hand on his wrist. He heard the distant yells of schoolchildren playing soccer on the other side of the valley. Bisley's son looked somehow different, awkward. Martin saw the pride and fear in his face and recognised it.

'Tell me something,' he said with great sadness. 'Do you hate what your father was?'

Jonathan Bisley gazed up at him. He shook his head with emotion, unable to speak. Martin stepped down towards him — and heard the shot. The bullet sang past his left ear. The glass door shattered. Nancy screamed aloud.

'Get down!' he yelled.

He flung himself on top of her, sprawling on the concrete steps. There were two more shots, from way over by the bridge. He heard a bullet ricochet off the railing.

Looking round, he saw Ishmael walk up the steps. One side of his face was red and glistening. There was blood coming through his fingers where he held his side. His rimless spectacles were dangling from one ear. Clumsily he tried to put them back on where the other ear had been. Then he knelt slowly on the step, toppled backwards and lay still.

Windows opened above them. Nobody spoke. Martin turned to Nancy.

'Are you okay?'

'I guess.' She wiped her eyes with the back of her hand, trembling. 'He damn near killed both of us.'

Martin shook his head. 'He didn't fire the gun.'

'He didn't?'

'Go back inside,' he told her in a low voice. He squeezed her hand. 'Please. Please do as I ask.'

He waited until she had gone. Then he went down to where Ishmael was lying. He turned him over.

Ishmael was dead. There was no pulse in the thin hand which still clutched his starred glasses. A papery dullness had settled over the pale protuberant eyes. But the mouth still accused him. It was twisted in a mocking, almost triumphant grin. *I've proved my point*, it seemed to be saying: *You kill*.

Behind him there was a screech of tyres as a car came fast down the service road. Footsteps rang on the pavement. He looked up. Three men were running towards him. One of them was Vanderbyle.

'You damn near killed us up there,' he snarled at the tall Texan.

'It wasn't us,' said Vanderbyle, breathing heavily.

'Who was it then?'

'I don't know.'

Martin stared at him, and then beyond him into the trees. Nothing moved. He had heard nothing, not even the crackle of brushwood. To the right he could see the grey-green span of the bridge that took Connecticut Avenue over the valley. They could have shot Ishmael from the bridge and got away. But the first bullet hadn't been aimed at Ishmael . . .

Vanderbyle was speaking, in a subdued voice. 'Whoever it was, I guess they saved your life, Mr Commoner. Bisley was gunning for you. We got word.'

Martin pointed downward. Ishmael's gun was still in his belt. 'Much chance he was given,' he said, bending down and picking it up. It was a 9mm Browning; it could put a hole through an ox. 'Why didn't you pull him in?'

The Texan opened his mouth to say something, then shut it again. He scowled up at the apartment windows. 'This ain't a peepshow,' he grumbled, waving his two men away from the body. 'Get something to cover him with.'

When they were gone, he addressed the DDO. 'If you'll come with me, sir,' he said. 'Maybe the Director can answer that better than I can.'

Martin looked round for Nancy. He ran back up the steps to the glass door, and paused. Nancy might be waiting behind it but he couldn't see her because the glass had shivered and misted. A touch could bring everything crashing down.

He reached out his hand towards it. Then he drew it back, and turned to where Vanderbyle was standing. 'We'll take my car,' he said.

* * *

Martin drove, following Vanderbyle's directions. Instead of heading back south, Vanderbyle took him out eastwards, along Harvard Street and Michigan Avenue, into a part of Washington Martin scarely knew.

He paid Vanderbyle no attention, but looked around him sharply, trying to get his thoughts straight. There were no large marble-white colonnaded buildings in this part of town; in fact no architect-designed buildings at all except for what the municipality provided — a hospital here, a library, a Catholic church, and once a cluster of college buildings. Instead they drove past housing developments, streets of shabby brownstones and several vacant lots in which the wrecks of cars lay stranded in the grass and the occasional house stood, tarpaulin tacked to its side walls, like a tooth in a rotting gum.

If Washington was a one-company town, these had to be the places outside the limit of its benefits. The folk he spent his time with — government officials, politicians, journalists, lobbyists, lawyers — they didn't live out here: it was too much like nowhere. It was too much like the real world, which went on exactly the same whether or not the Pope had been shot in Rome, or a satellite had taken off for Mars, or a gossip columnist had spread dirt about a member of the inner Cabinet. In these streets people had to stick around and get on or take the consequences, because they had no place else to go.

Abruptly he asked, 'If you didn't fire those bullets, how come you were just round the corner?'

'I was trying to find you. CI was supposed to be tracking you, but I had, uh, a communcications problem with them. And that English Special Branch guy, Pomfret, had rung me from the FBI someplace to say that Bisley was looking for you with a gun.'

'Maybe you should hire him. He seems more interested in my welfare than most of the people round here.'

There was no reply to that. After a minute, Vanderbyle said, 'You turn right at the next intersection.'

The neighbourhood was an industrial one. There were warehouses, grimy pre-war structures, on either side of the street. Near the end, they came to a high brick wall, its whitewash yellowed and flaking. Painted on the wall in tall green letters were the words NEW AND WORN APPLIANCES. US SCRAP METAL CO. GUARANTEED DESTRUCTION OF CONFIDENTIAL RECORDS.

'In here,' said Vanderbyle.

A wooden gate swung open. Martin drove into a big empty brick-paved yard surrounded on all four sides by long sheds in which old vehicle chassis and bits of rusting machinery were heaped towards the rafters. Half of one of the sheds had been converted into site offices. Vanderbyle directed him to pull up in front of them.

'I'll be right back,' he said, when he had escorted Martin into the main office. Left alone, Martin went to the window and looked around. There was no-one in sight.

The yard, he could tell, had been cleared for a helicopter pad. The Agency operated several places like this, switching them round as an elaborate security precaution. This one he hadn't been to before. If they wanted him dead, like Bisley father and son, this was the perfect place for an execution.

He glanced around the office. A cheap metal desk took up half the space. An adjustable chair was in front of it and a wooden hard-backed chair on the other side. Two filing-cabinets stood side by side; on top of one of them was the October issue of the *Scrap Metal Gazette*. A calendar on the wall had a picture of a naked blonde with a tyre round her ample hips. The caption underneath announced RENOLDS TYRES — FOR THE BEST RIDE.

A telephone cord ran from the wall into one of the desk drawers. Martin tried it. It was locked. He got out his penknife and was working the lock, when the door opened.

It was the General. He was carrying a small black attaché case. He marched forward, and shook Martin warmly by the hand.

'Thank God you're all right,' he exclaimed.

Martin gazed at him blankly.

'We've spent the last couple of hours trying to get hold of you,' the DCI went on, settling himself on the far side of the desk and gesturing Martin to the chair. Martin walked past him and stood with his back to the door, so that the DCI had to turn to face him.

'Vanderbyle informed me that one of the kidnappers was gunning for you,' he said with a cough of embarrassment. 'I asked him to check on Max Hemming's arrangements, but Max is due up in Warren with your kidnappers. So —'

'So you've just killed my best witness,' Martin broke in. 'The

269

one person who could clear up this mare's nest. You could have pulled the poor bastard in any time over the last twenty-four hours, but that would have loused up your case against me. Well you don't have that problem any more, General. I'm resigning. Effective from today.'

'Wait a moment.'

'Don't worry. I'll make it easy for you. I'll say I'm resigning on health grounds. Delayed shock, symptoms of stress, call it what you like. But the way I see it, you want me out because I'm holding up BeeSting and the Israelis want someone's head on a plate. It's been reflected in the attitude towards my testimony, in every damn thing that's happened since I got back —'

'Martin!'

The DCI had risen to his feet. His back was plainly hurting him, from the way he straightened up. His eyebrows bristling, he glowered at his Deputy. 'If you'd wait to hear why I came . . . it was to apologise to you. I appreciate the way you feel. I'm mighty sorry. I've already ordered an inquiry into why Bisley wasn't pulled in before he got so close. But I want to ask you for your patience and understanding.' He was eyeball-to-eyeball with Martin now, a familiar ploy. 'Think about it. The Agency's never had somebody at your level kidnapped before. BeeSting was on heat and frankly we were shitting in our pants. We had to bear down hard. You'd have done the same in my position.' He let his eyes drop. 'As it is, the heat's off. We're handing over the pictures, and the Israelis have let Fisher go.'

'Since when?'

'Since right now. I've just been on the phone myself to Jerusalem to tell 'em we've got all the kidnappers captured or dead.' The General's face tightened into a smile. 'I'm proud of you, Martin. BeeSting was your idea; it looks like it's going to hit the jackpot.'

'Yes,' said Martin. He walked slowly across the room, frowning. This talk about Fisher was baloney, it had to be. Nothing happened that quickly. It confirmed what he'd suspected all along — that the General had been bluffing him on Fisher. It wasn't the Israelis playing dirty: it was the Agency deliberately keeping the BeeSting plans in cold storage until they could be sure of Martin's innocence. The Israelis could have let Fisher go some time ago (a day? two days?) and Martin had been given what the British called a barium meal — fed with false information, to see if he would pass it on to the Soviets. From what Geoff Maclaren had told him at the Arlington Y, Geoff was in on it too.

A sudden movement made him turn his head. The Director was opening the attaché case. He upturned it over the desk and shook out six tapes.

'It's all yours,' he said.

'What are they?'

'They're all the records that exist of your interrogations. Do what you want with them. Destroy them.' He looked steadily at Martin. 'I'm not accepting your resignation. I want you back beside me.'

Martin picked up one of the cassettes. It was as light as a shell-case. All Grueller's hard work, tossed on a tabletop like a pack of cards.

He said, 'You're forgetting something. Ishmael and the others could still have been put up to it.'

'Who by?'

'I don't know.'

'You can cross Traill off. Yes, I know your views on Traill. I share some of them. But he's clean on this. His tip-off on BeeSting came from the State Department, after our NSC meeting. I should have guessed that right away, Knowing State.'

Martin grunted. There was a faint buzzing in his head, which grew louder, until it became a vibrating roar which shivered the tapes on the table and shook the filing-cabinet drawers. He went to the window. The chopper was landing in the scrapyard, blowing up iron dust.

He felt a hand on his shoulder. The General had joined him at the window. 'I'll have your clearances ready as soon as you get back from identifying these little bastards,' he said. 'If you're still worried about backbiters inside the Agency, we'll get to work and shake them out of the trees. Frankly, I don't think you'll have any trouble.'

Martin nodded, absently. Someone in the Agency had told Moscow about Oman and Agent Orange and the business in Greece. Someone had tried to kill him to stop him shaking them out. That added up to a whole lot of trouble. Through the window he watched the chopper blades slicing through the air, with a sound like downhill skiing very fast on dry snow.

'I think you should know something else.' The General's voice

271

lowered, his mouth close to Martin's ear. 'Between ourselves. I've submitted my resignation to the President, effective from April first. I'm putting in a strong recommendation that you should take over the job. It's about time the Agency had an in-house Director again. I think you'd do a darn fine job.' He put up his hand. 'Now don't say anything. I'll see you on board. Just take your time and think about it. Okay?'

Martin accompanied him into the yard. The DCI was stooping slightly, as though, in making public his decision to resign, he no longer had to maintain his ramrod back against age and infirmity. As they got to the chopper, the first few drops of rain began to fall out of a sky which had suddenly paled and clouded over. The General patted him on the arm and chuckled.

'Have I told you my favourite quatrain?' he asked:

> The rain it raineth every day,
> Upon the just and the unjust fella
> But more upon the just, because
> The unjust has the just's umbrella.

Looking to catch Martin's reaction, he chuckled again and turned on his heel. 'Get in before you get rained on!' he called over his shoulder, and strode away across the yard.

Martin climbed into the chopper. Vanderbyle was already inside. When he saw Martin he scrambled into the back seat to give the DDO room. Martin ignored him. As the blades whirred, and the machine rose into the sky above the capital, he went back over a scene he had replayed in his mind a dozen times: the gunfire on the back steps of the Devonshire.

There was no getting away from it. If the gunshots which killed Ishmael had come from the Connecticut Avenue bridge, there was no way he and Nancy could have been in the direct line of fire. No way from the trees, either, at least not so as to escape without being seen.

He had escaped death by a fraction. Just the one bullet. If Nancy hadn't been out there as a witness, he could be dead by now . . .

The helicopter turned north. The pilot ducked round and noticed Martin's expression.

'If you think that was turbulence,' he said, 'you ain't seen nothing yet.'

272

The road north from Pittsburgh wound for mile after mile alongside the Allegheny River. William was dozing when the FBI driver shouted back over his shoulder, 'Hear that? The Jews have done it again!'

'What?' William blinked wearily, rubbing his face.

'Listen.' The driver turned up the car radio. William recognised the tones of professional excitement which American newscasters employ.

'. . . *daring carbon copy of their night raid on the Iraqi reactor, six American-built F16 bombers attacked Pakistan's nuclear research station near Islamabad with pin-point accuracy. First reports coming off Pakistan radio confirm the Israeli claim of extensive damage to both reactors, putting Pakistan's nuclear program back by two or three years and wrecking hopes of an Islamic bomb by the mid-'80s. No word yet from the Government in Islamabad, but Pakistan has always denied Israel's claim that the uranium it planned to sell Libya and Syria would be enriched to produce bomb-grade plutonium. According to an Israeli spokesman this evening, his Government decided to act before Pakistan's reactors came fully on stream next month, in his words "to ensure the survival of Israel". There has been no response so far from the White House. But the State Department has issued a statement strongly condemning the pre-emptive strike, which it says will send shock waves through the whole of Islam.'*

'You gotta hand it to them,' said the FBI driver. 'No?'

But Pakistan was a small country a long way away. William had already gone back to sleep.

A railroad junction without a railroad. That was how the driver had described it. But by the time they got there, near six in the afternoon, Warren was already on the map. Newsmen and photographers milled among the cars parked in the narrow forecourt of the police station. William had to duck aside from cameras and microphones as he hurried past.

Inside the station, the atmosphere was hardly more restrained. Telephones were ringing. Men in bulky suits strode past on urgent unexplained errands. At the desk, the duty sergeant fended off questions from a red-faced man in a shiny parka, probably a local reporter who'd been let in as a favour. Two girls were whispering and giggling by the vending machine, infected by the mood of excitement. It wasn't every day that Warren captured famous fugitives even if, as was rumoured, they had surrendered themselves voluntarily. William half-expected to see bunting strung up under the flyblown fluorescent lights.

Meyer came out of the back to greet him. His expression was gloomy. 'We've got the spooks walking all over us,' he muttered. 'It's lucky I was here before them.'

'The spooks?'

'They've tried to get at the folksinger. Whoever he is. We're still checking up on his ID. But we've got him under police guard at the State Hospital while they take a bullet out of his shoulder.'

'Any news about Bisley yet?'

'Not that anyone's told me.'

'These two, have they talked?'

'No. Put them together and all they've done is sing.'

'Oh?'

'"He's Got The Whole World In His Hands" — over and over again. If I hear it many more times, I'm going to do something un-Christian. I'm hoping you can be a tad more persuasive.'

On a table near the vending machine lay a cheap guitar with a bullet-hole through the sound box. Beside it were two passports, a social security card, a clip of one-dollar bills, a packet of tissues, a penknife, a couple of tampons, a toothbrush, a wad of orange cards, an empty wallet and an empty purse.

'Is that all?' William asked.

'So far. We haven't found any drugs, but we're taking the car apart.'

William picked up one of the orange cards. 'FREE TICKET. ADMIT ONE', it said: 'To Spend Eternity In Heaven With Jesus Christ The Son Of God. PRICE OF ADMISSION: "Believe in the Lord Jesus Christ and you shall BE SAVED", Acts 16:31. EVERYONE A WINNER!' Turning the card over he read on the other side, 'FREE TICKET. ADMIT ONE To Spend Eternity In The Lake Of Fire With The Devil And His Angels. PRICE OF ADMISSION: To do nothing and ignore God's saving grace . . . "He that BELIEVETH NOT (in the Son of God, Jesus Christ) is CONDEMNED ALREADY", John 3:18. EVERYONE A LOSER.'

William pocketed his free ticket to heaven and followed Meyer across the charge room.

'Have they eaten anything?' he asked.

274

'Nope. We offered them ham and beans. They wanted a nut salad and carrot juice. No sale.'

They were in a corridor giving on to two cells, both empty, and a door at the far end. Two men in neat grey suits were talking softly outside the door. As Meyer approached, one of the men broke off and came to meet them. He had a pallor to his face, as if he spent all his time indoors. Twisting a gold signet ring on one pudgy finger, he glanced towards William and back at Meyer.

'I thought we agreed,' he said. 'I don't want anybody seeing them until we have word from Washington.'

'Mr Shusterman, this is Detective Chief Inspector Pomfret from England,' said Meyer, his tone unexpectedly deferential. 'He has full clearance from Washington. He'll be requesting extradition for the girl.'

It was not a name William had heard before. He felt himself being appraised, very intently, before the gaze dropped and Shusterman gestured them through.

When he saw them, William stopped in the doorway.

They were sitting side by side, in handcuffs, on hard-backed chairs against the far wall of the windowless room. Esther was pregnant, they hadn't told him that. Wearing a woollen gypsy shawl and a muddy blue skirt, she was resting her head on Luke's shoulder, humming tunelessly. The strap on one of her sandals had broken loose. Her long woollen socks had slipped down her thin white legs. Luke, dressed in blue jeans and an open-necked shirt, was inclining his head towards the girl. His eyes were squeezed shut and his lips were moving.

They looked defenceless, pathetic. The kind of kids who would think it a big deal to steal a Chevy for an hour and go joyriding. Probably they still didn't understand what Jonathan Bisley had pushed them into, and why they should now be sitting here guarded by men with guns after a police hunt that had involved more expense and effort than had been spent on their whole lives up to now.

And he had come all this way for this.

He turned to Meyer behind him and said quietly, 'Take him out, can you, and leave me alone with the girl. I'd like her handcuffs off, too.'

When Luke was out of the room, William went to shut the door. Shusterman was standing just outside, in the corridor, fiddling with a directional microphone. He frowned impatiently and waved William back into the room.

Esther was slumped in the chair, her eyes closed. When William shook her, she yawned and said in a faint voice, 'Let me sleep, man.'

'In a little while. When's the baby due?'

She opened her eyes a millimetre and regarded him. 'Are you a Brit?'

'Yes. I am. My name's William.'

'Are you taking me back with you?'

'It depends.'

'On what?'

'On what you've got to tell me.'

'I don't have nuthin' to tell you.'

'Yes you do.' He turned Luke's chair round and straddled it, resting his elbows on the back. 'You know, kidnap's a very serious crime in England. You could go down for five, ten years. They'll take the baby away. You help me now, girl, and I could get you off most of that. Maybe all of it. To bring up your child. What do you say?'

She didn't look at him. She closed her eyes and started to sing, in a thin, reedy voice.

'*We shall overco-o-ome, We shall overco-o-ome, We shall overcome one day-ay-ay —*'

'*Margaret!*'

It had the desired effect. Margaret Jones, alias Esther, stopped in mid-chant and blinked open her eyes.

'Your granny's very upset,' William went on sternly. 'She thought you were a good kid, she thought you loved your old granny. That's why she gave you her home, while she was sick in hospital. And this is what you do to her.'

Sulkily Esther scratched at a scab of dried blood on her leg. 'I ain't done nuthin' wrong,' she said.

'Kidnap and attempted murder —'

'It wasn't kidnap, it was *outreach*,' she exclaimed as if insulted. 'That's what Ishmael says, he said it was a chance to save his soul and turn a wicked man to God, like Paul on the road to Damascus. And we did!'

'Did what?'

'We put his life in God's hands, and God saved him.' She was triumphant. 'He made his peace with God. God accepted his

276

repentance. How else would he have got out of there?'

William was tempted to say, 'By good detective work', but thought better of it. Instead he asked her gently, 'Did you know who Martin Commoner is?'

'Of course I do. He's an agent.'

'An agent of whom?'

'Of . . . of the CIA.'

'And what's the CIA? What do the letters stand for?'

She scowled at him. 'Leave it out, mister.'

'Don't you know?'

'Look, fuck off, why don't you. He's killed people, isn't that enough for you? He's an agent, he's killed people, Ishmael says so. Why don't you ask Ishmael?'

'I will.'

Esther closed her eyes again. He stared at her: the long, lank hair, the pale, thin, intense face with its natural expression a disconcerting mixture of childlike innocence and cunning. Which was she more to be blamed for — the innocence or the guile? A poor weak creature, she had probably never been so strong or so sure of herself as she was now. The Jesus sect had done it. *Everyone a Winner*. If you knew you were going to be saved, what did breaking the law matter? Jonathan Bisley could have got them to do anything he wanted, so long as it could be dressed up as saving a soul from damnation.

Esther opened her eyes. In a whisper she asked him, 'Is Zed okay?'

'They're taking a bullet out of his shoulder.'

'Will he be able to sing?'

'I don't know. Why?'

'He's gotta sing,' she said in a quavering voice. 'He's makin' a record about us. He said that. It's what he said.'

'Did he introduce you to Ishmael?'

Before Esther could answer, Meyer had come into the room. Looking grimmer than ever, he beckoned William out into the corridor.

Outside, he gave William the news about Jonathan Bisley. 'It's been played right down,' he said, talking in an undertone although the two CIA men had disappeared. 'It happened two hours ago. The Washington stations are calling it "a shooting incident" and not mentioning Commoner, although our information is that he was on the scene. But they're giving out the name as Jonathan Lawrence Bisley and saying he was wanted on charges of assault and battery. I'm putting an extra guard on these two and the hospital.'

'What about Commoner?'

'He's on his way here. Shusterman just left to go look for his boss. He looked pretty sick.'

William nodded and said nothing. He went out and got himself a paper cup of weak tea from the vending machine. He should have had a sense of relief, but all he felt was anger at the waste and futility of it. It couldn't have been an accident, Ishmael's death. In his head was something Christopher Knight had said to him, plucking at his initialled cufflinks — *The most important thing about a principle, Pomfret, is that it can always be sacrificed to expediency.*

Of course, he had no way of knowing that Commoner himself hadn't been into it from the beginning.

He finished the tea and got himself another cup. It was as weak and evil-tasting as the first. Whatever happened he would be back in England soon, in fact as soon as the extradition proceedings had been initiated. Back in the land of strong tea and marmite and sausages and Yorkshire pudding. Back to Jenny and the kids, and the ins and outs on Hammersmith Borough Council and suppertime discussions on whether a loyal Social Democrat could be seen sending her children out of the State system to a private school. Meanwhile, after all this effort, what was his prize at the end? One tired, bewildered, delinquent little girl, who felt more strongly about something she half-comprehended than he felt about anything he knew and understood.

There was a commotion outside. William pushed the tea away and got to his feet. Martin Commoner came into the charge-room, Vanderbyle at his heels. Commoner strode across to William, and put out his hand.

'Always in at the kill, Inspector,' he said.

It was not the sunken, chalk-white face that had stared up at William from the demolition site on One Tree Hill. The colour was back in Martin Commoner's cheeks, the bags under his eyes had gone and he had put on weight. But there was something disquieting about him which William couldn't place at first. It could have been the nervous energy of the handshake, or the stare in his eyes, or simply that his dark suit looked incongruous on him without the tie which he had taken off and stuffed in his pocket. But no. He was wary, William suddenly realised — tense and wary, like an animal that has had enough of running.

Martin was deeply tired. Now that the adrenalin was ebbing, he was beginning to feel the effects of that morning's squash game against Geoff Maclaren. His limbs ached; his head throbbed. He felt like an old man. In the English detective's shrewd glance, he fancied he saw a hint of pity.

'Do I look that bad?' he asked William Pomfret with a smile.

'Not as bad as when I found you.'

'Thanks a lot. Are they here?'

Meyer appeared at his elbow. 'This way, Mr Commoner. An identification is all we need.'

Martin nodded. He looked at the Englishman. 'Do you mind coming as a witness, Inspector?'

The two of them, followed by Vanderbyle and Meyer, went into the cell corridor. Martin broke out into a sweat. He had rehearsed what was to come: now that the moment was upon him, it seemed an act of suicide. But he'd made his mind up. He'd had a good twenty years in the Agency. BeeSting had come off successfully. It was as good a time as any to go.

Esther and Luke had been locked in the same cell. They were on their knees on the cement floor, their heads bowed, mumbling the Lord's Prayer. Martin stared at them through the bars. Luke had a small bald patch on the top of his head: he'd never noticed it.

'Hi there,' he said, suddenly embarrassed.

Seeing him, they scrambled to their feet. Luke grinned and scratched his nose.

'Hi!' said Esther, without any semblance of shame. 'Are you okay?'

Martin did not answer. He went on gazing at the two of them. He felt neither anger nor forgiveness, nor even pity: but a blank, idle curiosity, as if he was looking through a window at something happening a long way down.

Vanderbyle coughed. Martin put out his hands and gripped the cell bars.

'I'm not pressing charges.'

'*What?*' Vanderbyle's voice was involuntarily high-pitched.

'Let them go.' He gazed at his abductors. Esther giggled.

279

'C'mon, Martin. All we need is an identification.'

He turned round and looked at them. Pomfret was frowning in puzzlement.

Allen Vanderbyle had flushed a mottled red.

'The people who abducted me are catspaws,' he declared flatly. 'They aren't the ones responsible for what happened to me. If you want to take it further,' he went on, addressing William, 'you're welcome to. As far as I'm concerned, you can set them free.'

He began to walk back down the corridor, without another glance at Esther and Luke. The Englishman stepped in front of him.

'I can't take the girl back,' said William Pomfret. 'Without your help I can't extradite her. You know that.'

'Can you honestly tell me that you want her back?'

The Detective Chief Inspector brooded. He had come a long way to nail these two. Martin scrutinised him, wondering where, between his police rôle and his sense of natural justice, his sympathies would lie.

He had not judged him wrong. Pomfret shrugged, his blue eyes focused somewhere beyond Martin, perhaps home in London with his young son and daughter. 'I'm just a policeman,' he said finally. 'I don't play hide-and-seek. You want her, you keep her. I've got a plane to catch.'

With that, William Pomfret nodded to them, turned on his heels and went out. Martin followed him. At the door he was stopped by Vanderbyle, who drew him quietly aside.

'Mr Commoner, I don't know what the deuce is going on here,' he said in his Texan drawl. 'But I'm supposed to find Max Hemming —'

'Yes, where is he?'

'That's what I was going to ask you. This gentleman from the Bureau, Meyer, says he left a message for me. Said to tell me he's "gone hunting for bear". Now do you make anything of that?'

Martin gazed at Vanderbyle without seeing him, blinded by a knowledge so sudden and complete that it came as a revelation. After a minute he shook his head and said huskily, 'Sounds like Max is on the track of something. Why don't you leave him be?'

'The General wants him back at Langley.'

'The General may be out of luck.'

Leaving Vanderbyle hesitating uncertainly, Martin made a

quick escape. The charge-room was full of cigar-smoke, and voices which fell silent when Martin came through. He hurried out of the police station and pushed through the crowd of pressmen, brushing aside their questions and smiling agreeably for the photographers. In his pocket were the keys of the Pontiac Vanderbyle had laid on to bring them into Warren after the flight from Washington. Well Vanderbyle could find himself another limousine. He got in and drove away.

For a time he drove through the homeward traffic of Warren commuters, making sure that he wasn't being followed. When he had calmed down, and his hands on the wheel had stopped shaking, he turned off the street and parked behind a Hickory House restaurant. The smell of food made him realise he hadn't eaten since breakfast. He went in and ordered the first thing on the menu, a platter of spare ribs.

It was nearly 7 pm. The questions he'd been asking himself since leaving the police station were beginning to find answers. He knew where Max Hemming must have gone; he knew why he hadn't told Vanderbyle. Max had gone up to Lookout Cabin, about 40 minutes drive away, high in the Allegheny mountains above the Chapman Dam. An old loggers' cabin, it was hired out by the CIA to senior Agency executives who needed to get away in the summer months — the kind of place you went for hill-walking, maybe a little shooting in the season. Martin had stayed here once in the mid-1970s on a summer hunting expedition with Max Hemming and a couple of other colleagues on Middle East.

Bear hunting. That was Max's sense of humour all right. it was the Russian Bear Max Hemming had an appointment with. If Martin was right, Lookout Cabin was the first stage in a long journey which would end in Moscow with a fanfare of publicity, a Kremlin medal ceremony, and the honorary rank of Major-General in the KGB.

It had to be this. Nothing else made sense any more. It had to have been Max from the start: tracking down Bisley's son, priming him to think Martin had killed his father and then holding him, holding him back, until the right moment came.

It was 7.30 by the time Martin finished his meal and got out to the car. The sky was darkening, and he still had to find the right road up into the Alleghenies. He took Route 337 east out of Warren over the railroad bridge. Almost immediately he doubled back on a minor road which crossed the Allegheny River and headed south into the National Forest.

BeeSting. One of the rare NSC meetings so top-security that even Max hadn't been able to get more than an inkling of what was going on. His masters must have gone stir-crazy, suspecting the worst, demanding to have the operation code-named BeeSting blocked at whatever cost, even having the Director of Operations discredited and maybe losing the best spy they had ever run in the CIA. So, like a falconer, Max had let Ishmael off the leash.

And Ishmael had failed him. The Soviets had played their part, releasing that information on US activities abroad which only a defected agent or spy could have given them. But Martin had survived; he had come home safely. And Max had no choice but to play through to the end.

He had nearly won. Using as pawns the people Martin loved and trusted, stepping up the psychological pressure inside the Agency and out, isolating Martin from his colleagues — it was a masterly performance. Not until the very last second had his nerve broke (though this might never be proved) — the moment when he had fired at Martin and missed, and turned his gun instead on Ishmael, the one person who could betray him.

It was too late after that. Max must have known the General would hold an inquiry. There was only one thing which didn't fit. Why had Max sent Vanderbyle the message about Lookout Cabin — a message only Martin could have understood? Max was trying to say something to him, something personal. Which was why he was coming up here alone.

He drove on, climbing steadily through the rust-red and yellow trees and the dark swatches of pine that lay between. Somewhere up in this wilderness, not much more than a year ago, David Bisley had met his death. The wind which had driven the light rain south over Maryland had left a clear pale grey sky, splashed with gouts of crimson in the west where the sun had sunk below the horizon.

There was so much to do up here. Trout and bass fishing. Hunting for deer, turkey and bear. In other circumstances he wouldn't have minded staying around. John was on vacation: he could get him to come up for a week, teach him how to hunt and track. How to use a gun.

The road was littered with pine cones; in the cooling air he could smell the dark resinous tang which he still associated with his Hagerstown outings as a child into the Catoctin Hills. He drove on in a kind of daze, trying to rearrange his picture of the man he thought he knew into this unfamiliar, dreadful pattern.

The coldness. The detachment. Those were the clues. It was vanity which had driven the Counter-Intelligence man on to work for the other side. It had to be vanity, an enormous over-mastering egotism which needed the spur of danger before it could be satisfied.

At Berkeley it had taken the form of egging the radical students on before informing on them. A dangerous innocence Martin had called it three days ago, after the General's dinner, and he hadn't been far wrong. But it wasn't the myth of American potency that had inspired Max Hemming. It was something deeper and darker: the obsession of the frustrated with order and symmetry, the desire to clean up the mess of a free society and direct it into something streamlined, smooth and powerful, like a guided missile pointed at the future.

That was what had impelled him forward, more than Soviet communism or anything you could call ideology. Having started his lonely climb, and got so near the top, he owed it to himself to see it through.

On the far side of the ridge Martin came to a junction and took the right-hand fork down towards Mayburg. The disused mine workings on the left were as he remembered them. He drove on another hundred yards, turned right by the telephone pole and bumped up the dirt track which led to the four-square timber cabin in the clearing.

There was a wisp of smoke rising from the chimney. Martin stopped the Pontiac some distance away, leaving the headlights on. Maybe he should have told Vanderbyle. It occurred to him now that Max Hemming could have laid this trail deliberately, much in the way that David Bisley had let himself be trailed by his son. Max could be lying in there with his brains blown out. Or he could have other ideas.

Before he got out, he opened the glove compartment and slipped Ishmael's gun under his jacket. Outside, he took several deep breaths, filling his lungs with the clean air. Behind the cabin the wooded hill rose steeply. The silence was absolute. As he walked in front of the lighted window, the dead pine-needles crackled under his feet.

The door was unlocked. The smell of stale beer and varnish in the hall-way brought back vividly that other time, five, six years before. Max had been the kid of the party. He'd shot his first bear. Martin had shown him how to finish it off Agency-style — crouching with feet wide apart, holding the gun in both hands, letting it sink of its own weight on to the target.

Martin licked his dry lips and kicked open the living-room door. The room was empty — just the embers of a fire in the grate. Keeping one hand inside his jacket, he went through the rest of the cabin, checking cupboards and the attic rooms. The head of Counter-Intelligence had gone. The mole had already silently burrowed underground. If he surfaced again it would be on the other side of the world, in an exile from which he could never return.

However, he had left one trace behind. Martin found it, stuck casually on the mantelpiece beside an old cartridge-case, when he was beginning to think that Max had never come to Lookout Cabin at all. A sheet of paper, folded over, on which were scribbled the words, 'MARTIN — THANKS FOR EVERY-THING'. Inside it, a TWA air-ticket made out to Martin Commoner. Its destination — Beirut.

Martin leaned back against the mantelpiece and laughed out loud. It was an insider's joke, of course. David Bisley had been framed that way — if indeed Max had set him up — and it had been the end of him. Max couldn't hope to work the same trick twice.

After a moment, though, his smile faded. Joke or not, they were compromising documents. What if Vanderbyle had found them? As it was, by not telling Vanderbyle in Warren about Lookout Cabin, Martin could be said to have connived in Max Hemming's defection.

Just as Bisley had been accused of aiding Mitchum . . .

He heard the faint noise of a car going past on the road below. Hurriedly, he blew up the embers of the fire and put the letter and the air-ticket on to burn. A week ago he'd have taken them back to Langley as curios — more than curios, as evidence that they might have been wrong after all about David Bisley. Not now. Not after what he had been through. He blew on the flames.

After a while, he roused himself and went to the 'phone, and dialled a Washington number. Nancy answered.

'I'm sorry,' said Martin.

'Why?'

'About today. Accusing you. I guess I was paranoid. It was all getting too much. Anyway it's over now.'

'Yes.'

'I'm sorry?'

'Yes it's over. With us. Martin you don't have to apologise. I know what you've been going through. It's not your fault. But I can't take any more.' Martin heard what sounded like a sob, but he couldn't be sure because Nancy recovered at once and went on steadily. 'I've been thinking all afternoon about us. I can't take your life, Martin. I've tried, and I'm no good at it. I need to trust people. You're stronger than me. I have to trust the people I love.'

'Nancy —'

'Please don't.' Her voice now was thick with tears. 'I love you. I can't argue with you. If I didn't love you, I wouldn't need you to trust me. But I know you mustn't ever do that.'

'But I do trust you. And love you. Nancy.'

'Please, Martin. Goodbye.'

'Nancy!'

The line had gone dead. Martin let the 'phone drop back. It was dark; the fire wasn't giving out any heat. Slowly he went to the grate; slowly he shovelled up the white ash and carried it outside. When he had made a little pyre of ashes on the grass, he dug a hole and buried them. It paid to be careful.

Stamping down the earth he heard a car again, maybe the same one, approaching from the junction on the Maybury road. It slowed down, passing the cabin track, and then picked up speed as it climbed the hill. It was time to move.

Is that what you do with your life, Dad? He should not have reacted the way he had to the scorn in John's voice. But it did come down to a straight fight, whatever they all might think. Vietnam and Angola had been proxy wars, skirmishes for the high ground from which to look down fearfully on the field of final combat. Only in intelligence, stealing out like sappers in the dark to mine the enemy's defences, was it possible to meet the real enemy face to face and know him for who he was. More often, in that universal darkness, you struggled in a weary confusion, not knowing friend from foe, until sometimes, as maybe now with Nancy, it was too late to say sorry.

285

He got into the car. Across the dark grey sky flew eight wild geese, almost on a level with him, heading south across the reservoir into the hills. There was work to be done at Langley. A big shakeout in Counter-Intelligence, for a start. It wasn't certain, yet, that Max Hemming had fired that shot from the bridge five hours ago. There could be others.

The war was not over. It never could be. But on one of its countless fronts a line had been made secure, a counter-offensive had been mounted. He gave a long, defiant blast on the horn, before putting off the handbrake and starting back out of the wilderness.